# ESCAPE WITH ME!

THE BAYON TEMPLE AT ANGKOR VAT

*Note the heads carved everywhere upon the towers.* *See p. 118*

# ESCAPE WITH ME!

## AN
## ORIENTAL
## SKETCH-BOOK

BY

OSBERT SITWELL

HONG KONG   OXFORD   NEW YORK
OXFORD UNIVERSITY PRESS

Oxford University Press

Oxford   New York   Toronto
Petaling Jaya   Singapore   Hong Kong   Tokyo
Delhi   Bombay   Calcutta   Madras   Karachi
Nairobi   Dar es Salaam   Cape Town
Melbourne   Auckland

and associated companies in
Beirut   Berlin   Ibadan   Nicosia

First published by Macmillan & Co. Ltd. 1939
First issued as an Oxford in Asia paperback 1983
Second impression 1984
Reissued in Oxford Paperbacks 1986

ISBN 0 19 583736 3

Printed in Hong Kong
Published by Oxford University Press,
Warwick House, Hong Kong

# ACKNOWLEDGEMENTS

I<small>T</small> should be unnecessary now to have to state how profound a gratitude, for the preservation and opening out of Angkor, all lovers of beauty must owe to the French authorities in Cambodia, or how much is due, in particular, to Dr. Marchal and Monsieur Victor Goloubeff for their investigations, and for the art with which they have been executed.

In the writing of Chapter V, I am much indebted to Monsieur Goloubeff for the benefit of his conversation during my visit to Angkor, and to Dr. Marchal, whose *Guide Archéologique* I have frequently consulted. For the historical facts concerning Greater India, I must, in addition, make my acknowledgements to Dr. Quaritch Wales, the author of *Towards Angkor* (Harrap & Co., 1937), which I have several times occasion to quote.

I owe a personal debt, which I should like here to acknowledge, to my friends Mr. Harold Acton, Mr. C. M. McDonald and Mr. Laurence Sickman — to whom I dedicate this book—for their kindness to me in Peking. But for the benefit of their familiarity with the city and with Chinese customs, and without their thoughtfulness, I should have seen little either of Peking or of the Chinese.

I must also gratefully proclaim my obligation to Dr. Derk Bodde for his translation of Tun Lich'en's *Annual Customs and Festivals in Peking* (Henri Vetch, Peking, 1936. In China, $9 : abroad, 13s. 6d. : in United States, $4.50) ; to Mr. Robert W. Swallow for his *Sidelights on Peking Life* (China Booksellers Ltd., Peking, 1927) ; and to my friend Mr. L. C. Arlington and Mr. William Lewisohn for their very delightful joint guide-book, *In Search of Old Peking* (Henri Vetch, Peking, 1935). Miss Corrinne Lamb's *The Chinese Festive Board* (Henri Vetch, Peking, 1935) was of much assistance to me in the writing of the pages on Chinese food.

I must, further, thank those responsible for permitting me to publish the various beautiful photographs which accompany the text. In particular, I wish to make the most appreciative acknowledgements to that distinguished painter of Chinese life, Mr. Thomas Handforth, for allowing me to reproduce several photographs of Peking scenes, which are only less exquisite than his drawings, and to Dr. Gustav Ecke for his remarkable photograph of the effigy of Kang T'ieh, the Eunuch General.

OSBERT SITWELL

# PREFACE

THE volume which you now open, Gentle Reader, is above all, in the phraseology of the day, *escapist* — or so, at least, I hope and trust, being pre-First-World-War by nature and by my age, pre-slump by disposition, and so a citizen of no mean city. I journeyed to China, for example, very largely to escape from Europe, but more especially in order to see China, and the wonderful beauty of the system of life it incorporated, before this should perish ; I did not go there to observe the form taken by the Social Struggle (though one could not help seeing the increasing grip in those days of the communist creed upon all the younger and more intelligent students of the Universities ; a result of despair, of the hopeless position in which China patently found herself), nor out of pure love of wandering, nor, alas ! in response to a request from my publishers to write a strong left-wing book about that country. Though I have long carried on a private, one-man campaign against stupidity, and the brutality and greed which are two of its symptoms, I am no soldier of a cause militant. The volume that has resulted, therefore, is intended for amusement, for a record and description, and was not created with instruction for its purpose. It is proudly free of any political aim (or any aim at all, I might say, except that of getting itself written) : though this is not to pretend that I have not my prejudices, or will not vent them, but to confess that these, if innumerable, vary, except in one or two directions where they have grown permanent, from day to day. Moreover, when they are political, they remain plain, wicked prejudices, without any need of justification or of being transmuted into virtuous aims.

The world, I know, is full of wickedness and folly (though more, I still believe, of the latter than of the former — indeed, the greatest instance of it ever so far recorded in history has taken place in my own lifetime) : but I have not for the moment the time, though often the inclination, to set it right. The chief duty confronting every author was — and still is — to use his eyes, to record what he sees, and what, because of them, he feels. Much of beauty and of merit yet remains in the old world ; let those who are blind to it prepare the new. (Who can regret sincerely that Holbein failed to give up his art in order to take a prominent part in the religious controversies of his day, that Botticelli, Michelangelo and Titian did not spend their time crusading on behalf of a United Italy, that Cézanne, by refusing to fight in the Franco-Prussian War, so skilfully avoided wasting a year or two, or that Watteau and Fragonard refrained from throwing down their paint-brushes so that they might prepare for the revolutionary struggle that lay ahead ?) In consequence, this is neither a communist book about Iceland or the Faroe Islands, nor a fascist volume about Spain. It is, in the main, concerned with China and Indo-China, and the journey thither : but I shall again essay, as on former occasions, to use the travel-book as a vehicle of a special kind, giving, in addition to the pages concerned with his present voyage, something of the passing thoughts and reflections, as well as memories, of the traveller ; further, I claim the right once more, as in former volumes which dealt with countries nearer home, to alight at random, as from the air, at any point convenient to me in space or history, and to be allowed to use the widest range of comparison for the enforcement of a visual image.

Moreover, the book that follows is approached, all through, from the visual and sensual angles, rather than from those of knowledge and learning : I hope, for example, effectively to describe Angkor, but I shall not endeavour to tell you the history of its kings, the details of its religious and social systems, or to dwell upon the conditions of the slaves who built the temples ; that must be left to those who, by the work of a lifetime, have qualified themselves to attempt it. Further, though I have seen nearly all the important monuments of Angkor and its district, I shall only concern myself with the few that were more significant to me than any others. . . . Again, with China, my judgments and impressions may, for all I know, be more *chinoiserie* than Chinese, for I cannot — nor in any case would I — divest myself of Western ideas and of the culture which, such of it as I possess, comes from the shores of the Mediterranean, and not from those of the China Seas. And so I remain a traveller, overcome with wonder at strange sights and events, but often, I dare say, not fully grasping their cause or implication. My understanding is that of the eye ; my only sure claim, to know and appreciate both beauty and character when I meet them.

But, nevertheless, while confessedly I am no sinologue, I grew, inevitably, to comprehend certain facts about China and Chinese life which are almost impossible to understand without visiting the country. Yet it is of Peking that I shall attempt, when the moment comes, to write, not of China, except in so far as Peking represents China : (I shall, too, continue to call it Peking, and neither Pekin nor the modern Peiping, for it is as Peking that I have always thought of it since I first read its magic name in childhood upon the programme of a pantomime). Even then, so vast is the subject that I shall only choose to write of those things which I feel I know, or of which I may have seen a unique aspect. I shall talk of the *look* of the Forbidden City (and try to communicate it to the reader), more than of its history, of which I know little : because its aspect must be more familiar to me than to most Europeans, since, until a comparatively short time ago, only an ambassador could enter it, and even he was supposed to spend most of his time in kowtowing and prostrating himself before the Emperor, rather than in observing the things round him. Whereas, during the four months in which I lived in this city, I think no single day passed except I wandered at least once in some part of the Palace, sometimes only for twenty minutes, sometimes for hours, and I have seen it in winter and summer, under rain and sun and snow. And the Forbidden City is the heart of that metropolis I came to know and love, in similarly watching its aspect change through the seasons from winter to full summer. On arrival there, all save the Forbidden City seemed a bare, Breughel-like world of brown lanes, squat and narrow, of ribbed brown roofs, and of tall, naked trees posing their neat but web-like intricacies above them against a deep-blue sky (except when a dust-storm whirled down from the Gobi Desert, carrying its load a thousand feet in the air, overcasting the sun with a thin yellow cloud, and insinuating a fine layer of sand upon every chair and table, and even between the pages of my notebooks), and of figures in padded blue robes, or patched blue canvas, and crowned, many of them, with triptychal fur hats that framed faces in a new way : when I left, it was a sighing, young summer forest, the gardens were full of blossoms and on the stone paving stood plants, moulded to the fashion of the trees on a Chinese wallpaper, and large earthenware bowls of goggling goldfish, engaged in their eternal skirt-dance of flowing fins and veils, while figures in the thinnest silk gowns fanned themselves beneath the tender, quivering shadow of young leaves. I stayed there long enough, in fact, to appreciate, where this city is concerned, the truth of what Dr. Derk Bodde says so eloquently in a preface to his translation of Lich'en's *Annual Customs and Festivals in Peking*.[1] " Indeed," he writes, " what the translator has felt most strongly in making this translation, and what he hopes his readers will feel, is the sentiment . . . of the essential oneness and harmony of man with the universe. It is a sentiment which permeates much of the greatest Chinese art and poetry, for in the Chinese, as perhaps in. no other people, has been developed a keen consciousness and awareness of the movement and rhythm of nature, as evidenced in the yearly rotation of the seasons. It is an awareness which has made them deliberately subordinate their own activities to that of the forces of nature, so that, as we read this book, we find such things as their foods, the clothes which they put on, and the lighting and taking away of their winter fires, all following in their times a course as rigid as that of the birds in their several migrations." . . . (This periodicity, so truly observed, is perhaps due in part to the reliability of the calendar, that is to say, of the climate itself ; for it is possible to predict the exact day of the second, and most severe, snowfall, of the beginning of the

[1] *Annual Customs and Festivals in Peking* as recorded in the *Yen-ching Sui-shih-chi* by Tun Lich'en, translated and annotated by Dr. Derk Bodde. (Henri Vetch, Peking, 1936.) This is a fascinating book, to which I shall many times have occasion to refer in the course of these pages.

great summer heat, and of the rains. These natural occurrences never fail them.) . . . Dr. Bodde continues : " Perhaps it is this subordination of man's will which has prevented China from achieving a science, for science is born from the struggle against, rather than the submission to, natural forces " ; a suggestion which, in that region where meaning exists under and between the lines, may strengthen the hopes of all lovers of China concerning the ultimate outcome of the present invasion.

# CONTENTS

## BOOK I

## EXOTIC VISTAS

### CHAPTER I

### CHAPTER II

### CHAPTER III

### CHAPTER IV

### CHAPTER V

### CHAPTER VI

# CONTENTS

# BOOK II
# PROSPECTS OF PEKING

# ILLUSTRATIONS

# INTRODUCTION

## THE CHERRY TREE

At night the heat lay over the Red Sea in clouds almost palpable. Everything you touched, the walls, the switch for the electric light, the sheets on the bed, the glass of water beside it on the table, was warm, and sleep was out of reach. In those hours it was impossible not to wonder if any country, even China itself, could repay such a journey.

It was curious, I thought, that China had always exercised such allurement, whereas the idea of India, despite its manifold and diverse marvels, continued to be repellent ; why, too, had Peking, above all other cities in the East, irresistibly attracted me ? . . . Partly, of course, because of the sensible explanations : that China, for several thousands of years, had, in fact, offered an alternative method of living — the only one in the world — to our own ; that Peking existed, a great and civilised metropolis, still ruled by native custom and ancient law, and not, like Tokyo and Baghdad and Bombay, made and governed in

3

the image of Manchester or Detroit, or, after the manner of Timbuctoo — another city romantic in the conception one held of it — merely a vast accumulation of mud huts, isolated from other, smaller, nearer collections of mud huts by enormous stretches of desert. I wanted to see Peking, to examine the system of life there before it ended (and I have done so), before one or other of the barbarian hordes who were so plainly planning its destruction, had compassed it. Moreover, if either the Japanese took it, or the Communists obtained open control, the Forbidden City would be once more forbidden in fact as well as in name, would become the home of a restored Emperor or a newly installed Commissar : whereas at present a tourist, even if he had lost in the matter of dress and ceremonial, forfeiting the chance of happening upon kowtowing, peacocks' feathers, pigtails and brilliant, fantastically embroidered robes, stood at an immense advantage over the past, and over the probable future, where the delights of architecture were concerned, for he was allowed to wander at his ease through the deserted gardens, courts and chambers of the great palace. . . . But there were, too, other reasons for my journey, and the moment I had chosen for it : for one thing, it was a way of celebrating my fortieth birthday, an ugly and all too indicative milestone. Besides, that year I did not know where else to go, could not make up my mind. . . . And so, one Sunday in November, having motored down for the day to see my brother in his country home, I complained to him of wanting to be off abroad, but of not knowing where to choose, nor how I could afford to travel at all : I certainly could not manage, at the then ruling rate of exchange, to stay long in France or Italy. And when he replied, unexpectedly, " Why don't

you go to Peking ? " my mind was made up, and I decided
to start as soon as possible. . . . As for the cost, it must
settle itself.

There had been, in addition, other influences, more
indirect ones, I suspected. . . . A certain love of the exotic
was, perhaps, innate in those of English blood, counterpart,
indeed, of our proud insularity : but it seemed too difficult
now to decide whether this streak in the national composition was responsible in the first place for our ancestors
going out into — and conquering so large a share of —
the world, or whether, on the contrary, it was the result
of these adventures ? Be that as it might, we had ever
been a people of wide ranging and, while covering the
whole globe, formerly with wooden echoes of our country
houses, and now with bungalows and wireless, and the
multiform benefits accruing from an enlarged credit system,
we had always brought back, too, from our travels various
objects that had caught our fancy and matched our purses ;
miscellaneous objects that still fill the lumber-rooms and
litter the shelves of innumerable mansions and cottages in
our land, so that every child grows up, from the time of
his first remembering, familiar with the idea of foreign
countries.

A love of travel, then, was in part hereditary, in part
acquired : but to disentangle the different predisposing
elements, embedded so far back in the past, required considerable skill and reflection. . . . This moment, however,
as I lay, turning from side to side in my bunk in the illogical
effort by so doing to escape the heat (which now entered
at the port-hole like the gusts from a machine for drying
the hair at a barber's shop), appeared to be the most favourable in which to attempt such a process, for it might serve

5

to distract the mind a little from its effort to get to sleep ; and so I allowed my mind to search the alleys that led back to childhood. . . . As a schoolboy of ten or eleven, I used to spend much of the holidays — for my father had been the victim of a lengthy and worrying illness, and my mother was continually travelling abroad with him — in the house of my paternal grandmother : while, before that, I had, of course, when a small child, constantly paid her long, and to me memorable, visits. She lived in a large, honey-coloured house in Surrey, then a country of commons and rich deep lanes, down which the carriages, with a top-hatted and cockaded footman on the box, rolled, rattled and bumped, taking the leisurely for drives, " to get a little air ", or for a condescending visit to poor and ailing ; a country of bare downs, yet virgin for the speculative builder, and of battered pilgrim churches. (It may, indeed, have been my boredom with these stone wrecks, to which from time to time we were encouraged to make expeditions, that has to this day left me with such a blind eye for the beauties of English parish churches.) An air of musical-comedy rusticity still smiled over thatched cottage and Elizabethan hall, and there existed, even, a few old farm-labourers, in smocks, with authentic Newgate fringes running under their chins from ear to ear, and very quavering, quaint voices ; moreover, the elder women of the village, in their voluminous black Sunday dresses, decorated with a large brooch, still curtsied to us as we passed on our way to church — the trick still worked here, evidently — so that the whole countryside had seemed very foreign to me, accustomed as I was to the sturdy modernity and independence of the North.

Nevertheless, I liked the place, though I did not in

those early days entirely approve of my grandmother, for she obliged me to attend family prayers in the dining-room after breakfast, and, further, refused to allow me during my holidays to read the *Daily Graphic* — one of the bright spots to which I had looked forward for a whole term at school, since I had found it to be full of the most entertaining news, strange stories of crime and passion, which were very exciting, though I did not thoroughly understand them. Worse still, she had wrested from me by cunning, by a mere ruse — for fear that I should cut off one, or all, of my fingers with it — an enormous pocket-knife which, besides two portentous blades, embraced every improbable and unnecessary sort of adjunct, such as a potato-peeler, a guillotine for slices of ham, an instrument for disembowelling apples and breaking lobster-shells, a saw for cutting through small branches, a gimlet, a sharp sword for piercing tins and ripping them open, and a needle specially contrived so that you might inscribe your unwanted name on glass ; a possession which had for a month or two constituted the whole pride of my career, and my entire claim upon the consideration and good opinion of my schoolfellows. Life would, indeed, prove difficult without it. . . . But all this I could not explain. . . . However, I gained my revenge, for my grandmother was deeply religious, but very evangelical in her outlook, with a great detestation of High Church practices : and when, the following Sunday, I was taken to Morning Service, with great presence of mind I astonished the congregation by turning to the east during the Creed, and, at mention of the holy name, by crossing myself with accuracy and fervour : observances which she remarked, but concerning which she scarcely liked to remonstrate with me, since she had always deplored my irreligious disposition, and had several times spoken to me about it, so that this, she could only hope, might be the token of conversion, a new and blessed ferment. . . . But, though I was by no means her favourite grandchild, and albeit she detected in my nature a mundane side which she disliked, seeing that I would be unwilling to forswear, either on my own behalf or that of anyone else, " the sinful lusts of the flesh " and " the pomps and vanities of this wicked world ", for the rest we got on very well together, and indeed with every year that passed I grew to understand her better and to become fonder of her.

She had seemed to me then to be very old, for she was between seventy and eighty, of great gentleness and of an imperturbable charm. Her resignation masked, it was clear, a will of formidable strength ; her lips were ever set in the smiling mode of the Mona Lisa, except that these lips were aged, and that the music which evoked her smile was one, I apprehend, issuing from that invisible world she was on the verge of entering, and of the existence of which she was so sure, rather than from the earth that spread itself visibly round her, and tangibly under her feet. . . . Her mind, indeed, was largely — too largely for my liking at the time — occupied with the next world (perhaps in itself a form of exoticism ?) ; and, in so far as she exhibited an interest in the present one, it betrayed itself in good works and in a surviving curiosity concerning foreign countries and manners.

This last was an enthusiasm I came to share ; easily explicable, too, when, for instance, you recalled that her father had run away from Eton at the age of twelve and, since no English regiment would, because of his youth, accept him, had joined the Portuguese Army, in order to

fight in the Peninsular War (the Duke of Wellington —
who was, I believe, his godfather — subsequently obtained
for him, as soon as he became old enough, an exchange of
commissions into an English regiment), and that, as a
young man, long before the era of railways, he had
several times crossed Europe from end to end, from
Portugal to Poland and Russia, in addition to having visited,
as I know from his diary (a dull book, alas, as that of a
man of action is apt to be), the most remote districts in
Southern Italy ; places which, even in these days of rapid
transit, myself had found sufficiently difficult to reach. A
very good-looking Irishman, with a singularly charming
expression, he had been gallant in the Regency manner,
though he had always possessed a very serious side to his
character : and a decade or so after the Napoleonic Wars
were finished, he married, and retired to spend his remaining
years — fifty and more must have lain in front of him, for
he lived to be eighty-eight — in a small manor-house in
Northamptonshire, which was the inheritance of his wife.
There five daughters were born to him, and as, later, in
Early Victorian days, he rode out with them, a groom
following, along the broad grass verges of the rustic roads
— their tall, crested elms standing up so high from the
hedgerows that they dwarfed this little group moving
swiftly as a shadow under them — he must often have
talked to them of past times, of his home in Ireland, of his
favourite uncle, the General, who, before he succeeded as
second Earl of Donoughmore, had been created, because of
his military feats, Lord Hutchinson of Alexandria and
Knocklofty (a title that in itself showed traces of exoticism),
and had been a boon companion of the Prince Regent's —
living, indeed, for part of the time, in a cottage in the

grounds of the Royal Pavilion at Brighton — of his own travels in France and Spain and Portugal and Germany and Holland, in Austria and Poland and Russia and Italy, of his friendship in Rome with Princess Pauline Borghese, Napoleon's lovely sister, with her slight, but perfect, body (immortalised by Canova) and her audacious, lively mind, and of her small and exquisite hands (her glove lay upstairs folded in a walnut-shell), though he never told them, I think, of his long and passionate relations with the celebrated Polish Countess, a beautiful woman married against her will to a man thrice her age, nor of how, many years later, she had died, a widow, leaving him all her possessions, including great estates in Poland ; legacies which he had relinquished at the wish of his wife. . . . But her portrait, showing her as a radiant creature with fair curls, arranged in the style of the Empire, was found in his library, framed in the inside cover of a blotting-book, some ten years ago, by his great-grandchildren.

My grandmother, then, had been brought up with her sisters in that very English house of grey stone, with thatched barns and stone-tiled farm-houses lying neatly disposed, as in a Flemish picture, upon the surrounding slopes : but it was full of relics of times gone by and of distant lands, including innumerable pictures of Turkish costume, brought back a century earlier by a member of the family, and a great deal of oriental china, so that, remote as the place was, she had pictured for herself many distant countries and had grown up to be a citizen of the world. . . . But, as a girl, or as a young woman, the great religious tide that followed the Crimean War had touched her heart, too (religion was in her blood, for her mother had been cousin to Bishop Heber, Primate of All India, and singer of coral strands), and foreign missions, Indian and African, Polynesian and Melanesian, had then come to reinforce, in their own direction, the already substantial claims to interest of " foreign parts ". Alas, however, travel, except for polite sojourns in France and Italy, had been denied her by circumstances, nor could she, as doubtless she would have liked, abandon her duties in order to help those who preached the gospel at the ends of the earth : because, at an early stage, she had been left a widow, with the responsibility of two children to look after, and a large country house, together with an involved estate. (She inclined, as an old lady, to adopt a somewhat dramatic view of her past troubles, for I well recall her telling me how, after her marriage, she and my grandfather had found themselves so badly off that they could only afford to live " over a little grocer's shop ". Much impressed, as all children are, by " hard-luck " stories, I naturally enquired where this modest home had been. . . . At first she showed some hesitation in answering, and then the truth transpired ; it was the three floors above Gunter's, in Berkeley Square !) And now that her children had grown up, and that she had, by her practical cleverness and ability to manage affairs, pulled the estate round, she had found herself too old to move very far away — people seemed to grow old so early in those times — and had settled here ; where, out of a few acres, out of gardens and lawns, surrounded by a double ring of ancient trees, she had created for herself a world.

Her heart was growing weaker every year — the machinery, as it were, was running down — and as she lay in a *chaise longue* in the Indian Room, with a fur rug across her legs, and a Samoyede dog, recently imported

from the Arctic Circle, one on each side of her, like the
lions at either hand of a Byzantine sovereign, her mind, I
imagined, was usually and equally divided between thoughts
of her own family (she took an extreme interest in the
doings of her sisters' children, and their children after them)
and the progress made by the various foreign missions
which she patronised. The Indian Room — the inspiration
for which had surely been derived from a chamber similarly
named at Osborne, wherein the Queen-Empress was wont
to receive visitors — was a large apartment, with a high
ceiling, painted mauve, with its walls lined with *meseri*,
showing scarlet monkeys disporting themselves among
flowers upon a white ground. Against these hangings
numerous carved Burmese figures jutted their hips of teak
and cedar-wood, and a great many Indian tablecloths
winked glass eyes at you. Vases of surprising flowers from
the hot-houses always stood on the tables, and one could,
furthermore, pedal out manfully upon an early pianola the
haunting, nostalgic waltzes, mazurkas and ballet-tunes of
Tchaikoffsky. There was also an apparently endless supply
of clergymen, young and old, who came to call, and to keep
us informed of the state of the neighbouring parishes.

Even the treats she offered us, or promised us, as children
were delightfully strange and new ; in midwinter, delicious
fruit (then a novelty) from South Africa ; or, if we were
" good ", she would, she told us, take us for a drive, to see
a new and super-wonderful pianola, worked by electricity,
in the home of a wealthy brewer who lived nearby ; or,
again, we might be taken to hear — the real thing, this
time — a musical prodigy whose face was green from
asthma, and who, we were told, could " play all Chopin
by heart " (I believe he is still doing it !). Or, best of all,

Mrs. Frampton-Stanwick *might* — she would not promise it — be asked to tea. . . . And this constituted, indeed, the chief, and much the most improbable, of the treats known to us : for Mrs. Frampton-Stanwick was a charming Yorkshire lady, of good family, albeit sadly addicted to the bottle, and, when asked to tea, would roll over to see us in her dog-cart, bringing always presents for us children, but still hilarious, with her voice still hoarse, her eye still bloodshot, from some historic, homeric *blind*. Inevitably, on her arrival, whole cohorts of timid curates, assembled for tea in the Indian Room, would dart away into a blank-tied and outraged outer nothingness. . . . And yet my grandmother, whose views were so strict, continued to tolerate, and even to encourage the visits of, this northern Bacchante. We never could quite explain to our own satisfaction why she received such preferential treatment (though we loved her, and were therefore delighted that her behaviour should be thus condoned). But reasons, no doubt, there must be, and of a charitable order : and we gathered later, in reinforcement of this surmise, that, as a result of mysterious happenings in a long-ago past, my grandmother honoured her and, in defiance of all her favourite curates, made excuses for her conduct.

There existed, too, other minor indoor treats. Along the passage from the Indian Room, beyond the Smoking Room (for smoking was still confined to a single room in the house), lay the Library, in which reposed many un-forgettable books, and ones, perhaps, appealing especially to the imagination of children ; among them, for example, old copies of the *Botanical Magazine,* full of folding, brightly-hued plates of cactus and orchid and tropical lily, and books of shells, hand-coloured, and volumes of Dickens, with the original Cruikshank illustrations. . . . And then downstairs in the hall stood a large cage, with a monkey in it. Alas, I was frightened of this capering creature, and, indeed, in those days hated the whole simian tribe, though latterly, since being informed of the events that led up to the massacre of the majority of the monkeys in Gibraltar — only a very few were allowed to survive — my heart had warmed to them. . . . For a moment I considered this new theme. . . . The streets of the fortress town are so narrow that the monkeys could easily swing from any window-sill in it to another opposite. One summer they took, suddenly, to stealing photographs, the glinting silver frames of which no doubt caught their attention, and to placing them in the rooms across the way. The havoc these tricks created was immense ; Colonel A would find that a photograph of his wife (" the Missus ") had disappeared, and would eventually locate it, either through his own initiative or the employment of detectives, in Commander B's bedroom : and *vice versa*. As a result so many altercations took place, so many scandals occurred, so many divorce proceedings were pending, that in the end, when the true criminals were discovered, it was felt that, for the honour of the Services, the monkeys of Gibraltar had better be suppressed, kept down to the minimum. . . .

But I must return, I felt, to my task of recollection. . . . The peacocks, both green and white, that strolled over the lawns, the rare, grey turkeys with which the farm was stocked and the black-and-white lambs, of a particular breed which my great-grandfather had introduced from Spain, all these I liked better than the ape. . . . In the kitchen gardens, too, the hot-houses contained unusual fruits and flowers, and, all through the winter, glass frames were full of large, single violets, deeply-scented blossoms ranging in tone from brick-red to magenta, and of the double ones, Parma violets, white and lilac, with curled and peruked heads too big for their stalks, until it appeared as though all these fires from glass-house and frame must succeed even in warming a little the frosty air outside, that laid mist upon each pane, making the colour within blaze more vaguely but with greater strength. And every spring one wondered whether the semi-tropical interests, as it were, of the owner might not serve actually to stoke up the immediate climate, for her house seemed to be quilted with *Banksia* roses, in neat shepherds' knots, and starred with huge magnolias, deep blanc-de-chine bowls, long before her neighbours' walls showed any signs of florescence.

From this distance, from this night on the Red Sea, all those fragments of time, long hours of waiting to be called in the morning, of waiting for the butter-yellow light to flood the room, of waiting, and of hearing the morning sounds, the turkeys gobbling in the distance, and cocks crowing, of our donkey braying from the stable, the harsh and idiot cries of the peacocks, the metallic noise of the carriage horses stamping, of footsteps on the gravel, and of rustic voices fresh from hours of silence, of long afternoons of flowers and music and of the faint, meaningless gold of the dying hours spattering old walls, and yet bringing out, to one's surprise, a comforting subcutaneous warmth ; all these had mosaicked themselves into a single period for me. . . . I must, however, have been very young, not more than six or seven, when one afternoon I walked by the Pergola in spring.

Pergolas were then, if I am not mistaken, newly invented, or imported, as a device for English gardens, and at that

moment I was obsessed, as children sometimes are, for a
week at a time, by one particular problem ; and on this
occasion it was the effort to trace a connection between
the meaning of words and the sound they make in human
mouths (for the most part a hopeless task !). Why, I
remember wondering — so it must have been in the spring,
in April — should the two syllables that composed the
word *tulip* — tew-lip, tew-lip, tew-lip, I repeated —represent for us this lovely, living chalice, with its sweet,
gold-dusted centre and its six pointed petals ? . . . Then I
saw the Pergola again with a new eye, viewed solely from
the point of view of the enigma before me, and repeated to
myself the empty music of its name (though I may have
pronounced it incorrectly, since the gardener always referred
to it as " Lady Sitwell's *Burglar* "). Regarding it now
with more care, as I posed this question of its relationship
to its sound, I observed, high above me, the coral buds
and blossoming of a flowering tree, a cherry perhaps, or
peach, and, as I looked, knew suddenly that it hailed from
China or Japan. Here, indeed, was a new problem to
ponder, a new puzzle ; how, especially when one had never
seen the land of its birth, could it be possible to tell, from
the habit of its growth and flowering, its shape and colour,
whence came a plant : for nationality, or race, was a human
attribute, and not, surely, a geographical affinity, applying
itself equally to man and animal, fish and vegetable ? . . .
But then, as a child, I did not know how the gentlemen of
the Far East, carrying their bird-cages, or with a bird held
on one arm by a chain, will examine a flower, will walk
round it, slowly appraising its points after the fashion of
English racing men examining a horse in a paddock, and
how, just in the same way that they peer into the black-

glazed, gigantic bowls of goldfish at the entrance to Pei-Hai, tallying with true virtuosity one golden fin, one sable veil or protuberant and goggling eye against another, so they will compare one peony, petal by petal, with its neighbour. Nor, as I lay there, thinking of this, was I aware (as I am now, owing to Dr. Bodde's exquisite translation of Lich'en[1]), that a retired Manchu civil servant, in about 1900, could, for example, — though he tells us that in addition another two hundred exist—specify at random one hundred and thirty-three varieties of chrysanthemum, and that, among them — to select a few — were blossoms named Honey-linked Bracelets, Silver-Red Needle, Peach-Blossom Fan, Eyebrows of the Old Ruler,[2] Concubine of the Hsiao and Hsiang Rivers, Goose Quills, Purple Tiger Whiskers, Ash Crane Wings, Spring Swallow in an Apricot Orchard, Snow-covered Cinnabar, White Crane Sleeping in the Snow, Azure Lotus, Jade Shoots, Egg Plant Blue ; and Golden-Hair Lion, Golden Phoenix Wing, Purple Dragon with Open Claws, Egret Crane Feathers, Azure Dragon-Whiskers, Lustrous Variegated Cloud-Dragon, Jade Spoon Stirring Broth, Autumn Beauty of the Hibiscus, Evening Sun on a Duck's Back, Lily on a Dazzling Day ; and Black Tiger-Whiskers, Golden Phoenix Holding a Pearl in its Mouth, Spring Dawn at the Han Palace, Red Mist, Half Water Half Sky, Bird's Talon Immortal, Intoxicated T'ai Po,[3] Phoenix Flute, Fragrant White Pear, Gold as One Likes It, Yellow Orioles in the Green Willow, Beehive, Quartz as One Likes It or Unicorn and Parrot ; names that reconcile me a little now toward the cairn-terrier-like horror

[1] See *Annual Customs and Festivals in Peking* as recorded in the *Yen-ching Sui-shih-chi* by Tun Lich'en, translated and annotated by Dr. Derk Bodde. (Henri Vetch, Peking, 1936.)

[2] The Taoist sage, Lao-Tze.            [3] Li T'ai Po, the great poet.

of this flower as we know it in Europe. . . . In fact, I did not realise how carefully all things are bred and grown for their purpose, of pleasing the ultimate almond eye of the complete connoisseur.

Nevertheless when, later on during that afternoon, now many years ago, I enquired the name of the tree and where it had been found, I learnt that it did, in fact, come from China ; an answer that inspired me with curiosity concerning this vast land, whose character was so powerful and original that it could thus mould objects, creatures and flowers to its liking, to its pattern.

As we grew older we became accustomed to hearing more of this strange country, for, in spite of his physical delicacy, the son [1] of one of my grandmother's favourite nieces was searching the more remote and unknown parts of China for hitherto undiscovered flowers. He could talk and read Chinese, and, in addition, had turned Buddhist ; a fact seldom mentioned in the house, since I apprehend that my grandmother and her sisters felt this conversion to be but a poor and ironic return for so much money expended upon carrying the true light to the heathen in foreign parts. . . .

But the heat now was growing intolerable, though this half-hour before sunrise was usually the coolest time. Even the slight effort entailed by recollection became impossible. . . . Now the mind must wander where it listed. Sitting up, I could see the dusty, low-lying outlines of the nearer African hills embedded in the first green and submarine light : and my lips turned to shaping phrases in which to describe them. How difficult, I thought, to describe

---

[1] Reginald Farrer, 1880–1920, who made many botanical journeys in Burma, China and Tibet, through regions where it was believed no white man could live. He died on a journey across the Burmese mountains. Author of *On the Eaves of the World*, 1917, and *The Rainbow Bridge*, published posthumously in 1921.

any landscape from just this distance, when it seemed more like a moon model, in relief — an effect no doubt aided by the circle of the port-hole — than actual territory, belonging to some race, and inhabited by living people. . . . And now, in this connection, I recalled my last interview with George Moore, and his obvious difficulty in grasping the facts of natural configuration.

It had been a delightful, and typical, occasion. He had written and asked me to tea, and then, when I arrived (I had not seen him for some time), he immediately explained his invitation by saying, " I have asked you to tea, because it appears that you have written a book in something *resembling* English ". . . . He then confided in me that he was writing a novel, the action of which he had laid in Sorrento. It was, he added, a book very different from his others. " It is about a man and a woman. He gives a museum to the town, and she is a nun. And she falls in love with him, and then — and this," he said, blandly smiling to himself, " is, I think, really rather original —, after she has been to bed with him for the first time, she turns to him and says, ' *At last* I have found something worth doing ! ' " . . . I did not venture to say that this sounded to me very much like the theme of all his novels, and in any case, he continued to talk on at once, asking me if I knew Sorrento. He had never seen it, and so found it difficult to master the plan of the town and lie of the country : it was holding him up. He wanted, for instance, to know where to place the museum. I answered that he could not have applied to any Englishman better equipped in this respect than myself, as I had spent a great deal of my time on that coast. Would I, then, describe the lie of the land to him ? " First of all,

Mr. Moore," I began hopefully, " there is a hill, a mountain almost, and then there is a valley . . ." — but, before I could finish, he cried out despairingly, " But if there is a hill, how *can* there be a valley ? " . . . It did not seem of much use to proceed with my disquisition, so I said, " Well, if you'd allow me one day to bring a map, and explain it to your secretary, I'm sure I could make it clear to *her*." . . . Accordingly, a week or so later, I received a note asking me to come round to Ebury Street the next morning at 11.30 and explain to his secretary the position of Sorrento. . . . I took the map with me, and half-way through my conversation with her, George Moore entered and sat down in a corner, facing us, but at some distance away. . . . At the end, I said to her, " Well, I think I've made it all clear, haven't I ? ", adding, rather fatuously, from a kind of nervousness, " and I believe *this* ", pointing at a small dot on the map, " would be a good place for Mr. Moore's museum ; it has such a lovely view." . . . Before she could reply, Moore had ungratefully interrupted, saying in a loud, cross voice, " Well, I'm glad *somebody* understands, for *I* do not understand a single word of it. . . . And as for the museum, I detest all views — but why a museum should have a view . . . ! "

Certainly the matter of description was difficult : a single phrase can mean a dozen different things to a dozen different people. . . . And yet, look at that Arab dhow sailing toward the sunrise ; it was precisely as Marco Polo had described such a boat six hundred years ago. One would recognise it, that was to say, from his description. . . . I thought of the dhow that, its crew first lighting a bonfire on deck, had, at immense speed, darted across our bows last night, and back again, for the sheer joy of its swiftness, I supposed ; it had swept the darkness like a phoenix, fabulous bird of these parts.

> " O blest unfabled Incense Tree,
> That burns in glorious Araby,
> With red scent chalicing the air,
> Till earth-life grow Elysian there !
>
> Half buried to her flaming breast
> In this bright tree, she makes her nest,
> Hundred-sunned Phoenix, when she must
> Crumble at length to hoary dust.
>
> Her gorgeous death-bed, her rich pyre
> Burnt up with aromatic fire !
> Her urn, sight-high from spoiler men !
> Her birthplace, when self-born again ! "

I intoned to myself, for I was sleepy now, as the light strengthened, and the sounds of washing and scrubbing and bumping began to spring up above my head, all over the deck. . . . And I thought of the Pergola, again, of the Chinese tree, of the house, now turned into a school, and of the old lady lying on her sofa in the Indian Room.

# BOOK ONE

## EXOTIC VISTAS

"Les espèces d'arbres sont nombreuses, des fleurs encore plus abondantes, ayant le parfum et la beauté. Les fleurs aquatiques sont de mille espèces, mais j'ignore leur nom. . . . Au premier de l'an il y a déjà en ce pays des fleurs de lotus.

"Comme animaux, ils ont le rhinocéros, l'éléphant, le bœuf sauvage, le 'cheval de montagne'. . . . Il y a en grande abondance des tigres, panthères, ours, sangliers, cerfs, daims, chevrotins, gibbons, renards. . . .

"Parmi les poissons et tortues c'est la carpe noire qui est en plus grande abondance. . . . Il y a des crocodiles, gros comme des navires, qui ont quatre pattes et ressemblent tout à fait au dragon, mais n'ont pas de cornes ; leur ventre est très croustillant."

*Mémoires sur les coutumes du Cambodge, de*
*Tcheou Ta-Kouan.* Translated by M. Pelliot

### CHAPTER ONE

## GOLDEN BOUQUET

" Where, like a golden bouquet, lay
Asia, Africa, Cathay."

Marseilles, as we left it behind us, lay plainly in the
grip of a blizzard. The lofty palm-trees seemed to spin
under its force like tops, and the golden islands which lie
round the coast had now assumed thin mantles of white
that matched the snowy crests of the enormous, pounding
waves. . . . We had chosen a French boat, because, in
addition to the chief point in its favour — that it constituted the sole direct means of reaching Saigon, our first
goal and the place whence it is most easy to visit Angkor —
the discipline to which passengers are subjected would
certainly be less severe, the food more palatable, than on
an English vessel. (Though in reality, for long, hot
journeys, Italian food is, in this respect as in so many others,
pleasantest, most suitable and most healthy, since pasta
and rice do not deteriorate, or have to be laid upon ice for
weeks at a time.) Moreover, Christmas was due at the end
of the first week's voyage, and here we should be able to
escape all the attendant celebrations, whereas a passage in

an English boat would have entailed either a churlishness
so resolute as to be worthy of a better — or worse —
cause, or else perpetual bouts of simple, communal Yule-
tide fun ; crackers, paper-caps, almond icing, toy trumpets,
conjurers, almonds and raisins tied with red ribbon, cham-
pagne, air-balloons and plum-pudding. . . . I recollected,
too, the last Christmas I had spent in an English boat, when
coming back from the United States during Prohibition
times, and the pleasures it had brought with it. Indeed, I
remembered only too well the middle-aged American lady
who had tracked me down on Christmas morning to the
bar — in a dark corner of which I had hoped to be a recluse
— and had sat on there drinking, and of how she had cried
bitterly toward luncheon-time. First of all she had confided in me concerning the loss of her family tree (a burglar
had broken into her villa in the South of France, a few
years previously, and had stolen it), and then of her family
fortune. Only a hundred and fifty thousand dollars a year
remained to her, it transpired. . . . But I must not think
that she was lamenting her lost riches : no, it was not that ;
it was because she was going to see her beloved son so soon
again, and because she was so proud of him, so proud — and
in consequence it made her weep. " And naturally, I'm
proud of him," she had added, simply. " You would be,
too, if you were his mother. Why, he's won every swimming prize at Eton and Harrow. . . . He's at school there,
you know." . . . In the end, her fondness so overcame her
that she did not go in to luncheon at all, but sat where she
was until dinner, and seemed very much annoyed when,
my appetite getting the better of me, I left her. . . . Everything that happened to her after that, was my fault, and if I
passed the door, she would, as though by instinct, open

one eye and direct its gaze reproachfully toward me. . . .
Here, however, such incidents could not take place : French
fun, which in any case applied itself to the New Year more
than to Christmas, was of a different quality.

For the first day, the boat had appeared deserted. . . .
Only after leaving the Lipari Islands behind us, and while
sailing between Italy and Sicily — those two lands I know
and love so well — in the green, homeric light of the early
morning, when it seemed almost as though this were the
first time of the earth being exposed, and it were waiting
for the sun to reveal its wonders, did the weather right
itself. As we watched, the sun touched the flat roofs of
Messina, a town again in its aspect : in this, very different
from the first occasion on which I had passed it, a few days
after the great catastrophe, to which its name was henceforth to be indissolubly attached.

Now, the sun had mounted in the heaven, and we were
sailing by Etna, under the gentle, swelling lines of its
imposing bulk, crowned by a snow-covered cone which
seemed to collect its many pastel tones from the sky of
winter azure. . . . The boat was beginning at last to come
to life, so that, in a moment or two, when soup was offered
to all the starving passengers, who reclined on their labelled
deck-chairs, it became obvious that convalescence was
well on its way ; though of course, as I have hinted elsewhere, with his national instinct for the *convenances*, for
doing the right thing at the right moment, the French
sufferer from seasickness makes no attempt to disguise the
nature of his complaint, but when in a ship, likes, on the
contrary, to parade his bottles of eau-de-Cologne and
brandy as well as a pallid or virescent face, in the same way
that he would wish to wear a kilt in Scotland or to eat the

appropriate *plats régionaux* of any locality in which he was staying.

Luncheon was at midday, and in the dining-room certain French characteristics now began to assert themselves. A prominent lawyer from Saigon, and his wife — a distinguished-looking couple, with a real structure to their faces, and with quick, intelligent eye — occupied the next table to ours. Both of them, from the first meal served to us, watched our dishes with feverish attention, and if the head waiter brought to our table any delicacy, such as caviare, that he had failed to offer them, they created a tremendous rumpus, the man shouting, the wife weeping, for they were at the same time greedy and democratic, sworn foes to the hideous spectre of privilege, whatever the form it might assume. Yet the scenes they created, they somehow or other contrived to make it plain, were in no way directed against *us personally*, only against the principle of the thing, so that we remained throughout the journey on friendly, if formal, terms, bowing, smiling and, when we passed one another, making the appropriate remark concerning the weather.

But it was on deck, now that the ship sailed on smooth waters, that you could best appreciate the difference between a French and an English passenger boat, both as a spectacle and in the life it sheltered. It was a different world. To begin with, a tremendous element of holiness, entirely lacking on board, let us say, a P. & O., entered into the picture ; there were groups of monks who, in their white woollen garb, seemed to belong to the canvas of some Neapolitan painter of the seventeenth century, and bearded priests — missionaries on their way abroad — and the still, calm clumps of nuns who, in their elaborate

wimples and with their wide Gothic sleeves, appeared to
be the very models that Van Eyck or Roger Van der
Weyden had delighted to paint against those blue, ves-
pertine landscapes ; figures that, in the stillness inspiring
them, yet bordered more nearly, perhaps, on statuary than
on painting. . . . They spent their time quietly enough,
the monks strolling on deck and talking to each other, the
nuns, sitting on wooden benches, reading aloud in stylistic
clusters, the folds of their voluminous skirts and their
airplane-like head-dresses taking up a great amount of deck
space ; but nevertheless they imparted to the whole boat
an air of placidity, of rustic goodness and unworldliness
that could not be for long dispelled by all the sounds of
jazz scraped out of travelling gramophones, or by the shrill
voices of the wives of French officials. . . . And yet, they
had something strange about them in these new surroundings, they surprised you each time you saw them, in the
manner of a picture by Georgio de Chirico : you could
reconcile them with almost any landscape, but, isolated
after this manner upon these blue and crested waves, they
seemed as incongruous at first sight as sheep separated
from their pastures, and installed, let us say, in a modern
flat. . . . Then another distinctive note was struck by the
bearded sea-captain, who, so unlike an English one, enjoyed
chiefly reading the books of Pierre Loti and of similar addicts
to local colour, and who, when in the bar, drank, not whisky
and soda, but absinthe, to which he added water, allowing
it to trickle slowly into the tumblers until they became
clouded as smoky crystal. . . . There were, too, of course,
a great many jovial, middle-aged French colonials returning
home, all of them short, with broad faces and low, bull
necks, accompanied by their middle-aged wives, still shorter,

their necks yet more tightly attached to trunks supported by very little leg, and with ankles of such hereditary width as to have saved their ancestors, no doubt, from the guillotine at the time of the Revolution. And each couple carried with it to the bar, in case a moment's silence should occur, a short, squat gramophone : (not that I have anything against a portable gramophone in a boat or in a hotel. It has become an indispensable part of every traveller's equipment : a method of retaliation in private life, similar to the use of a tariff between nations ; that is to say that if you have been kept awake until two in the morning by the playing of jazz records next door to you, the only means of preventing a recurrence of such trouble is to rise at seven and give a concert of modern music, Stravinsky and Prokoffief, for example. Moreover, in any place of resort, it constitutes a very sure defence against the bore, with his ineluctable booming). All of them had paid for deck-chairs ; for deck-chairs, also, were *de rigueur* in a boat. But, since they were too uncomfortable, no one ever attempted to rest in them for more than a brief, mistaken moment. They preferred — and no one could blame them for it — to sit here in the bar, or the " Winter Garden " outside, where they remained for hours, at intervals clapping together short, fat palms and thick fingers, and shouting " Boy ! " in order to obtain the attention of the slim, Annamite waiters, with their wide, shiny, black silk trousers, their white coats and beautifully shaped hands : they were ruder, more rough in their manner, I thought, to these servitors, if any order were incorrectly understood, than would have been the equivalent English officials or planters, who, at the worst, would seem to fail to notice, rather than to bark at them in this way. But, above all, the French long-distance boats are differentiated from those of other races by the whole vespiaries of jumping, hopping, skipping, running, shouting, weeping children which they contain.

So perpetually is the world informed that France has fewer children than any other European country, that it is a never-failing surprise to see — and hear — more children — and noisier ones — in French public gardens, French homes and French hotels than anywhere else upon earth : moreover, children so ingenious, well able to amuse themselves. Thus, as the weather became hotter throughout the voyage, they grew ever more inventive, devising special new games, such as, during the siesta hour, jumping, in turn, over and over again, in a particular spot just above your head, or dropping a weight, one after the other, in order to discover how many kilos each of them could lift. Meanwhile their Annamite nurses, in waxed, black silk gowns, with black, padded haloes round their heads, and teeth of black lacquer — so that, when they smiled, at first you saw nothing but a black and gaping hole — sat watching their charges with an air of mingled pride and resignation.

Tooth-conscious to the last degree, these ayahs spoke but seldom, and, when they did speak, attempted to screen from view their most interesting feature : by holding up a sheltering, yellow hand a little distance in front of the mouth. . . . And yet, there was no need for such humility. At home, in Annam or Tonkin, this ebony feature would be much admired, both for itself and as a sign of respectable origin. For black lacquer was practical, as well as decorative. The Annamites and their neighbours are the chief chewers in the world of betel, a drug, the crunching of which stains the teeth yellow : and, in order to avoid this blemish, every young child whose parents can afford it, has the teeth lacquered black in infancy. . . . And, of course, after a while they had begun to prefer this fashion — so hideous to European eyes — forced upon them by their habits, before anything that nature could achieve, and, in addition, to regard it as a sign of civilisation, of belonging to the true elect (in the identical way that a hockey-player considers a " hockey-thumb " on the hand of a new acquaintance, or, as for that, as an opium-smoker greets symptoms of the same vice in someone he has just met for the first time). Indeed, Mouhot, the engineer who discovered Angkor,[1] tells us that when a Mandarin from Tonkin was introduced to a person, from Penang, with ordinary teeth, he was much taken aback, and enquired of his suite, " Who is that man with the ugly mouth, and white teeth, like those of a dog ? " . . . But I suppose that in Europe their teeth had attracted attention of an unflattering nature : even in the boat, the eyes of the native stewards and waiters had been vitiated by European manners, and no one now said to them admiringly, " Really, darling, I believe your teeth are blacker than ever ! " . . . Hence, this new-born sense of inferiority.

As we neared the Red Sea, a certain air of nervousness began to manifest itself, both in the passengers and in the officers of the ship : for, at that time, despite the most stringent precautions, nearly every French boat inevitably caught fire when sailing through this piece of water. It was, in fact, " the thing to do ", *de rigueur* again, and, though they were not naturally nervous, the French feeling for the

---

[1] In 1860. For information concerning Mouhot and his discovery of Angkor see pp. 86-87.

*convenances* once more asserted itself. Two ships had been burnt out quite lately. The authorities, from the captain downward, were plainly terrified, and, in token of it, the great man himself took to consuming two absinthes where formerly one had served him. . . . As to the matter of precautions, intensely fussy little notices about the dangers of fire were suddenly placarded all over the ship, in order thoroughly to frighten any passenger who had hitherto escaped the panic, and we were forbidden, categorically, to smoke in our cabins or to throw cigarette-ends down on the deck. Ash-trays of the most inflammable substance, celluloid, or a special very soft and dry wood, were suddenly sprinkled everywhere to receive them. Moreover those curious, white-painted metal traps for the wind, resembling the gills of fishes, with which, in tropical waters, the port-holes of French steamers always bristle, became more than ever in evidence (no doubt they would have helped to incubate, and then to fan, the blaze, had it materialised). Further, Madame Lopez, the Algerian stewardess, who summed up in her generous range of black silk mountains the whole ancient African ideal of Motherhood, was always conjuring her bulk in and out of the cabins to see if any of her charges had yet set alight to themselves, and also kept a more than usually severe eye upon Geraint, the nimble, nitwit Breton steward, who constituted her chief worry, responsibility and joy. (The narrow, white corridors re-echoed always with her plaintive jungle-chant of " *Geraint . . . Geraint . . . Ge . . raint !* ")

One day we spent at Djibuti, that strange equatorial metropolis so soon to become a sound on the world's lips. Huge sea-shells littered the neighbouring shores, trumpets and spires and spiked tents in nacre, glittering in a dazzling green light : polished and scrubbed, and still more glittering, they could be seen again at the port, offered for sale, on small trays, by gigantic negro pedlars. They constituted, it seemed, all the articles of merchandise that the land bore, all its natural products — apart from the particular pride of the whole region, a few date-palms, which grew in regular formation round the house of the French Military Governor. . . . A dusty road, leading past them, took one to a town of low white houses, and, in the centre, a large square containing a few cafés with trellised shelters, in the cool shade of which dark-skinned waiters could be observed filling empty bottles of Evian and Vichy at a tap, sure death for several tourists. High over all the buildings floated the proud banners of the African dust, and beneath them were standing a great many people of various colours. Lepers were following travellers, importuning them, hoarsely promising to allow them to draw aside the veils from their faces if a suitably large sum were paid for the privilege : but, since no offers were forthcoming, they resolutely uncovered themselves without being asked, in order to levy their pitiful blackmail. Groups of giant, black-lead-coloured Somalis in white robes, their figures displaying the same tall, thin-limbed, broadshouldered elegance that inspires cave-drawings or Mycenean vases, were talking together, and Ethiops were selling picture-postcards of the coronation of the Emperor Haile Selassie — his delicate, fatal and iconic visage showing, perhaps, a slight resemblance to that of King Charles I — and of his hurriedly constructed palace, with its Hollywood *salons* and furniture. Further on, outside one or two low huts in the street beyond the square, a few nondescript natives were enjoying somewhat dusty siestas upon naked brass bedsteads placed on the mud pavement within the shadow of their shacks. . . . Otherwise there was nothing in this city of broken green lattice and wire-netting but the dust, and those shells that flowered alone on the low and sandy shore in glittering, equatorial light. . . . Devoid of all life, it appeared but a poor and empty gateway to a land described by Marco Polo as " full of elephants, lions, camelopards and a variety of other animals, such as wild asses, and monkeys that have the figure of men, together with many birds, wild and domestic " ; and where Bruce in his *Travels*, written five hundred years later, tells us that " innumerable flocks of apes and baboons of different kinds destroy the fields of millet everywhere ". . . . Though, as we left the town, I did, it is true, see a few white ibis pecking gingerly at the shells.

From the deck, just before dark, it seemed almost as though Djibuti no longer existed, as though the hours of fierce daylight had excoriated it, leaving revealed only the aching bones, dry and dusty but glowing, of this most sinister trading place. . . . How large a part, I thought, the light of the African sun plays in the infinite horror of African cities, as I have seen them, and yet how greatly it varies ! There are the white lights that play on Oran, city of half-castes and mean whites on the eternal fringe of things ; the scintillating, quivering mirages of the dried salt lakes that constitute an unreal approach to the desert city of Tozeur,[1] lying under the grape-bloom edges of the

---

[1] It was in Tozeur, I remember, that, when I remarked to a friend in English that the buildings of the town precisely resembled slums, my Arab guide turned round and delightedly said, " *Oui, c'est ça : tout le monde a dit qu'il ressemble beaucoup aux ' slooms ' !* "

sky, where it touches the sand ; even in so distant Marra-kesh, in many respects the ideal African city of water-lawns, cool, pillared palaces and orange groves, situated in a superb oasis between two snow-capped ranges, the strong rays momentarily expose an age-old squalor lying only just under the surface ; while, not far from Marrakesh, in Mazaghan, that city the very name of which sounds as though it contained within it the rolling of drums for executions, a curious yellow light runs like grease over the broken stone houses, and over the great Atlantic waves themselves, pounding so endlessly upon the deserted, thick yellow sands. But in this last town is buried infinite tragedy as well as horror, for it was once — as Djibuti, the full breadth of the continent away, is also said to have been — a great centre of the slave trade. The mono-tony of those grey, uninhabited houses — for all the white people engaged in this terrible merchandise were massacred by the natives some two centuries ago, and though their houses stand in the old town, no man will live in them — appears, in some way, to sum up for ever the tragedy of the gigantic, unformed continent, so that, while you regard these buildings, you seem to see the lines of drooping black figures, stretching to such a distance that the eye cannot follow them, back into the vast darkness which conceived them ; helpless, human animals chained together, the quick pulling the weight of the dead under an intolerable sun toward these waves which spelt for them, if they survived, a life as strange as if it lay the other side of death. . . . Djibuti was left behind by now, and we were back once more in the Indian Ocean.

That same evening, as I sat on deck again, after dinner, in an effort to keep cool, I was reminded of something I

had contrived to forget. . . . A suave and elegant French-
man, in a white-flannel, tropical evening coat, came up to
me to say that he and his friends knew how much Christmas
—the mere word, Christmas — meant to their " neighbours across the Channel ", and that, accordingly, it
completely spoilt their pleasure to see an Englishman sitting
alone and at his ease on such a night. . . . Would I not,
therefore, join a little party of some thirty people who were
gathering together to have supper at midnight ? . . . And
so my few, first days of peace — for we still had far to go —
were over : politeness obliged me in response — in response,
indeed, to such great courtesy — to sit up till four in the
morning.

The members of the party were drinking cocktails when
I joined them. The spokesman proved to be a doctor,
married to a beautiful Greek from Corfu ; a lady who
plainly must have inherited Venetian blood, for she showed
the suffused, flushed, golden fairness of the blonde Venetian
type, of Catherine Cornaro, Queen of Cyprus, for example,
or of Giambattista Tiepolo's daughters, whom you can see
to this day poised on clouds upon the walls and ceilings of
so many palaces all over Europe. There were also numerous
other couples, most of the women fair, and nearly all the
men of an athletic build ; in the stamp of so many French-
men since the war, as if, with victory, the type had reverted
again to a previous pattern.

Our talk proved halting. There was nothing much to
say : and it was extremely hot. When learning French,
the first thing you must acquire is the use of idiom ;
and what is idiom except cliché and platitude ? Thus
French conversation of this kind, except when it is the talk
of artists or *hommes de métier*, a little resembles the Chinese

(as I was to learn later). In both countries it is mere politeness to be unoriginal, and you must never indulge in any opinion that is unexpected, unless you wish to offend your hosts and fellow-guests. No . . . it is considered as a game, like whist or bridge, with fixed rules ; you must, of course, never revoke ; and when your neighbour proffers you the correct, and anticipated, conversational card, you must then produce its correct, and anticipated, answer. It must go snip-snap too, or a general feeling of discomfort will ensue. . . . One scarcely had to think, in order to talk, and my mind, apart from a certain preoccupation with the lateness of the hour — in which, it was obvious, re-sided its chief virtue in the eyes of the revellers, who would be able to go about for the next day or two, boasting to their less fortunate acquaintances, " D'you know, we did not go to bed till nearly five ! " — and with the tough-ness of the turkey, still blue-white from a long process of refrigeration, mainly concerned itself with the curious similarity of all the names of my new friends. Boutte, Boutin, Bouton, Boudin, Boudine, Bottin, Bottard, Bottarde, Botton, Boudhon ; how would it ever be possible to sort and separate them for the memory, as individuals, with different names and histories ? . . . And then suddenly my neighbour, Madame Boudin, did indeed say one thing which startled me, for, turning toward me, she remarked, " Ah, vous venez de Londres, Monsieur ? . . . Alors, vous connaissez Goldare's Green. C'est ravissant ! "

After this festivity, my morning walks round the deck every day had continually to be punctuated with polite halts, the rhythm continually to be broken with " Bonjour, Monsieur Bottin : Bonjour, Madame Bottard, comment allez-vous ce matin ? . . . Ah, ce n'est rien, un peu de fièvre,

*peut-être la chaleur."* " *Bonjour, Madame Bottin, Bonjour,*
*Monsieur Botton."* . . . The fear of fire, as the voyage
progressed, was happily abating. The wooden ash-trays
had been withdrawn, and the ship's officers were seen more
seldom in the bar. . . . But new symptoms were to be
observed. . . . As it grew hotter, more and more of the
women on board took to wearing blue-serge trousers, a
particularly warm and unbecoming dress (the reason that
women have not before adopted it, cannot be, surely, because they have not previously thought of it ?) ; but in
this instance it was largely due to a kindly effort on their
part to try and induce in the men the belief that they were
on a pleasure cruise, rather than returning — as, in fact,
most of the younger ones were — to a long period of
combined work and exile, or, as in the case of the youngest
of all, sailing East for the first time in order to undergo a
period of military service in the colonies.

Now we were nearing the coast of Coromandel, a name
so magical in both sound and association, falling on the ear
like a spell.

> On the coast of Coromandel
> Dance they to the tunes of Handel ;
> Chorally, that coral coast
> Correlates the bone to ghost,
> Till word and limb and note seem one,
> Blending, binding act to tone.
>
> All day long they point the sandal
> On the coast of Coromandel.
> Lemon-yellow legs all bare
> Pirouette to perruqued air
> From the first green shoots of morn,
> Cool as northern hunting-horn,

Till the nightly, tropic wind
With its rough-tongued, grating rind
Shatters the frail spires of spice
Imaged in the lawns of rice
(Mirror-flat and mirror-green
Is that lovely water's sheen).
Saraband and rigadoon
Dance they through the purring noon,
While the lacquered waves expand
Golden dragons on the sand—
Dragons that must, steaming, die
Of the hot sun's agony.

.    .    .    .    .    .

Still hotter grew the weather. Flying fishes skimmed the waves, but for them it was obviously out of the frying-pan into the fire, and they lapsed into their native element again. Forming groups by the prow, the nuns and monks would watch them silently, sadly, in the early morning, perhaps translating these watery undulations into the thick-leaved lanes of Normandy, with the birds flitting from hedge to hedge, and all the familiar sounds of hidden pipings and rustling leaves and of someone singing in the field, of the hour equivalent to this in France. . . . (A long time must pass before they could return home again for a holiday !) . . . Meanwhile they looked more than ever out of place in their heavy, medieval garments, so that in this light they assumed an almost visionary quality : and, as though, indeed, they were spectral in their nature, they would, throughout the day, never more be seen.

Downstairs, to sleep was out of the question, and Geraint was so overwhelmed that he sat on a chair in the passage, apparently in a coma, resolute in two matters alone : that he would answer no bell, and that motherly

Madame Lopez should undertake all his duties. (If he sat there, he thought, it was plainly no use her calling him. That eternal " *Geraint!* . . . *Ge* . . . *raint!* ") It became, too, I found, quite impossible to work in my cabin, even with the aid of a wind-catcher : and since, if I was to be able to stay as long as I wished in China — or, as for that, ever to return thence — it was necessary for me to earn some money, I used to sit on deck, at a table under an awning near the bar, every afternoon during the siesta hour, and write articles (the majority of which were re-published afterward in *Penny Foolish*).[1]  Indeed, I grew to like writing in that place, and trained myself not to heed the distant gramophone or dancing children. (If a writer is faced with any continual and insurmountable obstacle to quiet, such as a loud-speaker in a neighbouring hotel, or a crane working outside his window, the only method by which to conquer it is for him to pretend, little by little, that the sound helps him to concentrate ; but alas, if he does so, in the end he will find that he really cannot work without it.)  Finally, however, the temperature conquered even the high spirits of the children, and it became possible to write, with a fair measure of concentration, from two until half-past four every afternoon. . . . The only other survivors at this period of the day were two French-Canadian journalists, brothers, and jolly characters, but very unpopular on board because they were suspected of being Communists ; so unpopular, that audible remarks would be made about them in their hearing, since it was presumed that at each port of call, when they went ashore, it was to foment unrest, or even to plan insurrection, and, in this world of returning

[1] *Penny Foolish, A Book of Tirades and Panegyrics*, by Osbert Sitwell. (Macmillan & Co., Ltd., London, 1935.)

officials and rubber-planters, Communism was by no means held in as high esteem as in the *salons* of Mayfair or the salubrious model flats of Hampstead. . . . However, it seemed in no way to worry them. There they sat every afternoon, in their bérets — everyone else on board was by now wearing topees — working, with large glasses of beer in front of them. Often I wondered what, exactly, they were writing : for every now and then they would be seized with fits of such uncontrollable laughter that they would be forced to lay their pens aside and call for another *bock*.

The afternoons, then, became increasingly restful, though tea-time always brought a small influx to the bar and, just before sunset each evening, trouble would begin about *Le Rayon Vert*, the Green Ray. Recently there had been correspondence in the columns of *The Times*, and also, presumably, of certain French journals, concerning this mysterious and, indeed, mythical ray. . . . Accordingly, at the correct hypothetical hour, all the elderly gentlemen on board with any claim to scientific knowledge — and the French elderly gentleman who does not make such a claim for himself has surely never been born — would arrive on deck in a very important manner, carrying, hung round them, telescopes, opera-glasses, cameras, compasses, theodolites and any other instrument they could find which had the right look about it, and dragging after them tripods, camp-stools and metal stands : then, bridging their noses with special pairs of dark spectacles, they would proceed to stare back fixedly, but with a certain air of questioning and defiance, straight into the eye of the setting sun. After that, of course, green rays were visible to them in every direction, but, since each of these scientific enquirers had observed his particular one in a different quarter of the sky, this introduced into the data an element of doubt which led to an immense amount of quarrelling and bickering, fomented by the ladies, who, of a sudden, openly took sides in the matter.

Sailing-boats could occasionally be seen now, and one wondered whether they contained divers for pearls, for we were off the south part of Coromandel, the Malabar Coast, and I fell to thinking of Marco Polo's story of the pearl fisheries here, and of how the merchants always arranged for " certain enchanters belonging to a class of Brahmans " to sit in the boats accompanying the divers, and to utter spells, so that the numerous and ferocious sharks which haunt these waters should not attack them at their work. And at night these wizards only discontinued their magical labours in order that no thieves or unauthorised persons should benefit by them ; thereby, in fact, converting the sharks into a kind of special police force recruited for the pearl fisheries. . . . It is, I believe, a most beautiful land, but curiously unfrequented ; an enormous stretch of bays and beaches, sheltered by very lofty palm-trees, and with, every now and then, the gilded top of a pagoda showing above them. . . . The country, I was told by an English acquaintance of mine who has lived there for twenty years or more, is very badly infested by snakes : but he added that he did not fear them, since the natives had taught him to place a saucer of milk every evening in the garden for its own guardian snake : and, if you did this, the creature would not attack you, and would even protect you from the onslaughts of others ; a story quite as unexpected as any in Marco Polo's Travels.

The boats grew more plentiful as we approached Ceylon

(it was New Year's Eve, but fortunately I had proved such a dry blanket at the last party that the revellers refrained from asking me to join them), and the next morning we reached Colombo. . . . The European city was deserted, the shops shuttered. Only in the centre of the squares, and at the junctions of the broad streets, an enormous bronze effigy of dead general or statesman — looking strangely out of place in this air and light into which he seemed tremblingly to dissolve, an invader consumed from hour to hour by an intangible force that he had never foreseen — would appear to be acting as sentry, pointing vacuously down an empty street with a bronze baton or a sheaf of notes ready for the next speech. The large hotel near by constituted, too, this morning, a monument to dead dissipation ; the festivities of the previous evening had evidently only just ended, but now in an atmosphere of emptiness, stale cigarette smoke and dusty, trampled, paper streamers, they were dead, dead as Pompeii. One or two solemn-faced waiters, wearing combs in the coiled chignons at the back of their heads, and dressed in white linen, looked at us mournfully with the tragic, helpless eyes of the Cingalese. But they did not attempt to clean the room. . . . Something about their helplessness made me sympathise momentarily with Bishop Heber's unflattering lines on the inhabitants of this island : even with them in attendance, the place seemed empty, as though they were ghosts. Nothing would ever be done. . . . And yet, they had accomplished much in the past. Fortunately the Museum, beautifully situated in a park, was open, and fuller of interested human beings, I think, than any museum I have ever seen. All, too, were natives, crowds of jostling Cingalese, peering curiously and sadly at the bronzes made by their ancestors, and but lately discovered ; works of art of great magnificence, linking up with that lost civilisation which found its ultimate and finest flower in Angkor. Reflection, though, you would say, rather than thought or action, must, surely, be the forte of the modern Cingalese ; a kind of mystic mooning.

Inertia and emptiness prevailed again in those endless half-breed suburbs that always surround European towns in the Orient. Wooden bungalows, which might have been designed for the sole purpose of affording easy access to serpents, and many red-brick buildings, palpitated incandescently beneath their hot quilts of blossoms such as hitherto I had never seen, swags and trails and tresses of open-mouthed blue and lilac flowers, and cups in orange and flaming red. . . . But the native city, on the other hand, was filled with struggling currents of people, with a life so vivid as to leave far behind even such cities, to name only two of the most lively at random, as Naples or as Fez. (Perhaps inertia only comes into its full own when East meets West.) Bonzes hurried past in their yellow robes, and, more seldom, Hindu priests, with esoteric symbols tattooed upon temple or forehead, walked slowly by, a curious sense of power emanating from them. Bulky merchants, dressed like sham ghosts in long white linen sheets, rolled down the road at a swift pace in their rickshas, and formed superb monuments to the dignified tradition of oriental commerce, their cool urbanity and lack of expression contrasting with the feeble excitement of the shouting, sweating men who dragged them along ; in this, perhaps, a symbol of big business everywhere. Here there was no sign of resigned helplessness : it was a new world of shouts and cries and scents, and of music in new keys, of gigantic, high-coloured, very strong-smelling flowers, of henna and jewels, of white clothes and brown bodies, for the chief change to be observed here from Europe was the comparative nakedness of the majority : much more naked, for example, than at Djibuti. And, standing primly amid this welter of cheap life, a single, very restrained church, built by the Dutch at the end of the seventeenth century, struck a pathetic note of European idealism and reserve. . . . Yes, *idealism* : a quality which had led in the end, as was visible all round one, to the subjugation of lands as large as whole continents : but no one who had seen that church could doubt the existence of this virtue in the builders of it.

On the boat people said, " Well, if you *like* the heat, as you pretend, wait till you get to Singapore ". . . . But, when the ship reached there some days later, we found cool weather and such violent rain that we could not venture on shore. Nor was this merely the daily half-hour's storm to which the climate of Singapore invariably treats its victims : it had been raining after this fashion, we learned, for three whole days. Indeed, as we entered the harbour, it had been only just possible to see, through the drifting veils of rain, the diving black bodies of the very primitive, almost amphibious Malayan race that lives over these waters in thatched lake-dwellings, built of twigs, like nests, and balanced upon long stilts driven into the mud. And, in the port itself, the only warmth in the whole scene was imparted to it by the little rosy flames of the sprays of orchids that were being sold. . . . Nevertheless, in the sights and sounds round us, one could for the first time realise to the full the cosmopolitanism of the Orient. It was not, perhaps, so omnifarious a world as that of the

Near East, of Turkey or Egypt, or of Morocco, where reigns a religious internationalism which embraces as brothers all of Mohammedan faith of any colour, pink or brown or black, and where there has always existed, since the most remote times, the leavening influence of colonies of Jews ; but, notwithstanding, there were Arabs and Moors, doing conjuring tricks with infant chickens or showing rugs, Persians, Indians selling cigarettes, Burmese jewel-merchants, Siamese snake-charmers, Japanese spies, and, finally, the bands of Chinese coolies, wearing short blue canvas breeches and crowned here, against the heat, with large Aladdin's-hats of straw. (Now, in the rain, most of them had fastened old sacks round their chests.) Looking very tall and yellow among the smaller, darker people of these other countries, they worked in lines and groups along the harbour-front, hauling and heaving, and singing that coolie song to the accompaniment of which, no doubt, every magnificent feat of building and engineering in the extreme Orient, from the Great Wall downward, has been achieved.

In the space of four days we were at last due to reach Saigon. My French friends, who had made the journey several times, warned me of the dullness of the last two days of it ; a time occupied, they said, in steaming up the river with nothing to look at, except its banks. One might just as well be on the Seine, or, as for that, the Thames, they added. . . . At any rate, however, there were my fellow-passengers on board, to supply human interest : and no sooner did we enter the river-mouth than they began to exhibit the most singular and vehement changes in behaviour. . . . Several of the younger and more noisy of the men, who had hitherto sought self-expression in drinking, dancing and flirtation, became gentle and melancholy, sat alone in corners ; whereas the elderly and prosperous, who, some of them, had throughout remained a little aloof, reading quietly to themselves all the day long in deck-chairs, now turned ostentatiously assertive, and took to invading the bar, clapping their hands together and calling " Boy ! " with the best of them. (They had, I suppose, felt " out of it " in Europe, but were now nearly restored to a land in which their qualities and talents were appreciated.) The two French-Canadian brothers stopped writing and, quite oblivious, or perhaps merely careless, of their unpopularity, suddenly produced a camera and, to the general consternation, imposed a temporary regime of forcible photography, organising into unhappy groups all the people who chiefly disliked them — but who, for some reason or other, in spite of their hatred, found themselves unable to defeat so natural an inclination as the wish to photograph them, to perpetuate their likenesses in cardboard — asking their subjects to smile, and then, quickly, letting the shutter open and fall, as though it were, in truth, a guillotine. Stranger still, the Annamite ayahs, hitherto the personification of diffidence and shyness, now began to sit together in groups on deck, to talk, and even laugh, loudly : and, moreover, when they spoke, they no longer troubled to put a hand in front of their mouths, but boldly displayed their black-lacquer teeth in gold-lipped smiles. . . . They were returning to a country where men were men, and where ebony teeth were all the rage.

As for the river itself, the journey proved fascinatingly beautiful. Though the heat was yet greater, the light seemed to have developed a softer aspect, and on each side lay the jungle : no lofty and impenetrable flowery barrier, such as we were soon to see, but a low growth, floating above the water in gentle clouds of olive and sage and almond-husk and lime-green, seeming to compose, as it were, a perpetual thicket to screen the lovers, the shepherds and comedians, of Watteau and Lancret ; or, again, where sometimes a blush of pink crept into the foliage — perhaps, in reality, only called out in answer to the prevailing silveriness of the green — the river-bank suggested the wooded canvases of Fragonard, until one almost expected to see them lined with the blossoming hydrangeas that he loved to paint, or watch the great sailing barges starting, with a little shudder, upon their silken journey. This very delicate scrub may, for all I know, have been full — indeed, plainly it must have been — of snakes and tigers, and of mosquitoes carrying dreaded fevers with their bite, it may have been very directly inspired by a " Nature, red in tooth and claw ", but the general effect, indubitably, of these films and gauzes was that they had been created for dalliance rather than for mortal struggle, and through them and under them, dividing here and there into two broad streams where an island rode light as a feather, flowed these wide and limpid waters of green and silver.

As we approached the end of our voyage, the new and unforeseen characteristics developed by some of the passengers became more and more emphatically demonstrated, and there manifested itself, too, a general stir and bustle of excitement. . . . Saigon was, one knew, the representative in the East of French civilisation, gaiety and, above all, modernity. . . . It surprised us, therefore, when at last we reached the port, to find that there seemed to pertain to it something of the innocent, pioneer-industrialist atmosphere of the middle of the last century ; a lost and genial survival, comparable to some forgotten sugar port of the

West Indies. Or, again, we might perhaps have been a river steamer, arriving at a plantation town in the Southern States before the outbreak of the Civil War. There were the same diminutive cranes and odd-shaped engines, standing about for one obsolete purpose or another, and small red buildings lay huddled together under acacia-like trees, with deep green, emerald green, foliage that offered a competent and feathery shade. The quay itself was lined with little figures in white clothes and topees, come to welcome their relatives from France ; Monsieur and Madame Boutte, Docteur Boutin, Madame Bouton, Professeur Bottard and Madame Bottard, Madame and Mademoiselle Boudin, Monsieur Botton, all to be claimed enthusiastically in turn, as they pushed their way down the gangways. There were, even, little crocodiles of piously-dressed, slant-eyed, yellow-faced pupils to greet the nuns, and of lay-workers to greet the monks. . . . Only the two French-Canadians, genial but suspect as ever, were left to themselves, wildly photographing *gendarmes*, customs-house officials and departing passengers alike.

But as we drove into the town, it became plain that Saigon was, in fact, an achievement, unique, a French city flowering alone out of a tropical swamp in the farthest corner of Asia. Once there, within its narrow confines, it is as though, in the manner of the polite fiction adopted by embassies the world over, you stood upon the actual soil of France.

### CHAPTER TWO

SAIGON,
THE GREAT EXHIBITION
OF THE WEST

BUT there are differences, all the same. . . . In Paris, the Colonial Exhibition had but recently finished, and the general effect of Saigon was that it had been constructed as its antithesis ; a French Imperial Exhibition arranged for the Colonies, or, even, something larger and more important, a Western Exhibition organised for the benefit of the peoples of the Extreme East.

As though to instil, or further to emphasise, such a conception of the origin of the city, the styles — two in number — of its buildings, plainly derive from those that had dominated the two great Paris Exhibitions of 1900 and 1925 : scarcely any shop, house or office in the town can be attributed to previous or intervening years. To the first period belong, as a rule, the public buildings, ticketed all over in gold letters with the three world-famous tags of the Third Republic. Such, for instance, is the Post Office ; inside the scagliola halls of which, incidentally, in that accustomed smell of glue, cloves, hot ink and French cigarette smoke that is the prevailing and, as it were, correct official odour of French post offices in every part of the globe, the chief bureaucrats, with their Western pride, and the underlings and assistants with their Cochin-China obstinacy and resolve to adhere most formally to the few rules they know, contrive to make it quite as difficult to buy a stamp or send a telegram as anywhere in France itself. Again, such an important Art-Nouveau item as the Hôtel-de-Ville belongs to it ; an edifice boasting balconies which curve backward and forward into the tropical air in a most coquettish way, supported by enormous plaster caryatides, a hundred times the size of human beings, smiling very roguishly but looking singularly out of place in an atmosphere that bathes every vast cheek and nostril in a harsh and mocking light. The second period, on the other hand, Les Arts Décoratifs of 1925, claims the streets of low, marble-fronted shops, with their curved plate-glass windows, fashioned so as to look invisible, and their slick, chic, simple interiors.

The only permanent feature of the town, you felt — much more enduring here than alien marble, brick or plaster — were the trees, their shapes defined a little by cutting, which formed an avenue out of every otherwise shadeless street, and softened and broke up the light. Many of them, planted by the first French settlers in the time of the Second Empire, long before the present houses had been built, now reached as high as the eaves. Thus my bedroom, in a nest of green fronds, looked upon one of these cool alleys for the wind, suspended above upstretching, rough trunks, dyed with emerald stains : and they, at least, seemed permanent enough, even though they carried down them, at an infinite distance, the alien vistas of Versailles and Vaux-le-Vicomte : they would remain standing here, to outline a vanished town, long after Saigon had faded from memory. For except these trees, all the rest of it — the theatre, the Palace, the streets of shops, the Post Office — might disappear in an instant ; an order might come at any minute, it seemed, for the Exhibition (which could not now be counted as altogether a financial success) to be wound up, and for the gay, exotic exhibits — and those responsible for them — to be packed immediately and sent home.

Moreover, the moment for this act of withdrawal must, one presumed, be very near. The Foreign Devils' Great Exhibition seemed to be approaching its end : for the slump was reigning and, since the Indo-Chinese dollar had maintained its full value, having never been permitted to accompany its white brother, the franc, down the slide to safety, Saigon now found itself the administrative and commercial capital of the most expensive land in the world — except, perhaps, for Java and Sumatra. The white settler, in consequence, could sell nothing and had, in his turn, no money to spend. But, which made it much more difficult, the sense of prestige compelled him to behave as though nothing unusual had occurred and no catastrophe were impending. As a result, the smartly-dressed French shop-keepers had illimitable time on their hands, in which they could only stand, vacantly smiling, in their doorways, or occasionally turn round, to speak very sharply to native assistants, who were talking together in various tongues, none of which their employers perfectly understood, though they listened carefully. (Probably it was some abomination they were discussing : better to stop it, and so they interrupted again.)

These languages and dialects, it must be admitted, are many and varied : for Saigon embraces a fair proportion of all the peoples that live in Indo-China. The Cochin-Chinese (who inhabit Cochin, and in type resemble the Chinese, except that they are smaller and more golden) predominate ; and after them in numbers come the Tonkinois and Annamites, of a dissimilar, very slight physique, though they, too, approximate to the Chinese type. The Cambodians, also very numerous, show little affinity, on the other hand, even to their nearest relatives, the Siamese. (Besides being the most beautiful race I have ever seen, the Cambodians possess the most exquisite manners, traditionally one of the marks and relics of any high civilisation that has passed away : they differ, too, from those round them in the friendly attitude they display toward the French regime, being well aware that, but for this foreign protection, their more vigorous and war-like neighbours would long ago have consumed their land.) Then there are, of course, the Chinese who have migrated here recently, and some Malays : of whom there are several colonies spread over the country. For the most part, they, and their cousins, the Cambodians, dislike cities and cosmopolitan ways, preferring to live, like a race of predatory birds, upon the banks of a river, where they can fish. Thus you find them dwelling in their own villages, perched above the water on stilts ; in the thatched, South-Sea-Island cottages which the Cambodians also affect, and which exhale always, as you pass them, an odour most subtly disgusting — an acquired odour, as it were, for you infallibly grow to dislike it more every time you smell it — of burnt and rotting fish, the ingredients of a particular sauce so highly relished in these parts that it infallibly accompanies every single one of their dishes. . . . Finally, the country contains, too, the Lolos and the Moï,[1] the most strange indigenous and lost tribes, shy beings who resemble the drawings of primitive man, reconstituted from fragmentary skulls and bones, to be encountered in the pages of popular magazines ; but they are seldom to be met with, even in the hills, and scarcely ever in a town (though I hope to relate subsequently how I saw some of them in Hué). . . . Nevertheless, the influences of all these races, even of the last two, are to be felt in the present background, as much as in the art their lands formerly produced : and a waiter or a shop-assistant in Saigon may belong to any of the peoples mentioned except Lolo or Moï.

Thus in the principal barber's shop, a Cambodian youth, with the melancholy, finely-shaped head of all his country-men, was experimenting with new inventions for washing and drying, and dyeing, the hair — and, indeed, for almost everything else. The shop, playing its propagandist part as a unit in the Exhibition, was crammed with apparatus of various kinds, the most costly and elaborate contrivances such as you would find nowhere in Paris, London or New York, and its marble walls were lined with running waters of every description, with shampoo fountains and gushes of rose-water and eau-de-Cologne. And all this ingenious equipment, all this use of electricity, exercised over him and his fellow-subjects, and especially over the Chinese and Cochin-Chinese, an unrivalled fascination ; every moment spent in clipping and cutting and stabbing and plucking was a pleasure to him and to his confreres. Indeed, if only they had been allowed to do so, they would have enjoyed mowing every hair off the head of every customer with an

[1] See note 1, p. 133.

electric mower — and then, perhaps, the head off the customer as well : for these machines and their like combined for them the delights of both toys and instruments of torture (how they longed, many of them, for example, to attempt here the Lesser Slicing Method, formerly so popular at the Manchu Court), so that for the time being, while their clients were bound in white robes (Chinese mourning) and held, feet upward, in these magic chairs, which, at a single movement of a pedal, shot up and down, or whirled round at a great speed in the air, each bullied and badly-paid assistant became an oriental despot, like the Grand Moghul, still playing, though a fully grown man, in his nursery at Delhi ; an omnipotent Emperor who could, equally, amuse himself, if he wished, with Western toys or with inflicting agonies on those who had incurred his displeasure. . . . Alas, times were bad : there was so little to do, so few opportunities for either business or torture. . . . The cafés opposite were empty, the stationers could sell nothing but funeral cards. Only the bookshop next door appeared to be crowded ; a great many French housewives were examining there the magazines and newspapers, ostensibly to see which to buy, which were the latest arrivals from France, and to complain that there were none more recent, but in reality, to try to read them without having to pay for them, and, hardest of all, to memorise, for later use of needle and scissors, the newest Paris fashions.

Meanwhile, the streets, as always, were full of native families from the country — fathers, mothers and several children — grown-up and infant — who had journeyed hither to wander round the Great White Exhibition, peering and gazing and marvelling. . . . It was free, and it was quite unlike anything they had seen hitherto. Even the pavements were a matter of wonder to them. How ingenious these strange white people were, their eyes said plainly, plaintively ; but nevertheless, they were obviously enjoying themselves, enjoying their own surprise, and, at the moment, only the passing rickshas reminded them of their covert slavery. . . . The chief trouble that these enthusiasts caused was that — exhibitions being, as we all of us know, extremely fatiguing — when they became exhausted, they just sat down, wherever they were, upon the pavement, occupying the whole width of it. It was very tiring and hot, and so they rested there for a while, and made green tea, after which they would indulge in a short siesta, everyone resting with his or her head on somebody else's belly. This procedure, however, though innocent in the extreme, inevitably enraged the Annamite police, who very naturally felt that such a demonstration of native manners must in the end lower their own prestige. But in vain they would try to move their fellow-subjects on : the family parties could not see why they should not take rest and refreshment if they wanted, in their own manner : so they began to argue, and then fell to open insult. How fussy ! Trying to be a white-devil, dressed up in that uniform, and looking a sight, that's what it was ! . . . And why shouldn't a man wear proper clothes, if he can carry them off ? . . . Ooh, look at his boots ! Yah ! You stuck-up thing, you ! . . . And so answer and repartee would continue with increasing fury, until, at last, the police, remembering their powers, began to threaten to use force, and thus — until the next party arrived and sat down in a few minutes' time — won the first round.

However, the native parties, rising from the pavement and roaming on, soon forgot such disagreeable incidents, as they gaped anew. . . . They judged it critically, but they had to admit it to be a thoroughly fine, modern, first-rate show ; " something that is different ". (But the cost of it ! . . . Who found the money, they asked themselves ?) The chief flower-shop especially astonished them, even more than the barber's (of course, they were not permitted to enter, but they could peer in at the windows — and it was cheaper that way). The front was of dark-green marble, brought all those thousands of miles from Europe, and it sported a plate-glass window, with a sheet of real water running down the other side of it in cool trickles (they could have looked at that for ever !). But behind the glass and the water only a few, very unobtrusive flowers rewarded so much ingenuity and expense (as well display sparrows in an aviary !) ; two or three consumptive-looking Marguerite daisies, at four dollars a bunch, some marigolds, seemingly as indestructible as though fashioned of caoutchouc, and a few nostalgic sweet-peas, cornflowers and rosebuds, all evidently chlorotic, reared on ice. They could see here none of the tropical blossoms that grew in the neighbourhood in such profusion, no gardenias, tuberoses, or orchids, even ; none of the huge, highly coloured bowls and trumpets with which themselves were wont to decorate their temples, tearing them, first, petal from petal, and then rearranging them with wire, thus creating, after the manner of gods, whole new species of flowers to give praise ; none of the indigenous, jungle flowers that, lolling their large heads from tubs of water, could be bought, twelve a penny, from their gold-skinned vendors at every street corner in the town. . . . For what inscrutable reasons, they wondered, did these mysterious foreign overlords set so great a store on such sparse and withered stalks ; a religious significance, perhaps ? How strange ! . . . And what a curious land theirs must be, to produce such flowers — anaemic flowers — such buildings, and such people — anaemic people : above all, such people ! For these over-lords seemed always ill and cross, so why bother to come here ? (Surely, with all their riches, they could afford to stay at home ?) The slightest rise in temperature seemed to disturb them : they were always, it was said, swallowing lumps of ice. Sweat rolled off them, even when ordinary people were green and shaking with the cold. . . . So why come here ? How long do you think they will stay ? (Didn't Grannie say she could remember the good old days before they arrived ?) When will all these funny buildings be taken down ? . . . Well, I think it is time for tea ; sit down, dear, over there !

.        .        .        .        .        .

But, if Saigon appeared to be an exhibition erected for the benefit of the yellows, Cho'Len, about three miles away, constitutes, on the contrary, an exhibition for white visitors, a foretaste of China.

It goes without saying that Chinese colonists — not Cochin-Chinese, but Chinese who had arrived from the north, with all their own traditions, since the beginning of the French regime — had soon grown rich here, now that a government existed which allowed them to prosper and did not continually plunder them, except in the lawful direction of taxes. The very first impression of Cho'Len must be one of contrast with Saigon, for its thoroughfares were full of hurrying, busy people : here the slump did not evince itself. (In this connection, the amazing resilience of Chinese commerce has often been remarked : and a very eminent authority told me that in his opinion the reason for it was that the Chinese always approached commerce from the standpoint of the artist, rather than of the tradesman ; they delight in their virtuosity, and consider a pound earned and saved in bad times as a much more esthetically satisfying achievement than one similarly garnered in times of plenty.)

This miniature Chinese city — more Chinese, indeed, in some respects, as we shall deduce, than any in China — revealed in microcosm a whole civilisation. In the centre, the narrow shopping streets were hung, as though in perpetual celebration of a victory, with banners and pennons, bearing delicately placed inscriptions ; accounts, couched usually in terms of the highest poetical artifice and hyperbole, of the wares to be bought within on the counters. You could see for sale, too, many gay and delightful objects, toys and lanterns and fish made of coloured paper, and miniature trees and flowers. The alleys were crowded, with people strolling in the middle, and hurrying and running along the pavements. Nearly always in a Chinese street you observe people running, light-heartedly — not in order to be at their desks in time : and so it was here : an extraordinary animation prevailed, and the faces seemed masks of laughter.

On the outskirts stood several temples of Confucius, and, near the houses of the wealthy merchants, the shrines which the pious among them had erected to their ancestors. In the same neighbourhood, though spiritually in the opposite direction, Cho'Len had its quarter, filled with restaurants and opium dens and brothels. . . . To consider first — and on the first mention of opium, a theme that must recur as we reach China — the opium dens, they are an essential ingredient of a Chinese city *in the eyes of the sightseeing foreigner*. Thus, though the smoking of opium had

been prohibited in recent years throughout Chinese territory, such a veto by the Chinese Government in no way
defeats, of course, his expectation in the matter. And it is
for him that this town caters. (In its turn, the Chinese
mind must often have been puzzled by the European, and
in particular by the English, processes of thought ; first
of all we fight a war — or was it two wars ? — against
them, in order to compel them to smoke vast quantities of
opium grown in India ; then pressure of public opinion,
especially of Anglo-Saxon and Half-a-League-Onward
opinion, obliges the smoking of it to be strictly forbidden ;
and finally, the first question nearly every European asks, on
arriving in China, is " Where can I see an opium den ? ")
Nor, of course, in fact could such a dry enactment put an
end quickly to an age-old habit, that had, I apprehend, its
derivation in the climate of the Chinese Empire, and in the
diseases to which its tendency to run to extremes gave rise.
Never having myself smoked opium, I hold no brief for
defence or prosecution : but I believe, nevertheless, that
in China it was of considerable benefit as a sedative, and,
still more, as a mild disinfectant and prophylactic ; in the
prevention, for example, of the peculiarly severe colds
which are rife in the winter — the " Peking cold " is
notorious — and of the various forms of dysentery so
prevalent during the summer. In fact, it served very much
the same purpose in China that betel serves in these southern
countries, where every coolie chews it, in order to soothe
and fortify his nerves and thereby defend himself from the
equatorial heat. Moreover, the prejudice which exists in
the European mind against the use of opium is due, largely,
to the fact that when a European adopts the habit, he
becomes an addict and shows no sense of restraint, smoking

thirty or so pipes a day, just as a negro who takes to whisky may drink two bottles of it.

Opium-smoking, then, continues — or still continued — in China : but it could not be done openly, except in Chinese towns situated in various foreign countries. A year or two ago, it was undoubtedly easier, for instance, to find an opium den in New York's Chinatown, than in Peking ; though even at that time, Japanese agents — especially Koreans, who appear to serve as go-betweens in such matters — in addition to introducing such new and unquestionably pernicious drugs as heroin, were pouring great quantities of cheap opium into the northern provinces bordering on Manchukuo, in order to demoralise and ruin the Chinese people, and so give other, less intelligent, Orientals a better chance of establishing themselves there, both as a governing class and as traders.

Concerning the brothels, none such as these would be found in China, where the whole approach to sex is so slow and formal a one, so governed by ritual, that, while nobody is shocked if a Chinese man admires a woman in a house of ill-fame, he must yet adhere very strictly to certain rules that are always observed. Thus he must go and have tea with her every day, and recite poems to her for many months — a year, perhaps — before the conventions would allow him to enter into any more intimate relationship. Otherwise he could never hope to win her favour, and would write himself down as a boor, a coolie. . . . Common prostitutes,[1] to whom no decent Chinese would speak, are,

---

[1] It is not without interest that the Chinese, with their curious, sometimes rather sinister, sense of the practical, are said to encourage girls who have been born blind to become prostitutes. The implications of this are several. Lacking one sense, they are encouraged to gratify another ; their career keeps them occupied ; and since they cannot see their lovers, imagination has free play.

of course, to be encountered in the ports, but they, poor things, are objects of the most callous commerce : but there also exist, in the great cities of China, famous courtesans, who hold a position much superior to that of a concubine (who, it must be remembered, occupies a legal place in the household), and rather similar to that of the courtesans of the sixteenth and seventeenth centuries in Venice, women qualified by their education to discuss the arts and literature, and able, even, indirectly, to influence the course of politics. (Indeed, one of the most celebrated of these ladies, who, by her tact and charm, saved the Forbidden City from being burned down after the Boxer outbreak, was still living in Peking when I was there.)  And the greatest compliment which one Chinese gentleman can pay to another, whom he wishes especially to honour, is to obtain permission, at a price, to give a large dinner party for him in the house of one of these famous women. . . . But no trace of these typical traditions and customs is to be found in Cho'Len.  This is a miniature China arranged for the European — and American — markets ; a city seen through the eyes of some inferior French novelist of the 'nineties, his head full of stories of opium, of jade and Japanese geishas ; more obviously Chinese, or, at any rate, oriental, than any city in China, so that many American visitors, having seen it, feel henceforth (and how right they are !) that for them now to proceed northward, to Canton or Peking, would be sheer waste of their time and money. . . . Thus Cho'Len, too, remains an Exhibition.

Of a more genuine interest, I thought, than this model city, was another near by, of a kind quite new to me.  A branch of the river, curling round at an angle, flowed between Saigon and Cho'Len.  Upon its very considerable width floated a whole town of dark-painted barges ; one half of their decks serving apparently as gardens, wherein tall plants grew out of the tubs and tins placed there. The combination of repetitive shapes and colours, low tones of blue and black and sepia, of water and of green leaves and stems, in itself created an unusual and lovely rhythm of life : in addition, the actual line of each vessel, of its plants, and even of its solitary chimney, belonged to this land or to China, as clearly as did the eaves of any neighbouring temple in the country or in Cho'Len. The very columns of pale-blue smoke issuing from the chimneys seemed to dispose themselves against the sky in an individual and Chinese manner. A great din, a metallic and yet liquid-sounding roar, hung above this amphibious city, for the men in their patched blue clothes, here crowned with smaller straw hats like haloes, could be seen hammering and working on board, with an air of tremendous concentration, while their innumerable slant-eyed, plump, golden-faced children — all of them boys, it seemed — were banging in sympathy the surface of the water with palm leaves, or just yelling out of sheer high spirits. (The women, I suppose, were indoors, preparing rice of some sort, or were waiting on their smaller children, for every now and then the prevailing noise was punctuated by the wailing and shrieking of a baby, below, expressing itself forcibly in the sole international language known — and one, alas ! which we all shed as soon as we reach an age of understanding.) . . . Only at noon, and during the hours after it, when wise men sleep, an un-expected silence descended on the burning waters so that the blue spires of smoke, together with the carefully tended deck-gardens, alone pointed to human habitation. Other-wise it might have been just a cluster of abandoned, drifted barges. The dogs themselves, those lewd, loud-mouthed foes to quiet, then slept in silence, though occasionally stirring or twitching in their harsh, animal slumber, hunting through the fields of darkness — and each barge possessed its dog ; though for protection, I think, rather than for food, as some might suspect. (Indeed, the eating of dogs in these parts is not nearly so common as we like to assume, and when, some months later than the time of which I am writing, I asked a Chinese friend of mine whether it was true that he and his countrymen ate dogs, he betrayed all the irritation and anger of the gourmet misunderstood, and replied, " Of course not. Never — unless they have been drowned in a special kind of white wine, and left to soak in it, with the right herbs, for forty-eight hours.") In the afternoon, work began again : and continued until long after dark, when the boats would be lit with paper lanterns, and the sounds seemed clearer on the water. Even then, the children were singing and splashing about, for they seemed to stay up here, playing, as late as, formerly, they used to in the streets of Barcelona. . . . This system of life, then so novel to me — albeit but the first and most southern example of one that prevailed in varying degrees, throughout both Indo-China and China, in nearly every town built on a river — (and nearly every town there is built on a river), adds a notable and vital significance to the scene, and to the city itself, of which it thus forms an extension.

All the same, fresh as the place was to me, I found after a day or two that there was little to do in it. We had by now completed the arrangements for going to Pnom Penh and Angkor. As soon as the next motor returned from the ruins — for there was a shortage of vehicles — we were to be given it. . . . The pulse of life in Saigon,

as we have seen, was beating slow at present : once celebrated as " the Paris of the East ", it seemed now like the
West End of a city, when the owners of the houses are on
holiday. Inside the hotel, too, listlessness prevailed. The
most agreeable spot in it was one into which visitors were
never allowed to penetrate ; a long, rectangular courtyard,
of which from time to time one caught a glimpse, the
walls painted an apricot pink, over which hung the blue
sky. It led from the kitchen to the dining-room, and there,
at least, a little life manifested itself, for natives carrying
dishes on their heads, in brightly coloured clothes, hurried
across it, through two lines of gardenia trees in blossom,
and of shrubs that bore huge, yellow, trumpet-shaped
blossoms. At this one point, the Exhibition had lapsed :
for the rest the hotel was severely European, except that
the cold water was hot and the shower-baths did not work.
In the dining-room the food took an infinite time to arrive,
or stood for hours getting cold, on a table just out of reach.
The only person in the whole hotel who could arrange
anything so that it materialised, was a genial French
giantess, who sat, dressed in correct black, towering over
a trivial desk in the hall. She, at least, could impose her
will upon men and women, upon several waiters still lost
in opium dreams, upon Nature itself. A born organiser, a
female Kitchener or Lyautey, save for her intervention, the
life of the tropical marshes from which they had sprung
would, it seemed, already have reabsorbed the hotel and
the streets round it, smothering them in those films and
gauzes of sage and olive, pink and silver, that we noted
hanging over the river banks, and then filling their ruins
with the trampling and breathing of animals, the flutterings
of birds and butterflies and moths : there would have re-

mained of us, I think, but for her labours, only a few broken
stones and skeletons scattered in a hot and green inertia :
nevertheless, her continual expenditure of energy had inspired in her a certain disillusionment concerning human
character, its weakness and unreliability, and also, perhaps,
a mild contempt for human delicacy, for the feebleness of
the white body : everyone in the hotel seemed always to
be ill and to require her help.

Indeed, during this first visit to the tropics, I attribute
my own good health — which continued, in spite, no doubt,
of the many mistakes of a novice — to a deliberate neglect
of the classic English advice to newcomers : to drink no
alcohol until dusk, and, after that hour, to consume only
gin or whisky, never wines. I remembered, on the contrary, that William Hickey had survived to quite an
advanced age in India, drinking all the time incredible
quantities of claret, and without wishing to emulate him
in measure, I was — and am — convinced that Indian tea
has killed many more people than wine. I felt sure, too,
that the French settlers, who looked healthy enough,
would not be drinkers of tea — or of spirits : and, moreover, the food everywhere was obviously corrupt, tainted
with the taint of the tropics, and wine alone, with its
stimulating, yet soothing and antiseptic properties, would
be able for long to protect one from the hosts of germs that
prowl and prowl around.

Accordingly, I was careful to drink wine with every
meal. And that, perhaps, saved me. For, though there
were but few Englishmen in the hotel — few even in
Saigon (there were no golf-courses) — the few there were,
seemed for the most part to be ill. Even the Consul had
fallen sick, his place being occupied, temporarily, by a

junior colleague, whose advice, on various points concerning my journey, I went to seek from time to time. He was wise and helpful. And it was while waiting on one occasion in his ante-room, that I encountered a young English traveller who issued to me the following cryptic warning. " Did you see those three ladies, that left just as you came in ? . . . They're the Three Big Women from Hong Kong. You'll see them at Angkor, sure as sure. Can't avoid it, I should say. They are off there today for five days, and then they come back here again. . . . But, thank goodness, I shall be gone by that time ! "

Meanwhile, until we left for Angkor, what was there to do ? . . . One could, for example, wander round the town to discover the few mouldering relics that remained of the first colonists, little houses, erected before the influence of the two Exhibitions, in the style, as near as could be, that had prevailed in provincial France twenty or thirty years earlier, when the builders of them had been children ; honest, homesick, rather poignant little houses, now standing very low under the shade of the tall trees their owners had planted. . . . There was, too, the Museum, containing fine examples of Cambodian sculpture. . . . But the Zoological Gardens constituted the chief attraction, and I visited them early every morning. . . . To begin with, one was drawn thereto, because they were so carefully kept that an encounter with a snake seemed less likely in the Gardens than anywhere outside them : here, at least, they were kept in their proper place, and not allowed to roam. And then, all the big animals seemed to be at their ease, to feel well and happy, to be unconstrained in their demeanour as dogs in the English countryside. Even the elephants seemed, as it were, to plod the lawns with a lighter tread.

As for the birds, they were paragons and nonpareil. . . .
I suppose that similar creatures exist in heated cages in
London, and that their particular beauty here was derived
only from their better health, and from being seen in their
natural climate, but certainly they displayed a grace and
full-feathered elegance in which they seem to be lacking
when you meet them in the alien and confined spaces of
other latitudes. And what a relief it is, after the mousy
little favourites of the Georgian poets (for they still write
about them : the only difference is that now no one reads
what they have written), to come across these baroque and
flamboyant creatures, strutting, preening in so care-free a
manner in their native climate, brushing and pecking at and
spreading out their bustles and crinolines and panniers and
ruches of mauve and magenta and forget-me-not and flame-
coloured feathers, in a light that renders each separate
plume as sheeny and iridescent as water in a pre-Raphaelite
picture ; feathers which, by their dazzling audacity, proclaim their owners to be no dark-throated singing-birds,
but the somewhat ostentatious inhabitants of an elegant and
fashionable world of their own. They might have been,
it seemed, as they stood there — most of them, it is true,
on one leg — just putting the last touches to their toilettes,
pulling on their gloves, perhaps, before starting for ball or
opera. Certainly their appearance could be in no way
associated with so dull and earthy a thing as natural selection,
for they were — who could doubt it ? — the invention of
a specialist in fashions, but one raised by the power and
fantasy of his creation to the status of a god, a deified
milliner and modiste ; who had, too, outside his usual
province, been responsible for the design of several of the
flowers and blossoming trees in the neighbourhood.

I had to creep back to the hotel in the shade of the houses, for every morning, between ten and eleven, the heat, quite suddenly, would redouble its fervency, and it became unwise to venture out-of-doors again until after four : the sun flashed his wings with too blinding a brilliance, and every lustrous object, a motor-screen or a lamp, that caught the light, shone with a painful scintillation. . . . Apart from having luncheon, there was little to do in these indoor hours, except to lie down on the bed. It was often too hot to read : alas, unless I am ill, I can seldom, and only with difficulty, sleep in the day-time : and an *effort* to sleep is one of the most tiring things known to man. Accordingly, my mind near dreaming, but never quite reaching it, I would rest there, thinking of this strange Western town flowering alone in Asia, attempting to sum it up for myself, or, advancing a little into the future, I would try to conjecture how Angkor would look, to picture for my senses the actual, visual scene, the feel and scent of it, the mixture of jungle and stone : but this was not so easy, for almost the only representation of any of its buildings with which I was familiar, had been the " model " of Angkor Vat at the Colonial Exhibition.

Returning from such speculations to the present, to an agreeable, rhythmic nothingness, to taking in nothing but that present moment, I would fall to watching the delicate flutter of the leaves outside, those cool green bowers of which the room seemed an annexe, until, after a time, fragments of poetry would float and echo through the mind, partly because of its own inaction and need for entertainment, so that, on the perpetual edge of a slumber that would never materialise, it became free enough to project these verses, and partly from the heat itself, from the sound of the leaves sighing, or the glitter of the outer ones, which the sun clothed in armour, or the veining of the inner shadow they created with such a stabbing brightness. Always the poetry that came back to one in those moments would belong to the senses, rather than the intellect, and would bear with it a nostalgic odour ; such, for example, as George Peele's song from *David and Bathsabe* — a poem that, coming across a ravine of three and a half centuries to us, yet brings, in spite of its strangeness, the very breath of England in the summer, of the sudden rush of wind through the branches of tall old trees, and the consequent splashing and spattering of light, the swift alternation of breeze and sun, and light and shade, as when a cool flurry sends the leaves momentarily into silver flight, and then they recover their balance on the air, and all is calm again. . . . Even the recitation of it helped to keep one cool. Bathsabe is bathing, and sings to herself.

" Hot sun, cool fire, tempered with sweet air,
    Black shade, fair nurse, shadow my white hair ;
    Shine, sun ; burn, fire ; breathe, air, and ease me ;
    Black shade, fair nurse, shroud me and please me ;
    Shadow, my sweet nurse, keep me from burning,
    Make not my glad cause cause of mourning.
        Let not my beauty's fire
        Inflame unstaid desire,
        Nor pierce any bright eye
        That wandereth lightly."

How easily the words stay in the memory, and return to the tongue !

But no words, however beautiful, can for long temper the heat, or the spirit of the restless, and the renewed fluttering of the leaves drew me to the window, to look

out. . . . Below, in a wide space of green shadows, the
ricksha men, nearly naked, scratched and slept by day, as
they did by night, under the hoods of their miserable
vehicles, dreaming of endless cash to spend, like the white-
devils had, or, perhaps, of themselves being rolled along
at a smart trot by other groaning, sweating coolies. (After
all, everyone else here was carried, every sergeant, every
private soldier, every sailor : perhaps, then, the day would
come when they, too, would sit, in an attitude of perpetual
triumph and command, above their groaning human oxen ?)
Sometimes they woke, and chewed betel for a while, spitting
from time to time, till their lips were stained purple, and
their thoughts were soothed again by its aromatic freshness,
their eyes, as their mandibles moved slowly, gaining a
ruminative, melancholy calm. . . . What could they do,
they wondered, if they did not carry and drag these fat,
pink loads ? Miles and miles they must have covered,
many thousands of miles, at that rhythmic, swinging trot
(so much more resembling the gait of an animal than of a
man), with the sideways moving of the head at each pace,
as it were ticking out the minutes of their lives like a clock,
and with the sweat pouring down them in rivers. . . .
And yet, ordinary work was to them harder, because more
continuous. They could not, if they followed other trades,
be independent, and take a week off, when they wished.
Whereas, in a sense, this was easy money : and that was
why they did it, why they had dropped into doing it.
Ricksha-pulling was a kind of torturing refuge for the lazy,
because, when you had earned enough, your wants being
limited, you stopped for so long as the money lasted, and
slept and gambled as you liked. Life resembled that of a
dog, both when working and resting ; was more largely

a dream than a reality, for, when you were running, your mind was somewhere deep inside you, and lost, and when you were not running, you were sleeping. But the span itself was a short one : the money you earned was to pay you for the days of your life you had surrendered, as well as for the hours of your labour ; since, particularly in this climate, no ricksha coolie could hope, even if he wished it, to live for more than a few years.

All night they wait there, beneath the trees. Certainly in this climate it is no hardship to sleep in the open air, but there is little for them to do ; the weight of the Indo-Chinese dollar sits on the chest of every inhabitant of the town, nearly strangling him. . . . Even now that it is evening, the cafés are empty, though this is the hour at which, formerly, they were crowded, and, reputed to be the equal of any in Paris, the most famous restaurant in Indo-China — a dream of red and black lacquer, dreamt by a provincial confectioner in France — stands shut. At present, by the tables outside the cafés, in the *place* and in the streets, the aproned, golden-faced waiters pay scant attention to their few clients, but laugh and joke together in corners, flicking their napkins out occasionally at a customer, after a manner they had learned in the West. . . . But in an hour or two, at ten or eleven, it grows hotter again, till the heat seems to lie on the air like something tangible, and forces a few more white-coated figures out of their homes, so that they may sit here with iced drinks in front of them. It is very quiet, since there is no wheeled traffic now, and the occasional pad-padding of a ricksha makes little sound, so that it is easy for the clients of the two cafés opposite one another to talk, without shouting, across the gap made by the road. From time to time a beautiful Cambodian lady, with that pallid mask of such supreme delicacy, so exquisite in its subtle carving, and dressed in a blue silk robe, passes between them in her ricksha, or else two or three Chinese women, having driven here from Cho'Len, drift like leaves on their small feet — though here they are never bound — down the road, and the waiters fall silent, watching them. A nearing sound of singing announces the approach of two or three drunken French sailors, who reel happily along the street, their loud music waking the ricksha men, rousing them in a moment from slumber to a monkey-like, straining and uncomprehending eagerness. Just round the corner from them, where two streets join, a young Cambodian itinerant masseur is giving massage to a more or less naked friend stretched at full length upon the pavement. He plays tunes, as it were, on the dusky limbs, as though they were a percussion instrument. Close by, against the walls, the pails of tropical flowers, of tuberoses and gardenias and bavardias, and other larger and yet more waxen blossoms, the sprays and trails of orchids, look pale, losing a little of their colour under the electric lamps, though they still exhale clouds of fragrance, while their ragged vendors lie curled up, asleep, beside them.

### CHAPTER THREE

PNOM PENH

Motoring in tropical Asia was curiously unlike any form of travelling I had known before. The heat enforced a Daylight Saving Act of its own, compelling a start at four or four-thirty in the morning, so that a great deal of hurrying and packing had to be done in the green, sea-light of the dawn that filtered in through the trees. The long road that led to Pnom Penh, the present capital of Cambodia, and thence to Angkor, passed through semi-European suburbs and through those endless market-gardens, full of ragged huts, which seem to mark a French town in any part of the world ; a disappointing journey, because from this direction we did not enter the jungle for many miles, and were obliged to pass through league after league of rubber plantations, with their tall, well-drilled, shiny-leaved trees. Toward evening we reached Pnom Penh, and on the dusty further outskirts of it lay our large hotel, and the French Club surrounded by a wilderness of tennis-courts. Every now and then the dust sailed in great clouds above these miniature deserts of concrete, engulfing for a moment the alert herds of ricksha men, here much more active and happy, full of jokes and irrepressible laughter.

The *stupa* that crowns the pyramid hill, and the river, with long, umbrageous walks along its banks, are the two chief features of the city ; the river crowded again with boats, offering a rival town to the one upon its shores ; the *stupa* deserted, the hill asserting the dignity of immense age in the midst of very modern surroundings. But the museum constitutes the chief interest of the town, for it houses the principal collection of bronzes in Cambodia ; one far finer than any existing either in Saigon or Angkor. In these galleries the traveller begins to realise for the first time both the extent of Angkor, and its esthetic status, before ruin overtook it. Room after room is filled with these calm, bronze figures, with large, curiously shaped ears, and, playing round their mouths, that smile which so distinguishes them, and seems to have risen to their lips at some overtone from a world so distant that only their ears are attuned to catch the sound. But these beautiful images, removed from their surroundings, dead for so many centuries to all human contact, have become mournful, like the dry and dusty relics of Egypt ; even their smile has grown infinitely sad, and they can only be regarded now as so many disbanded heralds of that tremendous glory that stands recovered from the assaults of the forest, a grandeur that I shall attempt to describe in the next chapter. Lovely and, even, sublime as they were, they fail in the memory to attain to that same brightness, to that same incisive poignance as another altogether more transient and trivial impression of Pnom Penh.

It was eleven o'clock in the morning when we entered

the gates of the palace of the present Emperor of Cambodia. Silver spires and bells and slanting roofs crowded round the courtyard ; in the centre of it, a little to the left, stood a French bandstand, which, except for a touch of the Orient in the angle of its roof, might have been built in any provincial French town to shelter the brassy cackle of Offenbach. In it, the green-liveried band of the Emperor's bodyguard, crowned with plumed firemen's helmets, were immersed in rendering the strains of the March from *Aïda* ; East and West blended both in the music and in the architecture that re-echoed it. These people, so beautiful and stately in their own dress, were now altogether lost to sight in the grandeur of epaulet and helmet and braid and button. Nevertheless, their difficulty lay not so much, I think, in the mastering of the music itself, as in the effort to dominate the machinery evolved by western giants. They clung, like a fleet of monkeys on their bicycles at a circus, to instruments that were too large for them, to brazen serpents, to trombones and piccolos and oboes of gigantic size. It seemed as though they were engaged on the work of a lifetime, on a race, on a tourney ; if only they could, this time, correctly render the Grand March, they would have answered once and for all the challenge of the West and would remain ever after secure in their own self-esteem. With golden cheeks ballooning out from their slim faces, and slanting eyes intent upon the score before them or upon the angry gesticulations of their conductor, they raised a din that was most surprising in its cacophony, and that yet, when its percussions had tapped unrecognised upon the drum of a European ear, raised thereon, after it had passed, the ghost of the tune it was attempting. Similarly, perhaps, through the gongs and bells of some heathen temple, one might be able suddenly to recognise the familiar chiming of the village church, or the striking of Big Ben. The sun glared down upon the stones of the courtyard and upon the roof of the bandstand, but the crowd that watched and waited, intent upon the gestures and sounds served out to them, were undismayed, applauded loudly until they succeeded in obtaining the same item again.

Meanwhile, over the wall beyond the bandstand, a sacred pink elephant was regarding a similar congregation of reverent watchers with an infinite, primordial distaste. (Only one of these rare and august creatures had come out today, but others could be heard stamping profoundly near by in the royal stables.) The little crowd surrounding this huge, pale-rose-pink beast obviously stood in awe of him. Occasionally he trumpeted, as though to announce his opinion of the March from *Aïda*, but these impressive, if discordant, notes only served to punctuate the general disorder ; they edged away as he lifted his trunk, and whispered to one another ; edged closer when he was not looking at them, discussed his complexion and the various intimate details of his appearance and toilet. Everything about him, the performance of his every natural function, was hallowed, and therefore followed intently, and with the hush of reverence. . . . Occasionally he shifted the considerable weight of his roseate bulk from one gilded hoof to another : and you felt grateful to the beast for deigning to bear his own weight, for not expecting to be carried about in a palanquin ; because, to whatever degree of sanctity he had attained, he was both tyrannical and lazy — very lazy — ; of that there could be no doubt. Thus the greatest delicacies could be placed in front of him, all the things, bananas, sweets, fruits, of which the most refined

78

sweet-trunk could dream, and he would refuse even to look at them, unless they were held up to him on poles at the level of his mouth. . . . Others must do the work ; then, perhaps, he might deign to consume.

The palace itself is an injudicious mixture of East and West, red carpets, gold chairs, clocks and watches — innumerable clocks and watches — stuffed tigers and bright-coloured roofs, red and rose and gold. The Silver Temple, which has in it no touch of the West, is beautiful, light, as full of scales still quivering from the water as a fish's tail. Then there are, too, the collections of objects presented to the reigning Emperor by French and other monarchs, from the time of Louis XIV onward. Many of these consisted of the timepieces alluded to above, and oriental princes may well have concluded that these machines were the idols of the Western potentates, with their curious passion for punctuality, their schemes for dividing the day. But they were interesting, too, because of the way in which they reflect the distinctions in the characters of many dead personages. What a contrast, for instance, prevailed between the gifts of the Sun King and the great Emperor ! The presents of the first were calculated to impress the native prince with the importance of the giver : a peri-wigged and boldly outlined countenance stamped in bronze, and jewelled trifles all fashioned to indicate the grand monarch's own view of his own position ; whereas those of Napoleon were designed to insinuate as well as to impress. He sent toys and musical boxes, clockwork figures and wheels, set with brilliants, that revolved — as well as threats translated into bronze and silver. He bribed as much as he intimidated, and his nephew, Napoleon III, continued this tradition.

After a day or two we left Pnom Penh for Angkor, entering the real jungle for the first time. On each side of the road were prickly thickets of great palm trees, with leaves like the fans used for the entrance of the priests in *Aïda*. Except that they were bigger and more green, they seemed of the same variety that used, when I was a child, to grace the desert drawing-rooms of the very rich : palms of the sort first popularised in western Europe by Queen Alexandra and Sarah Bernhardt ; but here, tall and flourishing, they displayed nothing of that aridity which marked their presence in London houses. Later, these somewhat spiky groves were masked from sight by avenues of giant, green poles some hundreds of feet high, with festoons of rosy and mauve flowers falling in wreaths from one mast to another, as though this wide road had been prepared for the reception of the Sovereign. Sometimes the jungle would give way to plantations and fields, or a *Flamboyant Tree*, or that other tree named *The Flame of the Forest*, would shine in the hot sun of an open space, its branches turned to torches of coral. The heat came in great gusts down the road. But even this could not obscure the human interest of our journey, for it was upon this day that we were first able to observe, in all its strangeness, the character of our silent Cambodian driver. Very mild in manner, very gentle and wise, nevertheless the sight of a single dog appeared to drive him to fury. Directly he sighted one, he accelerated, and within a few moments had laid it out flat beneath his wheels. Nothing I could say — and neither of us could talk the language of the other — could persuade him to abandon this original sport. When we shouted, he may have thought we were cheering him on. Dog after dog lay stretched in the dust behind him.

It may be that he had been told of the sporting proclivities of Englishmen : or merely that he had long suffered some canine wrong ; be that as it may, all through this journey, and through the ones that followed, both in Cambodia and Annam, the reader must imagine to himself this sad diurnal line of corpses, accompanied by sudden, tragically annihilated barking.

We lunched at a rest-house in the forest, kept by an Englishman who talked much of home, and played such nostalgic tunes as the Londonderry Air upon the piano. A sense of mystery, of entering upon the beginning of one of Mr. Somerset Maugham's short stories of the Orient, immediately made itself felt in the atmosphere. Something strange and a little sad in the essence of this house communicated itself even to the casual visitor ; the feeling, too, of a benevolent and unseen presence.

Several people were present at luncheon, among them the French Resident, a chic young man, dressed, as only the French can dress, with a view to the dramatisation of his own career. As a further exploiting of it, he had placed in the garden a selection of wild animals which, so he said, himself had captured and tamed. He crossed the room to talk to us after luncheon, and then took us out to see panther and deer and monkey, having explained beforehand how domesticated they were ; that the panther never even growled, and could be let out of its cage, even, so that it could play with him. . . . But, the moment he approached, his voice was lost in the slinking brute's angry purr and roaring. It ground its teeth at the base of the bars, even tried to squeeze out between them, in order to get at its captor, the merest sight of whom evidently threw the animal into a frenzy. . . . Indeed, an hour later, when we left the place behind us, it could still be heard growling and gnashing its teeth. . . . I was sorry to go, for the little hotel was full of personality, and a certain beauty, even, pervaded its rooms and little rustic courtyards.

The radiations of a great city, notwithstanding that it has lain so long dead as to have become an object of almost biblical desolation, remain unaccountable. Angkor, in all truth, may be very far from not having one stone left upon another, but certainly the footprints of the satyr — and of the archeologist — are to be found within its holy places, and no tide of life, except that of the jungle, ever washes its walls today. Nevertheless, approaching it through the forest, for at least a hundred miles before the visitor can see its clustered, cone-like towers, the genius and immensity of this long-forgotten metropolis communicate themselves to him in a thousand ways, some obvious, some subtle and difficult to analyse and pin down. Still more dense grows the jungle, as though now it possesses a secret to guard ; and occasionally the fine, broad road driven through it by the French incorporates a huge and ancient causeway of golden stone, ending in a carved serpent, with rearing, fan-like head ; a causeway that, in addition to belonging clearly to some complete architectural system, but one never hitherto encountered, is constructed on a scale so much greater than that of the road itself, that he who passes it is at once obliged to deduce that he must be drawing near to some place of great former power and wealth. Moreover, through every opening in the trees, pools or lakes reveal themselves — often with stone staircases leading magnificently down to the water — or basins or reservoirs, albeit some of these have now become dry, or have turned into marshes. Very marked, too, is the intensification of wild life, though the animals that cross the road in front, from one side of the jungle to the other, run so far ahead, and travel at such speed, that it is impossible to identify them. Above all, the birds here assert themselves and their dominion ; and from the fact that the commonest bird, the very sparrow of this jungle, proves to be the peacock, in all its quivering, many-eyed glory of blue and green and gold, some conception of the fantastic and lovely plumage of the others can be obtained. . . . It should be sufficient to say that all the elegant habituals of the Zoological Gardens in Saigon are here to be noticed, indulging, as it were, in their country pursuits. . . . In the clearings, by the occasional wooden houses, even the poultry look beautiful, the cocks, with their proud combs and panache of piebald and green-black feathers, as vainglorious and combative as any in a Japanese woodcut or an English sporting-print : for here in the forest they are indigenous, and no doubt they thrive particularly, even when captive, in their native air.

### CHAPTER FOUR

## THE CITY OF THE
## KING OF THE ANGELS

At long intervals during many hundreds of years, rumours were current in Europe about the great lost city of Angkor, but during the passage of those centuries the whole of the Orient was a legend, a fable told to children by ingenious travellers. The stories of Marco Polo — which we know now, even when they are not accurate to an inch, to be so much truer than mere truth — were dismissed as false-hoods ; constituted, almost, a standard by which to measure probability or its reverse. " Great Princes, Emperors, and Kings, Dukes and Marquises, Counts, Knights, and Bur-gesses ! and People of all degrees who desire to get know-ledge of the various races of mankind and of the diversities of the sundry regions of the World, take this Book and cause it to be read to you. For ye shall find therein all kinds of wonderful things, and the divers histories of the Great Hermenia, and of Persia, and of the Land of the Tartars, and of India . . ." — so runs the opening to his account of his travels. Yet even he, Marco Millioni,[1] as he was called, who had seen the Tree of the Sun, the *arbor secco* or dry tree, that stood alone in a desert surrounding it on every side for a hundred miles, and under the shade of which those two battling Emperors, Alexander and Darius, had fought for the last time, who could describe the palaces and pleasances of the Old Man of the Mountains, that curious, haunting dream of the Crusaders, and had, indeed, known intimately and beyond dispute, Kubla Khan — to us of later generations a figure no less aureoled with the splendour of legend (in itself a kind of poetry) on to which great poetry has been grafted ; — even he had failed to visit Angkor, or to give an account of it by hearsay. . . . In the middle of the sixteenth century, however, came the first definite report : two missionaries, Fathers Ridadeneyra and Gabriel de Sant' Antonio, told of the apparition of some gigantic and singular ruins in the impenetrable fastnesses of the Cambodian jungle, palaces and temples, they said, which had been built " by the Romans or by Alexander the Great ". And toward the end of the same century, Father Chevreuil alludes to a temple " called Onco, and once as famous among the Gentile as St. Peters of Rome ".

As for the living inhabitants of the forest — those beautiful beings who, recalling the dignity and grace of the

[1] " And as it happened that in the story, which he [Marco Polo] was constantly called on to repeat, of the magnificence of the Great Khan, he would speak of his revenues as amounting to ten or fifteen *millions* of gold ; and in like manner, when recounting other instances of great wealth in those parts, would always make use of the term *millions*, so they gave him the nickname of Messer Marco Millioni ; a thing which I have noticed also in the Public Books of this Republic where mention is made of him. The Court of his house, too, at S. Giovanni Chrisostomo, has always from that time been popularly known as the Court of the Millioni." Ramusio's Preface to the Book of Marco Polo.

basalt figures of pre-dynastic Egypt, were yet then an oppressed and dying people, less numerous, it may be, than the images in their overgrown temples — they had forgotten long ago all their high, distinguished history : they knew merely that these soaring, tumbling labyrinths of golden stone, in the corners of which they yet worshipped, must be the handiwork of the gods ; their parents had told them so. . . . In the same way had the Romans of the Dark Ages, another people existing among the soaring ruins and crumbling monuments of a city that then seemed to have been created for a population of statues rather than of human beings, been content, as they gazed in wondering ignorance at the tremendous bulk of the Colosseum or the elegant yet grand perfection of the Pantheon, at the mighty span of triumphal arches and the sweep of aqueducts across the golden plain, and at the numberless tombs and titanic columns of an epoch that had already vanished from memory, to ascribe the construction of them to the old gods who had been driven out. Thus Henri Mouhot,[1] the French naturalist, to whose intelligence and pertinacity we owe the discovery — and very largely the preservation — of the lost city, tells us that by 1860 — the year in which he reached it — all traces of its history had passed into oblivion, though tradition maintained that Angkor had been the capital of a country that counted a hundred and twenty kings paying tribute and an army of five million soldiers. But even the inscriptions on the walls were indecipherable to the local sages. Indeed, when he questioned the natives and enquired who had founded Angkor Vat, " they in-

---

[1] See *Voyage dans les Royaumes de Siam, de Cambodge, de Laos et Autres Parties Centrales de L'Indo-Chine par feu Henri Mouhot, 1858–1861,* in *Le Tour du Monde,* 1863.

GENERAL VIEW OF ANGKOR VAT

variably made one or other of these four answers : ' It is the work of the King of the Angels, my Lord ', ' It is the work of giants ', ' We owe these buildings to the Leper King ', or, finally, ' They built themselves '." Mouhot himself writes of Angkor Vat that to look at it, after seeing modern Cambodia — the Cambodia of 1860 —, was to be suddenly " transported from barbarism to civilisation, from profound darkness to light ". He adds that to form any idea of the city of Angkor, it is necessary to try and imagine all the most beautiful creations of architecture " transported into the depths of these forests in one of the most remote countries of the world . . . incomparable ruins, the only remaining signs, alas, of a lost race, whose very name, like those of the great men, artists and rulers, who adorned it, seems destined to remain for ever hidden among the rubbish and dust ". And of Angkor Vat, again, he truly comments that " it could be compared very favourably with our most beautiful basilicas, and . . . is far more grandiose than anything built in the heyday of Greek or Roman art. . . ." Mouhot himself died a year or two after his astounding discovery : and the world must ever be grateful to him for his own immediate realisation of what he had found. Proving himself deserving of the apocalypse that had been granted to him, it was through his efforts that the boundary of French Indo-China was moved forward so as to include Angkor, and that it was thus saved to the world : for the Siamese, to whom it then belonged, were using the city as a quarry — just, again, as the Romans of the Dark Ages had formerly destroyed their great buildings. . . . Let us hope that, as he lay dying of a tropical fever contracted in this country, he may have judged that one instant of revelation to have been worth a whole ordinary lifetime, for he at least comprehended the magnitude of the gift to mankind of which he had been made the vehicle.

. . . . . .

Always, you will observe, the roads of our European thoughts return to Rome : and it must be admitted that a kind of verisimilitude is to be distinguished under the origin that the earliest of the monks attributed to Angkor, for of all the monuments of the East, those of the Cambodian jungle most nearly approximate to Western architectural principles. This is in no way to attempt to disparage their originality, or to pretend that, for all this, they do not appear very strange and remote ; but, when their geographical position and history are taken into consideration, it must seem curious that there appears to be so little of India, still less of China, in them, so much more of Ur and Babylon and Nineveh, of the great cities of Persia, Assyria and Mesopotamia, those vanished metropolises of winged lion and bull, of terraced pyramids and hanging gardens, from which both the later Imperial Rome and Constantinople, and through them, Venice, were descended, as much as the Byzantine cities of nearer Asia or the capital of the Sassanian kings. Thus the *idea* of Angkor, of its " sharpèd steeples high shot up in ayre ", is not unfamiliar to us : because the qualities which these ruins possess, in common, let us say, with Ctesiphon and Rome, though they plainly reached Cambodia from Indian sources, were not in themselves of an Indian origin, but of one even more remote in time. So often in the East you are made to feel that outside Europe the architectural spirit does not exist, that everything becomes a matter of pretty surface decoration indiscriminately applied, that, as with the constructions in stone or brick of Moor or Turk, though they often begin in a promising manner, they can never contrive to reach as far as the first storey without a powerful blunder of some sort or other being committed, that their owners, pashas and merchants, were never intended to indulge in more than ground-floor accommodation ; but these temples and palaces you recognise, directly you see them, as architecture, just as Mouhot did, wondering at " the genius of this Michelangelo of the Orient, who conceived such a work, who co-ordinated every part of it with the most wonderful art ". These buildings are Roman at least in their massiveness and grandeur of conception.

Moreover, even now, when several temples have been cleared altogether, or freed to a certain degree, of the surging invasion, there none the less manifests itself a most remarkable likeness to the Rome of Piranesi's etchings, the Rome of vast, broken arches tangled with the roots of trees, of fallen statues, and the drums and capitals of enormous pillars, lying beneath wildly clawing branches, of trophies, of old, dead roads, lined with tombs and shrines, from the splintered and broken cornices of which grow flowering weeds, wall plants, and, even, ilex-trunks : except that here all is exaggerated beyond the power of imagination, for the roots of trees are so gigantic that they enclose whole sanctuaries, the branches as thick as the bole of the Great Oak of Sherwood, while there are flowers and birds of the very existence of which no European could dream, and monkeys gape and chatter in the chapels, peering into the calm countenance of the Buddha or one of his saints. . . . So it is still, though the riot of fantasy must be a little reduced from the time when Mouhot first beheld the courts and towers of Angkor Vat, where, he says, " hardly a sound echoes but the roar of tigers, the harsh cry of elephants and the belling of wild stags ".

Let it be said immediately that Angkor, as it stands, ranks as chief wonder of the world today, one of the summits to which human genius has aspired in stone, infinitely more impressive, lovely and, as well, romantic, than anything that can be seen in China ; than, even, the Great Wall or the Ming Tombs. For, whereas in China it is in the strangeness of a mode of existence and of an art which offer an alternative to our own that the particular interest resides — in the fact, for example, that Chinese architecture, dependent for the most part on brightly painted wood, is yet in a sense of as abiding a nature as our own, because, if a building falls into decay, its identity,[1] if the will for it exists, can be reproduced exactly, and at no great cost : still more, that life, having been rendered to some extent fool-proof, was enabled in consequence, through so many thousands of years, to continue in the same mould, — here on the other hand, we are faced with objects of a kind more familiar to us, great and intricate organisations of stone and brick, complete even though in ruin, and all the more dramatic in their appeal because the civilisation to which they belonged, when compared with that of China, endured for so brief a period. Professional opinion, it is true, inclines sometimes to deny to the builders of these cities an entire comprehension of the use of stone as a medium (because, for many thousands of miles in every direction, only brick and wood had ever been used before), but were this criticism justified, their creations would long ago have been swallowed up, or dispersed under the never-ending and so vigorous assaults of the encircling forest. But, proof of the contrary, we have before us, still largely intact, the

[1] For the theory of Chinese permanence in architecture, see pp. 282-283 post.

material remains of a civilisation that flashed its wings, of the utmost brilliance, for six centuries, and then perished so utterly that even its name had died from the lips of man. Obviously the Cambodians were not in a position to build Rockefeller Centres of steel and concrete : but what their work lacks in knowledge — compared with that of modern architects — it gains in poetry, the poetry of conception, as well as of execution.

First of all, before proceeding to examine more closely these grandiose and imaginative works, it is necessary, perhaps, to disengage a little their history from its tangled web of myth, much as themselves, or several of them, have been cleared now from the parasitic romanticism of the jungle. . . . When Mouhot wrote, nothing at all was known of them ; and of the sovereigns who had ruled here, only the snow-white shadow of the Leper King had survived in the memory of the people. Mouhot thought that this ancient kingdom would never yield its secrets, but in the seventy years and more that have passed since his death, the work of scholars has thrown much light upon it. . . . The capital of the Cambodian or Khmer Empire — as " Khmer " merely means Cambodian, and acts only as archeological ballast to hold us to the ground, I propose at once to throw it overboard, and not to use it again myself (it may occur in quotations) during the course of this book — is known as Angkor Thom. Its temples, palaces and walls were constructed between the ninth and the fourteenth — but the majority between the ninth and the end of the thirteenth — centuries. It must, however, be remembered that in early times, in this quarter of the globe, cities were built, and abandoned, and rebuilt, in a most light-hearted fashion, and that though Angkor Thom is the one that has principally survived, there are, in addition, the remains of many others.

Specialists on the subject assert that today they can put an accurate date to each great relic ; but, despite the remarkable taste and judgment they have shown, to this claim I humbly beg leave to demur. For example, they began by assigning Angkor Vat to the first half of the twelfth century, then sent it flying back two hundred years to the tenth, and have now comfortably reinstalled it near where its career started : similarly, they first nailed the Bayon to the thirteenth century, then flung it back without warning to the ninth, and have finally relegated it again to the late twelfth century. And yet, lacking in this matter all authority, I find myself scarcely able to place faith in these ultimate dates : for there appertains to the power of correctly allotting a work to an epoch a quality, as in diagnosis, almost mediumistic, difficult adequately to explain on the level of what we know ; and, besides, were they correct in their latest transpositions, then the architecture of Angkor differs from that of all other cultures — is, indeed, the reverse of them — in that, beginning with delicate, sophisticated work, similar, let us say, to the creations of the Louis XVI period in France, it ends, five hundred years later, with the grand, primitive conceptions, such as the Bayon, that everywhere else would mark an earlier development of building. And I find that Henri Mouhot, who, being the first European of the nineteenth century to behold these wonderful remains, could know nothing of their history, and possessed, besides, little knowledge of architecture or esthetic equipment for their proper appreciation, nevertheless, since he was plainly a man of wonderful intelligence, immediately and as if by inspiration, grasped the facts relating to the epoch of the Cambodian temples, for he observes of Pnom Bakheng and its shrines (what has since been substantiated), that "... this building must be of far earlier origin than some of the other monuments. ... Taste was already finely developed, but ingenuity, will-power and motive-power were somewhat lacking ; in short, the temple of Mount Ba-Khêng appears to have been one of the preludes to this civilisation, as Ongkor-Wat must later have been its crowning glory."

In any case, however, owing to the investigations of the students in this field, we know that the civilisation of the Cambodian kingdom occupied five centuries, and was the heir in part of one of the greatest empires that Asia has ever known ; a dominion founded by a Hindu prince, who, as a young man, in the latter part of the eighth century, set out deliberately to conquer the world. Of him and his exploits, Dr. Quaritch Wales[1] writes : " This great con-queror, whose achievements can only be compared with those of the greatest soldiers known to Western history, and whose fame in his time sounded from Persia to China, in a decade or two built up a vast maritime empire which endured for five centuries, and made possible the marvellous flowering of Indian art and culture in Java and Cambodia. Yet in our encyclopedias and histories ... one will search in vain for a reference to this far-flung empire or to its noble founder. ... The very fact of such an empire's ever having existed is scarcely known, except by a handful of Oriental scholars. ..."

We are not cognisant of the name of this hero, because, owing to the laws of tabu, all Indian kings of that era remain anonymous to us : but he was known to his con-

[1] See *Towards Angkor*, by H. G. Quaritch Wales. (Harrap & Co., 1937.)

temporaries as Śailendra, or King of the Mountains (not to be confused with Marco Polo's Old Man of the Mountains, founder and head of the Sect of Assassins). His realm comprised the Malay Peninsula, Sumatra, Java and Cambodia, superseding the formerly celebrated empire of Funan : and for most of the information concerning it we are, Dr. Quaritch Wales tells us, dependent on the detailed accounts of their travels left us by Arab merchants of the time. (One of them, incidentally, records that our famous pantomime character, Sindbad the Sailor, in the course of his voyages found himself within the territory of the King of the Mountains and Lord of the Isles, and was received by that great potentate at court.)

The first King of Cambodia, then, of whom we can be sure — for there had been earlier monarchs of a more primitive kingdom, soon overridden — is King Jayavarman the First. His name signifies " from Java " (or more accurately, from the empire of which Java was then part), and he had been sent as a young man by his relative, the King of the Mountains, to rule over this country. With him he brought the particular Śailendra cult, which was to lead in time to such impressive architectural results : the cult of the God-King, " a kind of divine essence presiding over the destiny of the kings and resident in a *linga*, or emblem of Siva, which was enshrined in the sacred mountain ".[1] Owing to the flatness of the Cambodian plain, these sacred hills — which also, as a rule, served to mark the centre of the royal cities — had, except in a single instance, to be artificial, and in the course of the centuries were supplanted by the vast pyramid-cores of the great temples, which still, until the collapse of the Angkor

[1] *Towards Angkor*, by H. G. Quaritch Wales.

civilisation, retained at their tops sanctuaries such as had elsewhere been built on the mountains. (It was to these holy chambers, and, later, to a sanctuary in the Royal Palace itself, that the Kings of Cambodia must, according to legend, proceed every evening, in order to receive a visit from the Snake-Queen, who came to see him in the guise of a woman. If she failed to arrive, it meant that the hour had struck for the King to die : if, on the other hand, he did not wait there for her, disaster would overwhelm his kingdom.) In each of these shrines, too, was a *linga*, a phallic symbol still to be observed on all sides in tomb and temple and tabernacle, just as you might see similar emblems in Pompeii or Herculaneum. . . . Wound in with these central themes were the two religions of the country, Buddhism and Brahmanism : but, in Angkor, these two systems, elsewhere so often antagonistic, seem to have been in no way opposed, but, rather, to have interlocked one with the other. Evidences of both worships are to be found in the temples of each, and Siva and the Buddha have here become friends and neighbours.

Jayavarman I reigned sixty-seven years, having ascended the throne in 802. After his death the Cambodian kingdom threw off its allegiance to the Śailendra Empire, and became independent, and there followed through the next five centuries a succession of monarchs, rather difficult to differentiate, called, usually, either Jayavarman, Indravarman, Yacovarman or Suryavarman ; while all these sovereigns, as if in an effort to render themselves still more confusing, possessed, in addition, other styles bestowed upon them posthumously. But both these sets of names are, at any rate, known to us, even though the deeds associated with them have long been forgotten and we are scarcely certain of which great temple was built by whom. Looking at these vast monuments engulfed in the jungle, decorated with such art by their creators, and further endowed by nature with such a supreme quality of accidental and parasitic fantasy, the echo of lines from Spenser's *Ruines of Time* floats up to the surface of the mind :

> In vaine doo earthly Princes, then, in vaine
> Seeke with Pyramides, to heaven aspired ;
> Or huge Colosses, built with costlie paine ;
> Or brazen Pillours, never to be fired ;
> Or Shrines, made of the mettall most desired ;
> To make their memories for ever live :
> For how can mortall immortalitie give ?

Nevertheless, during a long period, the entire state centred round the persons of these princes, and, like the mighty rulers of Babylon and Assyria and, to a lesser extent, the Emperors of Rome, these tyrants occupied a religious and mystical, as well as a civil, position. Under them came a small feudal class of great wealth and importance, and then, at an infinite distance beneath, the Cambodian people, who lived in those remote times much as they do today.

Whole dynasties of kings ruled in undisputed power, and then, quite suddenly and without warning, they, together with the great and intricate system that they had created, and of which they were the crown, topple over and disappear into the darkness. Indeed, the end of this resplendent and curious civilisation is much more overgrown, more difficult to apprehend, than its beginning : for, after a certain date, no more buildings were constructed, and some temples, even, were to stand unfinished up to the present time. . . . The explanation of this collapse is said to be that the foreign and indigenous slaves, many of whom had been employed in carrying stone for these great works, took advantage of an attack by a neighbouring warlike tribe, the Thaïs, and revolted, slaying their oppressors, the King himself and the grandees ; and that, for two or three hundred years after this Bolshevik outbreak — until, in fact, the present Cambodian dynasty, originally of humble origin, had established its power — a general anarchy prevailed. . . . And at moments, withal, even in the hottest and most glowing sunshine — when colour is visible in objects, in stones and wood, that in more temperate climes have none — the terrible phantom of some indescribable massacre seems to hang over the ruins.

Meanwhile the great works of this culture still remain. In the jungle are nearly sixty square miles of ruins, centring round Angkor ; artificial lakes and basins and pools, moats and bridges, for this was a Narcissus-like beauty that loved to admire its own reflection in cool, flat mirrors of water laid upon the surface of a burning land. The four walls of whole cities now form a *hortus conclusus*, full of giant trees in blossom, of monkeys, and of animals more strange and ferocious, lurking in the tangled growth, nesting in the vast stones which everywhere lie submerged under the force of the vegetation that coils like a spring, about to leap up, or hangs down, making fresh roots wherever it touches the ground : and here, too, dwells an entire population of statues — yet more, no doubt, have fallen beneath the green tide and so are lost to sight — of images, and of the fabulous creatures of Hindu and Cambodian mythology.

And here, since I propose to treat of Angkor from the point of view of beauty, and not of archeology or iconography, and because, with this purpose in view, I intend in my descriptions to dispense with the exotic names proper to these beings and beasts, let me instance now the chief ones : the *Garouda*, the *Naga*, and the *Boddhisattva*, the *Apsara* and *Devatâ*. The *Garouda*, who resembles a gryphon — and to me will always remain one — is a mythical bird with a predilection for adopting human shape, while still retaining the head of an eagle, and wings folded back to display his arms. He is especially the foe of snakes, dedicated to their extermination, and in consequence is often represented in the act of grasping an enormous, many-headed serpent, which rears at his feet its inflated hood. This serpent is the *Naga*, deriving its form from the cobra, and constituting the most pronounced, as well as original and magnificent, theme in the symphony of Cambodian architecture. Everywhere in this world of water, the *Naga* acts as balustrade to bridge and causeway, and to the many bold flights of steps that, broken by imposing landings, lead down to lakes or up to temples. Its curving neck and the erect, proud hooding of its heads — seven, nine or eleven in number — display, as they raise themselves, one on each side of an entrance, all the vain grace of a peacock's spreading tail. The *Boddhisattva* is a kind of saint, in the Buddhist Mahayana doctrine. The *Apsara*, equivalent to a nymph, and given to dancing, flying and throwing flowers, is represented in bas-relief on many of the walls of Angkor, while the *Devatâs* are goddesses, the occupants of niches, and constitute an important architectural tribe. . . . Besides these beings, the favourites of the Cambodian builders, were lions, usually placed, again, on the stages of formal flights of stairs, and resembling kylins or Byzantine lions in their mock, smiling ferocity, and elephants, who, as they should, here occupy in decora-

DETAIL OF STONE ANGA, OR MANY-HEADED SERPENT
IN ANGKOR VAT

tion a position commensurate with their size. And, over all, floats the lotus, the emblem of the Buddha. . . . Thus, in future, though *Garouda, Naga* and *Boddhisattva, Apsara* and *Devatâ,* possess their own powerful appellations, and though we shall meet them at every step, I shall not mention them again by these names, because the alien music of their sound, the incalculable mystery it exhales, upsets the balance of every sentence with its weight, which must both impress and hold up the attention of the reader : so that, throughout the following pages, they will be reduced in rank, respectively, to plain gryphons, serpents, saints, nymphs and goddesses.

. . . . . .

To some of those who read these pages, Angkor will simply mean, I suspect — as I have owned it meant to me, until I went there — Angkor Vat ; of which a model, jostling the mud huts of Central Africa, and the wattle shanties of the Pacific islands, was included in the Paris Colonial Exhibition of 1931. . . . But, in fact, the " replica " of this great temple was an interpretation of Angkor to about the same degree that, if London were deserted, yet its foremost monuments were to survive, a model of the lantern of St. Paul's would represent, to the distant eyes of future generations of Cambodians and Chinese, not only the great cathedral itself, but also the architectural character of the rest of the city : for it was merely the topmost portion, the inner sanctuary, of one of Angkor's many great edifices, copied in plaster and dumped down in Paris amid the most incongruous neighbours, and without any connection whatever with the ground upon which it stood : whereas the chief wonder of this particular building resides precisely in that relationship, in the great system of moat and corridor and court and cloister and water-garden which lead up to it, and of which this central shrine, with its five towers, is the exquisite crown and culmination. Moreover, to my mind, there exist in this wilderness several other monuments — though none, perhaps, that, however gigantic, approach it in size — which rival, and even surpass, Angkor Vat in beauty. Thus, without fear that anyone who has once beheld it would ever dare to gainsay such a statement, the neighbouring Bayon can be said to be the most imaginative and singular in the world, more lovely than Angkor Vat, because more unearthly in its conception, a temple from a city in some other distant planet ; if Angkor Vat displays the nimbus of the sun, its splendour and vital majesty, the Bayon opposes to this the cold, ice-laden halo of the moon, a quality at once remote and hallucinatory, imbued with the same elusive beauty that often lives between the lines of a great poem.

Or, to take lesser works than these two stupendous temples, many of the little sanctuaries and chapels of brick and stone, scattered so plentifully through the forest, and belonging to an earlier epoch, are in a sense more perfect, their sculpture equal in execution and detail to the finest reliefs that line the walls of the larger buildings — but then there can be found in other lands shrines somewhat resembling these, and in spite of their beguiling grace, I am not concerned here so much for prettiness, or even for pure beauty, as for a loveliness that is new to us and adds its contribution to the sum of human genius. It must be admitted, however, that the greatest authorities on the art of this kingdom seem often to prefer the earlier and less characteristic work — perhaps because the discovery of it helps to emphasise the correctness of the historic theories they had evolved long before any such corroboration of their truth had been brought to light. (Sometimes, too, the belief hardens in my mind that those who remain for long in charge of beautiful things grow subconsciously to hate them, tend, in consequence, to care only for those among them that resemble objects elsewhere, and thus remove their guardians for a moment from the atmosphere round. This hatred can be accounted for, perhaps, by the silly transience of human life ; the Egyptian alabaster pot which the curator of the X Museum has just been obliged to purchase, though insensate, has already enjoyed a life of a hundred times his own span, and will, he knows, be prized and admired long after he has become dust, and his learned writings have grown obsolete, been forgotten — why, even the Chippendale chair upon which he sits before his desk will probably outlive him in the future, as it has outlived him in the past. Worse still, these dead objects in that section of a museum under the care of any particular official actually devour whole years of his flesh and blood : he is being forced, usually by economic compulsion, to sacrifice his life to them ; no wonder he hates them, that have changed him into so desiccated a being, drained of vitality ; no wonder he prefers those examples that escape from their category and remind him of things elsewhere, where life was sweet and he was on holiday. And though these considerations, fortunately, do not apply to men with a genius for their profession, such as Dr. Marchal and Monsieur Goloubeff, whose loving appreciation of the things under their care is evident in a thousand directions, nevertheless it must be remembered that, as a rule, those in charge of ruins in tropical countries possess a much more solid foundation for their hatred ; because not only are these long-lived inanimate stones the reason for their prolonged exile in remote countries, not only are they obliged to offer up to them hour after hour, ounce after ounce of their own bodies, as it were, but, in addition, the unhealthiness to a European of such a climate must, if he remain there long enough, inevitably shorten his life, so that the ruins are not only absorbing the few years allotted to him from the beginning, but will one day kill him outright — as these very ruins, perhaps, killed Henri Mouhot, their discoverer — or else leave him a hopeless invalid, confined to the cold monotony of a Bath chair existence in European spas.)

Nevertheless these chapels of the ninth and tenth centuries, even though often wrongly appraised, would in themselves be delightful wherever they were found, and the sculpture that adorns them is lacking altogether in that repulsive, greasy quality that so often mars Hindu works of art. For, while all the trade of Cambodia seems to have been with China, and though, as we know, the two empires were in continual communication, the only artistic influence ever to be detected in Angkor is Indian, the only analogy, with Maya art (for though the works of Central America must rank infinitely lower in the scale of human genius, there often, nevertheless, exists a disturbing similarity ; a similarity that led the late Dr. Thomas Gann to adumbrate his interesting theories — which, however, have not found acceptance — concerning a common origin for the peoples and arts of the two countries). Certainly this influence, and this resemblance, both exist : but, as certainly, the Cambodians were a people of the finest esthetic perception, and no Mexican, Javanese, Siamese or Indian temple or work of art can compare with their productions. Their genius permeates every piece of sculpture in the ruins.

Compare their carvings, for example, with those of their
neighbours and hereditary enemies, the Chams, and the
fineness of their quality, the difference between them,
becomes evident at once. Much Cham art is impressive,
but the hard, elongated faces of their statues demonstrate
an absolute want of life and originality : they seem made
only to be broken and set up in museums, and, when you
find them in their own sites, gain nothing from their
proper surroundings. . . . But let me once again quote
Dr. Quaritch Wales, a great lover of Indian civilisation,
and expert upon it, who yet writes of Cambodian art, and
of the Hindu influence upon it, in these very just terms :
" When the guiding hand of India was removed, her inspiration was not forgotten, but the Khmer genius was released
to mould from it vast new conceptions of amazing vitality
different from, and hence not properly to be compared with,
anything matured in a purely Indian environment. . . . It
is true that Khmer culture is essentially based on the inspiration of India, without which the Khmers at best might have
produced nothing greater than the barbaric splendour of
the Central American Mayas ; but at the same time it must
be admitted that here, more than anywhere else in Greater
India, this inspiration fell on fertile soil."

How well Angkor Vat bears out these words ! From
what I have said, when comparing it with the Bayon or
with the smaller sanctuaries, the reader must not conclude
that this great temple is just a variation on an old theme.
It is immense, superb, truly a work of the King of the
Angels, as later generations of Cambodians deemed it. . . .
For many miles before you draw near to it, you can distinguish in the distance its five cone-shaped towers, the
summits of which rise some two hundred and fifteen feet

from the ground, swelling and soaring high above the trees
— in themselves titans, boasting, many of them, a stature of
a hundred and fifty feet.  And then, suddenly, you find
yourself opposite the huge square moat which girdles the
whole temple. . . . At this point, as the newcomer obtains
his first vista of the entire structure and necessarily attempts
to relate it to his former experience, will come his first
surprise : in that the places whereof this great complex of
water-garden and terrace and court and corridor must put
him most in mind, as he takes in the symmetrical yet intricate
design before him, are Versailles and Caserta ; it is on an
identical scale, possessed of the same dignified and classical
organisation.  And yet, in spite of such an affinity, in spite
of its pleasantly secular, if imposing, air, and though many
have sought to see in it a palace, it seems to be established
beyond doubt that it was built originally as a temple and has
always served the same purpose.

Measurements tell one little, and I will soon abandon
the use of them, but it should perhaps be recorded that the
whole system of buildings bounded by the moat extends
for over a thousand and twenty yards long by some eight
hundred and forty wide.  The entrance is by a tall and
impressive stone causeway leading across the moat, full of
blue water-lilies and lotus in their season— the lilies have
the same blue and lilac tone as the sky—, and in it the
elephants are taken every morning to cool themselves,
plodding and plunging among the roots up to the top of
their huge grey backs, lifting their trunks into the air and
trumpeting their loud delight.  Floating above the land for
over two hundred yards, the paved terrace still here and
there retains its balustrade of stone serpents, while, in the
centre, its length is broken by a ceremonial architectural

ONE OF THE "LIBRARIES" OF ANGKOR VAT

feature of two staircases descending on each hand into the water below. The stone pavement, reverberant and crackling in the heat, sends up its dancing, trembling air into your face, and the sun scorches your back, so that in spite of the extraordinary beauty of the scene, you cannot but be glad to reach the outer gate, from which leads a cool corridor, winging it, and surrounding the whole enclosure. The porch itself, with a broken, cone-crowned tower and majestic flights of steps, flanked by rearing golden serpents, is superbly designed, but it is, perhaps, only at the moment when you have crossed under it that you can thoroughly comprehend both the familiarity and the strangeness of the building before you ; somehow familiar in the European construction of it, in the sense of its fountains and courts, of the device of false door and windows to aid the balance of the scheme ; strange in its motifs, so intensely Asiatic, in the bamboo formula, for example, of the bars of the false windows, and in the use of these elephants and serpents for the themes of the decoration. From here on each side of the inner causeway, which extends for three hundred and sixty yards, you can see the two " libraries ", so called, — of which the purpose is still obscure, but so European in their general appearance that, at first sight, they might well be taken for Roman works or for those of the later Italian Renaissance — the two water-lawns (one with its stone border still intact), groups of lofty palm-trees, their high feathery crests seeming always to move upon a breeze impalpable from below, and, finally, the cumulative effect of cloister and tower, and of endless stone roofs, their gables edged with stone flames, intersecting, rising one above another and mounting eventually up to the grandeur, greater still, of the five vast cones surmounting the five towers. . . . The interior wall of the entrance court is lined, too, with bas-reliefs of great beauty, as is the inner corridor when, in the end, you reach its shelter. In front of this immense gallery, raised to a higher level, is a colonnaded terrace bounded by a balustrade ; a stately terrace on which the King probably gave audiences, or from which, again, he may have watched the passing of religious processions.

The interior of the high-vaulted first storey constitutes, in fact, a sculpture gallery, filled with a continuous series of bas-reliefs of kings and priests and battles, and, above all, of dancing girls ; whole walls form a frieze of dancing figures, wearing the winged shoulders and head-dresses of the Cambodian dancers of today. Then there are illustrations, too, from the Hindu mythology, of, for example, the Sea of Milk and the struggle in it between the gods and devils, that constitute here so repetitive a theme, and of the fight of Rama to recover his wife, and of the army of battling monkeys that took his side, slinging stones at the opposing regiments of giants. Many of the figures that come to life out of the stone are highly polished, because since the wish to touch them is the very test and proof of good sculpture, the Cambodians, who like — and, one presumes, have always liked, from the beginning, right through their dark ages down to the present day — to walk here slowly, examining what they must regard as so many wonderfully told sacred stories, have patted and caressed the surface so often as to have imparted a gloss to them : further, being so simple a people, they have even spat out betel juice, to discolour the figures of the scoundrels, much as the villains of the old London melodramas used to be hissed, while the faces of one or two of the heroes have

STONE BALLET OF CAMBODIAN DANCING GIRLS

*Detail of relief in the great corridor of Angkor Vat*

been applaudingly touched with gold. . . . Every temple throughout the wilderness is similarly panelled, some with sculptures in high relief, others with flat, Assyrian-like figures, but all full of enchanting detail ; however, as I would wish here to confine description to general effect and atmosphere, I shall not, with one or two exceptions, mention them. Instead, they must be assumed by the reader wherever we go ; dancing girls, warriors, the armies of conflicting deities and devils, processions, kings standing upright on the backs of elephants, banners, music and the spoils of victory for Cambodia, chains and the bowed-down bitterness of defeat for the enemy : the art of this culture is essentially a triumphant one.

In this corridor, which seems to continue endlessly, so enormous is it, you might be walking at the bottom of the sea. The light through the openings, the green, mildewed darkness within, seem almost to impart a weedy movement to the figures, the lines and curves of whose bodies, swaying and trembling in, it appears, a pale, submarine phosphorescence, swell out of the stone with a certain reality. The height and angle of the vaulting, too, so steep, that if the roof were circular, it might be the inside of a witch's sugarloaf hat, help to intensify the curious atmosphere to be felt here : but still more does the overwhelming effluvium that pervades the whole length of the cloister, an odour of bats and reptiles, and of the habitations of men long buried and overgrown, left forgotten at the bottom of an immense forest, so that for many centuries no light ever reached them. Indeed, had it been necessary, I reflected while walking in it, for a great stage-producer to devise, let us say, an odour appropriate to the impressive, mournful yet slightly malign air of these mouldering perspectives, this, doubtless, was the one he would have chosen, the steam rising from the tropical equivalent of the Witches' brew in *Macbeth*.

> Fillet of a fenny snake,
> In the cauldron boil and bake ;
> Eye of newt and toe of frog,
> Wool of bat, and tongue of dog,
> Adder's fork, and blind-worm's sting,
> Lizard's leg, and howlet's wing. . . .

Only here the hell-broth would be distilled from fillets of cobra and krait, the eyes of alligators and the toes of many singular and unpleasant creatures that ordinarily we only see in the Reptile House of a first-rate Zoological Gardens, as well as from " wool of bat " : (for bats, giant bats, sleeping through the sunny hours, have become the normal inhabitants of the cloister). The ingredients, however, of the second verse, with its " Scale of dragon ", and " maw and gulf of the ravin'd salt-sea shark ", with its " Nose of Turk and Tartar's lips ", and " tiger's chaudron ", should be easier, geographically speaking, to obtain here, you would have thought, than in a cavern perched above grey boulders on a Scottish grouse moor. To " cool it with a baboon's blood ", for instance, should present but little difficulty ; while for those elements in the stew here unprocurable, others could be substituted. In the matter of the liver — " liver of blaspheming Jew " — failing the kidnapping of one of the several French-Austrian barons who were touring the country at the moment — and even they might not have been caught in the correct ripeness of their sacrilege — it would be best, perhaps, to throw into the bubbling, fire-scarred pot the liver of " blaspheming Lolo ". . . . Incidentally, it was revealed to me in a flash, as I repeated to myself the spell, how

Shakespeare had written one line, at least. He had sat down to compose this poem, but had found himself unable to complete the fourth line of the Second Witch's incantation; "wool of bat . . . and . . . and . . . and . . ." he had kept on repeating to himself, while a dog, near by, maintained a typically nagging, insane and vainglorious clamour, so that, whenever the poet was on the point of catching the dark, moth-like thought and rhyme that he wanted, this barking startled it away. Anger seized on him : he would have liked to tear the dog's tongue out . . . and then, suddenly, it came to him :

> Eye of newt and toe of frog,
> Wool of bat . . . and . . .

and . . . and . . . why, of course!

> . . . and tongue of dog,

. . . So, a touch of nature brings all writers, however good or bad, together : and, indeed, these deductions seemed to me much more probable than some of the inferences drawn by Shakespearian scholars. . . . But what a vista of suffering it shows ! And I dare say that Elizabethan dogs were of a yet more tenaciously noisy breed than our own, though, perhaps, less spoilt and fussy ? . . . With an eye now trained for the invention of newspaper articles, I considered the " caption ", as editors like to call it, " Was Shakespeare a Dog-Lover ? " The answer, I apprehend, must decidedly be in the negative (and this, in spite of the heading, would, alas ! deprive the article of any chance of popularity), for elsewhere in his work, dogs come in for much shrewd abuse : as, for example :

> . . . for coward dogs
> Most spend their mouths when what they seem to threaten
> Runs far before them. . . .

. . . No, he cannot have liked them, cannot have been a lover of " our four-footed friends ".

However, to direct our gaze again away from these peep-holes into the seventeenth-century poetic life of Britain, toward the Cambodian forests, since the jungle odour renders it difficult for anyone, not enured to it, to complete the tour of this vast rectangle, the fact that he has not yet visited the rest of the organisation to which it acts as prelude, serves on this first occasion as an excellent excuse for returning to the main door, or for climbing up one of the small staircases that lead to the second storey. The chief entrance to it is reached by a covered yard, full of Buddhist images, heaped together, and of a later epoch — they belong, probably, to a period a hundred years or so subsequent to the ruin of Angkor Vat. Few attain to any esthetic value, but the number and littering disorder of them, and even their likeness, one to another, bestows upon them a kind of interest. . . . Beyond lies a turfed courtyard, with two more libraries, symmetrically disposed, and from each of the corners a most memorable view of the central building can be obtained. The stairs in front are steep, abrupt and difficult in their ascent, very unlike the shallow, encouraging flights that marked the beginning of the lay-out. When you have mounted them, you see that the four basins that lie between the raised pavements of the second storey are of considerable and, indeed, of unnecessary depth, unless you accept the deduction (which various other details tend to support) that these, and the four spaces in the cruciform gallery below leading from the first to the second storey out of the turfed courtyard, were filled with water. Owing to the obvious delight — one, too, that, as we shall see later in the next chapter, bore, in addition, a practical and commercial aspect — displayed by the Cambodians in the use of water for decorative purposes, this need not greatly surprise us, though it would remain a feature that does not occur elsewhere in the other temples. . . . But then, Angkor Vat is a very original creation. . . . How lovely, though, if it were so, this water must have looked, cupped so high in the air, yet cut off from all lateral light, so that it must have radiated a deep and translucent blue that even the sky could not transcend ; how strange and striking must have been the reflections of the priests, as they walked in procession on the raised stone paths above, and of the five towers, plunging downward into these cool mirrors.

The traveller, climbing up steps that are more vertiginous than ever, to the central sanctuary, finds, when he reaches the summit, little to see within, albeit the view of the courts and corridors of the temple below, and of the encircling jungle beyond, is incomparable. . . . That which must chiefly impress him, as he looks down upon the elaboration of open space and mass, of sunlight and shadow, will be the sense of finely balanced proportion manifest throughout this gigantic and splendid edifice. Though permeated by a love of dazzlingly rich decoration, this is always kept in check, never allowed to run unbridled over wall and ceiling, as so often in other equatorial systems of architecture : it possesses strength and repose, as well as imagination and a power of fantasy. Here, gazing up at the lofty towers, or down, over fountain, court and corridor, terrace and paved esplanade, over the crossing lines of a thousand gabled roofs and exquisitely and boldly sculptured details, the main effect is one of supreme dignity : and next he will feel how curiously and fortunately combined in this great relic are ruin and survival. Almost whole — by far the least injured of the temples — so that nothing has been lost by decay, it has yet disintegrated just sufficiently to produce in the heart of the onlooker an overwhelming sense of age and past glory.

From this height, too, it is possible to descry the towers of Angkor Thom, in the depths of the forest, and even, here and there, the lines of its walls. . . . Below, scattered thickly under and above the mammoth trees, in that deranged, visionary world of Piranesi's, stand gates and walls and water-basins, niches and sanctuaries, sculptured islands lying on pools, terraces with a frieze of elephants cut out of the stone that supports them, magnificent stair-cases, flying on wings from one level to another, and descending to nothing, causeways across moats and canals from which, in the passage of centuries, the water has receded (assuming new and unexpected positions a little distance off), leaving the channels choked with water-flowers of such luxuriant beauty that, each time you see them, they take your breath away, while birds as gorgeous in their plumage as ever was the Queen of Sheba in her attire, stalk round the edge of marsh or pool or wade deep among the blossoms. From the exuberance of the vegetation, out of the festoons and wreaths trailing from the trees, appear roofs and shattered cornices, fallen stone beams of enormous size, great stones, like boulders, jutting out at insane, because purposeless, angles, carved heads of men and lions, horses and serpents, colossal statues on their splintered plinths, round the bodies of which have wound the long, snake-like coils of some parasitic tropical plant. Crowned with high, pointed tiaras, dancers extend their fingers in the significant gestures of Cambodian ballet from mossy walls under cascades of green leaves or sprays of

THE STRUGGLE BETWEEN STONE AND VEGETATION

*Detail of temple in the Angkor Thom Jungle*

flowers, and blossoms grow, too, from their pagoda-shaped head-dresses and from the round caps of the comedians and acrobats. The walls of whole towns and monasteries now form park-like enclosures : in them the fangs of the gigantic roots of a tree clamp together the sagging door of a sanctuary, or the immense trunk itself has split, to reveal the image of Rama, or some bas-relief of ancient triumph, while, in contrary process, the roots of other trees are disrupting a cloister, so that a man's bones appear beneath a stone slab. Nature and art are engaged every-where in ferocious battle, or merge in wild and inextricable confusion. Trees sprout like antlers from the heads of gods ; lions and gryphons, as though they were alive, peer through the fluttering screens of leaves. The prone image of the Buddha is being gradually raised from the ground by the force of the plants beneath his weight, and near by a stone Siva, destroyer and creator, is, in his turn, being destroyed by his creations.

Under a *Flamboyant Tree* lies a panel, sculptured with capering monkeys, and, as you look at it, high up in the branches above there suddenly swings into view a whole flight of them in the flesh, black velvet monkeys about three feet high, rocking and shooting forward with so airy and agile a grace, calculating each leap and bound with such nicety, that no expert skater or exponent of the waltz has ever been able to develop so audacious and delicate a mastery of rhythm as these inimitable artists of the trapeze. . . . Clawing feebly in their cages, or mocking the pleasure-cruisers, on their decks, in the Zoological Gardens of the great European capitals, these creatures never afford any idea of the perfection of movement of which they possess the natural secret, or of the marvellous acrobatic feats they can

accomplish ; whereas here, unhampered and free, dappled
and piebald with the strength of tropical light and shade,
they dance and bound through their native air with a
superb assurance. . . . (Looking at them, I became certain
in my own mind of the truth of a story I had read recently
in an Indian paper ; a story which illustrated, conjoined to
common sense and a wish to make the best of things, this
very quality. . . . It appeared that the monkeys in some
Indian town had become so *difficile* and prepotent, that it
was felt by all the townspeople that, whether sacred or not,
the city must rid itself of them.  Accordingly, though the
authorities had dreaded the scene that might occur, they had
been rounded up, one fine spring morning, without, it
seems, much difficulty, and had been then piled into waiting
lorries and taken to the edge of a jungle some hundred miles
away, where — for public opinion would not allow them to
be killed — they were to be marooned.  Arriving there about
tiffin-time, the attendants were surprised at the docile and
even pleased manner in which the simian hordes left the
lorries and swung their way into the shade. . . . It was, the
drivers felt as they sat down to luncheon, the very day for a
picnic : after an interval for rest and digestion, they were just
preparing to return, when the monkeys trooped back from
what they, too, had evidently regarded as a picnic, and resolutely took up their former places in the lorries.  Unable to
dislodge them, for they were numerous and determined, the
attendants had to give way and they were driven back to
the city, where their unexpected and stately re-entrance
caused considerable emotion.  They seemed to be bowing
to the spectators in answer to no apparent applause, and
had quite the air of exiled royalty returning home. . . .
And, after they had swarmed back into palm-trees and on

to the eaves of temples, they could long be heard chattering freely, discussing, no doubt, their enjoyable outing in the country.)

Beneath the swinging shapes, along the park-like alleys, Cambodian children, almost naked, their skins toning precisely with their jungle background, wander, carrying their rough archer's equipment, or pause suddenly, listening, with their arrows ready poised. They seem curiously unafraid, for, in addition to the birds and apes, leopards live in the green mists that veil the vistas of these kitchen-garden-like rectangles, but, albeit sometimes encountered, after the manner of all wild animals, they are said to be of a timid disposition. Indeed the forest is not frightening, and here for the first time I realised how much more alarming is an English wood than any jungle, and why ; it is empty, the loudest sound for which you could strain your ears would be a rustle, a scuttle or a sigh ; whereas these green depths are turbulent with life, which imparts to them a gaiety, the same air of bustle that you find in cities, and renders them altogether lacking in any quality of being haunted, or of unfathomable mystery, even though, at times, the actual volume of sound — as, for example, when carried on the back of an intense silence, or perhaps borne by a light evening wind to the higher terraces of a temple at dusk — is extremely startling.

But let us turn to examine the Porte de la Victoire, the strangest thing that can be discovered, as unearthly as the Bayon to which it leads : for this gateway constitutes the main approach to the ruined capital, of which the Bayon was the centre, and, like all the other entrances, like the temple itself, it is dominated by the repetition of a vast sculptured head, a lovely, smiling but enigmatic Cambodian face, though one raised to the power and beauty of a god, with features which, albeit infinitely more subtle, recall those of the jadeite masks of Mexico and Yucatan. So singular, indeed, is the visionary [1] effect of these heads, each surmounted with the lotus crown, that archeologists like to dismiss the king who built them as a megalomaniac : for here is something in the world of beauty of which they have never previously obtained even a hint. . . . And, to anticipate for a moment, as well as, for once, to examine the bas-reliefs, there exist in the Bayon, in the chamber next to the Eastern Entrance, some sculptured scenes in which a king is portrayed in single combat with various animals. In the first, by his own unaided efforts, he has thrown an elephant to the ground, and is grasping in his hand one of its hind legs ; in another he is shown contriving with equal proficiency the triumphant overthrow of a lion or some kindred beast, in spite of the sycophantic jostling of slaves round him, anxious to hold fans for him and parasols. These panels are said to represent King Yacovarman —

---

[1] In his stimulating and very interesting book, *Bali and Angkor* (Michael Joseph, 1936), Mr. Geoffrey Gorer has founded on this effect and similar ones a theory that Cambodian art was born of drug-taking. Now, though I am confident that the builders of Angkor took drugs, I do not myself think it is possible to relate their art to this habit entirely, any more than it would be reasonable to attribute the merits and faults of the Ritz Tower in New York to the cigarettes that the workmen constructing it no doubt smoked. In both cases, these were resorted to as a solace after hard work and an alleviation of a climate with a tendency to excess. Because our Western civilisation could not produce this particular kind of beauty, we have attempted to search for some peculiar reason that must account for it, intoxication or madness. . . . The lack of a European constructive sense is attributed to it : though this fault, due to a lack of knowledge and experience — and therefore, in reality, due, perhaps, to the short duration of this culture — is no worse than many of our own architectural faults to which we remain complacently blind. . . . Thus, too, one day when I said to a Moorish friend in Fez, " It seems so odd to us that you fill your rooms with brass bedsteads," he replied, " It is just the same as your filling your rooms with rugs. There should be no more than one in a room, we think."

THE TUG-OF-WAR, GODS VERSUS DEVILS OUTSIDE THE
PORTE DE LA VICTOIRE AT ANGKOR THOM

not the monarch who built this temple, but the founder of the original city on the same site — for such fights were a practice in which he is supposed to have indulged : but, since his distant " megalomaniac " successor, King Jayavarman the Seventh, erected them in the chief holy place of his later city, it is permissible to wonder whether he did not instal them here because he saw in these traditions concerning his remote predecessor a quality which appealed especially to his own burning imagination ; because himself was engaged single-handed in a yet more unwonted battle, one waged with masses of inanimate stone against time itself, and still proceeding to this day in front of our eyes ? Indeed he accomplished things in building of which no man, before or since, has ever dreamed, and though, in so doing, he broke many architectural laws — as well, no doubt, as the hearts of many Professors of Architecture, both then and now — his monument still stands before us.

All the gates of his city manifest the same very personal idiom as the Porte de la Victoire. Some display, at recessed angles, below the sculptured heads that in themselves form turrets, a motif of a tricephalous elephant, the triangles forming a graceful rococo curve. But this triple-gated entrance of which I write, the largest, has three square, crumbling towers, the most lofty, at the centre, rising nearly sixty feet from the ground, and crowned with four visages measuring at least ten feet in height, and gazing out, one toward each point of the compass. Below these bruised and battered countenances, over which trees of tremendous size pour their green torrents, and from whose faintly smiling lips, stained with lichen, spring many tropical weeds and flowers, stands a causeway. On either side of it are seated fifty-four stone giants, twenty feet tall as they squat, restraining or, as though taking part in a tug-of-war, pulling at, the long stone serpent with a multiple fan-shaped head, which forms the balustrade. The two opposing teams are recruited, one from gods, the other from devils, whose sullen, ferocious expressions contrast with the benevolent, calm-eyed determination of their antagonists. . . . Some of the figures had collapsed, and have only recently been re-erected, but the work has been accomplished with notable success. Outside other gateways a few similar giants remain in their original positions, but, as there are many gaps between them, you cannot, as you do here, comprehend the full design.

All the entrances, however, are but the announcement of a theme that finds a grandiose culmination in the Bayon, a temple originally dedicated to Siva, but transferred, before it was finished, to the worship of the Buddha. This Cyclopean bulk of stone, standing like a rock from which the ocean has receded, depends entirely for its effect upon the repetitive occurrence, the rhythm, of the colossal, gently smiling faces. So damaged by the combined assaults of time and the jungle are these towers that you cannot perceive immediately all the visages that they display. Indeed, the state of dilapidation into which some have fallen renders it difficult to be precise as to the total number of them, but there are between a hundred and sixty and two hundred. Many, however, appear only to assume their form while you are looking at them, in this fierce light dissolving back again, after the moment in which you had grasped their outline and contours, into ragged stony crags ; more than the handiwork of men, they seem natural crags, torn thus, carved by the wind into a likeness that will ever haunt the minds of those who come here. If you climb up to one of the platforms from which they spring, nothing will exist for you except these towers, at various heights and levels, above and below you, towers that turn always into strange masks, with an impalpable air of mockery, remote and not easily to be captured. And you should choose the sunset hour to visit them.

Many visitors will be watching at this time for the great ceremonial sortie from Angkor Vat of the bats inhabiting it, which, suddenly collecting each evening from every nook and roof and dome in the immense building, combine into a dark cloud of leathery wings and fly three times round the temple : [1] but actually to stand here, on one of the upper terraces of the Bayon, and merely to observe the shifting lights and colours of the tropical sunset play among these turrets, affords a spectacle infinitely more interesting and remote from experience. With every modulation they reveal new faces, or change the features and expression of those at which you are looking. They attain, now, to a numerical and problematic beauty, like that of a recurring decimal, that has no end, but goes leaping away into infinity, behind it trailing the indivisible progeny so soon to become itself. Never will you be able to penetrate beyond the barrier of this repetition, a similarity that yet alters as you attempt to focus it. No longer architecture, this temple has become a vast, prophetic poem, a vision such as was granted to William Blake. From here nothing else exists, except the sky, in which the evening star is now beginning

---

[1] In the last few years, these flights have stopped. "*Ils ne sortent plus,*" the guides explain, as though the creatures had experienced some overwhelming sorrow which discouraged them from going out in the world. And, indeed, as though to inflict a check upon the hordes of tourists, if they sally forth at all now, they fly singly ; but, for the most part, they remain resolutely indoors, in a kind of Faubourg St.-Germain seclusion.

to appear, and the moon, so clearly belonging to the same world as these crags : nothing else exists, even though the dying glory of the sun still rests upon the stones, throwing back its heat, and upon the jungle, whence come up to meet you on the scented evening air cries and chattering, and the sound of scuffling and branches crackling, which serve to emphasise the death and stillness, wherein only dreams can live, of this great building.

City beyond city, temple beyond temple, the ruins stretch into the forest. . . . To name only a few among the thousand monuments, a little way off you can distinguish the natural hill of Pnom Bakheng — the only hill for many miles round — which King Yacovarman, slayer of beasts, chose for the site of his sanctuary — wherein he was supposed to meet the Snake-Goddess — and also for the centre of his city of Yacodharapura. (For many years, though the boundaries were known, no centre for it could be identified : indeed, it was a temple, rather than a hill, for which the authorities were searching. Eventually Monsieur Goloubeff — an archeologist, for once, whose archeology resembles poetry — revealed the fact that this hill was the ancient capitol, and uncovered down its steep sides four tremendous flights of steps, flanked by lions ; steps, again, out of that world, tinged by nightmare, of Piranesi's. And these four staircases, facing the cardinal points, as well as constituting a most important architectural feature, are the admitted proof of his theory.) . . . The walls of Pra Khan enclose an area of about eight hundred and sixty yards by seven hundred and fifty ; in front of them lies a wide moat, and an avenue of gods and devils, similar to the one at Angkor Thom, leads up to each gate. . . . Then Pra Rup, a classical edifice, as it were, exhales, with its cut stones and terraces, a very European quality that, paradoxical as it may sound, recalls such buildings as, let us say, Blenheim or, even, the Pitti Palace. . . . Neak Pean, a floating shrine, built on an island — though the water is now only present in the wet season — offers us, on the other hand, the very essence of poetry. From a central basin rises this small oratory of stone, carved in the likeness of a lotus blossom : but since the whole of the upper part has been consumed by the roots of a giant tree, it is now possible only to distinguish the shape and carving of the base. . . . Ta Prohm, again, stands in the middle of another of those enormous, park-like enclosures that are so typical a feature of the ruins. Its numerous buildings and cloisters and flights of steps, huddled together, with none of the sense of proportion that marks Angkor Vat, for instance, seem but a haphazard collection, and yet, from their very disarray and multitude, to acquire a certain impressiveness. Moreover, no attempt has here been made to drive out the invasion of the jungle. Tree roots of huge, exaggerated size, bulky as a forest tree in northern latitudes, interpose themselves between the pillars of a cloister, cracking them as easily as a giant crushes a walnut with his hand, stone roofs are torn and twisted, and across some of the largest of them, even, straddle these tropical trees, bearing to them the same proportion as would an oak growing from a man's head. It is difficult for someone who has not seen it to picture so wild and ramshackle a confusion of animate and inanimate, of rampant green life at war with immobile grey death, golden death. Indeed, the stone itself acquires a kind of life from the struggle, for it is caught between two fires, branches stretching upward and downward to destroy it, so that the architecture, obliged thus to take part in a battle, seems here to assume a dynamic, rather than its usual static, aspect. The interior has grown dark, stained and shrouded, from this ceaseless combat, and, under the force of it, the numerous richly decorated reliefs have become endowed with a new if fortuitous power, looming in sudden bright swirls of light. . . . Once this was a monastery, as well as temple, and an inscription, said to date from the twelfth century, was found among these luxuriant coils and tumblings, held in place there by green arms and tentacles ; a tablet which helps to account for the dimensions of Ta Prohm, for it provides us with details concerning the establishment. Eighteen hundred priests and two thousand seven hundred and forty deacons officiated in the temples, and, in addition, there resided in the precincts two thousand two hundred and thirty assistants, of whom six hundred and fifteen were dancers ; while, altogether, sixty-six thousand six hundred and twenty-five persons, men and women, worked here in the service of the gods. . . . Or, let us look at the ruins of the Royal Palace, not so far away, in Angkor Thom, though little but the gates, and carved terraces and flights of steps remains. The famous Terrace of the Elephants still stands, consisting of a long, very lofty wall, with, carved on it in high relief, a magnificent procession of elephants hunting in a forest. Gone are the chambers and garden-courts above, though the inner sanctuary, and its beautiful sculptures, have survived, as have eighteen inscriptions, formulating the oaths of fealty to be taken by the highest dignitaries in the land to their monarch, King Suryavarman ; vows, some of which, so Dr. Marchal informs us,[1] are retained to the present day in the annual ceremonies when the Mandarins swear allegi-

[1] See *Guide Archéologique à Angkor*, by H. Marchal. (Messner, Saigon.)

ance to the King of Cambodia. . . . Near the Palace, too, an esplanade, one of the finest monuments of its kind in the country, half causeway and half a flight of steps, that incorporates the snake-motif at its best, sails far above human heads and descends majestically down to an empty lake. . . . Even today, its platforms and landings seem to be waiting to receive great state or hieratical processions. Indeed, the whole of Angkor calls out for magnificent ceremonies of its own kind, in the same way that Versailles demands a display of royal pomp, or the sweep of the Colonnade of St. Peter's evokes the ostrich-plume fans of the Pope and the robes and vestments of innumerable cardinals and priests and prelates.

### CHAPTER FIVE

AN EYE-WITNESS
FROM LONG AGO

In his account of Angkor, Henri Mouhot exclaims :
" What would I not give to be able to evoke the ghost of
one of those who lie beneath this soil, and to listen to the
story of their long era of peace and that of their mis-
fortunes. What matters could they not reveal who rest
for ever buried in oblivion ! " And, indeed, as the traveller
regards all the marvels disposed through the forest or
among the lakes, several problems, which he might imagine
he would continue to pose to himself in vain, are bound to
occur to him. On what foundation of wealth, for example,
were these complicated organisations built ; whence came
the money that paid for them ? . . . Or, what were the
people like who lived here, the King and his subjects, how
did they *look*, in what sort of outward and splendid style
did the princes and priests indulge ? . . . But some of these
and similar questions are now possible to answer. The
mass of the people precisely resembled, and even dressed
in the same way as, their descendants, the Cambodians of

today; of this we hold irrefutable evidence in the un-equalled series of accurately detailed bas-reliefs which Angkor contains. Further, and more unexpectedly, we can tell him of the exact appearance of the King, of the state in which the monarch moved, and can present, even, a picture of the royal procession, as it passed through the crowded streets of the ancient city, now lost in the forest : for, improbable as it may seem, an eye-witness exists to enlighten us. . . . Let us listen to him.

" The King prefers to wear a stuff worth a great deal, and the finest possible in colour and texture. He, alone, may sport a certain brocade of very thickly flowered pattern. As a rule, he puts on a diadem of gold, or, if he omits to do this, twists round his chignon a garland of sweet-smelling flowers, a kind of jasmine. Round his neck he carries a heavy necklace of large pearls, and on his wrists and ankles and fingers are bracelets and rings of gold, in which are set 'cats'-eyes'. He goes about unshod, but the soles of his feet as well as his palms are rouged. He holds a sword of gold in his hand when he leaves the Palace.

" The main building of this is magnificent, but its long verandahs and corridors, though bold, are rambling and without plan. They say the interior is sumptuous. The actual Royal Apartments are roofed with lead, the rest with tiles of yellow earthenware. . . . Above the Elephant Terrace stands the Council Chamber, with massive square pillars, and gilded window-frames, near which hang some forty or fifty mirrors. One is allowed to see the King go out with his chief wife and sit with her at the golden window of his private apartment. He has five wives, one for his private apartment, thus styled, and the other four for the four points of the compass.[1]  As for the concubines, and Girls of the Palace, I have heard their number estimated at between three and five thousand, divided into several classes, but they rarely cross the threshold. . . . Under these, rank the women responsible for the service of the Household, not less than a thousand or two of them. They are allowed to marry and to live where they like, and the roads in the vicinity of the Palace are always crowded with them, going to and fro ; they shave the hair on their foreheads, and mark the place, as well as their temples, with vermilion.  Only these women may enter the Palace.

" I have heard it said that formerly the Sovereign never left its precincts. . . . But the body of the new King is so thoroughly encased in iron armour, that no knife or arrow, even were it to hit him, could cause a wound ; and so, thanks to this precaution, he dares to appear in public.  I spent over a year in this country, and several times saw him go by in state.  Cavalry always head the escort, then follow the standards, the pennants and the music, and, in their rear, between three and five hundred Girls of the Palace, in flowered dresses and with blossoms in their hair, holding in their hands huge wax candles, which are alight even in the day-time.  More Girls of the Palace now bear the royal vessels of gold and silver, and a whole succession of ornaments, of many different kinds, and of which the use is unknown to me.  Behind, marches another company of Girls of the Palace, carrying lances and shields ; Amazons, these, who constitute the private bodyguard of the King. After them, come carriages drawn by goats, and carriages

---

[1] In this connection, it may be noted that nearly all the temples have — or had — five towers, one at each corner, and a somewhat larger one in the centre.

PART OF THE ELEPHANT TERRACE OF THE ROYAL PALACE AT ANGKOR THOM

*The wall is of enormous height*

drawn by horses, all ornamented with gold. The ministers and princes are mounted on elephants, and, going in front, scan the distance ; their red parasols are not to be counted for number. Next, the wives and concubines of the King drive by, in palanquins and howdahs (they have certainly more than a hundred parasols embellished with gold) : and behind them, erect on the back of an elephant — its tusks encased in gold — stands the King, holding in his hand the precious sword. Twenty white parasols surround the presence, and a squadron of cavalry for protection. Those who see the King are supposed to prostrate themselves and touch the ground with their foreheads : if they fail to do this, they are seized by the Masters of the Ceremonies, who do not release them without their paying for it.

" Every day the King holds two audiences for affairs of state. . . . The officials, or ordinary folk who wish to see him, sit on the ground to wait for him. After some time, distant music is heard issuing from the Palace, and outside it they blow on conches to welcome him. (I have heard it said that, as he has not far to come, he only uses a golden palanquin.) An instant later, two or three Girls of the Palace raise the curtain with their little fingers, and the King, with the sword in his hand, appears at the window. Ministers and people clasp one hand with the other in salute, and knock the ground with their foreheads. When the sound of the conches has died away, they may once more raise their heads."

Such is the description of the King and his court, given by Tcheou Ta-Kouan, a Chinese who resided in Angkor from 1296 to 1297, a period when the Cambodian Empire was still at the height of its splendour, and some eighty years before its mysterious destruction. The document, discovered in the Imperial Archives in Peking, was first published in Europe in 1902, translated into French by Monsieur Pelliot.[1] The history of its inception is, apparently, that the Son of Heaven of the day — one of the Mongol, " Yuan ", Dynasty, and, indeed, the successor of Kubla Khan — had decided to dispatch an ambassador to Cambodia, and appointed Tcheou Ta-Kouan, although in no particular official capacity, to accompany him. Soon after returning thence, he made this report, gathering under various headings, such as " *Inhabitants* ", " *The Language* ", "*Justice*", "*Maladies*", the appropriate items of information, intended, no doubt, for the perusal of the Emperor himself or of high officials of the Civil Service. In this wonderful survival and addition to human knowledge, the writer talks to us intimately and as though he lived today, albeit six and a half centuries have gone by, and the civilisation of which he tells us has vanished completely from the earth, except for these sad, amazing relics in golden stone.

As himself wrote, " Without doubt, the customs and affairs of this country cannot be completely known, but one was able to discern the principal traits ". . . . Certainly the picture we obtain from him of this extraordinary land, with its glowing, if top-heavy, system of life, is as distinct as though we were observing it for ourselves at the present moment ; a picture far clearer, for example, than any we possess of Ancient Rome, in spite of our being privileged to read the innumerable works that we possess of Latin authors who themselves belonged to that other lost world. How luminously the detail, for example, which he imparts to us,

---

[1] *Mémoires sur les coutumes de Cambodge,* etc., appeared in the *Bulletin de l'École Française d'Extrême Orient* (vol. ii). The present author has translated his own version of it from the French.

of the Girls of the Palace, raising the curtain " with their little fingers ", for the King to appear at the window, pierces the mists of history, and relates Cambodian dancing, so formal and traditional, to the outward ritual of Court procedure in the past.

Moreover we have reason to believe Ta-Kouan to have been an exact, and even scrupulous, witness, apart from the minor and occasional inaccuracies that prejudice of any kind inevitably entails in matters of observation. We must remember, of course, that the measure he applies to what he sees is a Chinese one, and that, after the manner of his countrymen in every age, he regards the people of all other nations as barbarians, being in consequence only too willing to believe the worst of them. His allusion to Angkor Vat, too, as being the tomb of Lou Pan, — a contemporary of Confucius and a famous Chinese workman who was in his lifetime employed by the state of Lou and is today considered as the patron saint of carpenters — seems curiously devoid of any possible foundation.[1] But, in order to test his usual precision, it is only necessary to read his account of the gates of Angkor Thom. It is near enough. He mentions that there are fifty-four genie, " gigantic and terrible ", on each side of the causeway, and the number, even, is a correct one. He often deals in similar details, the truth of which can be proved ; and he is nearly always correct. Thus, in the passage I have quoted, the parts relative to the King's dress, and to his wearing a chignon, can be tallied against the

---

[1] Monsieur Pelliot suggests that the explanation of this extraordinary mistake of Tcheou Ta-Kouan's is that, being ignorant of the Cambodian tongue, he was dependent for what he heard — as opposed to what he saw — on his compatriots. The long-established Chinese colony in Cambodia no doubt possessed here, as elsewhere, its own traditional stories, and perhaps one of these may have been concerned with the creation of Angkor Vat as tomb for Lou Pan.

representation of monarchs in this very attire on the bas-
reliefs. An interesting point, further, arises concerning
" the golden sword " of the King, to which he has numerous
references : Dr. Quaritch Wales [1] puts forward the suggestion (and to me it seems to bring immediate conviction
in its train) that this ceremonial weapon — according to
contemporary legend the gift of Indra — may be the
identical Phra Khan, or sacred sword of Cambodia, still
preserved with such care by the Court Brahmans at Pnom
Penh ; if this be so, one of the few relics of the Court of
Angkor to survive. Of such a theory we can possess no
proof : but ample corroboration exists of a great deal of
Ta-Kouan's evidence, and there seems reason, therefore, to
accept other statements of his, the truth of which, in this
so distant epoch, it is not easy to gauge. An authentic ring
can be detected even in his scandal (such as that the new
King, of whom we have just read, had stolen the throne
from his father-in-law by means of a trick, and had then
seized the rightful heir, his brother-in-law — who had
shown some symptoms of disquiet at this behaviour — and
after cutting off his toes, had consigned him for the rest of
his life to a dark and secret chamber) : and when, later on,
he descends to details — telling us, for instance, that the
parasols, carried over the heads of the princes and ministers,
were made of red taffeta from China and had fringes down
to the ground — we at once feel them, instinctively, to be
true.

For the purpose, then, of trying to focus a view of
Angkor as it was in the days when these jungle paths were
streets, thronged with people, I propose as briefly as possible
to concatenate the facts in my own order (as in the fore-

[1] In his *Towards Angkor*.

going passage, where the items dealing with the King were scattered through pages concerned with *L'Agriculture, Configuration Physique,* or *Les Habitants*), so as to heighten the effects, and not disperse them through repetition or an insistence on their being grouped under the original headings. Nor shall I hesitate to omit many details and descriptions, if they do not seem necessary to the completion of the more concise picture which is my aim : but those given will always be as near Ta-Kouan's own words [1] as I can reach through the medium of Monsieur Pelliot's translation.

" On each side of the bridge are fifty-four genie, resembling generals [2] in stone, gigantic and terrible. They hold in their hands as a parapet a serpent with nine heads, and look as though they were trying to prevent his escape. On the gates are five stone heads of the Buddha (the centre one is gilded), and there are stone elephants on either side of the doors. A golden bridge and eight golden Buddhas lie west of the walls : and the centre of the realm is marked by a tower of gold (another one is to be found above the King's sleeping apartments).[3] About a third of a mile to the north stands a tower of copper, of which the aspect is

---

[1] That is to say that the sentences will be often re-grouped : but within the enclosure of the inverted commas, I shall interpolate no words or remarks of my own.

[2] Chinese temples are guarded by the Four Heavenly Kings, sometimes called the Four Marshals : gigantic statues, usually made of brightly painted wood, with very red, angry faces, and eyes blazing with ferocity. These figures are said to represent four Generals who helped to unite the Empire in very early time, and had been, in consequence, deified. . . . The reference, no doubt, is to such images.

[3] Tcheou Ta-Kouan adds that, in his " humble opinion ", it was these golden towers that had been responsible for Cambodia's reputation for riches. Dr. Marchal (see his *Guide Archéologique à Angkor,* published by Messner, Saigon) opines that they were built of a light material, perhaps wood, covered in metal (in which case they would resemble many pagodas still to be seen both here and in Siam).

really impressive. . . . On the banks of the Eastern Lake are stone houses and a stone tower, in which reclines a bronze Buddha, whose navel continually spouts water. The Northern Lake has a square tower of gold, ten or so stone houses, and a golden lion and golden Buddha, as well as a bronze elephant, a bronze bull and a bronze horse — in fact it lacks nothing that could make it delightful.

" In this country, besides councillors, generals and astronomers (here many people, even women, are skilled in this art, and can foretell the eclipses of sun and moon), there exists, as at home, a whole horde of minor officials. Princes are chosen as a rule for the great offices of state. The most important dignitaries are granted palanquins and parasols in accordance with their rank. The chief ones are awarded a palanquin with golden shafts and four parasols with golden handles ; the next, a palanquin with golden shafts and one parasol with a golden handle ; those under them, simply a parasol with a golden handle ; while those still beneath have only a parasol with a silver handle. The parasols are made of red taffeta from China, with fringes sweeping the ground : but the *umbrellas* are of green, oiled silk with short fringes.

" Equally, the rank of the grandees determines the dimensions of their residences : they alone, apart from the King, may possess tiled roofs, and even then, over their family temples and private apartments only. The people would never dare to imitate them in this respect, and their houses are built of wood and roofed with thatch. Even middle-class families have no furniture or fittings in their homes. They cook rice in an earthenware pot, and make the sauce on an earthen stove. They bury three stones for a hearth, and help themselves to the dishes by using a coconut as a ladle. The rice is served on Chinese plates of earthenware or copper, and they help themselves to the sauce with leaves of which they make small cups that, although full of liquid, never let it run out. For spoons, they use smaller leaves, that can be thrown away when they have finished. Wine they drink out of pewter cups, whereas the poor use earthen bowls. (There are four kinds of wine : the first is distilled from honey and water, in half-and-half proportion ; the second from the leaves of a tree ; the third from uncooked rice, and the fourth from sugar-cane.)

" The grandees and rich people, however, in their homes, have silver and even gold receptacles, which they use especially on anniversaries, and on the ground are mats, specially imported from China, or tiger-skins, or the skins of panther or deer, or mats made from rattan, and lately they have adopted the fashion of low tables, about a foot high. They employ in their houses at least a hundred slaves, who do all the work : (even middle-class families possess from ten to twenty per household, and only the poorest of the poor have none). These slaves are aborigines from the mountain solitudes.[1] (There exist two kinds of

---

[1] The wretched Lolos and Moï, mysterious races which still exist today, and to whom we have referred before. Their fine figures can be distinguished, in the capacity of hewers of wood and drawers of water, on several of the bas-reliefs in Angkor Vat. Captain Henry Baudesson, in his *Indo-China and its Primitive People*, translated by E. Appleby Holt and published some years ago by Messrs. Hutchinson, estimates their total number at about 400,000, and states that " from the earliest times they have made their homes in the wooded uplands at an altitude which secures them from the fear of inundations ". He notes that, in addition to their beautiful physique, they possess a big toe which, " while preserving its prehensile faculty, is not detached from the other toes ". . . . " Generally speaking, the skin is of the colour of earth and varies between reddish-brown and dark yellow. It has a characteristic odour resembling that of a wild beast in good condition. There is an abundance of coarse black hair. . . . The forehead is low and narrow and sometimes terminates in a point. . . . The thick chin is

such savages ; those who understand the prevailing tongue — the ones sold in the towns — and those who can speak no language, and have never lived in houses. Followed by their families, carrying clay jars on their heads,[1] these last wander on the mountains : when they meet a wild animal, they attack it with a bow or spear, make a fire with a stone, cook it, eat it in common, and then go on again.) For a Cambodian to call a fellow-countryman, in the heat of a dispute, a ' Tchouang ' is an unforgivable insult. Even in a city, these slaves dare not show their noses outside the door, nor, in a house, may they sit or lie down except under the stairs. In pursuit of their duties, they may sometimes have to come upstairs, but then they must kneel, salaam and prostrate themselves, before they can proceed with their business. They call their master ' Father ', and their mistress ' Mother '. When they make a mistake, you may beat them, and they must not move : but otherwise you may have nothing to do with them. If they try to run away, you make a blue mark on their faces, or sometimes place iron fetters on their legs, or round their necks, so as to make sure of them. Their disposition is farouche, and, when wild, their poisons are very dangerous. In their own communities they kill one another a good deal."

At this point, Tcheou Ta-Kouan's complaints begin to emerge. In spite of certain superficial likenesses, which he notes with rapture, things in Cambodia, it is obvious, are in reality very different from what they are in China. . . .

the characteristic prognathous feature. The lips are fleshy and colourless. The prominence of the cheek-bones gives the face the appearance of a pentagon with the chin as its apex. The long and narrow skull places the type among the dolicho-cephalic races."

[1] Captain Baudesson also mentions the extreme value that the Lolos and Moï attach to earthen pots, and asserts that a red earthenware jar of large size was worth, in his time, thirty buffaloes.

" The women here age quickly : those of twenty or thirty
look as old as a Chinese lady of forty or fifty . . . but then
it is they who do the work, who attend to commerce. They
do not have proper shops, but a kind of mat, each occupying
a particular piece of ground, serves them as a place of
business, and it is said that for these pitches they have to
pay rent to a Mandarin. . . . The streets of the city are
crowded, but the people in general, though simple, and
willing to address a Chinese gentleman, when they see one,
as ' Buddha ' (later on, they will try to deceive him and
take him in), are only acquainted with the ways of the
Southern Barbarians.[1] They are coarse and very black.
One has to go to the Palace for true refinement. There —
and also in the noble houses — many of the women never
see the sun, and are as white as white jade. Everyone, from
the King downward, wears a chignon and has bare shoulders.
Indeed, even the best of them merely wind a bit of stuff
round their loins (the women never hesitate to expose their
breasts), except when they go out. Then they throw a
great sheet of material over the smaller piece. (As for the
stuffs they use, much of it is made in China and Siam, but
the most sought-after, because of its fine thread and texture,
comes from the Western Seas.[2]) The women tint the soles
of their feet and the palms of their hands ; but the men dare
not (because this is a privilege of the Sovereign). Both
men and women scent themselves with sandal-wood, musk
and other essences. . . . As for the priests of the three
different religions ; the Scribes [3] dress in the ordinary way,

[1] " Man ", a general Chinese designation for all savages of the Southern
regions.                                              [2] Bengal cotton.
    [3] " Les lettrés sont appelés 'Pan-k'i'." Probably the Court Brahmans, who,
for the ceremonies of the Palace and of guarding the Golden Sword, are called
" Bakous".

except for a cord of white thread which they attach to the neck as their distinctive mark ; the Buddhist priests, or Bonzes, shave their heads, wear, over a yellow skirt, a yellow robe that leaves the shoulders naked, and go bare-foot ;[1] the Brahmans dress like anyone else, except for a piece of red or white stuff wound round their heads. There are Brahman nunneries, but no Buddhist ones."

If Ta-Kouan is to be believed, the priests, whatever their clothing, were rather a handful. He permits himself to grow more and more shocked at the moral tone of the city : but, on reflection, it remains a little surprising that to one accustomed all his life to the ways of Eastern cities, customs and happenings of this kind should have come as so dis-tressing a novelty. The Salvation Army, the Y.M.C.A. and Y.W.C.A., and other similar and virtuous organisations, which now play so large a part in the daily existence of such almost legendary cities as Baghdad and Peking, were then still happily buried in the womb of time. . . . What, we cannot but ask ourselves, would Ta-Kouan have said if he had been able to read the *Arabian Nights,* or, worse still, Burton's Preface to his translation of it ? . . . However, let us turn to what he says, even though his frankness, and my English prudery, have obliged me to omit certain passages.

"It is the custom for parents to send for priests to deflower their little girls : if they are the daughters of rich people, this occurs between the ages of seven and nine, if of poor, sometimes not before they are eleven. A Buddhist or a Brahman priest is employed, according to which temple is the nearer, but certain priests have a regular clientele, and a regular tariff, consisting of presents of wine, rice,

[1] The same dress that they wear in Angkor today.

linen, silk, areca and silver plate. In the case of poor families, some priests refuse money (this is considered here as a work of charity!). The priest may only deflower one girl a year, and, when once he has been engaged for her, must refuse all other requests. On the night in question, the parents give a great banquet, with music, to their neighbours, and then, with palanquins, parasols and a band, they all go to find the priest and lead him back. Two pavilions are made of different coloured silks, and in one of them sits the young girl, in the other, the priest. It is impossible to tell what they are saying. The sound of music is deafening, for on this night you are allowed to make as much noise as you like. . . . When the day dawns, the priest is led home again, with palanquins, parasols and music. And the young girl has to be bought back from him, with presents of stuffs and silks, or else she will always be his property and will not be allowed to marry anyone else. . . . Sometimes in a single street as many as ten families have this ceremony on the same night : often their processions meet, and there is no quarter of the town where one can be sure of being spared this appalling din.

" Many men are to be found, moreover, who will marry women who have previously been their mistresses : the custom gives rise to no shame or astonishment. And the women, for their part, are most lascivious, so people say. . . . Thus, if a husband finds himself called away on business to distant parts for any length of time, all will be well for a few nights. But after ten or so have passed, his wife will not fail to make the complaint : ' I am not a spirit : why should I sleep alone?' Even to such lengths does their depravity extend ! . . . In this country, too, are a great many ' fairies ', who, in groups of more than ten, loiter every day in the chief piazza. They always try to lure on the Chinese, with a view to valuable presents. It is hideous : it is shocking !

" But then, neither debauchery nor gambling are treated as crimes in any way. . . . As to justice, formerly they did not make use of the bastinado at all, but only employed fines. For serious crimes, they neither decapitate nor strangle, but dig a ditch and bury the criminal alive : for lesser offences, they cut off fingers and toes or amputate the arms. . . . There are no inquests, but they indulge in Trial by Ordeal, a barbarous procedure.

" Then the people of this country are very often ill, largely due to their too frequent baths and washings of the head. They seem particularly liable to leprosy (there was even a ' Leper King ', but nobody thought the worse of him for it !). But, in the humble opinion of this writer, it is their amatory excesses, together with over-indulgence in baths, which bring it on (scarcely have they finished one thing, than they begin the other, so it is said). Everyone here washes far too much : the country is so hot that one cannot get through the day without several baths, and even in the night, one feels obliged to get up and have another bath or two. . . . The medicines are numerous, quite different from ours, and there are also witch-doctors who adopt the most ludicrous methods."

Like all his countrymen, Ta-Kouan enjoyed festivities, especially fireworks, and, albeit the celebration of the New Year occurred, from his point of view, in the wrong month — in November, instead of February or March — he was, in his love of junketings, willing to overlook this particular heresy. " At the New Year, a grand stand, entirely covered with lanterns and flowers, is erected in front of the Palace, and every night they build opposite it scaffolding and high masts, for the construction of four or five *stupas*. At the summits of these, they fasten rockets and crackers. (The cost of all these things is defrayed by the provincial governments and by the grandees.) When night falls, the King is requested to preside at the spectacle, and the rockets and crackers are let off. The rockets soar an immense height in the air, and the crackers, large as cannon, shake the whole city with their explosion. The Sovereign invites all the foreign ambassadors to be present, and Mandarins and nobles take part in the fête with candles and palm-leaves. . . . . This festival lasts a fortnight. But every month there is a gala of one kind or another ; Throwing the Ball, or a Grand Review (which means that the population of the whole country passes in front of the Palace), or the Washing of the Buddhas (the images are brought from all over the country for the purpose, and are washed in the presence of the King), Sailing Vessels on Dry Land, The Burning of the Rice (a favourite with women, who arrive from every direction by carriage or on elephant-back), or Dancing to Music, or Combats between Boars and Elephants. . . . The other festivals escape me."

.     .     .     .     .     .     .

We know, now, a little how the people looked and lived : but as we gaze upon these most spectacular and lovely ruins, at these towers and steeples lost in the green flood, at these gigantic terraces and gates and pyramids, at pools and bridges, other questions assail us ; we revert, again, to trying to surmise how all these monuments, and the life which they set off, were financed. We know what, in addition to silk, the Cambodians bought from China, for Ta-Kouan tells us : pewter, lacquer trays, blue porcelain, mercury, vermilion, paper, sulphur, saltpetre, sandal-wood, orris-root, musk, canvas, cloth, umbrellas, iron pots, copper utensils, oils, targets, wooden combs, needles and various kinds of Chinese matting ; but what did they sell in return, in order to be able to construct these enormous, fantastic edifices ; whence derived the vast revenues that buildings of such a scale, and furnished with such exquisite detail, even when the cost of them is known to have been reduced by slave labour, must inevitably have consumed ? . . . And the answer, which I have never hitherto seen stated outright in print, is one of the strangest and most romantic that can be imagined : from the *wings of kingfishers*. . . . Cambodian kingfishers were esteemed above all others in the Chinese market, because of their superior sheen and colouring, and were the chief source of national income : their flashing and iridescent feathers were shipped to Canton, where they were fashioned into those glittering blue and green tiaras, worn, until recent years, by every Chinese bride at her wedding, and which, though in China itself their sale has been forbidden, are still to be encountered from time to time, dusty and forlorn, in the dark recesses of English antique shops.

No wonder, then, that this was a water civilisation. We need no longer be surprised at the extent of the artificial lakes, the number of pools and moats and basins, or at the existence of the water-gardens and pleasances of Angkor Vat, their fountains raised so high toward the heavens, cupped and held up as though in offering to the gods, for over all of them dipped, skimmed and flashed then — as still to the present hour — the most exquisite kingfishers ; larger and with a more vivid tint of green, sea-green and lime-green and jade-green, than you can find anywhere else in the world. No wonder, either, that these towers and cornices tend to aspire, to take to themselves the angle and shape of wings, for on wings they were built, and out of wings they came. Did ever a city mirror a more true or more shimmering reflection of the source of its wealth than these feathers, which, as they gleam in the water, combine all the elements, the blue of the sky, the green of the jungle, the fiery gold of this sun ? For once these jewelled plumes have been transmuted by the magic of art into another medium, into something as beautiful as themselves and less transient. . . . And the civilisation to which, in a sense, they gave birth had, too, according to Ta-Kouan, assumed something of the tone of those birds, that, so lovely, yet line their nests with the rotting remains of dead fish, their horrible stench contrasting strangely with the rich lustre of their owners, flickering backward and forward over the water's sheen.

Ta-Kouan describes for us, as it happens, how the king-fishers were caught, the very methods by which they were snared. " In the mountains grow many strange kinds of wood. There in the clearings, the rhinoceroses and elephants assemble and live, and the rare birds, the curious animals, are without number. The most precious products are the wings of the kingfisher, ivory, rhinoceros-horn and beeswax. . . . The kingfisher proves difficult to snare. In the depths of the forest are pools, and in the pools, fishes. The bird flies out from the trees to catch one. Screened by leaves, a Cambodian crouches by the edge of the water, a small net in his hand : near him stands a cage, in which he has put a female kingfisher, in order to attract the male. The man waits till the bird approaches, and then captures him with the net. Sometimes he takes four or five of them

in a morning, sometimes not a single one the whole day."
. . . So wrote the Chinese traveller, toward the end of the
thirteenth century, when the Cambodian Empire was nearing extinction. . . . Perhaps in his day the kingfishers,
because too many of them had been caught during the
preceding three or four centuries, had grown rare: but now,
certainly, they have inherited the earth. Without fear of
evil consequences to themselves, they can benefit from all
these artificial sheets of water that originally came into being
solely that they might multiply, and then be trapped and
slain. . . . Thus the local exuberance and profusion of
bird-life comes to possess a new meaning.

All varieties of water-birds are now plentiful enough
here, more numerous than men : the forests, you would
say, are divided between them and the monkeys. . . . One
morning I was standing by the deserted moat of the Gate
of the Dead. In front of the entrance, some of the stone
giants still remain in place, but the water of the moat has
moved away, though there is still, on either side, a smaller,
flat pool of shallow water. It was very pleasant there, for
it was about ten in the morning and, at this particular
point, enormous and impenetrable barriers of leaves and
branches protected one from the sun, and even a little
damped down the heat, although the huge masks over the
gate, in themselves so cold and meditative, were bathed in
a fierce light that made every grain of their stone glitter. . . .
This, I reflected, must have been one of the busiest places
in the ancient city, and I tried to imagine the sentries and
groups of soldiers, the horses and elephants, the palanquins
and parasols of the grandees, the yellow-robed priests, the
chattering throngs, with their chignons and bracelets,
coming and going, rich men with their retainers following

them, and the naked beggars with clawing hands out-thrust toward them, the lepers collecting alms outside the gate. . . . At the present moment, however, the peace of the scene, and the beauty of it, were prodigious. Kingfishers clapped their wings over the water, and large tropical butterflies floated and glided and leapt on the hot, honey-sweet air : faint, contented purrings and cracklings issued from the jungle within the walls. A tall, wide-winged water-bird, a creation in salmon-pink and white and flame colour, with a touch of magenta and Parma-violet here and there, but, in spite of this outward ostentation, very dignified and like a policeman in mien and gait, stood, ankle-deep, in the pool ; fishing, I supposed, for he kept thrusting his neck down into the reeds. He stalked slowly, and with what Americans term " poise ". . . . It seemed as though an almost sinister silence had descended, there was no longer a sound, not a movement from the trees. Then, suddenly, while the bird's head was immersed in the water, a shriek of gutter-snipe laughter broke out from the branches, and a hundred or so very hard and pointed nuts, propelled by a hundred little hairy arms, cunning in their aim, shot out from the foliage at its superbly feathered rump. . . . The stately bird withdrew his head from the water as swiftly as he could without in any way impairing his self-respect, and uttered a sound that, though low in tone and couched, as it were, in diplomatic terms, distinctly signified protest and reproval, at the same time opening and shutting his broad and lovely wings. He made several menacing but rather pompous gestures, and looked as though, if this sort of hooliganism continued, he would bring the matter up before the League Assembly. . . . The monkeys, mean-while, were indulging in joy-flights in the branches, which rustled and swept low as they swung backward and forward, silently but in 2–3 time, from bough to bough. Then, their amusement exhausted, they became still and hid once more. . . . After a moment of tense, breathless excitement, they repeated their manœuvre : and, on this occasion, the bird, since he was on the watch and peering about him, was hit on the neck. He made an audible remonstrance, referring to Clause XVI, and uttered a further warning sound. He began to open his wings, but they were more for show, I apprehend, than for use, and the unfolding of these rather obsolete, if fantastic, pinions, required time and effort. Beautiful as they looked, the amount of business, the creaking and fluttering and beating the air, that were required in order to prepare them for flight, seemed, in truth, somewhat antiquated and absurd. The monkeys could no longer contain their delight ; they swung and turned somersaults and shrieked in the trees in an ecstasy, and aimed now quite openly and singly. . . . Slowly, a diminishing rocket of flame and rosy feathers, the vast bird made its spiral ascent, sailing away and up, high above the giant masks of gate and temple, over the most distant trees. His dignity was safe now. Stillness once more brooded upon the water.

### CHAPTER SIX

## LIFE AMONG THE RUINS

A WIDE, brown river crawls through Siemréap, some five miles from Angkor. Half Chinese, half Cambodian — and therein a typical village-town of the region — a great animation prevails in its wooden and wicker temples, under their winged spires and up-slanting eaves, in the busy open shops and in the streets by the water. Its surroundings are singularly pleasant, and the extra-mural banks of the river are lined with an oasis-like profusion of fruit and flower and vegetable, of banana-palms and fig-trees and papaw, all patterning, above a rich brown soil, their luxuriant, heavy-handed Corinthian designs against clumps of delicately poised bamboos.

Unfortunately the very convenient and comfortable wooden rest-house, situated just opposite the steps of the causeway that leads over the moat to Angkor Vat, and thus affording the visitor such wonderful views of stone tower and corridor and trees, of elephants and water-lilies, of gryphons and fan-headed serpents, had this year not opened its doors, owing, it was said, to an ingenious change of tactics on the part of its many scorpions. The only permanent residents of all the hotels here, these ingenious little creatures had learnt now to hide under shady ledges in the bathrooms, in order suddenly to spring out at the gallop and sting their unsuspecting victims with the greatest possible verve and venom.

First, therefore, I went to an inn, one of many, in Siemréap itself. But, though for these latitudes it was comfortable (and in these latitudes, because of the heat, the word *comfortable* of necessity implies what would be considered extreme discomfort elsewhere ; darkness, bare, cold floors, and beds and pillows so hard that they might be made of stone), the scent of that Malay dish I have mentioned, prepared from decaying fish, hung too hauntingly in the streets of a night and early morning, distilled by the cool air, and obliged me to move out of the town to a large new hotel, a mile or so away in the direction of the ruins. Here I obtained a fine room, a mosquito-net in perfect order (rare in a hotel anywhere), a bathroom, and a distant view of the towers of Angkor Vat swelling high above palm trees and jungle. . . . But my bathroom, too, possessed its peculiarities ; every time I turned on the water, I found the bath lined — absolutely black, no inch of white showing through — with insects ; species that were new to me and the very sight of which would, I suspect, have warmed the heart of an entomologist. One sort, I remember, consisted of little jack-in-the-boxes about an inch long : they were full of fun, and would stay quite still till you came near, when they would jump right up to the ceiling in one bound — an amazing performance, as though a man were to leap to the top of Mont Blanc — and buzz and whirr and bang and titter in a thousand different ways.

However, they were not venomous, in the manner of scorpions. . . . One evening though, as I sat downstairs after dinner in a corner of the large, airy, carefully decorated perspective of sitting-rooms, I beheld a dramatic rush of frightened women away from the centre, all holding their hair, as though to protect it from the assault of a maniac snipper, and with expressions of high tragedy clamped across their faces. Only twice before in my life had I seen such an effect : in 1920, when, while I was sitting outside a café in the Palazzo Vittorio Emmanuele in Florence, some Communists had tried to murder a Fascist, and the sound of the shots had sent the citizens of Florence, nervous because of their knowledge of the consequences of previous attempts of this sort, running from the square, knocking over chairs and tables in their flight ; and, before that, in my childhood, on a sunny afternoon some forty years ago, when, from the lawn at Renishaw, I witnessed the cutting down of an old elm-tree at the end of the avenue. Then, of a sudden, the women of the assembled house-party had rushed down the slope toward us, holding their carefully arranged heads of hair, with elaborate Boer-War puffs and curls and fringes, as hundreds — thousands, they seemed — of bats — verminous little creatures which were at that time held to be drawn by a peculiar sensual attraction toward the hair of women — swung wildly, blindly out from their home of centuries in the falling trunk. . . . So, too, they held their hair now, though more, I imagine, because it is a natural gesture of feminine terror than for any special fear of attack thereon. They resembled the crowd of a well-rehearsed, modern production of a play by Aeschylus or Sophocles, as, attended by their husbands, who ran after them, shouting soothing words of sympathy and affection, they left the rooms empty, so that I was able to perceive, at a safe distance, the cause of the commotion. . . . There, alone in the middle of the vista, a small black snake — a very poisonous serpent, too, I learned afterward — was wriggling on its belly along the marble floor. Now some-one blew a whistle. And, in a moment, a gigantic bearded Sikh, kept here for the particular purpose, had entered at a run, to engage in combat with this diminutive foe of so mortal an order. He wore a large turban, a long white robe, and in his hand he carried a very tall malacca mace, with a weighty silver top, resembling the staffs carried by footmen in eighteenth-century Europe. His feet being bare, he had to dance a little upon his toes to avoid the darting head of the black, venomous worm. However, to kill it occupied only an instant of his time : he struck it three times on the head with his mace, and then whipped its dead body out of the window, all in one dignified and graceful movement, doubtless born of long, and perhaps inherited, practice.

In this hotel, then, we stayed for many days, rising early each morning to wander among the miles of ruins, through parks and walled gardens of a maniac vision, until, at ten-thirty or thereabout, the heat of the sun became too great, compelling us to return home and not to leave shelter again until four or five in the afternoon. Then, when it became cooler, we would go to bathe about ten miles away, in a vast lake made by one of the kings who built these temples ; a piece of water so enormous that you could but seldom see across it, and of which the clear, green depths were so warm that you might easily, lulled by them, fall asleep while swimming, and, if far out, invariably found yourself overcome by lethargy, with no mind to strike out, back, toward the lovely shore, with its silver beach, bordered by waxy pink and white flowers, and, behind them, by the garlanded masts of the jungle. Then we would aim to be among the ruins again in time to hunt the sunset down the ranks of gods and devils, through the huge, tree-tangled gates, along the dark green, glittering avenues, above which every now and then rose a *Flamboyant Tree*, the branches outlined like a torch in its own phoenix-world of flame, or a vast trunk carrying antlers, bare of leaves but covered with yellow or sky-blue blossoms. . . . Even here, however, peace was not absolute.

The reader may recall the warning issued to us by the young English wanderer in Saigon, concerning " The Three Big Women from Hong Kong ". " You'll see 'em again at Angkor, sure as sure. Don't see how you can avoid it ! You mark my words," he had prophesied, with something of doom in his voice. " Better be amiable, too," he had added darkly, " or they'll have you bounced into the loony-bin before you know you've got there. They've got mettle, my word ! Regular all-in show they put on, when they're up against it : real, proper fighters, they tell me. I bet there are some pretty stiff letters from them in this office, if we only knew ! " . . . I had never hitherto been quite able to gather the official identity of " The Three Big Women from Hong Kong ", but here, sure enough, under the swags and tresses of these flowering trees, we found them in incongruous procession. First came the most important, the largest, who resembled a radiant personification of Britannia in some amateur theatrical performance organised by the local Women's Institute, or, perhaps, the bosoming, hearts-of-oak figure-head from a glorious ship of long ago :

then, following at a suitable distance behind her, as though holding an invisible train, walked her two companions, lesser — though, of course, only comparatively lesser — in stature and importance.

Whenever I met them — and this was very frequently — they laid their troubles before me. Imperturbable in appearance, they were existing, nevertheless, in a state of inward fury; because it had happened that, with the peculiar spite in little matters which Fate so often manifests, two rival giantesses, of similar temperament, from the United States, were staying in the hotel at the same time, and when, a few mornings previously, Britannia and her two ladies-in-waiting had descended the stairs — some decorative instinct urged them never to use the lift — in stately progress, they had discovered that the omelette they had ordered for their meal had already been consumed by, as it were, the American team. (They had only ordered an omelette — " Have you any omelettes ready ? " had been the formula,— instead of the traditional eggs and bacon, as a sop to foreign feeling. . . . And now, it had been wolfed !) Instead, they had found, placed in front of them, " some disgusting Yankee mess ". Both parties were angry, and neither — indeed, each of them prided itself precisely on not doing so — minced its words. " We never commuted for an omelette, and we won't be high-hatted by a Britisher. What happened was, we got it down before we knew better ! ", had been the transatlantic excuse; " *Where are our cereals ?* ". Britannia, never having heard of these comestibles, but being accustomed to reading the instalments of stories in *The Daily Truth*, thought that, in addition, they were accusing her of stealing a magazine or newspaper, and had, at once, sent for the manager and in his presence court-martialled the two Americans. But the worst of it was, they had not minded : they had appeared to enjoy the match, answering back and wisecracking to any extent. And so now, like those dancing in the old-fashioned " Lancers ", the two contingents, one at first not spying the other, would advance and then retreat precipitately backward down these green alleys in order to avoid a desperate clash, for which, at the same time, each was well prepared. . . . And, as Britannia told me of the latest encounter, avoided or entered upon, I used sometimes to think that I could catch the echo of high, cackling, simian laughter, drifting down from the leafy groves pitched so high above us.

Such were the lesser interests of life, as opposed to those of sightseeing. Moreover, it was during our stay here that we learned of the death of the Governor-General of Indo-China, killed in an airplane crash while flying home. Held in great esteem, as he was, by the entire population, native and foreign, the announcement that it had been decided to hold two services for him in Siemréap, one in the Catholic church and the other in the Buddhist temple, came as no surprise. The memorial service in the church, a tin Gothic edifice just outside the town, was timed to begin at the early hour of eight in the morning. It having been officially intimated that the authorities would welcome the presence of all visitors staying in the hotels, I arrived there on the stroke of the clock. Instead of a tolling bell, the vigorous banging of a gong both proclaimed the public sorrow and intimated to those whom it concerned that service was about to begin. Outside had assembled a crowd of well-fed Europeans in topees, gossiping in hushed voices. As I knew none of them, I entered the church at once, to find that the Cambodian congregation, huddled on one side of the aisle, had long assembled, and that, in spite of the continued beating of the gong outside, the service was already in full swing. A charming, but evidently rather vague, Annamite priest, resembling, with his thin beard and wise, benevolent expression, a Chinese sage, was conducting it in pidgin Latin, all the consonants softened and transmuted beyond recognition. Now the gong ceased its reverberations, and those who composed the white crowd outside stopped exchanging confidences and trooped in, quite unaware of what was happening, to find that they were late, so that they became stiff and consciously dignified under the eyes of the converts opposite, themselves plainly horrified by such a lack of punctuality and punctilio on the part of their fellow Christians. The noise and shuffling of feet did not seem to perturb the native Father, who continued to intone : but, just at this moment, the two Cambodian acolytes, in skirts and lace surplices, swung their censers in a very professional manner, only to find that they had forgotten to light the incense, so that they stopped and gazed dreamily about them. The priest looked indignant and taken aback, and, for the time being, the whole service broke down. Angrily he whispered to them in their own language, and sent them out to the vestry to make good their remissness, with a hearty and, under the circumstances, very natural, if rather unconventional, box on the ears. . . . So the service trailed on, with a strongly original and oriental flavour. The Latin, as I have hinted, would only have been comprehensible to an oriental scholar, and even the funeral music, from a harmonium, appeared, as it was played, to resemble much more closely a native dance than the ancient and sombre Western strains they were intended to represent.

After leaving church, we repaired immediately to the temple in the town ; a building which consisted of red, wooden columns supporting a winged roof. Screens of rush lattice hung from the pillars, but the sunlight, by this time strong as steel, soon found the chinks in this armour. Further, the entire population of Siemréap seemed to be pressed into this space or clustered together just outside it, impeding the entry of the air, and talking, groaning, singing, beating gongs and drums and thrumming upon stringed instruments to its heart's content. This service was impressive, but, also, had something free and unconventional in its conduct, unlike any worship to be found in temples elsewhere : for here in the jungle, the Buddhist faith, or philosophy, had assimilated various features from every cult that had ever existed in the neighbourhood, either in ancient or modern times. Thus, besides many features belonging properly to Brahminism and to Taoism, there were to be detected many signs of the former vicinity of the head-hunters, now confined fortunately to the islands. Masks of most ferocious expression grinned from the pillars, but the congregation had long forgotten the significance of these vestigial ornaments, once the bleeding, scarred and scalped heads of human beings.

By now, the heat was reaching its climax, slowing down even the tempo of the service, and as, sometimes, a gust of fiery air would be wafted in, it brought with it the drone of the countless winged creatures under the tall palm trees outside. . . . Indeed, as we left, the insects appeared to be holding a midday service of their own, such were the shrill and wiry crepitations, deep drummings and intonings ; a busy, reverent but rather meaningless sound of buzzing, and of castanetted whirring, twang and jangle, very similar to the music we had just heard performed.

The crowd this time dissolved quickly down the streets into the cool : only the yellow robes of the bonzes seemed to hold the light even in dark places, showing for some moments after their bare heads and necks and arms and feet had gone, merged in shadow. . . . It was too hot to walk, I decided : but, all the same, as I drove back, I noticed an old American lady, in a wig and tweed dress, ploughing her way through the dust toward the hotel. In her hand she carried a heavy suitcase, plastered over with labels ; " *Honolulu, Panama, Port of Spain, Madeira, Naples, Algiers, Venice, Athens, Constantinople, Colombo, Hong Kong, Yokohama* ", I read the iterations all over the brown fibre, so that no space remained ; " *Colon, Kingston, Lisbon, Gibraltar, Tangier, Trieste, Dubrovnik, Patras, Bombay, Shanghai.*" . . . This was, I found out afterward from the manager, the seventh world cruise (she had already visited Angkor three times in all) upon which, though over eighty and completely deaf, she had embarked alone. Nor can her knowledge of foreign languages have been sufficiently extensive to help her, for I heard her ordering dinner in French. " *Végétarbles, végétarbles,*" she was repeating angrily to a French *maître d'hôtel*. (Which shows, I suppose, that greediness was not among her vices, for, although a bad linguist, I have always found myself able to order dinner in any language, even if in other respects completely unknown to me. Moreover, ordering a meal in a foreign language perhaps tends to improve food : assuredly, since certain of the London restaurants, in order to placate visitors from the Midlands and the Middle West, took to printing their menus in English, there has been a lamentable deterioration in the quality of the food served.)

The very next day, the indomitable old lady was motoring many hundreds of miles to rejoin her cruise. . . . And like her, we must soon be off on our travels again, motoring northward to Annam.

But, after Angkor, a veritable wonder of the world, it is impossible even to talk of the remaining marvels (and very marvellous, in all truth, they are) of Indo-China ; the birds and beasts and flowers, the jungles and lakes, the cities, whether still humming with people or broken and interred, the numerous brick sanctuaries and towers of the Chams, and their sculptures, all would fall to a mere anticlimax, however ill-deserved. Yet I would like to discuss with you, Reader — how abrupt that sounds, Gentle Reader, Patient Reader, Critical Reader, Clever Reader, I hope not Angry Reader — many details of that journey. I want to describe the miles of lime-green mirrors for the sky that the rice-fields made on either side of the road leading northward, reflecting the images of castellated and turreted clouds, or a perfect blue vacancy, broken in some cases by the thin, shrill green shoots of the young rice, showing through them, as if the sky were bursting into bud, and I would fain tell you of the splendidly robed old Annamite Mandarin, who, having come from a great distance to attend a very elaborate funeral at Hué (the procession lasted for two hours), forgot it altogether, getting drunk instead at the hotel, laughing to himself and talking pidgin English and French with the greatest *bonhomie* to anyone within range, though even now, when in his cups, he retained a certain quality of personal dignity : the most wise, jovial and benign of Mandarins. I would like, too, to speak at length of the Kings of Annam, of the pomp of their Court in Hué, where alone survives in miniature the ritual of the

Emperors of China, of the red litters and palanquins, held
by four or eight bearers, that can yet be seen hurrying
through the royal park, of the eunuchs who still shamble
in droves down the broad terraces and walks, and of the
painted halls of the Palace itself, which, with their red
lacquer walls, gold dragons and huge porcelain vases, show
so marked a similarity to the exotic interior of the Royal
Pavilion which our own King George the Fourth built for
himself at Brighton ; of the River of Perfumes and of the
wide, shallow Venetian lagoons that lie toward the coast,
broad, peacock-winged sheets of water on which float a few
simple barks, like those you see in the canvases of Guardi,
and rosy clouds of flamingos ; and of the tombs of the
Kings, built from the end of the eighteenth century until
the present day, tall temple halls lined with marble, on
which are depicted in relief, in agate and jade and gold and
silver and precious stones, the favourite personal objects
of each departed monarch, such as pyjamas and, in one
instance, an alarm-clock (and yet these tombs are beautiful!).
I would like to describe to you the rocks and cloud-
entangled crags, with trees springing from them at unexpected angles and hawks hovering above them, of the
Road of the Mandarins, stretching for hundreds of miles
above a coast of crescent bays and elegant, slender, lofty
coco-palms, so that on one side you have the precise landscape of a Chinese scroll, and on the other an ideal South-
Sea-Island prospect. Particularly would I like to converse
with you concerning the short reign of that ambitious
monarch of mystery, King Raymond the First, an adven-
turer, it is said, of Belgian origin, who, during the nineties,
proclaimed himself King of the Jungle, and issued his own
coins and postage stamps, to be seen in the Hué Museum,

and eventually, on his return from Belgium, whither he had travelled to negotiate a loan for his realm, had to be suppressed by the French — or was he, I forget, assassinated on his arrival ? . . . All these things I must leave (only venturing to suggest, in doing so, that some other author, in search of a subject for biography, should investigate King Raymond and his reign) : all these things I must leave, I say, in order to take the reader with me farther north, because, after Angkor, there is but one thing, perhaps, that would not come as an anticlimax. We are in no mood for temperate zones and must hurry to the dry, frozen air of Peking, so far away. Nothing in China, or elsewhere, can compare, in its way, with Peking. But even there, we shall, as I have already warned the reader, discover no buildings so beautiful, so unexpected, so unearthly, as those of Angkor, though we shall, on the other hand, find, I hope, a diversity of life, a new and different form of beauty, an alternative way of thinking and living to our own, above all the continuance of a tradition from the remotest antiquity, to be observed nowhere else in the world. . . . And so, on this journey toward China, I will only stop to relate to you one small incident, trivial, but extraordinary enough, perhaps, in its way, to avoid bathos.

One evening, then, we were sitting on the terrace of the hotel at Hué, just as dark was falling and above our heads squadrons of mosquitos were humming, performing the rhythmic dance with which they greet the prospect of darkness and the sweet blood of foreigners. Our platform — that is a better word for it — stood just above the level of the broad embankment along the river and commanded a view of a fine modern bridge, of the walls and tiled towers of the Palace and of the old town beyond. Just in front of us were two ponderously cheerful tables of American men and women. . . . Suddenly a tumult arose, an immense outcry from the direction of the bridge, as a mob, like a moving knot of ants, came hurrying across it toward us, and out of it, spurning the disorder they were causing, burst four brown, dancing figures, two men and two women. They wore long hair down their backs, almost to the waist, and sported a minute loin-cloth made of rushes : otherwise they were completely naked. The men carried, and from time to time played, Pan pipes made of bamboo, instead of cane, and proportionately larger than those of Sicily. Both men and women showed the short noses and prognathous jaws, and the splendid bodies and carriage, of the primitive races. So, perhaps, had looked Adam and Eve from whom every mortal is descended — but the dance which they now performed would have created a sensation in any cabaret in Paris or, even, Algiers. Breasts and hips, legs and shoulders, buttocks and thighs, all were brought into play, the men facing the women. The American fathers of families at once realised what they ought to do, and, standing up, called across the table to their wives, " Mrs. Higginbootham, this is no place for a gracious American Mother ", and then shivered their way, backward, still watching, into the hotel, accompanied by their parties : but even these visitors were not so shocked as the people of the city itself, the Annamites and Chinese. " Moï ! " the gesticulating crowds shouted, shaking its fists, " Moï ! Barbarians ! Beasts ! Dwellers in outer darkness ! Get back to your mountains ! Pigs ! Elephants ! " The very policeman himself, controlling non-existent traffic so neatly from his rostrum, stepped down to join in. " Move on, there ! Get along ! Moï ! Brutes, be off with you ! " He was, I apprehend, as horrified as the crowd, for they all felt that this singular quartet was " letting down its side ", betraying Indo-China before the whites. " Moï ! " they screamed. " Moï ! Go back to your holes in the ground ! Hide your shameful ugliness in your native dark ! " Yet, as though some magic preserved them, no one actually dared to raise a hand against the dancers, who continued entirely to ignore the general disapproval, whether native or foreign. " If they can do it better, let them come up and try ", perhaps they thought. No one succeeded in moving them on. Still the oaten music, belonging to the world's dawn, continued ; still they squeaked in ecstasy, clapped hands, wriggled and kicked, shouted out words. " Hula hula ! " they seemed to cry, moving a putty-coloured, indecorous hip and rubbing noses and breasts, " hula ! Olé ! Ra Ra ! Lero lero, lilliburlero, lero, lero, bullen a-la ! " Intent on the artistic execution of their dance, they indulged in rippling movements of the muscles of the belly, and jigged and jiggled and barged. " Olé, olé ; Ra ! Ta-ra-ra-boom-de-ay, bullen a-la ! " they shouted, oblivious of the jeers of the now menacing crowd. Subtlety of movement and grace they may have subjugated, somewhat, to verve and abandon, but at any rate I am confident that they enjoyed those few, all too brief moments of self-expression and, too, of constituting, most decidedly, the centre of interest. Swiftly the dance ended, on a dying cadence. And at this very instant, alas, a posse of police swooped down and bore them off, struggling and panting — the women fighting as competently and bravely as the men — swept them across the bridge to safety, ahead of the pursuing and maddened crowd. They would, no doubt, spend a day or two in the lock-up, before returning to their fastnesses in the mountains, where the original inhabitants, the real princes of this country, so long enslaved and put upon, found themselves still at liberty to lead their own lives, and where, in the great open spaces of their heroic uplands, they were free to indulge in their own dances without interference, white or yellow ; where, perhaps, even, applauding crowds clapped hands in time to these, for them, delicious rhythms, where men were men, and no one would stoop to hiss or jeer, except a jealous rival. . . . The mystery, however, abides ; why had these primitive, inglorious, Karsavinas and Nijinskys — for great dancers they may have been in their own country — selected Hué for their display ? People of their race are shy, and shun cities ; why, then, had they *chosen* to come to the capital and perform for us outside the chief hotel ? They never asked for money (nor, perhaps, would they have found much use for it) : it was plainly a dance done for their own pleasure, and their own pride in their own dancing — though I think, I hope, that they needed an appreciative audience and, despite the general disapprobation, in us found one.

Certainly it was a rare occurrence, an unusual experience. I can still see them whirling and jigging in my mind's eye, and can remember how, as I watched the last fierce kicks of their simian can-can, my mind went back to the dancing, so very different, that I had seen at Angkor Vat ; the dancing of the people who had in the first place dispossessed and enslaved these poor Moï. . . . This art, on the other hand, the only one that had survived from the times of Cambodian greatness to give a new meaning to every sculptured panel in the temples, was all compounded of grace and subtlety and implication.

It had been a hot evening, and we had sat round the dancers on the stone causeway which crosses the moat of Angkor Vat. In front of us, a circle of small boys held, stretched out toward the dancers, sweet torches made of herbs, resin and rushes. These they knocked every now and again upon the pavers, so that the scent of them increased for the moment, and the smoky glow in which the dancers moved rose to a more fiery and quivering light. Within the circle, their faces whitened with chalk, immobile beneath high, winged headdresses, their whole attire having something of a flame's flicker about it, the figures moved rhythmically, nodding their heads or turning them from side to side, stretched out or unbent the joint of a finger, or drummed a foot in time to the strange music that seemed born of this scented darkness and of these jewelled, shadowy forms, showing beneath the faint but tremendous outline of tower and dome and carved stone roof.

A PEKING ARCHER IN HIS COURTYARD

# BOOK TWO

# PROSPECTS OF PEKING

" You must know that the city of Cambaluc [1] hath such a multitude of houses, and such a vast population inside the walls and outside, that it seems quite past all possibility.  There is a suburb outside each of the gates, which are twelve in number ; and these suburbs are so great that they contain more people than the city itself. . . . In those suburbs lodge the foreign merchants and travellers, of whom there are always great numbers who have come to bring presents to the Emperor, or to sell articles at Court, or because the city affords so good a mart to attract traders. . . . And thus there are as many good houses outside of the city as inside, without counting those that belong to the great lords and barons, which are very numerous.

". . . To this city also are brought articles of greater cost and rarity, and in greater abundance of all kinds, than to any other city in the world.  For people of every description, and from every region, bring things (including all the costly wares of India, as well as the fine and precious goods of Cathay itself with its provinces), some for the sovereign, some for the court, some for the city which is so great, some for the crowds of Barons and knights, some for the great hosts of the Emperor which are quartered round about ; and thus between court and city the quantity brought in is endless.

" As a sample, I tell you, no day in the year passes that there do not enter the city 1000 cart-loads of silk alone, from which are made quantities of cloth of silk and gold, and of other goods. . . ."

*The Book of Ser Marco Polo the Venetian Concerning the Kingdoms and Marvels of the East,* translated and edited by Colonel Sir Henry Yule, two volumes (Murray, 3rd edition, reprinted 1929).

[1] Peking.

### CHAPTER ONE

THE FIRST FIRE-CRACKER

W E first touched Chinese soil at the time of the New Year, which there falls between the middle of January and the middle of February, in accordance with the lay-out of the lunar year. This festival, of great antiquity, the most popular and lengthy of Chinese holidays, though officially abolished, together with the old calendar, many years ago by a spoil-sport Republican Government, can seldom have been better or more widely celebrated than upon this occasion. Only in Peking and Nanking were the rejoicings somewhat subdued, or disguised under some other label, such as a birthday ; in Peking, because that great city, as the former Imperial capital, is always a little suspect in the eyes of the true democrat ; in Nanking, because as, at that time, the capital of the Republic and the centre of the ascetic New Life Movement, which was then starting, the inhabitants felt themselves obliged to affect a certain, unbecoming austerity of outlook. Otherwise, throughout this vast and teeming land, that stretched from the Tibetan mountains to those seas upon which the typhoon rides its deadly course, and from the ice-bound rivers of the north down to the flower-sprinkled tropics, the people were greeting the New Year — the last one, if they could have foreseen it, of peace for a long period — in their traditional manner.

Alas, I was not able to visit the South, so I cannot tell whether in Canton the New Year continues to be observed in the same charming way in which it is described by an English botanist,[1] writing in the year 1847. The Cantonese decorated not only the outsides of their houses and temples with flowers, as well as with flags of every colour, but also the boats in which so many of the population lived, and this visitor, as he sailed up the river, met vessels in great numbers coming down, loaded with, amongst other things, branches of blossoming peach and plum, *Enkianthus quinqueflorus*, camellias, cockscombs and magnolias. . . . Certainly in the north, I suppose that the passing of a century has in some respects a little dimmed its glory. There was no longer an Emperor as apex and promoter of the proceedings.

Almost the first account we possess of a Chinese New Year is the description of one celebrated in Peking — or Cambaluc, as it was then called — in the thirteenth century ; (in Chinese history a comparatively recent date). The Emperor and all his subjects were entirely clothed in white for the occasion, and in the morning, the royal elephants, then five thousand in number, and caparisoned in rich stuffs with designs of birds and beasts on them, paraded through the

[1] *Three Years' Wanderings in the Northern Provinces of China*, by Robert Fortune. (Murray, 1847.) " Robert Fortune, 1813–1880, traveller and botanist. Visited China for the Horticultural Society in 1842 and the East India Company, 1848. The *Chamoerops Fortunei* (fan-palm) is named after him." *Dictionary of National Biography*.

streets, bearing magnificent coffers, filled with the Imperial plate required for a great feast later on in the day. These were followed by a multitude of camels, also carrying gold and silver equipment, and equally splendid in their harness and decoration. . . .[1] Well, there have been changes ; the elephants have at last gone to join their master, the Grand Khan ; with his dynasty, white disappeared as the colour of rejoicing — it had been a Mongol custom, imported by Genghiz — and red came into its Chinese own again. . . . To approach the present day more nearly, Tun Lich'en, writing toward the end of the Manchu Dynasty, in about 1900, tells us that " incense is burned to greet the spirits (who descend to earth at this time), and fire-crackers are lighted to show them respect, so that their noise fills the streets unceasingly throughout the night. After the greeting of the spirits, everyone, from princes and dukes down to the various officials, must enter the Palace to offer congratulations to the Court ; and on the conclusion of these Court felicitations, they go about paying visits to their relatives and friends, this being called wishing New Year Happiness. . . . Clothed in furs of sable and ceremonial embroidered robes, they mill confusedly about the streets, their carriages truly like flowing water, and their horses like roaming dragons in their numbers ! "[2] And, since each occasion in the Chinese calendar bears, connected to it by the indestructible link of palatal memory, the flavour of its own particular food, he adds that " Everyone on this

---

[1] *The Book of Ser Marco Polo the Venetian Concerning the Kingdoms and Marvels of the East*, translated and edited by Colonel Sir Henry Yule, two volumes. (Murray, 3rd edition, reprinted 1929.)

[2] *Annual Customs and Festivals in Peking* as recorded in the *Yen-ching Sui-shih-chi* by Tun Lich'en, translated and annotated by Dr. Derk Bodde. (Henri Vetch, Peking, 1936.)

day, whether rich or poor, of noble or humble rank, makes dumplings of white flour and eats them, and these are called boiled *po-po*. Throughout the entire country it is thus, nowhere is it different. . . ." And so, to a great extent, the feast continues : less glorious, it is true, but everyone still eats dumplings, and, as he has done for many centuries past, every householder still has a pair of Gate Gods, printed in the brightest hues on sheets of paper, and showing the two deities in full armour, with every kind of weapon, pasted on his doors as a protection against the events of the coming year.

In Shanghai the temperature was down in unfathomable regions below zero — a change for us after the tropics — but this seemed only to impart a greater zest to the celebrations. The first night the noise, reaching these tall New-York-like towers from the direction of the Chinese town, was prolonged and often indefinable ; but the sound of fire-crackers,[1] at least, could be distinguished, and must, no doubt, have been pleasing to the spirits of the dead, as well, I fancy, as to the great majority of the living. They were ricocheting in every direction, and with many subtle modulations of sound, so that, had I been the possessor of a properly trained ear, I should, in all probability, have been able to differentiate between the bang and hiss of the numerous varieties cited by Tun Lich'en as to be bought in the shops, and to distinguish Small Boxes, Flower Pots,

[1] The use of fire-crackers in China must go back a very long way. Many scholars think that Marco Polo makes a reference to the use of rockets, but the passage is obscure. . . . And, apparently, according to Dr. Bodde, before fire-crackers were invented, the Chinese employed, for the same purpose, sections of bamboo, which, when thrown into the fire, exploded with a loud bang. In this way, the ideogram " bursting bamboos " has come to mean fire-crackers. See note on *Pao-Chu*, p. 1, *Annual Customs and Festivals in Peking*, Bodde. (Cf. note 2, p. 167.)

Lanterns of Heaven and Earth, Fire and Smoke Poles, Silver Flowers, Peonies Strung on a Thread, Lotus Sprinkled with Water, Golden Plates, Falling Moons, Grape Arbours, Flags of Fire, Double-Kicking Feet, Ten Explosions Flying to Heaven, Five Devils Noisily Splitting Apart, Eight-Cornered Rockets, and Bombs for Attacking the City of Hsiang Yang, one from the other.

The next morning was grey, and a bitter, knife-edged wind swept this strange city, falling like a flail down the great modern boulevard which leads from the Liverpool-like wharfs and river-front, past the crooked, tortuous streets of the Chinese town, with its zigzag bridges and alleys choked with people, to the racecourse. The whole of this thoroughfare has, on one side, a pavement pitched above the road and nearly as broad as the road itself. Ordi-narily no block of people would have been permitted to assemble on road or pavement here, but today citizens were allowed to stroll and watch, to such a degree that progress was scarcely possible. Knot after knot, group after group, of Chinese, in European clothes and caps, in nondescript rags, or in their own quilted, padded winter robes, topped with fur caps, waited, laughing and talking, round the numerous attractions, until the wide pavement had become a mile-long stage, for actors, acrobats, mountebanks and charlatans of various descriptions. The scene must some-what have resembled a less elaborate Venetian carnival, save that here was no architectural frame, and that this grey blanket of cloud above us was substituted for the blue, autumnal, transparent sky of Italy. Down upon audience and performers, as in the ballet *Petrouchka*, drifted a few sad flakes of snow, occasionally increasing to a fine veil, melting on hats and shoulders. The noise was immense,

actors and female impersonators, singers, clowns and ventri-
loquists, all ranted and vociferated : conjurors shouted as
loud as they could, to divert public attention momentarily
from the movements of their hands contriving the crucial
sleight, and jugglers yelled in order to indicate their prowess.
The yellow, naked trunks of wrestlers gleamed sweating
through the thin snow, as they clutched each other round
the waist, the muscles of arm and neck and shoulder
standing out, and issued faked cries of rage or pain. Two
men in long blue robes with fur collars, one of them blowing
a trumpet, were leading along on a chain a heavily furred
bear, which growled and groaned and grumbled as it trod
heavily from side to side on two cruelly clawed feet that
were yet too delicate for its weight. Some of the turns
were elaborate, a scene from a well-known play acted in
the proper dress ; two actor-warriors, representing armies,
clanging their swords, one against the other ; a gang of
eight or nine acrobats turning co-operative somersaults, or
forming themselves into pyramids and towers. In the
middle of another inquisitive cluster, a man in a black robe
and a conical hat was giving an exhibition of the painless
extraction of teeth (a very old Chinese art, which I do not
pretend to understand, but to which, nevertheless, I constantly refer my dentist in London). There were, too,
stalls devoted to the wonders of Chinese medicine, to
witches' brews of beetles, sea-slugs and noisome verdure,
sealed up in huge jars (concoctions which, though un-
appetising, have, it is said, something of science in them,
effect their cures, though the healing art in China has been
very little studied by the West).[1] Professional story-tellers
banged their drums vigorously in several corners. Then

[1] See note on pp. 193-194.

there were singers, wailing to an accompaniment of lutes, and, for the children, Punch and Judy shows and marionettes, the booths decorated in red for the New Year. These last were surrounded entirely by the mothers and fathers, while their small boys of six or seven, in clothes padded like those of their elders, found themselves obliged to dart about beneath parental elbows in a vain struggle to see. . . . This was my first experience of a Chinese fair, and though in the course of the next few months I was fortunate enough to witness many of them, in the courtyards of temples, or outside their gates, or in ruined palaces, none remains more vividly in my memory than this New Year pavement fair at Shanghai.

Of Nanking, I will not write, except for two matters. I would like to place on record, as a matter of interest, that when, in the chief hotel, organised by my fellow-countrymen, I asked for a cup of tea, they brought me something that reminded me of a wet Saturday afternoon in a Hindhead boarding-house ; and that when, more explicitly, I then indicated that I wanted *China* tea, the reply came, " We only supply Ceylon and Indian here ". Eventually, in protest, I sent out for a cup of coolie, green tea to the street outside. . . . Secondly, it was while crossing the Yangtse on a ferry-boat, to go to the northern station, that I made my first acquaintance with Chinese garlic ; an unforgettable experience of the senses. It was singular that I had not noticed it at the fair in Shanghai : but I had not. Here, however, in the crowd, one was at once forced to recognise a sensation, which, for all my many travels in Greece and Italy and Spain, was unprecedented ; to compare Chinese garlic to European would be like comparing a gasometer to a violet.

As we journeyed north, the sky grew ever more azure, the fleece of the sun more golden, and the landscape began to assume the long, sweeping, bare curves of a Chinese scroll : bare and golden, each rounded hill was thumbed in with gold upon a sepia background. Moreover, in honour of the New Year, every village, with its simple brown houses and roofs of brown tiles or thatch, with its brown, walled orchards and farmyards, and its naked trees cobwebbed so delicately against a blue sky of an infinite depth, though not of an infinite softness, and every separate dwelling in this immensity of brown earth, was decorated with hangings of red ; hangings which, toward sunset, seemed to absorb all the colour that the winter had left, glowing through the dying, blue lights of the day.

As for the people who lived in this exquisite landscape, in any direction in which you looked, the vitality of this age-old race was asserting itself. . . . The country, you could see, was old and worn. It would be difficult to obtain a good crop out of this ground, intensely cultivated where-ever possible for four or five thousand years past, and swept, ever since man could remember, by great gales that took with them the most valuable part of the soil, but the life-power, the stamina and the intelligence of a people re-nowned for these qualities since the dawn of human history, remained undiminished, beyond the transmuting action of time, even — or, I am sure, of misfortune. The train, grind-ing its way slowly along the rails, stopping here or there for a breath of fresh air or an alien impetus of some kind to carry it on to the next station, afforded the passengers the chance of observing ; of watching, for example, the Chinese children running, or bounding in somersaults, like taut tops through the little squares, or of listening to their shouts and squeals of laughter as they applauded a New Year acrobat, who could be seen walking on stilts far above the level of the roofs of the scarlet-draped houses. In the background of the farms, pigs and chickens and ducks and horses were huddled together, but, out of these heaps of struggling and abundant life, it was always the vitality of the young human beings that triumphed (never have I seen more beautiful children than the Chinese, or ones who show more individuality at an early age), as, clothed in broad padded coats, they waddled and tripped and tumbled and jumped upon their short legs. And the vitality of the parents, though often worn down by circumstances of life, by hardships unknown in Europe, was the same, though shown in less exuberant ways. . . . Indeed, my first impression of the Chinese was of their readiness to smile ; even the most wretched beggar laughed as he asked for alms. Never have I seen faces less " impassive " and " inscrutable " than in China, for Chinese countenances, contrary to the English mid-Victorian and " Mr. Wu " convention, invented to afford sensual thrills to European middle-aged women, reflect the mood of the passing moment as vividly as the most expressive Italian face. They are a nation of laughing talkers, always talking and laughing. (It was, too, a surprise to find how tall are Chinese men of the north, tall and, in appearance, dignified, for all their smiles and chatter : by no means a little people, like the Japanese.)

At each station, the train stayed long enough for the passengers to purchase goods. Outside, crowds of Chinese vendors would be straining at the cement railings, shouting over them quick words of incomprehensible encouragement to prospective buyers, putting a hand through, with a paper lantern or a toy, or fruit, crab-apples in sugar or persimmons, sweets, silks and pottery, bogus bronze antiques, lovely artificial flowers, bowls of soup, melon seeds, or rice done up in leaves or, even, joss-sticks ; while the inevitable beggar would, equally, stretch out his hand in that sad, imperishable hope of charity which never leaves him, in spite of repetitive daily experience. And all this eager, shuffling crowd was dressed in blue. . . . Indeed, for the reader to be able to picture to himself any Chinese scene into which men and women enter, it is necessary for him to think of figures in blue ; everywhere, as I have said, the land was sepia and bare, touched with gold, everywhere the trees — often a huge, isolated old tree standing above a house — made cobweb-like patterns blown against a translucent blue, pale-blue sky, and everywhere, in town and country, moved and worked these vellum-faced figures in blue clothes, light blue and dark blue, faded blue and torn blue, blue patched with blue, green-blue and grey-blue and purple-blue and water-blue. And to whatever part of China he might go, this would be the predominant, the sole contribution to colour made by the human race : all wear blue, rich and poor, coolie and Mandarin, professor and farmer and porcelain-maker. Everywhere, for thousands of miles, they would be thus, until, travelling east, the traveller would see the Korean labourers and their wives dressed in black and white, moving like penguins through the fields, or outlined against a soft sky on the top of their gentle slopes, the men in long robes with transparent top-hats, the women in crinolines ; until, northward, he would see the yellow-robed Mongols, or, westward, the burnet-robed monks of Tibet. Meanwhile, the blue figures throng every station, and stand round the rails in the country to watch every train go by.

Though long, the journey proved less eventful than those in the know might have expected. The train was heavily guarded by profusely armed soldiers, and this we took to be an ordinary precaution of Chinese travel. But it was not so. Chinese trains, it was true, always carried soldiers as guards, but not such a number of them as upon this occasion. Reason existed for increased precautions. A few days previously — although we remained ignorant of it at the time — the bandits who infested the line had demonstrated a sudden change of tactics. Instead of ambushing the train and boarding it in the open country, they had made themselves look very respectable and had gone, separately, to Nanking station, where they had booked third-class tickets on the same train, sitting there in different compartments and reading the daily paper like any suburban business man on the Underground. But, as soon as the train had passed a given point about twenty miles beyond a certain station, they had drawn their revolvers, rushed out, overpowered the soldiers on duty in the corridors, shot a few in warning to the rest, and had then triumphantly proceeded to rob the intimidated passengers. Finally leaving their victims bound and gagged in locked compartments, they had dismounted in a very bourgeois, law-abiding way at the next station, where motor vans met them and the now surprising amount of luggage with which they appeared to be travelling.

On this journey of ours, however, there were no such alarms. The bandits had not yet, perhaps, sufficiently digested their booty to be obliged to devise fresh tricks or to resort to old ones. We walked, unmolested, to the restaurant-car from time to time, to eat a little rice or to drink tea — golden, honeyed and milkless — out of tall narrow glass tumblers. . . . The conductor had formerly served on the Russian Royal Train. (Only in China and Manchuria do your ears still catch a faint flutter of the old Imperial wings of the double-headed eagle.) . . . Two nights or three we passed in the train, between Shanghai and Peking, eventually approaching that great city in the morning light, through great clusters of gardens and decaying temples.

### CHAPTER TWO

SIGHTS AND SOUNDS
OF THE PEKING DAY

F ROM my room high up in the hotel — apart from palaces
and temples, one of the few lofty structures here, another,
which deserves mention, being the local home of the
Y.M.C.A. and assuredly one of the ugliest buildings in
the world — I obtained a first and most magnificent view
of Peking. The Legation Quarter, a conglomeration of
gardens, old temples and modern houses, lay behind me,
out of the picture, as did " The Chinese City ", so called.
But " The Tartar City " extended shining below, almost
untouched save for the structure I have mentioned ; the
same now as it had always been ; a sea of grey roofs surrounding the tall, vivid islands of the Forbidden and Imperial Cities, square and rectangular, one within the other ;
red-walled cities which occupied the centre of the picture
and, because of the obvious grandeur and beauty of their
temples, halls and pavilions, their moated gardens and
canals, vast courts and parks, overshadowed their setting.
Orange-tiled roof after orange-tiled roof, with bright green

and vermilion eaves, further emblazoned by the clear, clean sunlight of this pure air, stretched away toward two hills — the only ones for many miles round ; until, indeed, you reach the perfect contours of the Western Hills.

Both these tall mounds are artificial and have buildings on them ; the five summits of the nearer are studded with tiled pavilions, in which formerly the Empress and her ladies used to take the air, and see what was going on below them in the streets and alleys of the Palace ; while the further carries on its height a curious, white, bottle-shaped structure known as the White Dagoba, erected by the order of the Emperor Shan Chih in 1651, to mark the first visit of the Dalai Lama to Peking. Behind the White Dagoba, but still within the limits of the Imperial City, flashed in the sun a great sheet of water, the beautiful lines of its shores littered with derelict temples. This lake, famous for its lotuses, and the extensive wooded park which surrounds it, are known as Pei-Hai, or North Sea Lake. Now a public playground, it had once been the pleasance of Kubla Khan. " Between the two walls of the enclosure ", Marco Polo tells us,[1] ". . . are fine parks and beautiful trees bearing a variety of fruits. There are beasts also of sundry kinds, such as white stags and fallow deer, gazelles and roebucks, and fine squirrels of various sorts, with numbers of the animal that gives the musk, and all manner of other beautiful creatures. . . . There extends a fine Lake, containing foison of fish of different kinds which the Emperor hath caused to be put in there, so that whenever he desires any he can have them at his pleasure. A river enters this lake and issues from it, but there is a grating of iron or brass put up so that the fish cannot escape in that way."

[1] *The Book of Ser Marco Polo*, vol. i. p. 364.

The two hills are the two pivotal points of the city. Between them and my window, the Forbidden City showed in the foreground great halls, that, for all their gaily glistening eaves and shining tiles, were, in their lines and sentiment, as solemn and forbidding and grand as any in Moscow (just as Russia has in it something of China, so has China of Russia), as well as, farther away, toward the gate facing the nearer hill, pavilions blithe and delicate as flowers, brilliantly coloured little kiosks that seemed to float among their garden courts. The solemn buildings had all the monumental qualities of a Chinese bronze ; the little, all the grace of a Chinese drawing of a bird on a branch. . . . But already, while you looked at the Palace, you began to comprehend one fact, hitherto obscured, concerning the architecture of this race ; that their buildings are projected, I believe, with even more thought to their situation than are ours ; trees and gardens and water are even more part of them. It would be easier to think of Versailles without its elaboration of grove and avenue and fountain, than to think of any structure here without its adjuncts of moat and tree and terrace and curiously formed rocks. . . . In token of this, close to every building in front of me, whether vast or diminutive, magnificent and rugged, or gaily fashioned as a shell, could be seen the trunks of trees, giant or dwarf, the dark foliage of cypress or the smoke-like planes of the Imperial cedars, with their gnarled and twisted bodies. And through the branches of them showed the gleam of water.

Peking is still a walled city — or rather a collection of walled cities, Forbidden City, Imperial City, Tartar City, Legation Quarter, Chinese City, all have their walls. (Indeed, at the time I was there, the gates were made fast every night so as to defeat the schemes of bandits.) Thus, in places, could be seen, above the low houses of the Tartar City, its vast encircling walls, on which the visitor may walk; castellated walls, forty foot high, sixty-two feet thick at the base, narrowing to thirty-five at the top, being strengthened on the outer side at regular intervals of sixty yards by gigantic buttresses that project fifty feet outward; [1] and, soaring above them, the tops of their enormous gates, towers such as the Drum Tower, built by the Emperor Yung Lo five hundred years ago, from the materials of Kubla's Drum Tower, the Bell Tower near by, of similar origin and reconstruction,[2] and the haunted, double-cornered rectangular bulk of the Fox Tower.

Right through the city run the great thoroughfares (though until the abdication of the last Emperor in 1912, these remained closed to all but Imperial traffic) designed by Kubla Khan, and modified or rearranged by Yung Lo; though in reality this last claim may belong to the realm of patriotism more than truth, since the Chinese do not forgive foreign dynasties their good works, and, after they have

---

[1] For measurement, see *In Search of Old Peking*, by L. C. Arlington and William Lewisohn. (Henri Vetch, Peking, 1935.)

[2] The authors of *In Search of Old Peking* tell us that originally a kind of water-clock, called *The Brass Thirsty Bird*, stood in the Drum Tower. This mechanism derived its name from an upper jar, in the shape of a bird, from whose beak water trickled into a lower jar, fitted with a bamboo rod to indicate the four divisions of the hour. In accordance with its readings, a watchman used, in Mongol and Ming times, to strike a large cymbal every quarter of an hour. In the middle of the seventeenth century, however, the Manchu Dynasty abolished The Brass Thirsty Bird, installed a less imaginative water-clock, and substituted for the cymbal a drum, which now only announced the night watches. Whenever the drum sounded, the bell in the Bell Tower rang out an instant later. These customs continued into the days of the Republic, but latterly the Bell Tower has been converted by thoughtful local authorities into a cinema. . . . Marco Polo mentions the Bell Tower, before it was removed to the city walls, and that the ringing of the bell served as a curfew.

rid themselves of their alien tyrants, are apt to appropriate for one of their native Emperors the fine things the strangers have accomplished. Though so suited to modern conditions — much more adapted to them, indeed, than is the lay-out of the present-day London or New York — it was, then, of such impressive avenues and processional ways that Marco Polo wrote, nearly seven centuries ago, " The streets are so straight and wide, that you can see right along them, from end to end and from one gate to another " ; [1] down these broad roads, or others exactly like them, the elephants of the Grand Khan must have paraded for the New Year, previously described. And this sense of space, which inspired it, gives to the old capital a character entirely its own, decorative and metropolitan, very different from that of contemporary cities, whether in Europe, Asia or China itself : in no great town of this epoch can you find such a noble conception, thought out and completed. Elsewhere you would discover, whatever their beauties, only haphazard and ramshackle collections of houses and churches or temples, sheltering a teeming and contorted life : here, on the contrary, order and design abide, and the human body — man's natural measure for buildings or landscape — consequently obtains and sets a new proportion to its background.

Yet Peking has none of the dreadful impersonal quality of the more recently designed quarter of a European capital ; none of the coldness of the new Berlin, or of Haussmann's Paris : moreover, there is no lack of small streets, which are necessary, too, to the soul of a city. On the contrary, they are everywhere, in the Chinese City and the Tartar City ; but they are in their right place, not in the middle

---

[1] *The Book of Ser Marco Polo.*

of important routes. These *hutungs*,[1] as they are called,
are lanes of houses, never more than a storey high (for to
build higher would have been to trespass on Imperial privilege). This uniform squatness is only broken occasionally
by the lines of a tall temple, or by the squares of court or
garden : otherwise, beneath you, lie street after windowless
street of houses, with grey, ribbed roofs and, round them,
the intricate patterns, vein-like patterns, made by the
branches and twigs of bare, winter trees, while, high up
above, from every open space sail proudly the coloured
kites, red and blue and yellow, dragons and birds and
animals, flown by Chinese children. (All day long, from
dawn to dusk, these kites flutter toward the sky and strain

[1] *Hutung* or *hu-t'ung*. My friend Dr. Arthur Waley writes, " Hu-t'ung is the
transcription of a Mongol word, and has been in use in North China since the
fourteenth century. That is all that is known about it."

It is used of " certain streets outside the Forbidden City, where Mongolians
and other nationalities were allowed to have their residences. . . . No mention
is made of the Chinese, the Manchu conquerors apparently not wishing to openly
differentiate against those who, at times not far distant, had been the proud rulers
of the land. As far as my information goes . . . the term Hutung is confined to
North China, and is used largely in Peking and Kalgan, probably originating
in the latter place, which is so near the Mongolian border. . . . A Hutung
may mean anything from a miserable blind alley, containing a few dilapidated
hovels, to a broad street full of beautiful houses and official buildings. . . .
It is distinguishable from the main streets and thoroughfares by the fact that
it contains few, if any, shops and is essentially a residential quarter." (From
*Sidelights on Peking Life*, by Robert W. Swallow. China Booksellers Ltd.,
Peking, 1927.)

It is of interest to recall that the Empress Dowager, who ruled China for so
many years, was born and brought up in a *hutung* in the Tartar City, the Hsi La
Hutung, or Pewter Lane. Miss Yehonala finally left her home in this alley on
June 16th, 1852, to go to the Palace, with sixty other lovely Manchu competitors
for the position of concubine to the Emperor Hsien Fêng. She was chosen, and
became the Concubine Yi. . . . She only returned to her native *hutung* once,
when, after giving birth to an heir to the throne, she was allowed to visit her
family. All her relatives, except her mother, were awaiting the Imperial yellow
palanquin on their knees. But at the banquet which followed, even the mother
had to take a lower seat than her daughter, in spite of the laws of filial piety.
(See Arlington and Lewisohn's *In Search of Old Peking*.)

at their cords ; so that it becomes permissible to wonder whether the ingenuity which every small boy who can afford to buy such a toy, or who can contrive it for himself out of a piece of string and a piece of rag, expends upon the flying of it, may not, by the training it affords, constitute one of the secrets of the ingenuity and intelligence of the Chinese mind ?) [1]

If you descend into these streets you will find a blue figure or two in every alley, and the larger streets thronged, mostly with men ; young men hurrying about their business and old men, with scanty beards and with the happy faces of the old (for, in China, age is respected : perhaps because it is respectable), so different from the broken, sad look of old eyes in Europe. Here all wear the traditional dress of the Chinese, thick padded robes, some-times with fur collars, surmounted at this season with tri-angular fur hats, similar to those in the portraits of Flemish merchants by Van Eyck or his followers. In the *hutung* near by you see an old woman in black silk trousers and a blue, short jacket walking with difficulty, hobbling along with the help of a cane on her unemancipated feet, which all her life have been tortured and stunted, while, with her, but hardly able to endure the slowness of her pace, comes a young girl, similarly clad, with a jade flower in her hair, and with feet which, though never bound, are scarcely less small than those of her mother.

[1] From the tenth month onward kites called Aeolian Harps are on sale in Peking. " Small bamboos are tied to make the frame, which is covered with paper, and made into forms such as that of the flamingo, peacock, large wild goose, and ' flying tiger '. They are painted with extreme skill, and when children release them into the void, they can indeed make the eyes clearer as one strains to look at them." Some carry small bamboo bows, the strings of which hum, or gongs or drums which strike, in the wind, and can be heard according as the kites mount or sink in the air. (Tun Lich'en's *Annual Customs and Festivals in Peking*.)

From every street rise the sounds of gongs and drums being beaten in a thousand different ways (each with its own significance to the initiated), of flutes and pipes and multifarious cries, the wooden clack of rattles, the jingle of bells, the hum of the tuning-fork, the clink of metal on metal.[1] These indicate the presence of the ubiquitous street-vendors who supply Peking housewives with necessities and luxuries, the whole day long and right through the night, at their very doorsteps : and though the instrument, tuning-fork or drum, may be shared by a score of occupations, the effect of its playing differs as much as the trades it represents. There are, too, auditory tokens of that opposite kind of itinerant dealer, who wishes to buy ; the parchment drum of the ambitious seeker for jade and jewels, who taps out a special rhythm as he wails his wants, or, humbler and more easily gratified, the unaccompanied growl of " I will give money for foreign bottles, I also buy scrap iron and broken glass ". But the cries of the vendors were, of course — for supply always seems to me to outstrip demand — much more plentiful and heterogeneous than those of the purchasers.

It was not, however, until I descended to ground, after a week of my hotel, in a Chinese house situated in the Tartar City (a lovely house belonging to someone who became, in contradiction of the usual landlord-tenant quarrels, a most valued friend) that I grew aware of the full multiplicity of these cries and signals by means of percussion, wind and stringed instruments ; they were as numerous and diverse as the sounds of the insect world,

[1] For all the information concerning the street cries of Peking, in this chapter and in Chapter 8, I am deeply indebted to Mr. R. W. Swallow's most interesting *Sidelights on Peking Life* (China Booksellers Ltd., Peking, 1927).

of bee and moth and beetle and cicada, and the crepitations and whirrings of all those other nameless winged creatures of a summer night in a warm land. There, in the Alley of Sweet Rain — Kan-Yu Hutung — in that delightful and typical collection of rooms on the ground floor — all roofed with herring-bone patterns of grey tiles — and of paved garden courts, approached by a red door hidden in a blank grey wall in a grey alley, it was possible to distinguish every one of them. . . . And, notwithstanding my hatred of noise, I liked them — cries as well as accompaniments — from the first moment of hearing them, although, judged by Western standards, they would be ranked as by no means musical. It is true that I did not understand their meaning, but then neither did the majority of native citizens of Peking : for it is said that the cries of the western end of the city, for example, differ so entirely from those of the eastern as to be incomprehensible if transposed, one to the other, and, further, many of them are antiquated in style and language, and formalised beyond recognition except by those familiar with them. (Think, as for that, of how difficult it is to interpret the words of our only remaining traditional London street cry of " Lavender, sweet lavender ! "). . . . Be this as it may, I liked listening to them, and this narrow, grey lane, with its trees and grey-brown walls, was seldom without one of these strange and romantic cries — some of them, at night, seeming unearthly in the extreme — or of these other arrangements of notes and rhythms that gathered an indefinable quality, an added tinkle and tang and crispness, from the dry and sparkling air of Peking.

Many of these sounds continued until dawn ; a matter of habit, for, though the night-life of the wealthy Chinese is now more limited than formerly, Peking, like all great cosmopolitan centres (and, though it may no longer be the official capital of the Chinese Republic, it must always, whatever happens, remain the metropolis of the whole of middle and north-eastern Asia), has to cater for innumerable wants at all hours of day and night, and it was necessary for the vendors, between them, to cover the entire enormous ground space — about twenty-five square miles — of this vast town. A few go silently (and here silence, so rare, is almost the best identification of a trade) on their rounds, the seller of ankle ribbons, for example, or those who deal in shoes or shoe leather, or sell whips. Others cease their cries, or mute their instruments, at dusk.

Among this division, whose music dies with the daylight, can be ranked the barber,[1] who, unlike his European counterpart, does not open his mouth, but twangs at a tuning-fork with a short steel rod ; the seller of hats in winter and of fans in summer, who plays a huge, ingenious apparatus of bells strung on a framework of wire which

[1] The relation of the barber's trade to political changes, and the role he continually plays in them — quite apart from the conversations for which his shop is notorious, and which have often in the past been responsible for the acceptance of lies as the truth, and, in consequence, of much political mischief — are matters to which I have referred previously in a book entitled *Discursions on Travel, Art and Life* (Gerald Duckworth & Co. Ltd., 1931). Therein some account is given of the revolution in Naples in 1799, when the barbers incited the mob to attack the liberal aristocrats, because they had forsworn the use of wigs and had thus diminished professional profits. In Peking a similar connection is emphasised by the outfit of the itinerant barber. Mr. Swallow, in his delightful *Sidelights on Peking Life*, indicates that the Chinese barber has very much come down in the world now that the pigtail is no longer worn. In the early days of the Manchu dynasty, when that badge of servitude had just been imposed by the conquerors, the hairdresser was a salaried government official, though, in addition, he expected tips from his customers for the performance of his duties. The little painted pole, which he still carries, and on which he hangs strops and brushes, is a diminutive replica of those which, in the days of the Empire, denoted official authority, and on it he used to inscribe his licence. Mr. Swallow adds that the tuning-fork is said to be the vestigial remains of the large knife used for cutting off the heads of those rebellious subjects of the Son of Heaven who refused to wear pigtails.

dwarfs completely the portable store upon which it is erected ; the mender of porcelain, who, like so many of his brother hawkers, carries slung across his shoulders a pole, from each end of which hang his means of livelihood, and who rings a gong by means of pellets, which swing upon cords to the rhythm of his step ; loudest of them all, the Punch and Judy showman, with his booth, and with the clamorous gongs and cymbals that proclaim it ; the purveyor of pretty trifles such as especially recommend themselves to women, who manipulates a jangling contrivance with a wooden handle ; the sharpener of knives, who clashes long, rectangular metal plates together or blows down a trumpet ; the trudging quack doctor with his bell ; the clothier with his wooden mallet ; the seller of toys, which jog and dangle from the top of a tall stick as he calls out, " Buy, Small Man, they are lifelike, they have eyes and arms ! " ; the hawker of green-glazed jars, who shouts his wares and adds a proposal to take old ones in part exchange, and the men from Shansi, who offer, with deep-throated notes, iron pots such as are only made in that province ; the pedlar of kettles, who carries his goods slung from the end of a pole, and taps the curving metal belly of one of them, as he goes along, with a rod, so that it rings out like a bell ; the maker of " sugared horse blossoms " — a sweet compounded of sugar, oil and flour, plaited to resemble a horse's tail decked out for a feast day — who screams out his delicacies at the top of his voice ; the seller of wooden gourds, who bangs them together ; the fortune-teller, who divines character or prophesies the events of a career, according to his particular art, whether by the lines of your face, by judging of the manner in which falling grains of sand dispose themselves, by clairvoyance or augury, and who, to denote his approach, taps a piece of wood against the top of a short stick; or, another member of the large group devoted to magic, the blind palmist, who may choose to herald his coming either by playing a flute, beating a small gong, or plucking the strings of a kind of fiddle ; all these still their music with the coming of darkness, though they are not more numerous than those whose cries and crepitations continue throughout the entire night.[1]

[1] See Chapter 9, pp. 328 ff.

### CHAPTER THREE

## CHANG AND THE CHINESE

It must have been during the morning of the second or third day of the first week spent in the house in the Kan-Yu Hutung that, as I wrote near the window, an intermittent music floated down from the sky and drew me out into the court to see what it could be. High up, alternately dark or smoky against the blue dome that in this atmosphere appeared taut and brittle as glass, a flock of birds was manœuvring. When the creatures sped in a straight line the music came low and regular, like that of a distant rocket in ascent, only fainter, but with each turn in their flight it grew of a sudden stronger, and seemed to contain a note, also, of menace such as I had heard in no bird-song heretofore. I could not quite solve the mystery. The birds were too high up for me to be able to identify them, and I judged it singular that this fluting should be at its loudest during the very moment of their circlings and loopings : could it be due to the pleasure, perhaps, which they took in their own evolutions ? . . . At this instant Chang, my Chinese servant, came out, and remarked in a gratified voice :

" Master worry and puzzle : has not heard pigeons make whistle music before ? "

And, indeed, I had not. . . . Nor had any of my friends acquainted with China ever warned me of it, or told me of the technique the Chinese employed, of how they tie whistles to the bodies of the pigeons, so that the rush of their flight produces these strains,[1] or of how a boy, carrying a flag of some colour which, through training, the birds are able to recognise, runs along the ground far beneath them, to indicate the line of their passage, to keep them aloft as long as their owner wishes and, finally, to guide them safely home again. Indeed, our friend Lich'en, to whom we have recourse so often, appears to have regarded the entangling of pigeons with musical instruments as a duty, for he announces categorically,[2] " Whenever the pigeons are let out to fly, bamboo whistles should be attached to their tails ". He goes on to explain that the instruments are of two kinds, the first, the *hu-lu*, being divided merely into large and small whistles, while the second comprises subdivisions of a much more complicated and diverse nature, including, under its designation of *shao-tzu*, whistles of three pipes clamped together, or of five, or eleven or thirteen double pipes, of some with obstructed openings, and of others that consist of many large tubes surrounding

[1] Messrs. Arlington and Lewisohn, in their *In Search of Old Peking* (Henri Vetch, Peking, 1935), say that to the Chinese the appeal of this sort of pigeon-flying, apart from its music, consists in " watching the flock circling round, sometimes standing out black against the sky, and then suddenly almost invisible, according as the sunlight catches them . . ." (p. 228).

[2] This and subsequent quotations, as well as the list of names of pigeons, is taken from Tun Lich'en's *Annual Customs and Festivals in Peking*, pp. 22, 113-114 : but sometimes, in the list, I have taken the liberty of altering from plural to singular, for the sake of sound, or for the consistency of my book ; from *Purple jade wings* to *Purple Jade Wing*, for example.

a single large one in the centre. "When the pigeons wheel overhead," he continues, "their sound rises even to the clouds, containing within it all five notes.[1] Truly it gives joy, and a release to the emotions ! "

The emotions to which, in my case, it had given release were those of surprise and bewilderment ; but then, how, before reading the delightful pages of Lich'en, could I have known the extent to which the peristeronic art had been cultivated in Peking, any more than the strange ways in which the birds had been employed ? For example, in former years, some of them were taught to steal. They were trained to fly, directly they were set loose, straight to the Imperial granaries and swallow as much of the finest rice as their crops, artificially distended, would receive. When these " Food Distributors " — as, with the Chinese sense of euphemism, they were termed — returned home from their raids, they were dosed with alum and water, and made literally to disgorge their booty. After being washed, the rice would then be sold. The proprietors counted on a flock of a hundred pigeons bringing home fifty pounds of rice a day.[2] How clearly has this device been invented by the same race which evolved the ingenious use of the cormorant for fishing !

As for the numbers of pigeons, they were countless, dividing the sky of Peking with the kites flown by children. Their varieties, also, were many. Among the more common, Lich'en enumerates the Dotted One, Jade-Wing, Phoenix-Headed White, Two-Headed Black, Small Ash-Black, Purple Sauce, Snow Flower, Silver Tail, Four-Piece Jade,

---

[1] Of the Chinese scale.
[2] See *In Search of Old Peking*, by L. C. Arlington and William Lewisohn, pp. 227-228.

Magpie Flower, Heel and Head, Flowery Neck, and Taoist Priest Hat, while in addition to two very rare kinds with plumage the colour of gold, the more select comprised Toad-Eyed Grey, Iron Ox, Short-Beaked White, Crane's Elegance, Azure Plumage, Egret White, Black Ox, Bronze Back, Mottled Back, Silver Back, Square-Edged Unicorn, Blue Plate, Striped Sandal, Cloud Plate, Purple Black One, Purple Dotted One, Parrot-Beak White, Parrot-Beak Spotted, Purple Jade Wing, Iron-Winged, Jade Circlet and Wild Duck of the Great Dipper. . . . I like to think that those I saw so high up, wheeling and whistling, were a flock of Square-Edged Unicorns, or, if common they must be, of Phoenix-Headed Whites ; but probably they were only Magpie Flowers.

One thing, at least, was certain about this new form of entertainment ; to whatever variety the birds may have belonged, or whatever the method of their training, Chang enjoyed, even more than the music of their flight, my obvious surprise at it. Though tall, with an almost epis-copal dignity of mien as he swept in and out of the rooms in his long robe, he liked to giggle to himself a little when-ever a white employer plainly betrayed his ignorance. It was not a rude titter. Pleasure, it is true, entered into the composition of it, but the chief emotions conveyed were those of pity, and of fear concerning how my lack of know-ledge of the world and its ways might not next evince itself and thereby, perhaps, damage my career. . . . Thus I remember, a day or two after I arrived, calling him into my room to help me deal with a singular monster that was clattering about on the floor with a noise, as it sidled and darted, like a walking coal-scuttle ; an enormous, crab-like beetle, encased in a cuirass of green bronze, a full two or three inches across, and with strongly armoured legs and feet. Indeed, it had frightened me, for its whole appearance was so baleful that I thought it might possibly be mortal to man. . . . Chang paused to identify this dragon, and then remarked with an air of immense superiority, " Master no like ? . . . Very much prized in Chinese medicine." [1]

[1] The Chinese science of acupuncture, though long neglected by Western science, is now receiving considerable attention, chiefly from French doctors. It consists, in practice, of stabbing deeply, with a sharp needle, let us say a sympathetic nerve in the foot in order to cure a pain in the head.

Where medicine is concerned, the Chinese doctors make use of their own pharmacopoeia, developed empirically through a score or so of centuries, and some of the ingredients they use are naturally disconcerting to our ideas. They believe, too, in administering enormous quantities of weak medicine, usually in liquid form, as opposed to the fashion of concentrated drugs in small compass prevalent in Europe and America. They consider that, apart from the better physical results they obtain by this method, the psychological effect of having to drink two or three tumblers of medicine at a time is much more beneficial to the patient than that of swallowing quickly " a tablespoonful in a little water, thrice daily after meals ".

I quote the following interesting account of how, far from any possibility of finding medical aid, Robert Fortune (see footnote on p. 166, preceding) was cured of fever when staying with a priest in the temple of Tientung, near Ning-po, by a Chinese practitioner, whom he called in " with considerable reluctance ". (From *A Residence Among the Chinese*, pp. 103-104. Murray, 1857.) He had been ill for some time, and when the doctor entered, was " in bed with a burning fever ". In spite of never having seen an Englishman before, the doctor evidently understood our island nature, first of all by forbidding him, even when he was better, to bathe every morning in a cold stream, and subsequently by endeavouring to persuade him to moderate his diet.

" He then despatched a messenger to his house for certain medicines, and at the same time ordered a basin of strong, hot tea to be brought into the room. When this was set before him he bent his two forefingers and dipped his knuckles into the hot tea. The said knuckles were now used like a pair of pincers on my skin, under the ribs, round the back, and on several other parts of the body. Every now and then the operation of wetting them with the hot tea was repeated. He pinched and drew my skin so hard that I could scarcely refrain from crying out with pain ; and . . . left marks which I did not get rid of for several weeks after.

" When the messenger arrived with the medicine, the first thing I was asked to swallow was a large paper of small pills, containing, I suppose, about a hundred, or perhaps more. " Am I to take the whole of these ? " I asked in amazement. " Yes ; and here is a cup of hot tea to wash them down." I hesitated ; then tasted one, which had a hot, peppery kind of flavour, and, making up my mind,

Nevertheless, sympathy was to be felt mixed with his contempt. (Poor barbarians, they know no better. Must try and help, must try educate.)

And, indeed, I found that talking with him undoubtedly aided my education. Whatever may be urged against servants — and I refuse, not from snobbishness, or from anything but an esthetic feeling for the use of words, to insult them by writing " domestics " or such bastard terms as " lady help " or " gentleman assistant " —, that they undermine self-reliance in those waited upon, and encourage servility in those that wait, that such labour degrades man, and all the rest of that pompous humbug which recurrently emerges into the correspondence columns of the daily press, it must be allowed that in former days, when a country gentleman lived in a house peopled with servants, they acted as a conductor from his earliest years between the son of the house and the workers. From them he learnt

gulped the whole. In the meantime a teapot had been procured capable of holding about three large breakfast-cups of tea. Into this pot were put six different vegetable productions — about half an ounce of each. These consisted of dried orange or citron peel, pomegranate, charred fruit of Gardenia radicans, the bark and wood of Rosa Banksiana, and two other things unknown to me. The teapot was then filled to the brim with boiling water, and allowed to stand for a few minutes, when the decoction was ready for the patient. I was now desired to drink it cup after cup as fast as possible, and then cover myself over with all the blankets which could be laid hold of. . . ."

After this, there was no recurrence of the fever, and a precisely similar treatment administered three days later completed the cure.

Fortune adds, ". . . I am inclined to think more highly of their [the Chinese doctors'] skill than people generally give them credit for. . . . When I first came to China, a celebrated practitioner in Hongkong, now no more, gravely informed me the Chinese doctors gathered all sorts of herbs indiscriminately, and used them *en masse*, upon the principle that if one thing did not answer the purpose another would. Nothing can be further from the truth. . . . Being a very ancient nation," he continues, " many discoveries have been made and carefully handed down from father to son which are not to be despised. . . ." In China I have heard it stated that one particular medical secret, of how to cure some special illness or disability, may form the patrimony of a whole family ; the members of which, therefore, will under no circumstances consent to disclose it.

how others lived, and how they talked and felt, just as he learnt French, let us say, from a French nurse or governess. Thus the wisdom of the aristocrat, if he should chance to be wise, and his folly, if he should chance to be foolish, had equally been learnt below stairs, in pantry or living-room. And the wisdom, if it survived, was one that cannot be learned from labour-saving devices, however enlightened the age. (It may be noticed, too, that true wisdom — as opposed to cleverness — seems to have flourished no less in times when few people, comparatively, could read or write, than in the present day, when all can read papers and write books.) And still, for those writers and artists who cannot give all their time to exchanges of intimate confidences in public-houses, and are equally determined, too, to take no part in the " Class Struggle ", servants represent a store of popular feeling and consciousness with which it is well to keep in touch. . . . Thus from observing the ways of Chinese servants, I grew to understand certain things about China and Chinese feeling and, through talking with them — and, more especially, with Chang —, began to appreciate several points in the national character ; such, for example, as that method of indirect approach to a subject, which comes so naturally to the Oriental, but remains so alien to our unsubtle minds.

It cannot be denied, I think, that this habit of the indirect approach in speech has its drawbacks for those not accustomed to it. The Chinese is always on the look-out for it, expecting it from the foreigner as much as from men of his own blood. And so it was, that, one day, when I was handed by mistake some letters addressed to my land-lord, and laid them down on the table, saying to myself idly at the same time, " Well, I wonder what they are about ", Chang naturally concluded my words to be an injunction to him, and, before I had realised what he was doing, had torn open the envelopes and was informing me of their contents.

Often, too, from talking to him, I obtained in part a conception of how the Chinese regard the various actions of men, placing thereon a value entirely different to ours. Thus, one morning, he remarked to me, by way of opening a conversation :

" Master interested in army ? "

" No."

Not at all discouraged, he continued proudly, " My uncle a General in Chinese Army."

I betrayed no surprise, for it was proverbial in the foreign colony here that, since the Civil Wars had started, every Peking houseboy boasted a father or uncle who was a General on either one side or the other ; sometimes on both.

" Uncle very patriotic man," he went on.

" I am sure he is," I replied commendingly.

" Yes, the Japanese they offer him one whole hundred thousand dollars to help them."

" And he refused it," I said, finishing the sentence for him.

For a moment I saw the shocked expression that always appeared on it when his sense of thrift was in any way thwarted, cross his face, and then he cried out with anguished patriotism,

" No, no, Master ! He take money, and then run home."

" *Malbrouck s'en va-t-en guerre*," I sang to myself happily, for I seized his point. Always it had been my opinion that the great Duke of Marlborough had proved himself twice as good a patriot — and commander — as the

ordinary English general, if it were true, as tradition maintained, that, besides vanquishing Louis XIV, he had first
accepted from him large bribes to let the French win ; for
in that case he had inflicted upon the Sun-King a double
defeat, one financial, the other in the field. And I had
regretted accordingly any attempt, even by pious descendants, to palliate or dispel such stories, whether myth
or reality. An example of this kind should not be destroyed.
During the last war, how often had I not wished that the
English generals, models of national probity, would both
accept bribes from the Kaiser and be content to sacrifice
fewer English soldiers : for, after all, a man who has bought
a battle expects to win it, and will be twice as dismayed when
he sees that, far from being dormant, the troops of his
enemy intend to win. " *Malbrouck s'en va-t-en guerre !* "

But, to return to our conversations, one day, several
weeks later, I said :

" Chang, can you find a photographer for me ? I want
him to come here to take a group of all of you in the
courtyard."

" Very easy for me. I own photoglaphic business —
but no one know."

(At this point it should be added that, when the photographs were finished, anyone who saw them would have
been able at once to guess the secret. Every other face in
the group came out lined and seared, whereas the camera
man had, with a terrible sycophancy, touched up Chang's
countenance to that of a Chinese Adonis. Contrarily, his
enemy, the cook — a genius in his own way — who, old
and by no means handsome, possessed a certain presence,
as of a philosopher, a certain air of ponderous and austere
benignity, combined with intellect, that gave him, except

for his colouring, somewhat the same appearance as the late Lord Haldane, was transformed in it into the likeness of a malicious and idiot gnome.)

" Very easy ", Chang repeated.

" But, good heavens," I said, interested at once, for by this time we were on very good terms, and I was consequently surprised that I had heard nothing of this concern before, " you've kept very quiet about it. Next, you'll be telling me you've got another business as well."

" Yes. A photoglaph business in Jehol, and two silk business with brother in Mukden."

" Is that all ? "

" No. Two silk business in Tientsin, and one fruit business with nother brother in Harbin."

" And others as well, I suppose ? "

" No : no more : no more stores : only two restaurants in Shanghai and one, very big, in Hong Kong."

" But you must be a rich man, Chang ; why do you work like this ? "

" In Peking this no time for big people : this time for little man. Make myself small. . . . And not rich, not rich at all. Price of eggs dleadful now : twelve a penny ! "

Nor, I am persuaded, were his enterprises by any means confined to those he had named. (I suspect his brother's farm, concerning the merits of which I used to hear frequently.) Moreover, he had other possessions.

A few days later, he had come into my room and had hovered about with a peculiar air. I could tell, from experience, that he wished to approach me, and I could see that he was turning some problem over in his mind. But when at last he spoke, his meaning was so remote from usual domestic matters that, in my stupidity, he found it for a considerable time difficult to make his meaning clear to me : but I can only suggest here the amount of his circumlocution. . . . It appeared to him that I walked too much for my health. It was very tiring, and he was sure that I was not strong. No one who used his brain should walk much. . . . Besides, it was silly to walk. Why walk, when you could drive ? People here looked down on pedestrians : and Chinese servants thought that, if a European used his feet, it was because he could not *afford* to drive. (Many Chinese servants very wicked, look out for nasty things to say. Hollid servants in this street. . . .) Gradually it became plain, however, that his acquaintances were taunting him with serving a master who could not afford a motor, and that, as my personal servant, he felt humiliated. He had, I think, suffered considerably and quite genuinely. . . . And now he was circling nearer and nearer to his object, which was to tell me that he owned a motor (though this again must constitute, of course, a secret between us), and that, if I feared the expense of hiring one — or if, as he put it, I found the cars of Peking inferior to those to which I was accustomed — he would be delighted to place it at my disposal for so long as I liked, free of charge, if I would just pay the cost of the petrol. Then, when I wanted to see a temple, I could drive there, allowing him to occupy the seat next the chauffeur, so that he could be recognised, and all this unpleasant backbiting would stop. . . . After this, we often went out for trips together.

It was an open motor : and I think, too, that he enjoyed taking the air — the Chinese love picnics and expeditions of any sort — but had hardly dared previously to be seen in it, lest, without me, inquisitive fellow-servants should solve the mystery of its ownership. And there existed, I

am sure, a further reason for his liking to drive with me ;
he could not endure the uncertainty as to where I might
be going. For he manifested a full share of another national
characteristic, intense curiosity. This directed itself im-
partially to all things, whether important or unimportant.
. . . For example, the only times I ever saw suffering
plainly written upon his face, occurred when he knew I
was going to dine out, but did not know where or with
whom. Deliberately, I would at first tantalise him, but in
the end pity for his obvious distress always overcame me,
and I would enlighten him — except on one occasion, when
the spirit of scientific enquiry hardened my original resolve
*not* always to give way to Chang in this fashion. One
ought, I felt persuaded, to keep him in ignorance, if only
once, in order to see what he would do, how he would deal
with this new situation. . . . So I said nothing. Just as
we were leaving the house, however, he came up to me,
walking very fast, and said, frankly, imploringly, as if
placing his whole future in my hands, " *Please* tell me
where Master dine. No one know. Can find out nothing
from nobody. . . ." So plainly was he at the end of his
endurance that, even then, I could not find it any longer in
my heart to refuse him the information. . . . And, as it
was, the state of suspense to which for a whole day he had
been subjected, must have wrought on his nerves more than
I had realised at the time. The next morning he fell ill
with a short, very violent attack of influenza, and had to
swallow whole demijohns full of ancient remedies, and be
treated by a Chinese doctor with acupuncture before he
recovered. It had, I suppose, lowered his power of re-
sistance. Nevertheless, considering how ill he appeared to
be, he was about again remarkably quickly.

These talks and incidents are reproduced solely because, reflecting upon them afterward, they appeared really to afford a clue to the outlook and working of the mind, where both political and everyday conduct is concerned, of the ordinary citizen of Peking. Just as one has only to exteriorise such processes, to look at a goldfish, a flowering tree or a Pekingese dog, to be convinced, once and for all, of the difference between them and their equivalents in Europe, so with the ways of thinking which, over a long period, produced these objects and creatures. . . . Thus, for example, I do not believe that either Emperor or Republic, or any General, was ever popular in Peking. It must be remembered that the former Emperors of the Manchu Dynasty were never " Chinese Emperors ", as they are often loosely called, but Emperors *of* China ; originally they had belonged to one more of the several foreign dynasties, ruling over savage tribes, which had imposed themselves by force (and the Chinese, though tolerant, despise both foreigners and force) for a term of two or three centuries upon a peaceful people ; while, on the other hand, the Republic was a new idea (and the majority of Chinese are by nature violently opposed to new ideas). As for the Generals in the Civil War, one was as good as another. And so, in Peking, all kinds of flags, in addition to Imperial and Republican, were always, though ingeniously hidden, kept in readiness in nearly every house, in case they should be wanted : for, to the Chinese, the way of the Vicar of Bray is the Path not only of Wisdom, but of Virtue, and I am only surprised that there is not a temple to that ecclesiastic among those countless shrines to strange gods that are to be found everywhere in Peking. Because you should, they hold, as a matter of principle,

accept, and adapt yourself to, events and not hurl yourself
suicidally against them. . . . Thus the citizens of Peking
are willing to hang out any flags required by expediency,
and to render unto Caesar even the things which are not
Caesar's, if he demands them. Whichever — or whoever
— entered the city in triumph would be received with
triumph ; but it would signify nothing, except a certain
characteristic enjoyment of pageantry. For the rest, people
will fall in with almost any plan for their own domination,
or regeneration, because they know that in the end it will
fail. They have seen so much in the long life of their
country. Upon one thing only are they united and
resolute ; they will not allow outside events to break in
upon their lives. Even so rigid a faith as Communism, if
for the sake of convenience it had temporarily to be
accepted, would find itself powerless to alter the national
character : on the contrary, the national character would
very soon modify Communism to suit itself, or even
assimilate it, as it has always assimilated foreign conquerors.

The professors and students alone are patriotic in the
Western sense of the word patriotism : and the young
students, tired of the picture of national disintegration
which the course of their lifetimes has afforded them, often
incline to Communism as to the only new and untried faith :
but they are young men and women with a mind for ab-
stractions. All that the ordinary Chinese, and, not least,
the ordinary citizen of Peking, demands or desires is to be
allowed to proceed with his own life in his own way, and,
further, to be allowed to adapt his natural artistry to his
trade (it must be repeated that he approaches every trade,
whether boot-making or banking, from the angle of the
artist). Thus no system can flourish here for long, unless it

allow the average man sufficient scope for his instinct for profits, and for an individuality so intense that it makes itself felt in every child at the earliest age.

That toward the Japanese, the Chinese entertain a profound hatred and allied feelings of fear and contempt, I have no doubt (and yet, since each comprehends the other much better than he will ever comprehend a European — or the nearer Indian — there is always the possibility, if temper calms and megalomania recedes, of an understanding between them). Even when I was in Peking, a year or two before the unprovoked Japanese assault on China, the Japanese were already entrenched there, constituted already the real executive and motive-power. Their soldiers marched everywhere, wearing pads over their mouths to guard them against alien contamination, I suppose. But by the Chinese they were treated as a secret, as something it was scarcely decent to see or mention ; much as, in Wells' *Time Machine*, the underground cannibal workers, who eat them, are treated by the aristocrats living on the surface.

. . . Yes, certainly they hated them : in illustration of it, I recall a curious incident. The Japanese, as we used often to be told in the days when they were our allies, are a brave little people : sometimes, however, their bravery entices them into trying to ride horses and drive machines that are too big for them (it may be, even, that China falls into this particular category). Never, then, shall I forget the rapture of a Chinese taxi-driver who was taking me to the Legation Quarter, when, in passing, we saw a diminutive Japanese soldier, on an immense, very powerful motor-bicycle, lose control of it and charge at tremendous speed into a Japanese guard outside the Embassy of Nippon. The behaviour of the sentry, thus battered and pinned against the wall, was heroic. An expression of silent pain that was almost ecstasy took possession of his face, and he did not even utter a groan. . . . But meanwhile my Chinese driver was laughing so much that he had been obliged to pull up at a corner and have his laugh out. Nor do I think that in this case it was due to the Chinese concept of pain as a fit subject for laughter (a psychological phenomenon to which I shall allude again shortly). No, I watched him, and I believe the idea which prompted this reaction was : " The Japanese *will* be overbearing : they will try to do too much (they've no repose) ; they have the advantage over us of being stoic, of *liking* pain and to go out and meet it half-way. . . . And now one of them has got it, right enough, and from a brother dwarf : that's the best of it ! Let's hope it will be a lesson to them."

To generalise again, the Chinese and the Japanese are like the French and the Germans. The Chinese are witty, in their lives, in the things they make, if not in their conversation ; which, as I have written on an earlier page, when comparing it to the talk of French people, resembles a game of cards. I pull out this card, a philosophical tag, and you pull out the opposite one, that you know by experience is the reply to it and will take the trick. For hours, they will sit upright on chairs, a hand on each knee, waiting the cue, and thoroughly enjoying their own skill in platitude. Originality here would be bad manners. Not even the most brilliant Chinese mind would care to show his quality in company. Nevertheless, their outlook is compounded of wit ; and, in addition, they are original, self-indulgent, fond of food and good things and gossip, kindly and deeply attached to their families, interested in the arts and commerce, and, though brave, too fond of life to wish to die unnecessarily. The Japanese, on the other hand, are loyal to a fault, but possess the same order of tact and wit for which the Germans are, and always have been, renowned throughout Europe. Both nations, to coin a word in the German fashion, are corn-tramplers. Nevertheless, the Japanese are clever with their fingers, if not with their minds ; but they are austere and ascetic ; as individuals, kind, but tyrannical the moment they put on a uniform, state-owned after an early age, afraid of ideas ; while their greatest aim and happiness consists in being killed for their country and getting everybody else (some of whom are not so keen on it) killed too. . . . Yet, it must be confessed that, in times past, no nation has produced finer works of art.

But though in so many traits the Chinese resemble the French, on the other hand, as yet they lack their patriotism, which leaders as diverse as Joan of Arc, Louis XIV and Napoleon have cast into an imperishable mould. . . . No doubt, if the Japanese are in Peking, the people of Peking will be nice to them ; because, as I have said, they want to proceed with their own lives and their own business and, in the course of these, to receive as little molestation as possible. In the long run, the historic result of invading China will repeat itself. . . . One day, when I was in London, at the beginning of the Chinese-Japanese war, I asked a Chinese friend of mine, a professor, who was having tea with me, " Dr. Sung, what do you think will happen in China ? " He replied, " Mr. Sitwell, I think and hope that our troops will win in battle ; or perhaps — for it is a large country — through the use of guerrilla tactics. But, if they do not win, then the Japanese will win. At present there are seventy million Japanese and four hundred million Chinese : so, after their victory, there will, instead, be four hundred and seventy million Japanese, of whom four hundred million will be Chinese. . . . You see ? "

Even should Japan temporarily succeed, she will never be able to transform the Chinese character or outlook. Nor, I apprehend, will national misfortune, even if overwhelming, ever rid the Chinese uneducated classes of the contempt they entertain for foreigners and, not least, for the Japanese. It is an innate sentiment, persisting from the most remote times, when the word *China* meant the Middle Kingdom ; the centre of the world. . . . Even so late as the reign of George III, the Emperor Chia Ch'ing remained convinced that England was a vassal state on the fringe of his Empire. Indeed, I think that one of the saddest and most singular events in history occurred in 1840 when China, still sure of her invincibility, first collided with a great modern industrial power at Hong Kong and found, to the amazement of the Emperor and his Mandarins, that she was hopelessly surpassed in might by a barbarian state : but nothing would ever persuade the Chinese people of it. They could, and would, never place belief in such a state of affairs. The supremacy of Chinese life and of Chinese ways of thinking is a certainty of which the Chinese mind never has been — and, I think, never will be — disabused. The contempt they cherish for " lesser breeds without the Law " is at root a moral one. As readers of the *Satyricon* of Petronius, for example, are aware, no moral condemnation can exceed in strength and virtue that entertained — I had almost written, enjoyed — by the addicts of one vice for those addicted to another.

Thus we are shocked by what seems to us, often, the cruelty of the Chinese, their insensitiveness to the physical pain of others, their laughter at it. Certainly that laughter

— though chiefly among the uneducated classes — exists. I remember, for instance, going one day to a shop in Jade Street, kept by a most dignified old jeweller, always arrayed in imposing robes, and with a beautifully trimmed beard. I had on several occasions bought things of him, so that we were on friendly terms. But, upon this particular day, in going out I bumped my head rather badly against the low lintel of the door, and, turning round suddenly, when the proprietor imagined I was out of sight, observed him doubled up with laughter, level with the counter, so great were the spasms. . . . Similarly, one morning I asked Chang to pour some hot water into a glass I was holding : in so doing, he poured a few drops, almost boiling, by mistake onto my hand, and laughed so much at my conse-quent moment of agony — while repeating over and over again the words, " Velly, velly solly " — that I had to relieve him of the kettle in case, in a paroxysm, he should spill the rest of it. . . . Yet I believe the laughter that pain arouses after this fashion in the Chinese to be merely an instinctive reaction. I do not think they find it really *funny* : but they laugh, just as we might give an exclama-tion.

But we are not more horrified at such traits than are they by certain of ours ; our insensitiveness to, and neglect of, our ancestors, our lack of respect for the old. Our vices seem particularly despicable to them when matched against their own. . . . Opium-smoking was at that time against the law (indeed, until the arrival of the Japanese, it had really decreased). It would be idle, however, to pretend that none existed. But even those Chinese who never indulged in it and who altogether condemned the practice, were wont to compare it favourably with the manner in which Europeans drank whisky and cocktails. The habit of opium,[1] they would maintain in argument, if smoked in moderation, a few times a week — and especially on Sunday afternoons, two or three pipes, in the manner of so many of the legion of Peking antique-dealers — keeps a man free in the winter of those dreadful " coolie colds " (for which the city is justifiably famous), and in the summer, from dysentery. But to drink, like the Europeans do, day in and day out : *that* is dreadful ! . . . Of course Chinese gentlemen sometimes get a *little* drunk on Chinese wine (but then Chinese wine is so healthy, one drinks it only to keep well). A little too strong, sometimes, that is all ; it nevertheless possesses properties that make Chinese drunkenness different, a thing of poetry and good fellowship. But women allowing themselves to drink it ! And cocktails ! Yet in a way this scandalised contempt has in it a quality of tolerance.

Let me quote Chang twice again, in an attempt to convey this outlook. . . . First, before proceeding further, it must be taken into account that their profession occasionally obliges Chinese servants in the employment of Europeans to see life in its most unpleasant aspects ; they are under the orders of people who often fail to treat them with consideration, regarding them — and without any desire to make a secret of it — as members of an inferior and subject race, " a set of Chinks ". Moreover, at the best, European manners in distant parts of the world always tend, too, to sink to colonial standards : I mean, they are manners of the heart, the most touching of all, but without elegance ; whereas the Chinese of every class prize above all subtle and elaborate courtesy, which, cultivated for centuries, has

[1] See pp. 60-62.

even evolved an entire rhetoric of its own. I doubt if they
have much respect for the European and American kindness
and plain-speaking with which, equally, they often come
in contact. They are disillusioned.

Yes, sometimes it is more disillusionment than contempt. . . . Thus one day a note arrived from Mrs. Lulling-
Cheetham, a well-known, long-established resident in
Peking. It ran, " Dear Mr. Sitwell, I have just been able
to obtain, from impoverished members of an old Manchu
family with whom I was brought up, some wonderful
specimens of old silk. And since I think that you, with all
your knowledge and taste, may be interested, I send them
round to you by a servant, who unfortunately speaks no
English : but their prices are clearly marked on each roll
of material, ranging from 120 to 150 dollars a yard : very
reasonable, I think you will admit, when one considers how
rare they are, how hard to come by. All of them have the
Emperor Ch'ien Lung's cypher worked in at the corners
and sides. I send them to *you first*, so that you may have
your choice. Please choose the ones you want, and send
the others back to me by hand, as they are precious. . . .
Indeed, if it were not to oblige old playmates fallen on bad
times, I would not care to have them in my charge. . . .
They are too valuable. . . . And one never knows whom
one can trust nowadays, does one ? . . . But you'll think
me cynical, I fear. Yours very sincerely, Lily Lulling-
Cheetham."

The silks were pretty enough : but Chang hovered in
an airy way in the background, and presently, knowing
that his confrere spoke no English, kicked one roll with his
foot, so as to expose the price, and said to me in an off-hand
manner, as though talking about the weather, " Dealer who

supplies those silks to Mrs. Lulling-Cheetham, friend of mine : makes them himself in Nanking, and sell here for five dollars and a half a yard each ! No good."

But, also, I can give an instance of the contempt, tolerant contempt. . . . I was alone at dinner one night, when, as Chang filled my glass, he said suddenly :

"Major Champing-Chudbury, late master, him very angry with Chang one night."

"Really . . . I'm sorry to hear it. I hope you had given him no cause for complaint ? "

"Angry because not like me carry Mrs. Champing-Chudbury upstairs."

"Well, why did you do it, then ? "

"Because she could not walk."

"Poor creature ! " I said, "a cripple. . . . But isn't that *like* people ? He ought to have been *pleased* and *grateful* to you for helping her, and instead he was angry ! . . . Though actually, I believe, he was right in a way — because, if they can use their legs at all, it's supposed to be better to make them *try* to walk. . . . Otherwise the muscles atrophy."

"Mrs. Champing-Chudbury, she try walk, all right : but no good. Tellible fall ! Hear it all over house. House shake like quacker.[1] Fall velly heavy and hurt herself bad." (At this point, Chang laughed so uproariously that he had to stop talking. . . . As soon as I could make myself heard, I replied.)

"How dreadful, *poor* woman ! "

"And then she fall again, upstairs, as soon as I put her down. . . . Major Champing-Chudbury, him furious this time, he shout and he yell."

[1] Earthquake.

" But how unfeeling of him to be angry, just because she was ill."

" And it take a lot — oh, you should see, a great big lot — to make her ill too. Most of that day, she walk as if the sea were crawly."

" How very unkind of her husband to behave like that when she'd been ill all day. Very unkind, I call it."

" No, Major very kind man. Very patient, but no like empty bottles. Seventy-two empty bottles in cupboard downstairs, besides what Major find in bedroom. And Mrs. singing all the time like the prayer for Universal Peace in the Lama Temple. . . . Master not seen Lama Temple ? There's a rumour there is fair there tomorrow. . . . Perhaps Master and Chang go in motor ? "

" There's a rumour " was the proper indirect way of announcing something of which you were certain, and had long been forewarned. . . . And so, once more, I accepted his suggestion. . . . It proved an experience. This Temple is one of the largest in Peking. The Emperor K'ang Hsi first saw the light in the ancestral palace which formerly occupied its site, but, because no palace wherein, in the Chinese phrase, " a Dragon was born ", can ever again be the dwelling-place of mortals, according to custom he converted it into a temple. Moreover, being interested in Tibetan Lamaism, he dedicated it to that creed, and placed it under special Imperial patronage. For that reason, its numerous buildings are all roofed, after the same manner as the Forbidden City, with yellow or orange tiles.

The next day, when the motor drew up at the gates of the temple, the cries and music of the Devil-Dancers, who perform, only at this fair, once a year, could be heard right across the three intervening courts, all of vast extent. The crowd of pleasure-seekers — for such, rather than devout, their demeanour showed them to be — behaved as though it were a Rugby-football scrum ; but one on an immensely enlarged and, from the point of view of the possibility of violence and inflicting injury, improved scale. Pent up for a while, just as we entered, it broke like a flood through the heavily guarded gates. Police with batons and thonged whips and long poles laid about them, but got as good as they gave. They were swept through into the second courtyard, in spite of their weapons and the vigorous use to which they put them. Here fighting, all against all, began in earnest : there was more room, and, at the same time, more people to join in. The struggle centred round the tall, square black marble monument which stands in the middle (a tablet on each face gives the history of Tibetan Lamaism in four languages, Chinese on the north, Manchu on the south, Tibetan on the west, Mongolian on the east). Chang edged his way round the outside of this swearing, swaying, screaming, banging multitude, making himself " look small ", and by some means or other contrived to sidle into the inner court, taking me with him, without either of us incurring a scratch.

Here, surrounded by a mob of excited Chinese spectators, the Devil-Dancers, in carved and painted masks and rich, fantastic dresses, were whirling round and indulging in various significant antics to the sound of gongs, drums, trumpets and stringed instruments. The lamas, however, who were not disguised after this fashion, but, clad in their ordinary robes, instead gazed intently at their brothers, appeared scarcely less interesting and unusual. Those garbed in yellow came from Mongolia, those in murrey from Tibet, and their bearing, the expression of their faces, were both remote and uncouth, yet sly and challenging. Their manifest poverty had about it, too, for China, an unusual ferocity. In fact, their presence here seemed hardly less alien than that of their five terrible gods in one of the halls behind them ; the Five Defenders of the Law, as they are called, who include among their number the adored goddess of the Red Sect of Lamaism, with her black, gory face and necklace of human skulls, Kali, to whom the Thugs made their sacrifices, and Yama, the God of Death. . . . Besides these monks, others — for the monastery contains a whole army of them — were swarming in the Hall of the Wheel of the Law. Some were merely watching, or only joining in to the extent of uttering short, sharp yells at regular, rhythmic intervals, while those actually taking part squatted cross-legged on the floor, turning prayer-wheels and howl-ing — so they gave out — for Universal Peace. . . . I hope it *was* for that purpose, because I subscribed a sum toward it. But I nearly withheld my pence, for, judging purely from the sound, I had my doubts concerning it at the time. And the course of events in the subsequent few years seems to have borne them out.

The whole scene, the temple, the monument, the lamas, the dances, formed a good instance of the cosmopolitanism of Peking ; to which I shall have to allude several times in the course of the next few chapters. Like all citizens of Peking, Chang himself was cosmopolitan by tradition : but, though tolerant of foreigners, and curious concerning their ways, in his heart only the Chinese and their customs abided. Within these precincts today, he enjoyed, as did all his fellow-countrymen who composed the audience, the noise, the shouts, the music, the spectacle, the sense of occasion. . . . But I doubt if he really approved.

Mongolians and Tibetans, though former vassals, were outlandish : to them he offered the same contemptuous tolerance, combined with curiosity, that he bestowed as much upon myself as upon his former employers, the Champing-Chudburys. For all that the rites were celebrated in Peking, this fair to him remained a performance given for foreign devils by foreign devils.

The air of Peking was full of this combined contempt, tolerance and curiosity ; an atmosphere that puzzled me, for I was sure I had known something like it before ? . . . But where had it been, that great city, with an utter lack of faith in anything, yet full of superstition, abounding in temples, empty, except at the annual fairs, full of decaying works of art and of crowded streets and restaurants and theatres and shows of every kind, the centre of an empire gone to seed ? Could it have been Vienna that offered the parallel ? . . . No, not like this, a different disintegration altogether. . . . I sought to recapture its identity, but for a long time it perplexed and evaded me.

### CHAPTER FOUR

## THE WEALTH OF YESTERYEAR

Perhaps, I thought, by trying to picture to myself Peking and its surroundings as a whole, roughly sketching in as well as I am able the background and foreground, it may be possible to identify this curious sense of a familiarity with similar conditions ?

Here was a huge city, a great metropolis set in a gold and sepia plain which extended to the shadow of lovely, blue hills lying light as veined bubbles upon the horizon. Their steep slopes were covered with temples, many of the smaller ones now converted into country-houses for summer use by Europeans resident in Peking, and this change of purpose had been accomplished without any protest from the faithful, should such still exist. Disused temples stood in every other direction — I say *every*, but, owing to the increasing number of bandits in the nearer countryside, we were only able with safety to penetrate to some twenty or thirty miles along two broken-down roads ; down the rest, it was wiser to turn back toward the walls after a mile or two ; Taoist Temples, Lama Temples, Buddhist Temples, Temples of Confucius, Temples of Agriculture and the Azure Cloud, temples to the God of Fire, the God of War, the God of Literature. Some of these places of former worship were surrounded with immense courts and cloisters, decaying and overgrown, while in the shrines themselves the rows of gilded, fat-bellied gods had been hurled from their places, lay powerless and in the immobility of death, deep in white dust ; others were small and well cared for, with huge old trees hanging lop-sided above them, and little garden courts set ready for the spring, the peonies covered with matting, the shrubs only waiting for the first fine weather, the eaves brilliant with paint, the old bronzes and carvings in perfect order, the gods glossy and well groomed. . . . But how few were these in comparison with the monuments in disintegration, which, after a year or two of very picturesque decay, vanish utterly, vanish now week by week; though many of the sites they occupied were far older than the present city of Peking, some going back to the third and fourth century of our era, while nearly all the building upon them belonged to Chinese history.

The temples were as diverse in style as in their history and the cults they served. There was often about them, too, as we have already noticed in the Lama Temple, that cosmopolitan tinge continually to be noticed in religious systems. (Just as the Church of Rome carries Rome with it to London and New York, South America and the Pacific Isles, so Buddhism wafts to this cold north the balmy air of Southern India and Ceylon.) For instance, a little way off the chief road to the Western Hills, only two or three miles beyond the Hsi Chih Mên, with a vast old Gingko

A TYPICAL GATEWAY OF A TEMPLE IN PEKING

*Note the rock and trees in the foreground*

standing on each side — its trunk, in the manner of a Greek column looking more lofty because of its artful entasis, being of a texture and surface unlike that of any other tree — stood an Indian vat, a miniature five-towered edifice related to those we have seen so recently in Angkor, and unlike any other building you could find for many thousands of miles. It was not so beautiful as the Indian vats, nor so lovely as the Chinese temples round, but as it stood there, its colours glowing in the frosty sunlight, it looked indescribably exotic, had the interest of something lost and forgotten in a country far from its home. Near by, on the other hand, was an inhabited temple, very neat, except for a garden full of those natural rocks in agonised shapes [1] by which the Chinese set such store ; so full, indeed, that walking among them proved difficult, as in a maze, and it was best to look down upon them, and upon the bushes of yellow *Forsythia* in full bloom, which seemed entirely to fill up with their growth the paths between them, from a belvedere poised above on an angle of two walls ; *Forsythia*, that lovely first torch of spring, which should, even though the spelling of its name is not precisely identical, now be divorced from a sound so cluttered in the mind with sagas. And in contrast, again, to this neat temple and blossoming enclosure, we found, a mile or two away across country, with no path leading up to it, an immense monastery that had lately been used as a barrack by one of the contending semi-bandit armies. (These mysterious bodies of men had remained in the district long after hostilities were universally supposed to have ended, requisitioning supplies on the authority of their arms alone, and doing as much harm as any foreign army could have achieved in the way of general

[1] See pp. 292-293.

wantonness and destruction.) The troops had not long gone, and it had only been re-occupied about a month before by a young monk who had chanced upon it in his wanderings, just after it had been deserted. Now he was piously at work on the immense — and, one might have thought, heart-breaking — task of reconstruction he had given himself, of clearing away tangles of barbed wire, and broken logs of firewood that had, a year or two before, been magnificent groves of cypress, of mending and painting, of assembling once more those idols that were not too shattered to be beyond repair, and of tending their altars. A very friendly and simple creature, his faith was in the process of moving mountains with extraordinary ease. The manner in which, in so little time and with efforts totally unaided, he had contrived to re-introduce a little order into gardens and courts, and to renew completely the air of peace and contemplation that had formerly existed here, was in the highest degree remarkable and to be praised, but he remained quite unconscious of his own desert. He could, I am sure, see no merit in the fact that, alone, and living on nothing except the little bread or rice with which the people of the neighbouring village provided him, he had succeeded already in restoring to this beautiful and historic place its soul. A quality infinitely lovely and pathetic instilled his labour, and I often wonder whether circumstances have allowed him to finish his work.

Alas, hundreds of other temples had not been so fortunate. On every mound in the flat country, on rocks of fabulous elegance, on every crest, from ascent to ascent, of the Western Hills, rose lofty pagodas, of stone, of brick, or, in one or two instances, of faience. Nor were these pagodas the simple, slender stalks that their name, through

long acquaintance with Chinese eighteenth-century porcelain, suggests ; many of them were stout, complicated,
many-floored constructions of the Ming period or earlier,
bearing on their polygonal sides magnificently sculptured
reliefs, though all were marked by that particular tapering
away into the sky which is partly responsible for this preconceived idea of their delicacy. Long forgotten had been
the saints whose bones reposed beneath their foundations,
and now no devout ever came, as in years past, to visit
them, though the few bells that tinkled in the knife-edged
wind from their eaves and the cornices of each storey could
still make their thin, sad music travel a long way off. That
these towers had been loaded with bells was something
that, I know not why, I had never been able to believe,
until, in a brown, winter village, with snow on the ground,
and boys in fat, blue coats skating on a pool, I suddenly
heard drifting down to me from a distance this remote
and bitter jangle. But only a score or so of these inverted
bronze cups hung there now, though formerly a single
tower — the White Cloud Pagoda — of thirteen storeys,
standing in a courtyard of a temple half a mile out of
Peking — was a-tinkle with as many as three thousand four
hundred bells, which, it was said, could, when conditions
were favourable, be heard a full mile off. . . . But the days
of such profusion were over, and, when I went, just beyond
the village, to look at this tower of music, the first I had
heard, the arms and legs and heads of statues and many tiles
of the deepest blue, were lying smashed at its foot. Not even
the Peking dealers in antiques had troubled to come and steal
them.

Everywhere in the surrounding country were ruined
gardens, basins of water that had dried up, broken fountains,

the stumps of fine trees, ornamental lakes which were now frozen mud and arid rushes that crackled in the wind. The Summer Palace remained in good order, but even Dragon Pool and Jade Fountain were only just holding together, on the verge of dissolving, and all else was sinking beyond the power of resuscitation (and this, remember, is written by one accustomed to the crumbling monuments of southern countries, and only too well aware, from what he has seen in his own lifetime, that restoration is often the favourite weapon of Siva the Destroyer, and can achieve more in a few weeks than can whole centuries of decay). The Temple of Heaven has not suffered, for it is a modern building — though none the less lovely for that — having been burnt down, and rebuilt after 1889, in times when attention was still paid to the past, and its creations : but the Altar of Heaven, which goes back to the founding of Peking and, apart from its long history and the symbolism of the ceremonies for which it was built, is one of the chief objects of beauty in the whole of the Orient, will disappear, like so many other irreplaceable works of art, within the space of a few years. Its very simplicity, the nakedness under the sky of this triple-terraced circular platform, with its wonderful carved balustrade of white marble, renders it, if continually and consistently neglected, all the more liable to disaster. The sacred groves of cypress, some said to have been planted by the Emperor Yung Lo in the early fifteenth century, have been hacked down for firewood by soldiers and peasants, and temples of great esthetic value and historic interest lying within the Park, as it were, of the Altar of Heaven, have been converted into police stations and public offices.

Soon little more will be left of temples and altars, of

pagodas and monasteries, than of Yüan-Ming-Yüan, the Old Summer Palace, which formerly stood outside the grounds of the present Summer Palace built by the Empress Dowager. There, until the Anglo-French armies burnt it in 1860, and looted its treasures in order to take mementoes home to York and Lille and Roubaix and Surbiton, existed an edifice that, with its grounds, ranked as one of the marvels of the world. This, as Mr. Sacheverell Sitwell has written elsewhere,[1] was the opposite to *chinoiserie*, an oriental variation on Western themes. A unique episode in the history of taste, it was ordered by the Emperor K'ang Hsi, and carried out by Chinese architects and workmen under the superintendence of the Jesuit Fathers. Of palaces and pavilions, of formal and landscape gardens, nothing remains now but a dust-heap, in which the small children of neighbouring farmers play, throwing large stones at the few plumed helmets and trophies that remain, and battering at the balusters of a marble bridge — as I saw them doing during my first visit to the site — for the sheer joy of the thing, with a ram they had made of wood. Even the Europeans, who were so curiously responsible both for its creation and destruction, never think it worth while to

[1] See *Spanish Baroque Art* (Duckworth & Co.) by Sacheverell Sitwell, Chapter VI, for further details. In 1737, the Emperor Ch'ien Lung united the buildings erected by his two predecessors, and entrusted the general plan to Fra Castiglione, the celebrated painter. The Jesuit Attiret, Ch'ien Lung's special European artist, writes of in 1743 : " The whole façade seems to be nothing but windows and columns ; the woodwork is gilded, painted and lacquered ; the walls are of grey brick, well shaped and well glazed. The roofs are covered with glazed tiles, red, yellow, blue and violet. . . . The canals are crossed by bridges of very varied form. The balustrades of some are of white marble, well worked and sculptured in bas-relief. In the middle of the large lake rises, on a rock, a little palace with a central point that the architect chose as giving the finest view of the whole park. . . . In the Emperor's apartments can be seen the most beautiful things imaginable in furniture, ornaments, paintings in the Chinese taste, antique vases, porcelains, gold and silver cloths and silks."

drive there to see what is left, and, if asked about it, reply vaguely that it was " not at all Chinese " and " rather odd " — for they only admire the earliest and most primitive works, Stonehenges in bronze and pottery as opposed to Trianons. And yet, a visit is most rewarding, though scarcely a stone is upright or on the surface, for every piece of ornament, broken column or mask, has a quality, original, strange and exquisite. The actual disposition of the ground, the little, low artificial hills, the streams, the remains of bridges, all exhale an atmosphere that only lingers in places that have been superlatively beautiful. Long after the site is forgotten, and the last fragments of stone or marble have sunk into the ground, future generations will wonder at the enchantment that emanates from this small stretch of varied country, with its pleasantly flowing streams.

But if the palaces seem to have obtained the worst treatment from Europeans, the temples seem to have suffered most from the inhabitants of the country itself, and from members of the faiths they celebrate. Nevertheless, the peasants, from whom monks and priests, as well as soldiers, are recruited, continue to be pious in the traditional way. Wandering across the brittle winter fields, that disintegrate at each step into whirling clouds of dust, one would often pass a small piece of ground, a family holding, in which had been planted several sticks with, attached to them, pieces of white paper — or, if possible, red. On these were usually scrawled some characters. At first, I took them to have been placed there to scare off the birds, but soon I learnt their real purpose, that of messages to the spirit world, to convey to parents and grandparents the intelligence of the birth of a new male descendant.

In spite of their piety, however, in spite of their prodigious labour and their natural cleverness and ingenuity, their lot is a hard one ; the prey equally of rapacious brigands, money-lenders and tax-gatherers. In consequence — and as a result, too, of the desolation that has fallen on the larger buildings and more important monuments of the country-side — the general feeling of this beautiful and romantic landscape was one of sadness and expectancy. Everyone, both here and in the city, was waiting ; waiting for some event.

But directly you set foot in Peking, the sensation of melancholy vanished, was, in fact, precisely reversed. . . . Once within the walls, in spite of bad times, revolutions and daily alarms, a great exhilaration prevailed. Perhaps the gigantic old walls themselves afforded a false, ostrich-like feeling of security. (Certainly at night the fact of all the gates being locked and barred against the bandits, as in the European Middle Ages, in no way impeded the general gaiety of restaurants, streets and theatres, induced no depressing sense of being imprisoned for your own safety — though, in this connection, I recollect an American visitor enquiring of a friend of mine, resident in Peking, whether it was true that the city gates were shut every evening at nine, and, on this statement being confirmed, exclaiming, " Well, I can tell you here and now, we wouldn't stand for it in Detroit ! ") . . . Assuredly there was nothing in the state of affairs at the time to justify cheerfulness. Its reasons, therefore, must be sought in the national temperament ; perhaps, also, in the certainty that the climate affords, the knowledge that the winter will be dry and clear and sparkling, that the snow will fall three times, for so many days just when it is expected, that it will be safe to go for picnics in April, but that the real heat will begin in May, and thus, on through the calendar, until the end of the year ; but still more in the way in which the city has been laid out, in its fine and airy perspectives, its trees and parks and palaces, and shops. But it can be traced, too, to the certain air of luxury and cosmopolitanism which pervades it, and has always pervaded it since it was built : for much of what Marco Polo writes concerning Cambaluc remains true of its descendant, modern Peking today. There exists the same vast population (even though latterly it has a little declined), the same great numbers of foreign merchants, travellers and provincial fortune-seekers. " To this city also are brought articles of greater cost and rarity, and in greater abundance of all kinds, than to any other city in the world. For people of every description, and from every region, bring things (including all the costly wares of India, as well as the fine and precious goods of Cathay itself with its provinces). . . . Round about this great city of Cambaluc there are some two hundred other cities at various distances, from which traders come to sell their goods and buy others for their lords ; and all find means to make their sales and purchases, so that the traffic of the city is passing great." [1]

Let us enter in the middle of the morning, when peasants cluster about its gates, pushing past one another in their eagerness to reach the city, and scores of carts with wooden wheels are still lined up, waiting for official permission to creak their way through. Just inside the gigantic, nail-studded doors, men in faded blue tunics and trousers are sitting before vast mounds of pottery, jars and bowls and plates, secured by thick webbing, and are in the interminable process of haggling over them with gesticulating farmers'

[1] *The Book of Ser Marco Polo*, vol. i. pp. 414-415.

wives. . . . But the scene is still too rustic for us, since we have already watched these people driving along the roads within their self-spun veils of dust : so now we turn our feet toward the broad, old thoroughfares and streets of shops in the Chinese and Tartar Cities.

The pavements are thronged, and the northern sun spatters both the moving people and the many static surfaces of paint with the flat, sparkling discs of a picture by Canaletto. Everyone is talking, laughing, shouting, buying or selling. Carts are rattling and jolting, and cattle are being driven through the best streets by swearing farmers' boys, armed with long sticks. A line of heavily laden, double-humped camels, proud but melancholy, are making a progress down the sandy track at the side of the broad road just beyond the Palace Walls, engaged on the endless journey that is all their lives, to Tibet and the Himalayas and back again, and are bowing their necks and turning their heads, as they pass, as though in stately acknowledgement of cheers. Their drivers trudge, two in front of the caravan, two behind, in fur-edged, blue clothes with round blue caps, their Kalmuck features yellow, bored and expressionless. European ladies, the wives of diplomats, holding handkerchiefs to their noses against the spirals of the dust or possible contagion, are being drawn in triumph toward the Legation Quarter by trotting ricksha men (Scotty and Spot and Jock, their dogs, are waiting in the hall to welcome them with rasping barks which remind them of home). The pavements are hidden, so thick are the people, mostly Chinese, endlessly diverse in type, for every province, even the most distant, has here its representatives.

In no matter regarding the Chinese are Europeans so mistaken as in their idea that all of them look the same, with yellow skins, flattened noses and up-turned, slanting eyes. Here they vary from the tall, stately people of Peking, of a pale yellow, to the small, lightly built, more deeply golden people of Canton. Many have aquiline features — and this applies particularly to the Mohammedan population,[1] who came here at a late period from the western boundaries of the empire, and to members of the Mandarin families, who possess more prominent features than the coolies. (Every day the visitor to Peking detects the differences in feature and colour more distinctly ; but from the first they are unmistakable. . . . And in the course of time, in addition, his own eye alters where Europeans are concerned. . . . For example, one morning, after I had been in China for three months, I passed one of the gates of the Forbidden City, and observed, standing in it, a group of men. I thought, " How strange, they exactly resemble the paintings of Europeans on Chinese plates of the eighteenth century ! " . . . And then, suddenly, I realised that they were just ordinary Western travellers like myself, but that I was looking at them with eyes accustomed to Chinese men and women, animals, flowers and objects.)

Occasionally, we may see a Mongolian prince, in a flamboyant robe of yellow and purple brocade, and a chieftain's hat, with a feather in it, who is plainly visiting Peking for the first time in his life, and, as we pass, he peers right into our eyes — for we are the only white-devils he has so far ever encountered — with an insuperable aversion, inquisitiveness, and utter lack of self-consciousness. Or, scarcely less effective in their dress, because, though less elaborate and splendid, their clothes are more wild and tattered, we may meet a group of Mongolian clansmen —

[1] See pp. 250-252.

their faces precisely those wrongly attributed by Europeans to the Chinese in their entirety. These have come to sell droves of ponies — that absurdly resemble those T'ang pottery horses so many of which have found their way from tombs to London drawing-rooms — and having sold them, to spend the resultant money, and also a sum, previously saved up for several years for this purpose, in Peking. (Always they carry their money straight to Jade Street, to buy jewellery, their only form of investment, and the shopkeepers, informed beforehand by underground channels of the day of their arrival, invariably, in order to do good business, prepare and adopt the same stratagem, with reason confident that it will never be discovered. Aware that these clownish tribesmen possess a magpie-like impulsion toward the theft of any brightly glittering objects upon which they can lay their hands, the cunning Chinese goldsmith will leave within easy reach a few scintillating baubles of no value, and pretend not to notice when they disappear, for he knows that, once they have been allowed to pocket them, the strangers, in their ignorance, and in their secret delight at having already got something for nothing, will be willing to pay the most exorbitant price for the articles they buy in the ordinary way of business.) Sometimes, again, groups of priests or lamas from the Monastery walk by, or by chance we may catch a glimpse of the curtained litter and accompanying large retinue of the Panchen Lama of Tibet,[1] at present paying a visit to Peking in order to

[1] In 1933 the Panchen Lama of Tibet sprinkled holy water over many thousands of people in Peking and Annam, and was continually and lavishly entertained by the Government.

Apropos of this, not long after, another Tibetan, Nola Kotuhutu, while a guest of the Canton Government, publicly declared his ability to protect the people against poison gas by incantation.

have talks with prominent officials. . . . In addition, the spectacles provided by the pavement, the quarrels and the laughter, the groups talking, the children running along with their kites, the beggars planning together their acts of whining blackmail, are countless and novel of their kind. At every street corner, too, coolies are gathered round portable stoves, eating rice and drinking their green, thick tea. Moreover, the objects for sale on the kerbs, offered by vendors carrying trays or in some instances seated on the pavement itself, the lanterns and artificial flowers, the Mongolian buckles like rough, Merovingian jewels, the sweets wrapped up in coloured paper, the balloons and toys and pieces of silk, the little painted boxes and printed calendars, are hardly less charming, and certainly no less gay, than the objects to be bought near by in the shops.

These are without number. . . . I have lived a great deal in Italy, and can remember the hundreds of antique shops, full of lovely objects, in Rome and Venice and Florence, and the scores in the smaller provincial towns : but never have I seen so many as in Peking ; at least ten thousand, I should hazard at a guess, all equipped with enormous staffs. How these establishments carry their over-head charges, by what means they pay their assistants, I cannot imagine. Directly a stranger crosses the threshold, eight or ten boys in grey robes stop their gossip and come trotting out to meet him from an inner room, with that same expert air with which a troupe of Chinese jugglers runs on to the stage to receive applause. And very beautiful are many of the bronzes and pieces of lacquer and porcelains, the stone heads of the Buddha or his hands, the bulls' heads in jade and glass beads, the screens and silks and eighteenth-century European clocks, which they sell : even the modern imitations, where they can be told apart, are charming, if expensive. . . . Then, not far from my house, were collected, each with its own shop attached, nearly all the factories wherein are made the celebrated Jade Trees. . . . These miniature and precious trunks, a foot or half a foot high, with berries of cornelian or quartz or topaz or amethyst, with leaves of jade and blossoms of crystal, clear or smoky or mauve or pink, are no less effective and grotesquely lovely than when their prototypes were first fashioned many centuries ago. And in bare rooms running round a courtyard, and lit by the bright sun of Peking, it is possible not only still to buy them, but also to watch them being made.

But the real, growing trees, to be bought in florists, situated for the most part near the Hata Men,[1] are even more fantastic and full of poetry. These shops offer in midwinter a synthesis of spring and early summer as the Chinese see it ; to enter them is comparable to finding yourself in the fabulous flowery groves of a newly discovered continent, where all the species that grow in your own garden have been transmuted, through thousands of years of cultivation apart, into new forms, the flowers into new shapes, and invested with new and strange tones of colour, while within this small space has been condensed, also, the scent of whole orchards in an enchanted spring. . . . Here, indeed, the Chinese have indulged in their " peculiar propensity for dwarf and monstrous growth ", as a former

[1] The Hata Gate is a very good instance of the age of many of the Peking names, so often erroneously believed to be no older than the founding of the present city by the Emperor Yung Lo. It is named after a Mongol, Prince Hata, whose palace was on a site in this neighbourhood during the preceding Yuan Dynasty, and goes back to some two hundred years earlier. See *In Search of Old Peking*, by L. C. Arlington and William Lewisohn.

traveller [1] termed it. These little blossoming trees (for the shops deal in plants more than in cut flowers), each crooked, bent branch in such perfect grotesque relationship to the next, so well balanced and inevitable that no other position for it would seem possible, might well have constituted the model for every Chinese decorative artist of the last twenty centuries. Furthermore, by no means the least pleasure to be derived from visiting these caged orchards was to watch the real Pekingese customers making their purchases. First, they would walk round the shop, examining all its contents, apples and quinces, peaches and cherries with their heads in little rosy clouds or bowed under a load of snow, orange-trees, bearing at the same time their blossom and their fruit, some of these glowing like lamps, others green-bronze and nestling hidden in their glossy foliage, and little formal bushes of button roses, wistaria plants, about two or three feet high, coiled and serpentine, their drooping fragile clusters the colour of storm-clouds or an etiolate white. Having fixed his heart upon one particular example, the prospective buyer would then peer down at it for ten minutes at a time from every angle, appraising after this standard and his own experience its various faults and perfections, haggling inimitably over the price demanded — which seldom, even for Europeans, ranged up to more than four or five shillings — and pointing out to the blandly unconvinced shopkeeper a blemish, here, upon a petal, or a possible failure of line, there, in a twig.

It was a lengthy performance : but then it must be remembered that, by the custom of ages, the Chinese esthetic has been applied to flowers as much as paintings

[1] See previous note on Robert Fortune, p. 166, note 1.

or sculptures, and that the cultivation of these winter trees constitutes an art,[1] and a very ancient one. By the employment of this code, in addition to the very important question of symmetry, no plant and no single blossom can be allowed to belong to the category of the beautiful if it presents an ugly, or even an untidy, appearance at any stage of its development ; however lovely it may be in flower, it is admired proportionately to its state of perfection in every season of the year, in bud, or when the petals are falling, or when the tree is bare, as much as in full bloom. Never must it look dishevelled or miserable. And for his own self-respect, it is necessary for the customer to bear all these points in mind before deciding which plant to buy.

According to Lich'en,[2] they are called " Hall-Flowers " in Peking, because, being a favourite present for the New Year, they stood in the hall of nearly every house there at the time of that festival. Peonies, plum blossom and red-peach blossom, jasmine, begonia and lilac were all for

---

[1] Robert Fortune describes the manner in which these trees were grown. In *Three Years' Wanderings in the Northern Provinces of China* (Murray, London, 1847), he writes : " Stunted varieties were generally chosen [for cultivation], particularly if they had side branches opposite or regular, for much depends upon this ; a one-sided dwarf tree is of no value in the eyes of the Chinese. The main stem was then in most cases twisted in a zigzag form, which process checked the flow of the sap, and at the same time encouraged the production of side branches at those parts of the stem where they were most desired. When these suckers had formed roots . . . they were looked over and the best taken up for potting. The same principles . . . were still kept in view." The pots contained very little soil, and the plants were given only just enough water to keep them alive, but if anything occurred to break this severe regime, they quickly reverted. " Whilst the branches were forming," he continues, " they were tied down and twisted in various ways. . . . Sometimes, as in the case of peach and plum trees . . . the plants are thrown into a flowering state, and then, as they flower freely year after year, they have little inclination to make vigorous growth " (pp. 96, 97-98).
[2] See Tun Lich'en's *Annual Customs and Festivals in Peking*.

sale at that season (January and February), being reared in hot-houses by methods introduced into China during the Han Dynasty. . . .[1] Certainly the love of these trees — which, just as much as any other medium, afforded a means of self-expression for artists — seems to have permeated the whole Chinese people from very early times, and the reason for it, I think, must be sought in more than one direction. . . . First of all, they honour ingenuity in itself, and are proud of it, being willing, moreover, to occupy hundreds of years of human life in struggling toward the — to them — perfect gold-fish or Pekingese dog or plant ; and, since professions were largely hereditary, the production of such a living work of art would be the easier in that this ideal passed over the years from father to son, and every succeeding generation had been bred and grown up with it. In addition, Nature has bestowed upon them a sense of the grotesque which no other race possesses to the same degree ; a sense continually manifested in all their productions. And, finally, it must be sought, too, in the Chinese reverence for age. They love old people and old things. And, since their small houses cannot contain a four-hundred-year-old forest tree or a two-hundred-year-old fruit tree, then they must tame them to domestic size, and be content with the ingenious semblance which results. . . . An anecdote told by Robert Fortune [2] well bears out this last contention. He tells us how he dug up, on the hills near Hong Kong, a most singular example of a Lycopodium, a pretty little plant which often shows a likeness to a miniature tree. He took it back to the Gardens,

[1] 206 B.C. to A.D. 264.
[2] *Three Years' Wanderings in the Northern Provinces of China.* (Murray, London, 1847.)

where he was keeping the other plants which he was collecting for the Horticultural Society. " 'Hai-yah,' said the old compradore, when he saw it, and was quite in raptures of delight. All the other coolies and servants gathered round the basket to admire this curious little plant. I had not seen them evince so much gratification since I showed them the ' old man Cactus ' (*Cereus senilis*). . . . On asking them why they prized the Lycopodium so much, they replied, in Canton English, ' *Oh, he too muchia handsome ; he grow only a leete and a leete every year ; and suppose he be one hundred year oula, he only so high* ', holding up their hands an inch or two higher than the plant."

Old age, convenient size, and, above all, perfection of grotesque form are, then, the attributes which the Chinese gardeners and florists still cherish. Often I left the shop feeling that I had earned their contempt by a neglect of the rules, had been trapped too easily by the scent of an orange-tree or by the pallid beauty of a magnolia. Nevertheless, though weakness thus made me unable to abide by it, I could grasp, every now and then, the Chinese point of view, which had enabled them to produce these lovely creations. Even more astonishing, however, than the way in which they could bend and reduce whole trees to an esthetic formula, I found their success with more transient things, such as flowering bulbs. To these, swiftly growing and short-lived, the century-rule could not be applied, and sleight-of-hand must serve instead : thus narcissi and jonquils, for example, are grown in flat, shallow, square pots, their bulbs being planted upside down, with only stones and water to nourish them, so that they are obliged to conform to the same elegant, if tortured, standards.

All these shops and trades help to impart an air of

luxury long installed : yet the general impression of the streets outside is one of great business activity, more than of wealth. . . . The older Manchu nobles, many of them formerly very rich men, now seldom cared to go beyond their gardens, so greatly, if they walked abroad, did they suffer from the sense of their unpopularity and loss of power, and so deeply did the general disintegration — as they saw it — that had occurred since the fall of the Empire sadden them. There were still large fortunes in Peking belonging to Chinese merchants, or to the descendants of nobles or contractors who had managed to profit greatly under the old regime. But Shanghai or Hong Kong provided a safer refuge for them, and many of those rich by descent — as opposed to those who, engaged in commerce, were unable to leave the city in which they transacted business — had there found sanctuary. Even in Shanghai, however, it was necessary for them, for fear of being kidnapped, never to leave their homes without an armed escort of two White Russian giants. . . . It was pathetic, therefore, to notice how these true natives of Peking, though conscious of the danger to which, notwithstanding the continual presence of their bodyguard, such a visit exposed them, could seldom resist returning for a few days, every three months or so, to the city of their birth and upbringing. The long journey there and back, and their ensuing peril, they found well worth while, if only for so short a time they could breathe their proper air and visit favourite restaurants to eat dumplings or Peking duck.

And here, since food plays so important a part in the life of Peking, we must take a cursory glance at its restaurants (a subject in itself worthy of a whole book). But it must be remembered that those to which we now turn our attention, though not all of them expensive — and indeed, by Western standards, often very cheap — are intended for the well-to-do.[1]

In China as a whole, the food differs entirely from province to province : and this heterogeneity is not so much regional as national, the cooking of the Peking district and of Shansi, of Canton and Szechuan, being as dissimilar as the dishes of France and Rumania, Poland and Italy. For the small, ordinary dinner in house or restaurant, the Peking provincial system is the most suitable, being plainer and better adapted to the climate, for the food of Szechuan or of Canton — though each excellent — is by its nature richer and more complicated. In the same way, the straightforward dinner to be obtained in house or restaurant here is to be preferred, from a gastronomic point of view, to the feast, of which, though it may not be openly acknowledged, the whole menu — and especially such costly essentials to a banquet as Shark's Fin or Bird's Nest Soup — has been designed by tradition to serve an aphrodisiac rather than a palatal purpose.[2] But, though the actual food of the neighbourhood may be the most pleasant and healthy for every day, Peking once more exhibits its metropolitan — or, rather, cosmopolitan, for China must be re-

[1] For these pages concerning Chinese food, I must make, once more, my grateful acknowledgments to Messrs. Arlington and Lewisohn (*In Search of Old Peking* — see chapter, p. 267, entitled " Wine, Women and Song "), and to Mr. R. W. Swallow (*Sidelights on Peking Life* — see chapter, p. 53, entitled " Feasts and Restaurants "). I must also thank Miss Corrinne Lamb for the help she has given me by her book (*The Chinese Festive Board* — Henri Vetch, Peking, 1935) ; I must not omit, also, to thank my many kind friends in Peking, European and Chinese, for their invitations to dinner, and unnecessary exhortatory encouragements to eat and drink more than was good for me.

[2] All the same, Bird's Nest Soup is delicious. It is now mostly a synthetic product.

garded as a continent more than a country — character ; by
sheltering within its walls hundreds of restaurants representative of each province. Many of them, moreover, have
been famous for two, three or, even, four centuries :
(considerably older than restaurants in the West ; the most
ancient of which were in Paris, founded in order to keep
themselves alive during, or just after, the Revolution, by
chefs formerly in the service of great noblemen who had
been banished or guillotined). Though, with the removal
of the government to Nanking, the former capital had lost
a little of its culinary glamour, it is not to be wondered
at that it remained — and no doubt to this day still remains
— the paradise of the Chinese gourmet, for its restaurants
are celebrated throughout the East, and the number of
them in existence is variously computed as between six
thousand and nine hundred.

Nor in China is this regarded as any evidence of greed ;
no such vice exists. Cookery ranks there as an art.
Further, the Chinese vaunt that, though, alas, painting,
the drama, sculpture and music are all in decadence, this,
one of their great arts, still survives in all its pristine
splendour. And, indeed, it is this approach toward their
meal, so admirable in many respects, that renders it far
from easy for a visitor to obtain any recipes : because if,
for instance, he enquires of a Chinese chef there, " How
much chicken-liver do you put in ? " he will receive the
reply, " As much as you judge to be right for it ", instead
of the precise European answer, " one and a half ounces ",
or if he asks, " And for how long do you cook it ? " will
be met with, " Until it seems to you perfect ", in place of
the expected " for twenty-five minutes over a slow fire ".
And this rejoinder is dictated by no desire to defeat curi-

osity. No, it is the response of an artist ; so might a painter talk if someone put to him the question, "How long does it take you to finish a picture ? "

But art enters, also, into the placing as well as cooking of a meal, great attention being paid to the sites of many of the restaurants. Thus, though the positions of the majority are due merely to convenience, some stand on the shores of lakes or streams, and many within their own gardens, by the side of flowering trees or under the shade of some gnarled and massive trunk : nearly all possess terraces and courtyards, entirely painted, gay with pinks and greens and blues and reds ; moreover, now it is permitted, as well, to give dinner parties in one of the canopied Imperial barges,[1] so that, while floating among the lotuses of the North Sea Lake, fortunate guests can sample at their ease the art of a chef formerly in the employment of the Empress Dowager.

The newcomer should be warned that if he wishes his dinner in any restaurant to be the best that it can supply, he should order it *at least* forty-eight hours beforehand. . . . As for the serving of the meal, nothing could be more simple : and the simplicity is from choice. There are no napkins, no tablecloth, no cutlery and no waiting : but there is a Chinese alternative for each. . . . The usual hour for dinner in a restaurant varies between six and seven-thirty, and every party is accommodated in a separate room. On arrival, a cup of hot tea is drunk : another being consumed immediately before, as well as immediately after, the meal. The guest finds by his side a small bowl of rice, to accompany the whole of the ensuing dinner, together

---

[1] The end-papers of this book are reproduced from a wall-paper which the Empress Dowager used for the decoration of the Imperial barges.

with a diminutive saucer of brown soy, Chinese alternative for salt. Each set of eight or ten small dishes is placed on the table, and the diner helps himself to what he likes with the aid of chop-sticks, which are retained during the entire meal. Little bowls of different kinds of soup are handed to him twice or three times in the course of it, for they are supposed to aid digestion, and Chinese wine is served throughout. Directly dinner is over, small, coarse towels, dipped in boiling water and then squeezed out, are brought round, and each person wipes with its damp, steaming surface his hands and face. (The habit is physically comforting, but since two or more guests usually share the same towel— and in theatres, where they are thrown considerable distances in the air across the auditorium, from one person to another, often five or six— these warm cloths form one of the surest mediums for the spreading of those several dreadful infections of the eye so rife in China.) The guests then rise from their places and seat themselves at another clean table on the opposite side of the room, where they find dessert and sun-flower seeds, and drink the after-dinner cup of tea and continue with their wine.

The whole great land of China contributes to the fare of Peking : but its own unrivalled materials are ducks and sheep, to which the presence of a very small quantity of salt in the soil of the meadows and the water of the rivers just outside the city imparts a special flavour. For this reason, no doubt, the Pei-I-Fang, outside the Shun-Chih-Mên, specialises in Peking Duck, famous throughout the East (but the birds are here kept in a dark room and artificially fattened), while the celebrated Cheng-Yang-Lou, outside Ch'ien Mên— a restaurant which has been open for nearly three hundred years — offers, as the feature of its winter menu, mutton grilled on an iron plate : though in the summer they abandon this for crabs fed on sesame seed. The numerous places which specialise alone in Peking mutton, are usually kept by Mohammedans [1] : then there is the Peking dumpling, to which several references have been made in these pages, an inexpensive local dish, popular with every class and almost exactly similar to Italian *ravioli.* Indeed, the Chinese in their fondness for *pasta*, of which innumerable kinds are to be met with, and for rice, very much resemble the Italians.

Since the city is so full of restaurants, and since, as a rule, they boast an immense repertory (the Chinese systems of food including hundreds of different recipes), it would be useless to attempt the enumeration of either one or the other. . . . I here append, therefore, only a few favourite dishes, beginning, in one restaurant, with a soup said to be made from stock over sixty years old ; Fried Prawns ; Turnip Cakes à la Shantung ; White Fungus cooked in Wine ; Tortoises' Eggs ; Bamboo Shoots with Shredded Ham and Sea-slugs, à la Szechuan ; Boiled Bear's Paws ; Scalded Mutton ; Fried Fish-lips ; Roast Turtle ; Minced Pork and Cabbage with Mushrooms and Bamboo Shoots, served in rind of Bean Curd ; a kind of black Caviare, boiled in vinegar and red pepper ; Stuffed Chicken ; clear soup made from the lips and gills of fish, Baked Water-Chestnuts, Sweet-and-Sour Fish, Chicken Velvet ; Ducks' Tongues with Bamboo Shoots ; Chicken with Walnuts ; and Pudding of the Seven Heavenly Flavours. . . . It will be noticed how often bamboo shoots, one of the most delicious and poetic discoveries of the Chinese, figure in

[1] See pp. 250-252.

this list. . . . Of the other items, Sweet-and-Sour Fish is particularly good, and a very usual dish ; for it, a carp is generally chosen, and cooked in vinegar, sugar and Chinese wine. Chicken Velvet is Szechuanese and consists of chicken breasts pounded up with cream. The Pudding of the Seven Heavenly Flavours, the most appreciated of all Chinese *entremets*, contains numberless ingredients, including lotus roots, on a foundation of millet. As for the Stuffed Chicken, it sounds innocuous and usual, but Messrs. Arlington and Lewisohn [1] give the following account of its preparation. " After the entrails have been removed it is stuffed with various condiments and hung in the air for several months, with feathers intact. When thoroughly dried, the feathers and condiments are removed, and the chicken is stewed. Makes very good eating. . . ." To some, perhaps, these dishes may sound outlandish ; but how would the detailed description of the content of a Vol-au-vent Toulousien (than which no name could be more ethereal) sound, if duly catalogued : Cocks'-combs and Chickens' Gizzards, sliced up with Mushrooms and Ducks' Liver ? . . . One fact remains ; Chinese food *is* excellent : though to some — and to myself among them — the best European food seems better.

Concerning the accompanying wines, though often agreeable, it would be idle to pretend that they can bear comparison with our own. They are usually made from rice — though some have, instead, a basis of corn — and so, since they take a very long time to mature, forty years is by no means too old for them. Nevertheless, by taste and bouquet they are correctly classified as wines rather than as spirits, and the most pleasant of them are reminiscent,

[1] See Arlington and Lewisohn's *In Search of Old Peking.*

both in flavour and colour, of very dry, pale sherry. Chinese wine is always served hot out of a pewter or china wine-pot (resembling, but smaller than, a teapot), and a good many, seven or eight, little cups of it are drunk during dinner. Though the idea of drinking *hot* white wine may not appeal at first to the European, it is, notwithstanding this prejudice, the correct concomitant to these particular dishes, carefully calculated by long experience to match them and bring out their flavours, and, in addition, while being in itself palatable, produces an enlivening effect. . . . Among other wines — apart from these white ones — that can be drunk, are some both flavoured and coloured with pomegranate, with bamboo leaves or with lotus flowers. Another, similar to these, which I liked, but which is very strong and often handed round like a cordial after meals, is a pale pink " Pai-kan ", somewhat in the nature of kirsch, except that it tastes of roses instead of cherries. . . . A fierce wine which, so far as I know, I have never sampled, is Kao-Liang, distilled from millet, with pigeon-droppings added to give it body.[1]

Finally, before taking leave of a restaurant, we must notice the noise and laughter issuing from other rooms, and especially from one large dinner party of men, who, between the courses, play those mysterious games which the Chinese so much enjoy ; games that consist for the most part in throwing out your arms and fingers in front of you, and shouting, while the forfeit or prize — I was never certain which — consists in drinking, straight down, so many glasses of wine.

An ordinary dinner, but of an elaborate order, costs much less than anywhere in Europe : but *feasts* are very

[1] *In Search of Old Peking.*

expensive, because of the delicacies considered essential to their nature, out of compliment to the guests. Thus Shark's Fin — which is the special part of a very special shark's fin — is dearer than the best caviare in London, Paris or New York. . . . Though, therefore, both the city and the country round were in a state of disintegration, the rich man could still proceed to his banquet in Peking without hindrance, in much the same way that in Rome, not long before the sacking of it and its consequent collapse, the wealthy patrician would still be carried in his litter from his villa in the Campagna to some feast in the city, where he could consume his favourite Dormice Baked in Honey or Nightingales' Tongues.

Moving from the heated rooms, and from the heating effect of food and wine, into the frozen night air of the winter street in Peking, the rich man will find knots of beggars waiting for alms outside. . . . Of these, not the least pitiful, but certainly the most menacing, will be Russian ; former officers in the Imperial Army, who have somehow found their way across Asia, and now, ragged, hopeless, desperate and demoralized, spend what little money they can extort from passers-by on drink and drugs, and who, since for so long they have been under the starvation line, become mad on a single glass of vodka, so that their behaviour is often braggart, aggressive and menacing. . . . But the Chinese beggar, for all his woes, is philosophic by nature : he recognises the right of the rich to spend money, and of the poor to beg rather than work. A pleasure-lover himself in his miserable way, he understands the rich man's love of enjoyment of the same sort. (Money spent on rare books or pictures he might, on the other hand, a little resent.) . . . And so, the bodyguard of Midas was employed to protect him, not against the poor, but against the contending political, and piratical, generals, against thieving governments — or, if you prefer it, against virtuous governments who disapproved of the manner in which his fortune had been acquired, and so meant, in consequence, if they could catch him alive, to bring a charge against him, and see that it was taken away from him and applied in other, less contaminated, directions.

The poor are so tolerant, then, that they will even tolerate the rich, just as the irreligious here tolerate the devout. But, since most of the Peking amusements that are left — apart from the theatre — are linked with religion, and since, further, the religious side has been almost completely forgotten, this is more easy to understand. Yet formerly the rich, too, provided entertainment for the poor. The people of Peking love spectacles, and, in the times of the Emperors, constant ceremonies were staged for them to enjoy. The Emperor might pass on his way to the Summer Palace, or to sacrifice at the Altar of Heaven, and there would be the procession to watch. Or, for instance, on the sixth day of the Sixth Month, the Imperial Elephants were taken down to the moat outside the Tartar City to be washed, and all Peking made holiday for the occasion. Then the inexorable Chinese calendar always imposed upon the rich certain details of costume, recurring at regular dates in the year, to which the populace could look forward. Thus the nobles of the Court, and those officials entitled to wear them (no ordinary person, however wealthy or influential, was allowed to don them), adorned themselves, on the first day of the Eleventh Month, with sables, known here as " jackets turned inside out ", and discarded them with equal punctuality, in favour of silver-fox furs, on the ninth day of the First Month. And the Bodyguard outside Ch'ien Ching Mên and the state gates of the Forbidden City would, too, come out in sable jackets on a particular morning in the Eleventh Month.[1] But all these free spectacles have now vanished from the scene, leaving the loafer (of whom, as in all great cities, there are considerable numbers) disconsolate, for the road-drill does not gladden his heart and ear as it does that of his confrere in London. . . . Only religion is left him for the comfort of his eye, if not of his soul. He has less to look at, but looks at it just as much.

For example, though the extreme pomp of weddings and funerals had been officially discouraged by the Republic, the demand for it in the hearts of the people is strong enough to defeat any quantity of government decrees. Down the great avenue of the city one still sees the long processions of mourners in white (some of them incorporating at a small rate of pay the loafers themselves), carrying long sheaves of white artificial flowers, or the splendid red litter of a bride, with its retinue of attendants in scarlet clothes, both heralding it and following behind it. And then there were always the fairs, perpetual fairs. . . . The crowds, stopping to give alms before they enter, are pouring into the courts — at other times deserted — of the temple of the day. According to their means, they buy sweets and apples, and silks and antiques, and badly cured furs, and paper lanterns, and Western hats and, even, chickens and small, grunting black-and-tan pigs, squealing and rocking on their short legs. The background of arches and painted eaves and tiled roofs, of decaying shrines and old trees, sets off the animated bustle of the jostling, pushing groups, always with an undercurrent of small children hit-

[1] See Tun Lich'en's *Annual Customs and Festivals in Peking.*

A CONTORTIONIST PERFORMING IN A TEMPLE FAIR AT
PEKING (T'IEN CHIAO)

ting and running beneath their elbows, while the sun flickers over them its flat, golden light, as though a boy were playing with a piece of mirror.

Many of these fairs last for three or four days, but the identical " first-night audience ", as it were, of beggars will always be present on the opening morning, spending the previous night as best they can, on the ground outside. And it must be admitted that, by their various states of anomaly, by their thick winter paddings of rags and patched blue trousers, and by their faces, some empty of feeling like that of a simpleton, others cunning or tragic in the extreme, with eyes fixed on an unknown point beyond the physical horizon, they succeed in imparting a note of morbid interest to the scene, fitting in under the wings of dust that rise on the wind from the disintegrating buildings, and against the background of broken walls and temples and ancient cedars, with the same certainty with which the Neapolitan beggar accords with his coloured domes, cloisters and volcanoes. Further, it is interesting to note how some curious but un-erring instinct always prompts them to choose for their swarming the visitor by nature the most nervous of atten-tions from such a living collection of rare diseases and acci-dents of birth, the most easily nauseated by them. But they are quite jolly about it, cackling with laughter, and winking at him their suppurating eyes, as they throng round, flourishing their stumps and thrusting upon him their most secret sores.

Indeed, for all the obvious misery of their condition, they seem a jovial enough band, continually shouting and laughing, except for an occasional professional moan. . . . But the least pitiful and heart-rending of them, present on every occasion, was a healthy old couple, man and wife.

He was bearded and plump, with a shrewd, good-humoured, rather rustic face ; his wife was thin, with amused old eyes, while her clothes bore some semblance to the covering of human beings : blue trousers, blue coat and black cap. The openness with which they dared to prepare their turn was in itself diverting. First they would choose a suitable position, and then, after sprinkling herself with several handfuls of dust (fortunately for their act, at a fair always easy enough to find), it was her part to lie down. She would remain quite still, as though in a faint, or perhaps dead, while he would stretch himself along the ground at right angles to her, with his head pillowed on her stomach, groaning for hours together in the most pitiful manner. The whole scene was delightfully counterfeit. Nobody for a moment believed that anything had just happened to them ; it was obvious, on the contrary, that, as such things go, they were both of them — but especially the old man — quite comfortable. Yet though, plainly, nothing was permanently wrong with either of them, few passers-by could resist contributing a few coppers toward their maintenance. . . . The protagonists themselves, I think, thoroughly enjoyed these outings, and often I used to see them in the evening, after it was over, having a cosy bowl of bamboo soup together at the stall of a street-vendor.

While these crowds are struggling through the doors of the courts, their faces a little red from the cold, their eyes turning everywhere, like the eyes of birds, so as to miss nothing, the innumerable temples in other parts of the city will be completely empty save for the rows of shining-faced gods, lacquered and gilded, or the statues of saints and holy men. The Four Heavenly Kings,[1] whose gigantic

[1] See note 2 on p. 131, *ante.*

wooden images, twenty foot high or more, and painted in very strong colours, guard the entrance to every Buddhist temple, standing in a kind of gate-house, two on each side, their faces respectively a ferocious red — like that of our own generals — white, blue and black, their eyes blazing, their swords ready in their hands, now posture to the empty air. (I always found these guardians very disconcerting to the ideas I had previously formed concerning Buddhism ; they in no way suggest contemplation or peace, but rage and vengeance.) Not even a solitary beggar lingers outside in the winter sunshine. The altars have no food on them, and the breath of incense that still hangs under the painted rafters and red and blue ceilings is due, merely, to all the sticks burnt in these halls during many hundreds of years past.

Thus the tolerance that at present prevailed was evil as well as good, being born of an absolute state of disbelief and of not-caring, as much as of a broad mind : moreover it was accompanied by an enormous amount of superstition. Not only does the Peking mind, even the most free-thinking, abound with portents, omens and magics, but many ghosts haunt it, together with will-o'-the-wisps and fairies.[1] These ghosts are more harmful than ours, for they are perpetually, in order to gain their own freedom, luring and driving men to their death, or even, with true simplicity of plan, killing strangers by the shock of their materialisation. Continually the drowned thus rise on dark nights to misguide the feet of human beings and lead them into the water : while evil spirits exist who build up round men invisible rooms, thus walling them up alive, and others

[1] The reader anxious to know more of these beliefs is advised to read chapter xii of *Sidelights on Peking Life*, by Robert W. Swallow.

who urge them to hang themselves, actually holding the rope in position for their victims (one of these lives in a garden in the Legation Quarter !), or Demon Barbers come and shave off a man's hair while he is asleep, so that it never will grow again. Idols in temples can be possessed, and so can living people ; these last often by dead relatives, who impose upon them their ways of speaking and tricks of manner. Of fairies, the fox-fairy is the most usual, and, though by nature intensely mischievous, aids mortals more often than he injures them. (The Fox Tower was formerly badly haunted by these fox-fairies, and one is said to live, too, in the Temple of Heaven, but he is an exception to his tribe, epicene and malignant. He appears either as a beautiful woman or good-looking man, and friendship with him entails death at no very distant period.) Snake, badger and hedgehog, though not as influential in the spirit world as the fox, are also to be mistrusted on psychical grounds : their powers, as opposed to the often helpful activities of the fox, are those of the poltergeist, throwing stones and rattling doors and windows : and victims must remember that the professional exorcizer who can deal with a fox may be powerless with a hedgehog, and so it is important first to identify precisely the species. Finally there is an innocuous but unpleasant ghost, a black patch, without arms, legs or head, who likes to wander about at night. . . . Against these ghosts and evil influences there are many remedies, such as biting the tip of the middle finger and smearing the intruders with the blood from it, or rubbing your hair very violently : while a mirror over your door will defeat spirits that want to enter it, then thrown awry in their orientation. A lion on the roof cornice is also said to be of some use.

GUILD PERFORMERS OUTSIDE THE GATES OF PEKING

Strict in their superstitions and superstitious observances, the Chinese have always been broad-minded where religion is concerned. For centuries the people of Peking, as a whole, have been in the habit of attending any temple for which they felt in the mood, whether Confucian, Taoist or Buddhist : for if Confucius continued to offer a philosophy to the philosophically-minded, the other two religions afforded opportunities of indulging in the most ample polytheism. Thus it is indicative that in one building [1] alone in the Imperial City, there is a circular hall which formerly housed a thousand Buddhas, now, alas, utterly vanished, while the edifices at the side, originally constructed in the sixteenth century, still shelter a very divergent body of gods and goddesses, including in their select ranks the Twenty-Four Dragon Kings, regnant over such elemental features of earth and universe as sun, moon, mountain, rivers and air ; the Twelve Dragon Gods, who control the Goat, Monkey, Cock, Dog, Pig, Rat, Ox, Tiger, Hare, Dragon, Serpent and Horse of the Zodiac ; and the God of Thunder and Goddess of Lightning.[2] Nor must it be forgotten that in Pei-Hai, not so far away, stands the Altar of Silkworms, where sacrifices were offered to the God of Mulberry Trees, and that next to it is another altar where the Empress used to preside, offering sacrifices to the Goddess of Silkworms. There also existed in the city formerly, a temple to the God of Horses : a worship which the English mind finds no difficulty in accepting.[3]

Polytheism itself has now given way to superstition, and when the modern men and women of Peking visit a temple, except for a fair, more often it is to have their

---

[1] The Ch'ien Shêng Tien in Chung Hai.
[2] Arlington and Lewisohn's *In Search of Old Peking*.    [3] *Ibid.*

fortunes told according to some ancient system of augury, evolved through the centuries from the placing of the holy images, than for worship. . . . On the other hand, should something suddenly go wrong in their daily lives, the same people will often suffer a sudden, if transient, conversion, becoming for a short time extravagantly, abjectly devout. And for this, their friends would neither despise nor respect them, but would, with quiet conviction, await a recovery as swift. . . . Only the Mohammedans of Peking still adhere with an extreme severity to their creed and its tenets.

The Mohammedan community affords another example of the cosmopolitan derivation of the people of Peking, as well as an excellent instance of its romantic survivals. These Moslems often present, as I have said, a different appearance from their fellow citizens ; which deviation may in part be responsible for their unpopularity. Their history, though, is more probably the cause of it ; they are for the most part descended from prisoners taken at the outer borders of the present Chinese Turkestan at the time of the campaign there in the reign of K'ang Hsi.[1] Thus, in addition to being originally of alien blood, their status at first was practically that of an enslaved nation, until, by the gallantry they showed, they established their value as soldiers of the Emperor, and were rewarded by an improvement in their lot and tacit permission to worship in their own way.

Another reason, however, for the undeserved lack of esteem in which they are held by the populace, can be traced very surely, like that of the Quakers in England during former times, to their commercial success. They possess a certain reputation for making good bargains and for keeping business in the hands of their co-religionists :

[1] 1662–1723.

by those who distrust them it is even said that nine-tenths
of the antique dealers of Peking are of this faith. But the
people of Peking leave them in peace, though they dis-
approve of them and incline to mock them. Thus, alleging
that they manifest too great a partiality for meat, their chief
district has been named Niu Chieh, or Cow Street, in the
same way in which, in the eighteenth century, a street full
of Quakers might have obtained the name of " Tea Lane "
or " Cocoa Alley ".[1] And this way in which they were
treated has left a sure mark upon them, quite as definite as
their own heredity, and has made them into a peculiar
people, set apart. Yet, though proud of their religion,
they betray a singular unwillingness to admit to it. They
have their own large quarters in the city, with the appropriate mosques : yet, when I asked a native of Peking who
was working for me — and whom I knew to be a Mohammedan — to explain to me where I could find the chief
mosque, he affected not to know and only vaguely to be
aware of its general position, though undoubtedly he worshipped there every Friday of his life. . . . Similarly, when
I arrived in the quarter only inhabited by Moslems, it was
very curious how little the people in the streets knew about
the locality : none of them could possibly direct me. . . .
Eventually I found it for myself, a large but very discreet
mosque. From the outside it pretended to be a Chinese
temple of the familiar type, with old trees, tiled roof and

---

[1] Still more they condemn them for manifest partiality for mutton. In that
most amusing as well as informative of guide-books, Arlington and Lewisohn's
*In Search of Old Peking*, the authors write : " Occasionally, out of pure spite, a
Chinese opens a pork shop opposite that of a Mohammedan butcher and, in
order to frighten off the sheep that are brought to the Mohammedan shop, has
the picture of a ferocious tiger painted across the front of his own shop. The
other then retaliates by hanging up a large mirror in which appears the reflection
of the tiger that will then, of course, devour the pigs ! " (p. 220).

slanting, brilliantly painted eaves ; but once you entered
you found yourself in a whitewashed mosque, crowned
with a shallow dome, and containing a high pulpit ; such
a place of worship as you might expect to find anywhere
between Marrakesh and Baghdad, Timbuctoo and Sarajevo,
but scarcely in this so distant part of the world.

It will be seen, then, that the tolerance in matters of
belief of Peking is no new symptom (though the decay of
the Chinese national religion was not to be observed in
other times), and the number of different faiths that took
advantage of it was very considerable. As I looked round
the mosque, therefore, it rather surprised me, bearing this
liberty of faith in mind, that there appeared—though Marco
Polo speaks of the presence of Israelites in China, and a
mention of them in Cambaluc, the forerunner of Peking,
occurs in the pages of Marignolli— never to have been a
Jewish colony here. . . . On the other hand, I enquired
of a most eminent Chinese philosopher and scholar concerning this point. He confirmed that the Jews had never
lived here, but told me of an interesting encounter with
one a few years before. A Chinese from Turkestan had
appeared at his door to try to sell him some antiques, and
had produced a card on which was printed, in Chinese
characters, the name Li-King. . . .[1] Gradually, as they
talked together, a quality in the aspect of the stranger—
although at first he had seemed typically Chinese, and was
dressed in the usual robes— as well as in his name, began
to make an impression on my acquaintance, who had lived
much in Europe and America. Finally, he asked him
straight out, "Are you not a Jew ?" . . . And Li-King

---

[1] I cannot remember correctly the first syllable, but the second and, in this
case, all-important is correct.

STROLLING JUVENILE PLAYER.   PEKING

immediately with pride admitted it, stating that his patronymic, " King ", had originally been Cohen or König, and that his family had moved eastward from Europe in the time of the medieval persecutions, and had, since the middle of the fifteenth century, been settled in Chinese Turkestan. In proof of this assertion, moreover, he took out of one of the cases which he was carrying with him a family Talmud, printed in Chinese during the seventeenth century.[1]

But, if there were no Jews in Peking, another but smaller parallel to the history of the Mohammedans can be produced from the record of the Cossack colony, Albazin, on the Amur River. Its members had long been in the habit of making incursions into Chinese territory, and of looting,

[1] The best-authenticated instance of the presence of Jews at an early period in China occurs at K'aï-Fêng-Fu in Ho-nan ; where three lapidary inscriptions exist concerning their arrival, although each gives a different date for it. Made in 1489, one of them declares that seventy Jewish families found their way here between the years A.D. 960 and 1278 ; the second, dated 1512, that the Hebrew religion reached here between 206 B.C. and A.D. 221 ; while the third, written in 1663 (by which time the colony had, in any case, been long established), bounces the whole claim back to the eleventh century B.C. !

On the other hand, oral tradition among the Kaï-Fêng Jews claims that they penetrated to China through Persia, via Khorasan and Samarkand, during the reign of the Han Emperor, Ming-Ti (A.D. 58–75) ; perhaps in flight after the Siege of Jerusalem. . . . What appears undoubted, however, is that the original Synagogue here was built in 1163, rebuilt in 1421, and again in 1653 after a disastrous flood.

The first Jesuit missionaries in China, that very remarkable body of men, sent back to Europe the initial news of the presence of this strange colony. The famous Matteo Ricci having received a visit from a young Jew of Kaï-Fêng, a missionary was despatched there soon after. A little less than a century later, two other Jesuits visited it, and brought back plans of the Synagogue. . . . In 1760 the Jewish merchants of London sent a letter, written in Hebrew, to their brothers of Kaï-Fêng, and a Jewish merchant from Vienna visited them in 1867. . . . Not long after that date, however, these Chinese Jews fell on such hard times, that they were obliged to demolish their historic Synagogue, since they found themselves too poor to repair it. The tablet, formerly over its entrance, which bore in gold characters the name ESZLOYIH, or Israel, had been removed to a mosque. The survivors seemed likely to be absorbed into the rest of the population. (See notes by Sir Henry Yule and Dr. Henri Cordier, *The Book of Ser Marco Polo*, vol. i. pp. 346-7.)

and, in consequence, K'ang Hsi had been obliged to quell them. The prisoners included thirty or forty Russians, with a priest among their number, and the Emperor, when they were brought to Peking in 1685, granted them land and a small temple, close to the grounds of the present Russian Mission in the North-East Quarter of the Tartar City. They, and their descendants, remained loyal to the Orthodox Church, and priests were sent from Russia to attend to them. Nevertheless, they intermarried with Manchus and became physically identical with their Chinese neighbours, though it is said that families bearing Russian names still dwell in the neighbourhood. . . .[1] In the same way, though not because they had been taken prisoners, but because it was the policy of the Manchu Emperors to encourage them, the Mongolian Lamas had been given their own temple here, the *Mahakala Miao*, with its double roof, and in this sanctuary are still obliged to read the Buddhist writ in the Mongolian tongue.

The mosque, eclectic building though it is, possesses a kind of beauty ; from it emanates a strong sense of piety, of fasting, washing and the severe code of the Prophet. . . . Notwithstanding, the Temple of Confucius, " The Temple of Great Perfection ", though altogether lacking in the spruceness and cleanliness of the mosque, and wanting, too, in the excitement of the secrecy of its location, much transcends it in loveliness. Built in the middle of the fourteenth century, by Chih Chêng, last Emperor of the House of Kubla, it is, compared with many of the Sage's Temples, of relatively modern date : but with its long and admirable terrace — called the Moon Terrace — of white marble, its dark cypresses and clear pool, it merits the boast

---

[1] Arlington and Lewisohn's *In Search of Old Peking*, p. 177.

expressed in its name. Sanctity, philosophic calm and benign virtue, such as I have never felt elsewhere, seem to pervade every corner of it. Yet scarcely more than two or three visitors wandered in the vast green enclosure or in the garden courts between the halls, and even they had chosen it more, perhaps, in order to enjoy the warmth of the winter afternoon sun than from any religious sense — or they may have been Chinese connoisseurs come here to inspect the ten celebrated " Stone Drums ", made in reality of black granite, and by many authorities supposed to have been carved about a thousand years before Christ. Until a month or two before, they had stood upon the verandah here, but alas, like so many other of the portable treasures of Peking, they had now been moved, stone replicas being set up in their stead. . . . But the air of peace and beauty which is to be perceived here, through the skin as well as the eyes, seems older than any temple, older than the Stone Drums, co-existent with the first shoots of green things growing from the earth and the first stirrings of life. . . . (So, always since visiting this temple, Confucius has seemed to me connected with the idea of the survival and beauty of ancient things which are yet very much alive : and thus an incident that occurred a few weeks later greatly delighted me. . . . I was walking with a friend in the grounds of the Summer Palace, crowded with beautifully dressed Chinese, for the Lord Mayor of Peking was giving a Garden Party. We passed a very pretty and elegant Chinese girl, and when I asked who she might be, for her appearance had great distinction, my companion told me that she had recently made her appearance in Peking, and was the newest descendant in the male line from Confucius, who was born in the year 550 before Christ.)

Places like this are empty, and those temples, of the greatest interest and beauty, which surround Pei-Hai are crumbling away, hour by hour. Yet temples with no esthetic or historic association, so long as they have some trick attached to them, are full. I remember visiting one such, outside the city : wherein each day of the year is represented by the figure of an Immortal, and, according to the gesture and expression of the God presiding over the day of your birth, a person skilled in the art will essay to tell your fortune. . . . This building is consequently crowded, yet, were it to fall into a state of bad repair, I doubt whether any help would be forthcoming. It would continue, merely, to be thronged until it had actually dissolved beyond the state where any fun could be derived from it. . . . Nobody would care, not even the superstitious : it would affect them no more than the vanishing of their monuments and memorials, unique and irreplaceable, worries the antiquarians who, while they deplore it constantly in speech, make no effort to prevent it. To the same degree as those beyond the walls, they decompose and perish day by day, so that some of the most precious works, guarded with such care by previous and more reverent generations, had completely disappeared during the last few months. . . . But that they saw these processes of disintegration at work in all the buildings round them, in no way impaired the gaiety of the crowds, any more than would private or national misfortune in ample measure.

The circumstances and state of this deposed metropolis and its surroundings, the spirit of the people, this vivacity of a very old city-bred population (albeit one ever able to draw on the life-power of an immense country — for the streets of Peking, like those of London, remain paved with gold to the ambitious rustic or provincial mind, and so all roads in Eastern Asia still lead to Peking), this fainéant pride in its monuments, this desire for pleasure and contempt for barbarians, assuredly all these seemed strangely familiar. . . . And then one day, suddenly, I realised it was something of which I had read, not which I had seen ; the Rome of Gibbon and Gregorovius, just before the official adoption of Christianity : not, as in the Dark Ages, when, after repeated sacks, Rome lay empty, but when it was still the greatest city in the world, when the arrogant Romans believed in nothing and the great temples, decayed, stood empty all day long, when Isis was worshipped as much or as little as Jupiter (just in the same way that gods from the Hindu Pantheon were assembled here), when the rich were still carried to their feasts and the poor still enjoyed their circuses and their fairs, still thought of themselves as privileged, beings apart, living on the tribute of the world, each individual proudly murmuring to himself, in this long-drawn-out process of death through which he and his city were passing, " Civis Romanus Sum ! ".

*CHAPTER FIVE*

THE FORBIDDEN CITY

" You must know that it is the greatest Palace that ever was." [1]   So wrote Marco Polo of the Forbidden City of his day. . . . But now, as in Rome when no longer the centre of the Empire, the great Palace stands empty and, except for the tourist, who is for the first time free to wander in it, the loss is all the more considerable because in both capitals the Palace was the city ; the whole machine having been planned for ceremonies and created with a view to the best effect that could be obtained for Imperial comings and goings.   Its dresses, fantastic in the extreme, the elephants and horses and chariots and palanquins and eunuchs that constituted its furnishing, these were all part of it, belonged to it as petals to a flower.

Even the parks and gardens pertained here as much to the Palace as its contents. . . . Let us therefore look, first, at two features of its landscape.   In a previous chapter [2]

---

[1] *The Book of Ser Marco Polo*, vol. i. p. 363.
[2] See Book II, Chapter 2.

I have attempted to describe a little how the palaces are disposed. The cities fit into one another ; the Tartar City, low and grey in the winter or a sea of green branches in the summer, surrounds and sets the Imperial City ; of which the Forbidden City composes the walled, square kernel, extending as far as the base of the first of the artificial hills I have mentioned. This, with its five orange-tiled arbours placed in the exact five positions for the best views, is known as Coal Hill ; because the earth taken out of the moat when the Ming Emperor Yung Lo excavated it at the beginning of the fifteenth century, in order to construct, or modify, the Palace, was piled up here on a foundation of coal, previously kept in storage on the same site. More-over the mound possessed a definite and, to the Chinese mind, very necessary purpose, being heaped on this spot, in front of the northern entrance to the Forbidden City, in order to ward off evil influences from that direction, just in the same manner that a devil-screen protects the approach to any ordinary Chinese house. . . . At its foot are many buildings, with orange and yellow tiled roofs, the colours of the eaves dimmed and powdering (and among them can be seen the Hall of Imperial Longevity, wherein the reigning Emperor used to sacrifice on New Year's Day to the por-traits of his innumerable predecessors, of former dynasties as much as of his own). Westward, the Imperial City extends in lakes and parks, all bearing appropriate buildings; and with a true sense of Chinese symmetry, the second artificial hill, that of the White Dagoba, stands balancing Coal Hill, a little way back, by the side of the Pei-Hai or North Sea Lake.

Of this hill, we know more than of Coal Hill, for Marco Polo leaves an unmistakable account of how it looked in the thirteenth century, and of how and why it had been, not long before, created. And, that we may comprehend the elusive atmosphere that clings to these places, even in the present day, this passage must be quoted : for a sense of antiquity, of history, permeates and pervades the air, often strengthening a suspicion that the Forbidden City itself, as well as the lay-out of Peking, is older than local antiquarian authorities will admit, or than the facts, as we know them, would justify us in believing.

"Moreover on the north side of the Palace . . . is a hill which has been made by art from the earth dug out of the lake ; it is a good hundred paces in height and a mile in compass. This hill is entirely covered with trees that never lose their leaves, but remain ever green. And I assure you that wherever a beautiful tree may exist, and the Emperor gets news of it, he sends for it and has it transported bodily with all its roots and the earth attached to them, and planted on that hill of his. No matter how big the tree may be, he gets it carried by his elephants ; and in this way he has got together the most beautiful collection of trees in all the world. And he has also caused the whole hill to be covered with the ore of azure, which is very green.[1] And thus not only are the trees all green, but the hill itself is all green likewise. . . . On the top of the hill again there is a fine big palace which is all green inside and out ; and thus the hill, and the trees, and the palace form together a charming

[1] *The Book of Ser Marco Polo*, vol. i, p. 370, note 12. With reference to " ore of azure ", Sir Henry Yule appends a footnote, in which he informs us that in the original it reads " Roze de l'açur ", and that a mineralogical authority gave it as his opinion that it must stand for *roche de l'azure* ; which interpretation Sir Henry adopted. The same person suggested to him that it was probably a term loosely used for blue carbonate of copper (which assumes a green tone in the presence of moisture, and would account for the concolorous appear-

spectacle ; and it is marvellous to see their uniformity of colour ! Everybody who sees them is delighted. And the Great Khan has caused this beautiful prospect to be formed for the comfort and solace and delectation of his heart." [1]

These two hills, now more brown than green, break the level of the city, as the above discursion concerning one of them has broken the level of my prose. . . . But I am far from apologising for it, because, at the beginning of this book, I explained how I regarded it as a special medium, and how I hoped to travel through its pages as I liked, at my own discretion, as I have travelled outside them, and certainly if the reader has possessed the patience to accompany me thus far, and if I have been able in any way to afford him the extra vista it has been our object to derive from our flittings, then I am sure that, from his kindness, he will not resent the two further digressions, little artificial hills in print such as those we have been examining, that lie in front of us before we are free to visit the Palace in order to regard it, just as we might regard a picture, for its beauty alone.

Nor, as a matter of fact, is its claim to this quality unconnected with these matters. . . . In the latter part of the eighteenth century, the Rule of the Picturesque decreed that anything that attained to the marvellous or the horrific through its proportions or from the circumstances surrounding it, also belonged, by virtue of this exaggeration or intensity, to the realm of beauty. And, though this esthetic,

ance which was such a source of delight), and recalled to him another similar Imperial whim ; that Nero had employed powdered siliceous carbonate of copper for making his circus green, in compliment to his favourite faction, whose colour it was.

[1] *Ibid.*, vol. i. p. 365.

in its full implications, has long been abandoned, something of truth still remains in it. . . . " You must know that it is the greatest Palace that ever was ", we have seen Marco Polo write, though he had journeyed to Peking from Venice, at a moment when its own incomparable, lily-like palaces were rising day by day out of the lagoons which mirrored their growing. " The building is altogether so vast, so rich and so beautiful that no man on earth could design anything superior to it. . . ." [1] It is plain that this vastness and richness of which Marco Polo speaks, as well as the history of the Palace, and the curious rites that belonged both to its founding and, throughout so many centuries, to its daily life, cannot but enter into the general impression of it, adding to it a romantic or *accidental* beauty.

First of all, then, let us talk about the elephants ; in themselves a very good instance of that cosmopolitan, and even exotic, atmosphere to which I have alluded several times in the last chapter, and which Peking seems always to have enjoyed. Certainly, except in so far as such beasts exactly match the scale of these buildings, we should never have expected to find them carrying out a diurnal routine in these northern surroundings : as soon encounter them, we might think, in Moscow or Stockholm. . . . They are, however, said to have already been trained for use in the state ceremonials of the Emperors of the T'ang [2] and Sung [3] Dynasties. And Lich'en [4] goes so far as to state, in this connection, that, during the reign of Tao Kuang

---

[1] *The Book of Ser Marco Polo*, vol. i, pp. 363-364.
[2] T'ang Dynasty, A.D. 618-906.
[3] Sung Dynasty, A.D. 960–1279.
[4] See Tun Lich'en's *Annual Customs and Festivals in Peking* as recorded in the *Yen-ching Sui-shih-chi*.

(who died in the year 1850), an elephant still existed with tusks encased in bronze that had been cast a thousand years before ! This, I apprehend, only constitutes one more elephant story : though admittedly the vast creatures seem to have enjoyed all the privileges and respect attaching to old age in China, for, during the nineteenth century at least, they ranked as Princes of the Empire and derived the same remuneration. But, to revert to earlier periods, we have, on a previous page, seen them march past, their trunks swaying with a military swagger, as they bear aloft the plate of the Emperor Kubla on their way to the banqueting-hall in preparation for a feast. And, owing to his lameness, the Emperor, when he went out hunting, was always carried upon the backs of four elephants " in a fine chamber made of timber, lined inside with plates of beaten gold, and outside with lions' skins." [1] Marco Polo [2] estimates the number of elephants at 5000, again ; but this may merely be another of his " Millioni " exaggerations, for the Ming Emperor Hung Chih, who built their stables, only planned to accommodate forty-eight of them. (On the other hand, the Grand Khan ruled over such much larger southern dominions than any of his successors, and, through his family connections, wielded over others a kind of suzerainty, that it may, equally well, have been true.) Their duties were, as we shall see, for the most part complicated, but not onerous : though the Manchu Dynasty placed a certain responsibility on them, for both the Emperors K'ang Hsi [3] and Ch'ien Lung [4] deputed these animals to carry the revised Imperial Genealogical Register, amended every few years, back to the Temple of the

---

[1] *The Book of Ser Marco Polo*, vol. i, p. 404.    [2] *Ibid.*, vol. i, p. 391.
[3] K'ang Hsi, A.D. 1662–1723.    [4] Ch'ien Lung, A.D. 1736–1796.

Imperial Ancestors in Mukden for safe-keeping.[1]

Alas ! the Elephant Quarter, as it was called, no longer exists, having been pulled down to make way for parliamentary buildings (a far whiter elephant, so to speak, than any of the beasts which preceded it). But it was immense, and so elaborate that it possessed its own temple to the Elephant God. The stables were still in use in the last decade but one of the nineteenth century. Lich'en[2] informs the reader that in 1874 and 1875, the Kings of Annam twice sent a tribute of six or seven elephants, " very fat and sturdy ", and that the populace " used to delight in their peaceful appearance, and rejoiced as they passed along the road " ; but that after 1884, in which year one of them went mad and ran amok in the crowd, they disappeared from the contemporary scene. And this seems a pity, if only because of their having been for so long a feature of Peking, and, more especially, because " when spectators would enter [the stables], the elephants could make a sound through their trunks as of conch shells ".

Their service was of two kinds. One consisted in drawing along the chariot of the Emperor, upon very special occasions : the other was more complicated. Facing each other in pairs, trunk to trunk, six of them took up their position at daylight outside the Wu Mên, the chief gate of the Forbidden City. As soon as a bell sounded, these palatines knelt down until all the officials who were on duty had entered the Palace. But, when the last one had disappeared, they then rose and crossed trunks, so as to prevent any unauthorised person from making his way in ; a posi-

[1] For this information about the elephants, as for much that follows, I am again indebted to Arlington and Lewisohn's *In Search of Old Peking*. See pp. 165-167 of their book.

[2] See Tun Lich'en's *Annual Customs and Festivals in Peking*.

tion they maintained until, the levee having ended, they considerately lowered their trunks again for the Mandarins to leave.

As befitted their rank, these beasts acted only under the direct commands of the Son of Heaven. "If," write Messrs. Arlington and Lewisohn,[1] " an elephant fell sick whilst on duty, the keeper at once sent in a memorial to the Emperor, who wrote out a slip ordering the sick elephant to be sent back to his quarters and another one to take his place. The Emperor's order, it is said, had to be read out aloud for all the elephants to hear, as otherwise not one of them would move. But if the order was read aloud the elephant next for duty would step forward and follow the keeper to his post. If an elephant injured any one of the public while on duty, or otherwise misbehaved himself, the Emperor would order an appropriate punishment. If it was to be a whipping, two elephants would wind their trunks round the offender and force him on to his knees, so that the keeper could flog him ; when it was over he would rise and bow several times, as if thanking the Emperor for the punishment. . . ." Or, if it were merely a minor elephant-ine offence, the culprit would be degraded to a lower rank.

The keepers were Annamites, and their posts were hereditary : but, though doubtless well paid, pride in their office did not prevent them from trying to make extra money out of their charges. . . . One method of doing it was by selling the elephants' dung to the ladies of Peking, who, after washing it, used the resulting liquid, when it had been strained, as a shampoo : for it possessed the local reputation of being able to impart a peculiar brilliance to the hair. . . . Another way they attempted was to cut

*In Search of Old Peking*, p. 165.

down the elephants' supply of cooked rice, always handed
to them wrapped up in their daily bundles of rice straw.
But the animals had formed their own ideas concerning
the honesty of the keepers, and, after each of them had
carefully weighed his bundle with his trunk, and found it
— and the keeper — wanting, they created such havoc that
their guardians had to take refuge in a trench, kept ready
for this purpose, outside the stables.

Now we approach the other, less superficial aspect of
Palace life here : for, though all Peking could come to
watch the elephants (when, for example, they were led
down, on one day in the year, in July, to be washed in the
moat, a very popular occasion, as we have said), there were
other things more secret. . . . Just as Coal Hill was constructed to guard the Emperor Yung Lo's Palace from
spiritual mischief, so was the whole of the Forbidden City
designed on geomantic lines. All its palaces and temples are
therefore founded in sorcery. It is safe to say that no hall or
pavilion or kiosk was allowed to be built anywhere within
the boundaries of the Imperial or Forbidden Cities at any
time, without its proper position being first most carefully
calculated by augury. Long before the Ming Dynasty
founded the present Palace, Kubla Khan employed at his
Court magicians and astrologers (here great additions to the
science of astronomy eventually accrued from their black
arts, just as, in the West, the search for the Philosopher's
Stone in the end brought to birth modern medicine).
Marco Polo says that five thousand magicians lived in
Peking, clothed and fed by the Emperor — apparently a
favourite number with that traveller, but one perhaps
merely intended to convey the idea of a great quantity. It
constituted their duty in return to forecast the weather and

events of each year, and determine when it was auspicious to go out. . . . We may, however, wonder how much that enlightened Tartar Prince believed in it himself, and how much of the system he merely inherited, for in the Eighth Month of 1292, Korean wizards and Shaman women were admitted to the royal presence in order to cure the Emperor of his old enemy, gout : but when they seized his hands and feet and began reciting spells, he could not stop laughing.[1]

Yung Lo, of the ensuing dynasty, who is supposed to be the founder of the present Peking, is said to have consulted for his plan an eminent astrologer, Lu Po.[2] The thaumaturge handed the Emperor a sealed envelope containing the plans of the new capital, based on the recognised principles of his magic. The city was to represent No-Cha, a mythical being with three heads and six arms, and a corresponding space or building was allotted to each part of his body. . . . Thus, to take a few instances, No-Cha's head — or heads — is the Ch'ien Men, the principal gate of the Tartar City (through which the Emperor used to be drawn by his elephants on his way to sacrifice at the Altar of Heaven, the supreme ceremony of the Chinese Year) ; an open gutter, now covered over, in the West City, represents his large intestine ; a well in the Western Section of the Forbidden City, his navel ; two gates, facing the Yellow Temple and the Black Temple respectively, symbolise his feet, treading on " Wind and Fire Wheels ", while the red painted walls of the Imperial City constitute his red silk stomach protector.

[1] According to Palladius. See footnote by Dr. Henri Cordier, vol. i, p. 408 of *The Book of Ser Marco Polo*.

[2] For the full geomantic chart see Appendix B, pp. 337-338, in Arlington and Lewisohn's *In Search of Old Peking*.

With the advent of the Ch'ing Emperors, from Manchuria, the strength of the various prevalent systems of magic was augmented with fresh currents of low-caste sorcery from the North. There was a great indulgence in Shaman rites and sacrifices, semi-devil-dances and other Berchtesgaden tactics.[1] The strange, sub-arctic antics of the Shaman, belonging by their nature to tribal worlds of Lapp and Eskimo, of underground huts, piled up with snow, and of blubber-smeared bodies, now took place, in strict privacy, within the lovely, civilised halls and courts of the Forbidden City. They were held between three and four o'clock in the morning on Imperial birthdays, in the presence of the Emperor and Empress, and none but Manchus might participate in them. . . . After the " Guardian of the Nine Gates " had given a signal, a man cracked a whip three times, the great drum of the Palace sounded thrice, and then, to the sound of music, the Emperor mounted his throne. The performers, with appropriate masks and high, feathered hats, were divided into two sides, one dressed up in black sheepskins, the other in bearskins, and a horseman in a strange and complicated dress, crowned with a tall, plumed helmet, rode between the two ranks, firing arrows at them. At last some individual would pretend to be hit, and the rest would then career off. . . . There were other forms, too, of this childish witchcraft. Sometimes these grown-up men would put on costumes with different-coloured flags attached to the back

[1] In *The Book of Ser Marco Polo* Dr. Henri Cordier has a note concerning Bon-Po Lamaism, a form of Tibetan Lamaism. " The Bon-po Lamas are above all sorcerers and necromancers, and are very similar to the . . . *Shamans.* During their operations, they wear a tall pointed black hat, surmounted by the feather of a peacock, or of a cock, and a human skull. . . . Their sacred symbol is the *svastika* turned from right to left 卐."

of their necks, would fasten stilts with bells to their feet, and would proceed to prance on hobby-horses, jingling round the courtyard before the Emperor, and occasionally pretending to neigh. Or, again, they would dance round a sort of sacred maypole, hung about with old bones and strips of meat left over from the sacrifice : a wooden post which still stands today in its place on a marble terrace outside the Palace of Earthly Tranquillity. . . . After these revels, the performers would usually sit down to a hearty bump-supper, as it were, and would compete among themselves as to which of them could eat and drink the most.

Right up to 1911 the same systems of magic continued their sway. And, indeed, in 1908, when the Empress Dowager died, her body, after being dressed in robes of state, embroidered with the Imperial Phoenix, and placed in a coffin which she had commanded always to stand open, ready for her, and being then removed to the Hall of the Imperial Phoenix in the Middle-Sea Palace, was kept waiting there for burial for nearly a year before an auspicious day could be found for the ceremony.

Certainly an immense amount of mumbo-jumbo and pious flummery took place : but we must not allow the romantic ideas with which they are connected, nor the actual silliness of the practices, to influence us in our judgment of Chinese architecture, even though in many instances it was based on them. For the theories, however absurd or however exemplary, by which an art is inspired seem but seldom to improve, to degrade or in any way to modify the art itself. Ruskin's water-colours are no finer for the whole volumes of theory that laboured to produce this single feather from a peacock or leaf from a strawberry plant ; the Escorial is no less impressive for being built in the form of St. Laurence's gridiron, and Seurat's pictures are no less miraculous because of his unfailing advocacy and use throughout of the semi-scientific and worthless doctrine of *pointillisme*. (He was a superb artist, and thus, if he had chosen to paint with a spoon, as Goya did upon occasion — or, as for that, with a toothbrush or a gramophone needle or anything else to hand — the results would have been equally satisfactory.) Great art is always produced *in spite* of the difficulties the artist himself puts in his own way. And so, had the Chinese architects been commanded to build the Palace in the shape of a dragon or a toadstool, or even, had such a thing then existed, of a motor-bicycle, they would no doubt have created just as magnificent an edifice.

We must not, therefore, let this tendency to hocus-pocus on the part of its inhabitants divert us from a proper appreciation of the Palace, which both was born of it and served as background for it, any more than we should permit the names of its gates and chambers, lovely and fantastic in themselves, to heighten for us, through the partiality they induce in our minds, the quality of the buildings to which they have been given. But certainly we should know of them ; such names, to choose some from one section alone of the Forbidden City, as Pavilion of the Imperial View, Jade-Green Floating Pavilion, Hall of Pears and Pondweed, Pavilion of Ten Thousand Springs, Porch of Red Snow, Palace of Pure Affection, Palace of Benevolent Prospect, Palace in Honour of Talent, Flowery Moon Gate, Hall of Vast Virtue, Pavilion of Equable Autumn, Hall of Vigorous Fertility, Pavilion of Pleasant Sounds, Porch of Combined Harmony, Pavilion of Favourable Winds, Hall of Controlling Time, Studio of Pure

Fragrance, Rain Flower Pavilion, Hall of the Basis of Propriety and Tower of Auspicious Clouds, or, to instance a few others from the kiosks and palaces on White Dagoba Island in Pei-Hai, Porch of Olive-green Kingfishers, Pavilion of Perpetual Southern Melodies, Studio of Salubrious Peace, Pavilion for Watching the Spring and Peaceful Cottage among Coiled Mists. . . . (The Pavilion of Perpetual Southern Melodies carries to me the cooling, icy percussion of marimbas over hot, parrot-haunted lagoons, while the Peaceful Cottage among Coiled Mists suggests a picture by Salvador Dali — except, perhaps, that then it would be called in the catalogue " Peaceful Mists among Coiled Cottages ".)

.    .    .    .    .

If you divide the Forbidden City into two, the southern half roughly comprises the main halls of state, while the second, the Nei Ch'ao or Inner Court, contains the pavilions and living quarters that I have mentioned as being so opposed in spirit to the great apartments. Both sections I have visited many times, under snow and wind and spring calm and great heat, and the particular quality of beauty which each part manifests leads me to choose a different kind of weather by which to see it. First, for the frosty beauty of the great courts and the dark sumptuousness of the State Apartments, I should select a typical Peking winter day of bright, yellow-fleeced sun in a blue heaven, of an intensely animating cold (which makes the crowds in the fair we have left talk and laugh more than ever, though, as well, it causes their teeth to chatter) ; but, for the appreciation of the residential quarters, and the facets and adjuncts of the Chinese life they represent, gay as the drawing of a flower or a bird upon a Chinese paper, we must have a spring day, a morning from that brief season, enduring only a fortnight, that falls, very regularly, about a month later than the Feast of Excited Insects, and is all too short, since, in it, after a winter when every twig and piece of earth looked hard and dead as iron, the year suddenly leaps into life, and the lilac and shrubs and fruit-trees rush within the space of a few days into intoxicating flower and scent.

On each of these two visits it is our sad task to remember — though indeed this makes itself obvious enough — that the furniture and china and bronzes and paintings we see are not those that belong to the Palace. The scale and proportion of the first of these walls, courts and chambers of state are stupendous, massive with a grandeur for which no man will ever find himself prepared ; the gardens and pavilions of the second, gay and light as air. How much greater still, or how much more delightful and fantastic, must the effect have been before the treasures that so peculiarly belonged to these places had been dispersed ! For there is now nothing to help them, or to furnish them. A few things still remain in the immense courtyards, enormous bowls of gilt bronze — dating back, for the most part, to the times of the Ming Emperors — bronze dragons and tortoises and lions ; otherwise every object of value — of the tremendous value, moreover, that the Imperial collection, the greatest collection of Chinese works of art in the world, possessed — has been torn out of its setting and cast forth, their place being usurped by tenth-rate objects collected from palaces elsewhere ; oriental, late-Victorian furniture imported from a famous London shop for her personal use by the Empress Dowager, or bad European clocks of the early nineteenth century (again, some of these can be delightful, but the best ones have, too, probably been moved

away). . . . In fact, the Imperial and Forbidden Cities
have been sacked, just as truly as Rome was sacked : but,
on this occasion, the crime was committed, not by barbarian
invaders, but by their own impious government ; a theft
all the more atrocious and impossible to condone, because
the things removed so intrinsically pertained to the Palace
and to one another, often had been designed for it, and
could never, even were they again assembled together, look
a thousandth part as well elsewhere. (The excuse advanced
by the culprits was the fear that these incomparable objects
might fall into the hands of the Japanese ; — who would,
whatever their faults, most certainly have looked after and
appreciated them. As it was, many of them arrived at
Shanghai, their temporary destination, smashed and shattered owing to faulty packing : because, though the Chinese
pack better than any nation in the world, the contract had
been so often sub-let at a profit, by one firm to another,
that the packers finally employed could not at the price
obtained properly execute their task. Other items disappeared altogether on the journey.)

The sculptures and paintings and carvings and textiles
and porcelains thus raped were nearly all of transcendent
beauty as well as historic interest ; of that pure loveliness
or grotesque magnificence to which Chinese art at its best
always reaches. Whereas, some of those that remain — or,
rather, that have been brought here — detract actually from
their surroundings : for it is a very singular fact — and one
that we must notice, before we have proceeded any further,
in spite of the intimidating thunderings and squeals of
Western authorities and collectors of Chinese art,—that the
Chinese, who possess perhaps the finest natural taste of all
races and who still apply it with the most success to the

273                                                              T

common objects of everyday life, have nevertheless, through many centuries, made and admired, equally, the ugliest possible concoctions of metal and colour, or of silk and kingfisher-wing ; top-heavy *cloisonné* enamels and dust-collecting screens. To this, perhaps, their ingenuity led them. So that the paradox arises that, while in countries like England [1] nothing really ugly was created or to be bought before the year of the Great Exhibition in 1851, in China, the land of perfect taste, the most hideous objects had been made, lauded and collected for a full thousand years ; while, on the other hand, when, long after, with the coming of the Industrial Revolution and the eruption of the Middle Classes, the whole of Europe and America had given itself up to the pursuit of ugliness as beauty, in China artist and architect and humble artisan continued, without any load of duty, and without a Ruskin to mouth them back into the first-class waiting-rooms of morality and antiquity, to produce instinctively, and gaily as a bird sings, scrolls and pavilions and porcelains that were exquisite.

Alas ! the objects that remain in the halls merely clutter up the space, whereas those that have vanished imparted to it proportion and perspective ; just as did those strange beings who flaunted among them, the Emperor himself, in yellow silk embroidered coat, moving awkwardly on high, stilt-like heels and talking in that special, high, Imperial voice that had taken, it was said, two thousand years to evolve as a pattern, his wives in their magnificent long-

[1] I express this opinion with natural hesitancy since I have read, in the pages of the French magazine *Minotaure*, an article by Professor Herbert Read. In this, with all the weight of his authority on such a subject, the Professor states, if I understand him aright, that evidence of artistic taste in England has been negligible during the last four hundred years.

sleeved jackets, the Mandarins in glittering robes, with pigtails and peacocks' feathers, the guards in their sables. But all have gone, and we find, before us, a great architectural model, relying now no more upon the things it still contains [1] than upon its adjuncts of sorcery and poetry.

Yet magic and poetry of its own it will always possess, so long as it continues to exist : and, above all, an overwhelming feeling of immensity and of antiquity. Looking up at these tremendous walls, of chamber and guard-room and stable, it would indeed be a brave man who would with confidence care to pronounce the precise date of their building. Many of these edifices have been burned or destroyed, and then rebuilt, several times within a century : some are known to have been remodelled by the first Manchu Emperor, Shan Chih, in the middle of the seventeenth century ; others are said to have remained untouched since the reign of Yung Lo in the first half of the fifteenth century. Others, again, conceivably — and, in my view, probably — existed as they are today some hundred and fifty years before the time of this Emperor. So many things that here appear to be old, turn out to be, comparatively, new ; so many that look new, to be immensely ancient. Who, for example, unless his mind were stored, previous to his going there, with the history of Peking, could possibly presume that the broad and modern lay-out of the

[1] Some of these did, as a matter of fact, belong to the Emperor Ch'ien Lung, who was a great collector, and seems to have possessed a genuine flair for ugly objects. He occupied the heart of the Chinese eighteenth century, and in his reign of sixty years contrived to amass numbers of things so hideous and spiritless that it is difficult to believe that they can have been made in his Empire, and especially during a period characterised in China — and everywhere else — by its grace. In spite of his great love of learning and poetry (he was, as every stone and piece of wood in the grounds of the Cities, and for miles round, testifies, an indefatigable poet and calligraphist), he seems to have been drawn irresistibly toward any kind of pointless complication in art.

275

chief thoroughfares of the Tartar City was the creation, in reality, of Kubla Khan ? And no one denies the authenticity of many other buildings of the same epoch in the Tartar and Imperial Cities. . . . Similarly it cannot, I think, be controverted that — except for minor details, such as that, owing to changes of dynasty, and, with them, of religious practice, the use of white has long been abandoned, being kept now for the colour of mourning — the account which Marco Polo leaves us of the aspect of the Great Palace in Cambaluc in the latter part of the thirteenth century, reads just like a description of the Forbidden City as it remains today.

" In the city of Cambaluc stands the Palace of the Great Kaan, and now I will tell you what it is like. . . . It is enclosed by a great wall forming a square, each side of which is a mile in length ; that is to say, the whole of it is four miles round. It is also very thick and a good fifteen feet in height, whitewashed and loopholed everywhere. At each corner is a very fine and rich palace, with a similar one half-way between them. This great wall has five gates in its southern face, the middle one being the state entrance of the Emperor, and inside it is a second wall enclosing a space somewhat greater in length than breadth. In the middle of it is the Lord's Great Palace. It has no upper storey, being all on the ground floor, except that the basement stands some three feet or more above the ground. This elevation is retained by a wall of marble, raised to the level of the pavement, five feet in width, and projecting beyond the base of the Palace so as to form a kind of terrace-walk, on the outer edge of which is a very fine pillared balustrade. On each of the four sides there is a great marble staircase leading to the top of the marble wall, and forming the approach to the Palace. Its roof is all coloured with vermilion and yellow and green and blue and other hues that are fixed with a varnish so fine and exquisite that they shine like crystal, and lend a resplendent lustre to the Palace as seen for a great way round. Inside, the ceiling is very lofty, and the walls are entirely covered with gold and silver, and adorned with representations of dragons, in relief and gilded, beasts, birds, knights and idols. And on the ceiling, too, is nothing but gold and silver painting. . . ." [1] It would scarcely be easy to give a more graphic picture of the present Palace, apart from the fact that, owing to the carelessness and meanness in such matters of the Chinese Republican Government, many of the eaves are losing their colours, and the roofs, their tiles. If, then, Kubla's Palace presented this identical appearance, is there any reason to doubt that, with the faithfulness to tradition which ever distinguished the Chinese, it represents the type of Imperial Palace as it has existed for a thousand years at least, since, let us presume, the days of the Sung, long before Peking was built and when China was governed from other capitals ?

Always it had been from halls such as these that China had been ruled. And, as if to strengthen this impression, the Imperial Seals, draped in long, empty, yellow silk hangings, are still shown dustily in one of the smaller rooms. Perhaps some of them are replicas that have lately been substituted, it is impossible to tell ; but, ostensibly, the

---

[1] Here I quote a version, much abbreviated and rearranged for my purpose, from *The Book of Ser Marco Polo*, pp. 362, 363, 364. I have left out of it all the, for the moment, unnecessary corroborative details, concerning the use to which the various rooms and chambers were put, retaining only the descriptive side, with, for the furthering of it, the archaisms (viz. " hath " for " has ") modernised or removed. For old measures, " palms " and " hands ", I have substituted the equivalent " feet ". Otherwise it is faithful to the book.

oldest of them was the official signet of the Emperor Ch'in Shih, who built the Great Wall of China in the third century before Christ. . . . Moreover, for nearly five centuries, every road throughout the Empire ended in this present vast complex of buildings. And in it, during the whole of that half millennium, flourished the same tremendous palace organisation of pomp, of wives and concubines and officials and eunuchs, that had originally existed in the palaces of the Kings of Persia and Babylon and Syria and Ur. Nebuchadnezzar and Artaxerxes and King Darius the Great had lived in much the same kind of state and splendour as the last Emperor of China, now Emperor of Manchukuo.

Approaching the Palace from the Legation Quarter, you will first cross the track of the camels on their journey from Siberia to distant India and Tibet, and then you will see before you one of the great ceremonial arches, of heavily ornamented and painted wood, with three openings and a tiled roof, called P'ai Lou, that are so decorative a feature of Peking. (Handsome in themselves, they nevertheless must bear always, to the eyes of those acquainted with the churches, and Church, of England, an unfortunate resemblance to lych-gates ; bastard — if I may use such terms in this connection — triplets of a lych-gate. It is as though an English clergyman had gone mad, turned heathen, and were yet unable to rid himself of his old architectural complexes.) Beyond this, are four low, marble bridges, crossing a shallow, straight canal, and two winged, elaborately carved columns of great height, called in Chinese " Flowery Signposts ". . . . These pillars, in addition to their own beauty and impressiveness, can boast an extreme historical interest, in that, just as was the system of life within the Palace, so are they the last descendants of a long line. Similar pillars stood outside the royal palace in Nineveh, and possibly, later, in Rome.

These may be of alien descent ; but on their top, how-ever, they both carry lions, than which nothing could be more Chinese ; real Pekingese lions, the likeness of lions as they would have looked if only the Chinese had, through a thousand years or so, found the opportunity of breeding them.[1] Similar delightful beasts, of varying sizes, in stone as well as bronze, are on guard upon the terraces in many of the courtyards. . . . Nor, though the system they sheltered for so long may, in the first place, have been of foreign derivation, could any buildings — albeit these are much more massive and structural than one who has not seen them in their actuality, even if acquainted with photo-graphs of them or with apparently similar work elsewhere, could anticipate — be more Chinese than this vast series of roofs and courts, which now open up as you enter the gate, these stout pavilions balanced above their castellated walls, these guard-houses and libraries and lofty halls, or than the texture and carving of the marble balustrade before us. Indeed, the decoration of this, the reiteration of the clouds, is superb, resembles no other in the world, seeming as typical of the nation which produced it as are the gently sloping, flat marble panels near by, with extravagant dragons cut upon them in shallow relief, down which, in former times, the palanquin of the Emperor was carried, while his retinue descended the twenty-eight steps on each side. . . .

[1] Inside the gate are two more winged pillars surmounted by lions. Messrs. Arlington and Lewisohn, in *In Search of Old Peking*, say that the closed mouths of these two animals, facing north, indicate that, in the event of the Emperor having left the Palace incognito, strict silence concerning it should be maintained by those in his service ; while the open mouths of the others, facing south, symbolise their intention of reporting to the Sovereign on his return any malpractices that have taken place, on the part of the Court Officials, during his Majesty's absence.

And we must notice, further, how great a part calligraphy, most valued of all Chinese arts, plays in the general effect ; the beauty of the signs over the doors and of the numerous inscriptions everywhere, and how, too, Chinese decoration continually declares its connection with Chinese hand-writing.

You must picture to yourself immense deserted court after immense deserted court, spacious enough for the most splendid ceremonials. Each large building, or group of buildings, is flanked by smaller arcaded cloisters, of great extent — cloisters that seem to call for occupation by the Imperial Guard, for the sight of their uniforms and the sound of their cries. In front, in the middle, a high, slanting-roofed hall, tiled with orange or yellow (the tiles change from one colour to the other with the play of the light), stands pitched like a tent on triple-decked terraces of white marble, that seem, in the same way that the arcades evoked the Imperial Guard lounging in the light of dead suns, by their beauty of modulation and colour and surface, to demand groups of Mandarins in Court dress, kowtowing like painted tortoises before the Emperor himself. . . . So strong and so strange to us are the rhythm and perspective of these courts, that it is pleasant to spend hours on the terraces of different levels in the same courtyard, in spots only a few yards away, observing the differences of view and perspective to be obtained from them.

Across the first and greatest of the courts, runs down its marble channel in a wide and most delicate curve, the cele-brated canal, Golden Water River, with three fine marble bridges crossing it. To me, for one, observing this prodigi-ous enclosure, it always seemed that, in the fortress-like grandeur of the edifice behind, in the line of the canal and the poetry of its waters, flickering reflected sunlight under perfect spans, in the workmanship and design of the balustrades, in the vista of lofty, superb halls in front, with their scarlet and green eaves high in air, and still above, in the vista of roofs fitting, one into another, with supreme art, the Palace reached its culmination. The theme is one of ascent, flowing and progressive from flight of steps to flight of steps, from terrace to terrace, from lower deck to upper deck, from one building to another. The similarity and slight difference between court and court, roof and roof, outline and outline, invests it with the depth and immensity of a night sky when, gazing at it, you try to identify a single star. Yet each court constitutes a world of its own, remote in feeling as the moon ; a world wherein nothing happens except the ceaseless, clock-like sweep of cold, golden light from east to west, across it, across the marble floors, across the broad and shallow flights of steps, across the canal, lying like a scimitar below, across the cracking, sagging terraces, their surface dry and powdery with age.

As we stay here, gazing about us, and noticing how one court leads, with line and colour, into the next, we begin to grasp a little the difference between the Western European and Chinese conceptions of architecture : for each offers to the other, as do the two methods of life of the races who evolved them, a complete alternative.

To begin with, the Chinese is the only fully developed system of polychrome architecture extant : no other (though many have done so in the past, Greek and Gothic among them) now relies upon colour for a full half of its effect. Then European is the art of mass and contrast, Chinese that of harmony and balance. Angkor, for instance, so eastern in its placing and decoration, yet depends for the achieving of its magnificence upon contrast more than harmony (and it is for this reason that I have so insisted throughout the pages concerning it upon its *European* aspect ; the details are oriental, while the structure is western). But here court opens out of court, hall out of hall, united by a marked symphonic similarity. It is an art of suave and subtle modulation, intensely civilised and well-bred, as against one of opposition. The risk — as a rule triumphantly avoided — which through its very nature Chinese architecture incurs, is of monotony ; that to which European is liable, of extravagance. The Chinese buildings aspire to the same extent, but are humbler in that they do not attempt the soaring ambition of Gothic, or the gesticulations, the rhetorical questions to Heaven, of Baroque. In another respect, as well, Chinese architecture strives less. It does not, as we do, build for eternity. (In the same way, the Chinese does not aspire to the same degree as Western man to *personal* immortality, to the striving of an enlarged ego to survive *as an ego* and dominate through eternity, but relies, instead, wholly on a modified, articulated survival, from father to son, for countless generations.) Soaring, thousand-year-old towers of carved stone or reinforced concrete — as though even stone by itself did not afford a sufficient chance of survival — are alien in spirit to the Chinese builder (though modern circumstances may oblige him temporarily to use a medium foreign to him). On the contrary, he accepts fate ; fires, earthquakes, plundering by armies and the massacres they recurrently inflict ; and plans his edifices so that, when they have been burned down — which, the experience of four thousand years has taught him, happens every hundred years or so —

they can very easily and precisely be repeated, and will seem, on the contrary, never to have been injured. (Indeed, a notable fault of Chinese architecture, as well as a notable merit, and one which we have had cause in the last chapter frequently to deplore, consists in its transience : it can disappear, melt into nothingness as easily as, on the other hand, it can be renewed.) Thus the great reverence which the Chinese possess — or until lately possessed — for antiquity in a building, comes from a knowledge of how difficult it is for any building to achieve it : and this also explains a little, I think, the occasional surprising want of accurate knowledge on the part of the Chinese connoisseur concerning the date of some of his most admired and precious temples. . . . It is very old — or it looks very old : both are the same to him. And should a building truly prove to be of great age, he is agreeably surprised. . . . So would he regard the Palace ; it looks very old, it is very old. . . .

A tragic air broods in these bright, cold courts, fanned by arctic winds and yet so much sadder for the warmth and light of this sun, which, enclosed after this fashion by stone and marble, contrives to impart a certain heat, enough to make the blood thaw from the heart of winter. And in each hall, with its tall, red columns and gold ceiling and coloured walls, broods a painted, gilded and shimmering-eyed beauty, like that of a peacock's tail, in which the Manchu Emperors seem still angrily to live and move, as might a wasp in the heart of a ripe nectarine. . . . Nevertheless, as you look out of the door, at square vista after square vista, slanting roof pitched beyond slanting roof, no thought asserts itself — as it must, for example, in the Palace of the Old Seraglio in Constantinople — of the dramas, more often melodramas, enacted against this background, of the tyrannical and not seldom hateful characters of the rulers, of the sinister plottings of the eunuchs, or the resultant murders and tortures, nor any stain of that Imperial hocus-pocus, skulls and owls' feathers, tainted so plainly with both witchcraft and infantilism ; no, the Palace represents in perfection the serene character of the people ruled, their sense of order and, formerly, of piety, their ingenuity and permeating poetic consciousness.

I have been fortunate enough to see the Forbidden City under snow, and it was a sight unforgettably lovely. The huge buildings floated upon clouds, were borne up by them, like the Hospital of St. John the Baptist (the only building said to have been designed by El Greco himself) in the master's famous picture of Toledo and the landscape surrounding it.[1] The glory that shone from the ground (for it seemed now as if more light came up from the earth than down from the sky) imparted a brilliance beyond belief to the interiors, to the great red pillars, up the length of which golden dragons clawed their way, to doors and frescoed walls ; and still more glittering was it outside, where it reverberated up against the flashing eaves which supported the quilted tents of snow covering the roofs. Below, the white terraces were now whiter still, beneath their soft loads of swansdown : and this expanse of whiteness still further exaggerated the size of hall and of court. Even the moats beyond were padded out of sight, the canals extinguished ; and in the gardens, the dark foliage of cypress and cedar made startling patterns, of lace and fans and cubist needles, over the light ground. From the walk round the top of the Guard-House, floating high above walls and roof — a

[1] This picture was, until the Revolution, in the Casa del Greco in Toledo.

walk, like that in the gallery of an Italian Romanesque cathedral, just wide enough for one person — the more distant towers and gateways of the Forbidden City appeared sombre and isolated by this whiteness. . . . But astonishing as were the reversals of appearance undergone by the great buildings, it was the delicacy of the nearer details that, by this new emphasis placed upon them, triumphed ; the flowers painted upon a shutter, the bird or crag upon a panel, were now luminous and melting as the snow itself. In this chapter, I have tried to dwell upon the solidity and massiveness of Chinese architecture, because that is a side of it with which those who have not visited China — and above all Peking — are necessarily unacquainted : but it is the other aspect, of Chinese art and Chinese life, which we now approach.

*CHAPTER SIX*

THE PHOENIX TREE

Here we exchange the winter for the spring, and the great apartments of state for the residential quarters of the Imperial Family, of the Princesses and Concubines and Ladies-in-Waiting.

I decided to walk, for it was a delicious morning, and there was a stir in all the narrow lanes ; a ferment, due to the fine weather, which seemed to make the sellers cry their wares twice as lustily, and the customers to buy twice as much. Moreover, there were newcomers ; the seller of gold-fish, for instance, who, with plaintive voice, was singing the praises of the flashing fins and goggling eyes in which he dealt, while the water in his tank swished a little, from side to side, as he walked. Then there were men offering roses, and, though they were not yet out in Peking, small bunches of peonies of two varieties, called " Concubine Yang " [1] and " Doltish White ",[2] and others who carried large baskets of cherries, piled up and glittering.

[1] See Tun Lich'en's *Annual Customs and Festivals in Peking.*     [2] *Ibid.*

. . . At present, little fruit had appeared in the streets, and the cherries were but the forerunners of countless others ; strawberries and peaches and plums. Then would follow melons. (Just as water-melons remain the choice of the poor, so that, in their season, you will see their black-spotted, cut-up quarters, that look as if their substance had been dyed scarlet, for sale on barrows everywhere in Peking, in the same way, among those who can afford them, sweet melons are most in demand ; favourite kinds being Green Skin Crushables, Hami Crisps,[1] Dry Golden Droppers, Old Man's Delight, Wei Pulps,[2] and Sheephorn Honeys.) And, after them, grapes, announced as being " sweet as sugar ". . . . But, in default of these summer delights, which would so soon be here, the cry of the vendor of a kind of ice re-sounded all day long down the Hutungs.

> " I give big helpings of *Fallen Snowflowers,*
> Cool, sweet, good to drink,
> They soothe your thirst and put out fires." [3]

Nearer the Forbidden City, these sounds died down, and in the wide old roads beneath its walls everything at this time of morning, between nine and ten, was quiet ; but happily quiet. Only the occasional, rhythmical padding of a ricksha man was to be heard in them. By the broad moat, the birds were singing hosannas within shrill bowers of transparent young leaves, poised far above even these high, ancient, pink walls. An old gentleman, wearing a very elegant, black silk robe and a black billycock — the only billycock I saw in the whole of China — was pro-

---

[1] See *Annual Customs and Festivals in Peking.* Dr. Bodde notes that Hami and Wei are both places in Chinese Turkestan.　　　　[2] *Ibid.*

[3] Adapted from Mr. R. W. Swallow's translation of the cry in *Sidelights on Peking Life.*

menading slowly up and down in the sun, sheltered from the spring wind by the wall. In his hand he carried a bird in a cage, for birds are taken out for walks on spring mornings in China, as naturally as are dogs in England. Indeed, had I been out here at sunrise, I should no doubt have noticed, even at that early hour, various of them being given their outings, for the voices of valuable singing birds are reputed to lose in power and sweetness unless, in suitable weather, allowed to greet the dawn. (Being delicate, and the air fresh at that hour, they are conveyed in cages draped with cloth. . . . Nor need this custom of singing at sunrise fall too hardly on the bird-owner who is by nature a sluggard, for he can utilise the services of a professional Peking bird-airer.)[1]  This bird, however, was not singing for the moment ; so presently the old gentleman sat down on a fallen trunk lying by the water's edge, and took the little creature out of its prison, so that it stood on his extended forearm, clapping its wings and preening itself, and at once added to the great chorus of song in the branches above its own jets and spurts of pleasure and contentment. . . . But it never attempted to join its fellows, or the other, further flocks that lived opposite, over the moat, in the fan-shaped, smoke-grey leafage of a grove of ancient cedars.

Drawing near the gates of the Forbidden City, we enter it this time from under the shadow of Coal Hill. Soon we have crossed the threshold, and are walking down huge, interminable passages, straight and wide as the road to sin, that run between tall red walls open to the sky. These were known to the former inhabitants of the Palace as

---

[1] See chapter entitled " Various Professions " (p. 79) in *Sidelights on Peking Life*, by Robert W. Swallow.

" streets ", and are in direct communication with the part of it we have already seen. Traps for the sun and light, these long basking-places for lizards are in themselves impressive, running the whole stretch of the City, so that the stranger finds the ends of them continually receding into infinity, and in time notices the new, small measure of his own height against the walls. Turning to the right out of these corridors, however, as soon as we can, we discover, instead of those immense and frozen courts of a mathematical beauty that we visited in the winter, painted clusters of little gardens and patios and pavilions, gay as an air by Mozart, twisted rocks and clear pools, old trees set as though they were jewels, and fountains, smiling, stone lions and pots of flowers and lattice-work screens and small terraces under pink and green canopies of wood, and trellises that weave the light with shade, and rare shrubs and huge bowls of gold-fish. In the walls dividing the courts are set windows of fantastic shape, that transform the vistas seen through them (since every frame makes its own picture, and the view, for example, through a circular window is very different from the same view seen through a pointed or a square one). And the formality of the great corridors that enclose all this lightness makes it seem all the more enchanting, just as, perhaps, their vast scale tends to produce the impression that these courts are smaller than their actual proportions.

Certainly the Family Temples that flank some of them are large and stately : but even their height and dignity only add to the joyousness of these worlds where all nature is reduced for our delight. . . . Inside the pavilions, it is true, the furniture that remains — apart from one or two musical clocks — is poor, and the paint peeling. There are a few pieces of carved red lacquer, with squat, bow legs, some thin porcelain, and European furniture that once belonged to a family of missionaries ; but the colours of the rooms, the flowers that seem breathed, more than painted, upon silk, the dragons that are radiant in their menace as butterflies, the little mirrors and looking-glass pictures, are insouciant as the day outside : for undoubtedly it is the garden just below, and the day that prospers it, which are the chief impression of these rooms. That is to say, the exterior is more important than the interior ; and for the proper comprehension of a palace or a garden of this sort, the fact is not without significance.

Here, for the first time since arriving in China, we begin, also, to grasp how the idea of *chinoiserie* seized on our ancestors. . . . Nevertheless, it is no easy matter to attribute such buildings and objects to the correct date. Elsewhere, the prevalence of a similar feeling would indicate the middle of the eighteenth century. This particular sensibility, I mean — this particular response to nature, a response at once gay, natural and, in a way, artificial, — gave us the art of the middle and late eighteenth century in Europe. But here, on the other hand, it is often to be detected in things made at least a thousand years earlier, as much as at any subsequent period. Thus, two or three of these fragile little pavilions were constructed in the reign of a Ming Emperor, and so are three or four hundred years old. Further, several of the trees, set in stone borders, have inscriptions attached to them which prove their age to be greater than one would expect.

And now, since here the exit to a room is more important than the entrance, let us continue to look outward. The sun, for so early in the year — it is still April — im-

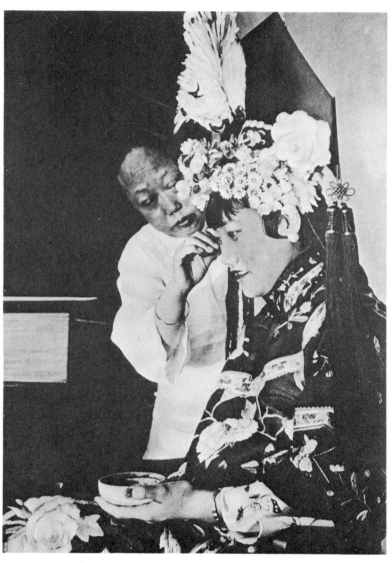

A MANCHU GIRL IN PEKING, BEING ASSISTED TO DRESS
BY HER MAID

parts a considerable warmth, and the cascades of flowers, of green whips and tresses, pour down the weeping trees. Huge bushes of yellow, button-like roses stand beneath raised wooden balconies, and wistaria droops mauve and smoky showers over every trellis, or grows independently, its writhing coils supported by stout staves painted a coral pink. Emerald-green lizards flicker across paths from under rocks or bask uneasily on wall-tops, for the spring has entered into even their cold, reptilian blood, and, though the singing of the birds in the bushes here is more intimate, not of so polyphonic an order as in the bowers overhanging the walls, it is none the less vivacious and full of high spirits. The whole of this world of green things focusing the sun-rays, of pavilions and pillars and balconies, their tones, faded but glowing, with pink and green and scarlet and blue, of moss and rocks and pools and flowers, seem to have grown together, coeval and tangled. (And this, indeed, is the impression of every garden in China, being as true of the courts of the temples in the Western Hill as it is of a Peking town garden.)

Here, more than Central Park outside the wall, and once the chief pleasure-ground of Imperial times, is for us the best place in which to try and understand the Chinese garden. Up till now, in the winter, it has been difficult to comprehend, for it has consisted of a little dry earth, a bare tree and a deformed-looking rock. But now it is easier, and these courts, though in fact much bigger than the ordinary Chinese garden, and though, too, they differ from it because they cling to no landscape, are yet not, like Central Park, too big for our purpose : they are typical enough. Indeed, if we dare to use a word in England so weighed down with Art and Craft and Greek dresses and Peasant

Pottery, this is a garden city. And, since the Chinese garden is everywhere part of the Chinese house, it should, bearing this always in mind, be carefully examined.

The most pronounced obstacle to its understanding is the Chinese love — whereto allusion has already been made — for those contorted rocks to be seen in every ambitious Chinese garden, whether belonging to house or temple or palace. (How greatly the Chinese would revel in Stonehenge, how many fruit-trees would they plant in its centre and with what numberless coils of wistaria vines drape the supported, horizontal boulders !) They must be crags grotesque or sinister, worthy of exhibition in the surrealist museum, natural objects with a kink, born with a likeness to something else, to a mountain, to a man or a thing he has fashioned, to an animal, an insect, even : and the more fantasy the stones betray, the more complicated and extravagant their resemblance to, let us say, an ant-eater, a microscope or a motor-car, the more they esteem and wonder at it, being willing to pay for a single such object several hundreds of pounds. The Chinese mind is curiously haunted in several directions by this admiration of resemblances, whether resulting from accident or intention. Thus, for example, in Pei-Hai, on the Island of the White Dagoba, an inscription written by the Emperor Ch'ien Lung specially praises a predecessor of the Sung Dynasty for having brought to this hill " many rocks from the South and placed them here in fanciful positions to make them look like dragons' scales ".[1] . . . It is a love which we, I believe, shall never share for long, only during a passing surrealist phase : but to Chinese eyes, perhaps, no more strange than the English national addiction to herbaceous

[1] *In Search of Old Peking*, p. 87.

borders, in which they see merely an outrage committed on nature, the running-riot of unsubtle and barbarous minds, blazing with a desire to achieve colour, or a whole painting where one stroke of the brush would have better achieved the purpose. And so, let us leave it.

Other features come more easily to our taste. . . . Robert Fortune, writing of a garden in Canton, has a passage applicable equally to one in Northern China. Despite the slight contempt he always evinces for everything that is not Britisn and Victorian, he truly herein succeeds a little in explaining the principles to be grasped before we can hope to appreciate a Chinese garden in a *Chinese* way, as opposed to a *European*. " In order to understand the Chinese style of gardening it is necessary to dispel from the mind all ideas of fine lawns, broad walks and extensive views : [1] and to picture in their stead everything on a small scale — that is, narrow paved walks, dwarf walls in all directions, with lattice-work or ornamental openings in them, in order to give views of the scenery beyond ; halls, summer-houses and alcoves, ponds or small lakes with zigzag walks over them — in short, an endeavour to make small things appear large, and large things small, and everything Chinese."

This summing-up is, in many respects, just. The realisation that space is relative, that large effects can be achieved in small compass, is thoroughly Chinese. (The Japanese exaggerate it still further, until it assumes a recognised symbolism. . . . Thus, when I looked at a Japanese garden, about the size of a small table-top, in a monastery, and asked what a minute piece of rather white sand near the middle, with a herring-bone pattern scratched

[1] *A Residence Among the Chinese,* by Robert Fortune. (Murray, 1857.)

on it, might be, the monk replied, rather angrily, in a manner strongly implying that any averagely sensitive person would at once see the resemblance for himself : " That, Honourable Sir, is moonlight on the Gobi Desert ".) And it must be remembered that this ability for forgetting, or overcoming, actual dimension, is further emphasised in the little courts of the Forbidden City by the fact that the view to be obtained here is not of a misty hill, with, beyond, a bamboo thicket by a stream, but only of the miniature prospect framed by the walls of the next enclosure.

In another book,[1] Fortune again reverts to these theories, and at the same time gives us some telling details of the arrangement of the garden of a Mandarin in Ning-po in Northern China.

". . . The building of artificial rockwork is so well understood, that the resemblance to nature is perfect, and it forms a principal feature in every garden. . . . The small courts . . . are fitted up with this rockwork, dwarf trees are planted here and there in various places, and creepers hang down naturally and gracefully until their ends touch the little ponds of water which are always placed in front of the rockwork. These small places being passed, we are again led through passages . . . when the garden, with its dwarf trees, vases, rockwork, ornamental windows, and beautiful flowering shrubs, is suddenly opened to the view. . . . It must be understood, however, that all . . . is very limited in extent, but the most is made of it by windings and glimpses through rockwork, and arches in the walls, as well as by hiding the boundary with a mass of shrubs and trees ". . . . In nearly all his descriptions of gardens,

[1] *Three Years' Wanderings in the Northern Provinces of China*, by Robert Fortune. (Murray, 1847.)

though in this one it is omitted, he refers to how *Chinese* they look : and indeed the strength of the Chinese national flavour always surprises the foreigner, however well he may have prepared himself for it.

But I think a very important point about the Chinese garden, and one that influences it deeply and applies to it no less than to many other aspects of the national life, he fails altogether to mention. Indeed, I have not seen it ever stated in relationship to this art. In the preface I quoted, more fully, a passage from Dr. Derk Bodde [1] in which, among many admirable and revealing words, he writes : ". . . in the Chinese, as perhaps in no other people, has been developed a keen consciousness and awareness of the movement and rhythm of Nature, as evidenced in the yearly rotation of the seasons ". . . . In Europe we have, of course, our spring gardens and autumn gardens : but it seemed to me, when I was there, that the Chinese gardens were, above all, a vehicle for the seasons, a channel cut for them to flow down, as a channel is cut for water. To vary the metaphor, gardens, in fact, were the formalised means of self-expression humbly offered to Nature by man. In the winter, it is true, they are utterly dead, more dead than ours, but, for the rest, each piece is set, and flames out with the month and with the season. When the great rose-bush is in flower nothing else exists, it has the same relation to other plants and flowers as the full moon to the stars, and stone and marble and pavilions and green trees are there to do it honour. When, later, the peonies on their terraces, or the lotuses in the pool, open out, they again, each in turn, clearly constitute the only reason for the garden : everything must have been designed for them : but within a

[1] See Tun Lich'en's *Annual Customs and Festivals in Peking.*

295

week after their fading, a hitherto unnoticed magnolia decks itself with China-white blossoms that turn in a few days to a tawny vellum, and it becomes plain that the whole machinery of house and garden has been fashioned round this dark, glossy-leaved mast of full summer. Each season is thus afforded the means of a perfect self-expression. It is impossible to exaggerate the importance, too, of other, smaller adjuncts, all of which go to the production of the effect ; bird-cages, flower-pots, stone lions, fountains, the correct tones in the paint, the right shade from the trees, chosen because of their shape, for their position, the exact placing of the water so that it assumes the desired colour, the precise angle of the paths, the appropriate resemblance in the natural rock, the most effective gold-fish bowls, and, above all, the finest gold-fish, selected upon their points by connoisseurs, in the same way that a prize bulldog would be judged in England. (The Chinese, I am sure, would love and admire the bulldog — almost a dragon-dog — its straying, straining eyes and curious legs.) In fact, as Robert Fortune remarks, here is the endeavour to make everything Chinese : and in nothing is the prolonged attempt more obvious than in these grotesque, finny monsters ; to whom, indeed, Western writers have paid latterly so many tributes of horror or admiration (one of the best and most descriptive of which occurs in Mr. Peter Quennell's *Superficial Journey through Tokyo and Tibet*) that I hesitate to add another leaf to the weedy wreaths of their fame. Nevertheless, they are an undoubted part of the Chinese garden.

Hundreds of years of careful breeding have gone to the making and perfection of these diverse types, at once monstrous and foppish, the counterpart in the piscine world of dwarf trees in the arboreal. It is not certain in what particular epoch [1] the Chinese first began to show their interest in them, for gold-fish are native to the rivers of China and are still to be found therein, swimming wild and free and undeformed. They were said to have been reared, though, since the twelfth century in the small ponds that yet existed not so long ago in the vicinity of the Altar of Heaven, and formerly there were dozens of similar ponds, all stocked from them, in the neighbourhood of Peking. Now, however, they are for the most part raised in wooden tubs, and the pools are dry. But, notwithstanding, the demand for them must still be very great. They are to be seen everywhere, sold in the streets, or swimming at their ease in house and garden. In the Fifth Month, the beginning of which varies between late May and June, an awning is hung overhead in the smaller courtyards against the heat of the sun. Then " the pomegranates come into flower, so that their fresh lustre dazzles the eyes. Householders all have them arranged in their courtyard together with oleanders. . . . Between the pomegranates and the oleanders there must always be a large earthenware fish-jar arranged in a symmetrical way, with several gold-fish swimming inside. In practically every house it is like this, so that there is a Peking proverb which speaks of ' a mat covering overhead, an earthenware fish-jar, and a pomegranate tree ', thus mocking at their uniformity." [2] Moreover, to prove how essential they are still considered to the Peking house in summer, it may be mentioned that for the feeding of their gold-fish many of the richer citizens employ a pro-

[1] I am indebted again to Messrs. Arlington and Lewisohn, from whose *In Search of Old Peking* this information concerning gold-fish is derived.
[2] See Tun Lich'en's *Annual Customs and Festivals in Peking*. This was written about 1900.

fessional gold-fish tender, part of whose duty consists in netting from pools and watercourses the animalcules upon which these burnished, gleaming creatures feed. An arrangement can be made with him, by which he will undertake, besides the supply of their food, to change the water when necessary, and to be responsible, generally, for their health and comfort. His profession is one which probably exists nowhere else in the world : [1] for nowhere else is the gold-fish so important.

Near the entrances of Central Park and Pei-Hai stand whole lines of great bowls, their inhabitants being appraised, point by point, for hours at a time, by enthusiastic amateurs. Like all creatures highly bred, they are delicate, and great care has to be devoted to them. For so long as the weather is cold, they remain indoors. Thus they have only just made a welcome début, their appearance being as eagerly awaited as, for instance, is the opening of the flat-racing season in England. Here, on the contrary, in each of the courts and gardens of the Forbidden City, there are no more than two gold-fish bowls, brown-green bowls of glazed earthenware — large and deep as an Italian terracotta garden pot — placed on a terrace or balcony. But, though they have but so lately taken to open-air life, the flashing denizens of these still waters look as happy as though the Empress Dowager herself were still able to keep an eye on their welfare. Wandering from bowl to bowl in the different courts, we observe the varieties ; some are gold, and some are silver, and some are scarlet with black markings, some are striped and barred like wasps and some are all of black velvet, with gold pouches under the eyes, some have trans-

---

[1] See chapter entitled " Various Professions " (p. 79) in *Sidelights on Peking Life*, by Robert W. Swallow.

parent scales and some are of sepia velvet spangled with gold or silver, some have a fuzzy, churrigueresque repetition of tails, or tails like diaphanous crinolines, some have fins that have become antennae and streamers, and all of them have eyes that are yet more fantastic than their bodies ; protruding, bulbous eyes, eyes at angles, swivel eyes, eyes at the top of their heads, eyes like those of dragons, eyes like those of German Princes in the eighteenth century. . . . So they float, goggling at time itself, flickering and turning, clad in their draperies of sable and gold, engaged, some of them, after the manner of Salome, in an eternal Dance of the Seven Veils. Except that the single strand of their grotesquerie unites them, they might all of them, with their glorious heraldic titles of Red Dragon Eye, Five Colour Stripes, Blue Dragon Eye, or with schoolboy nicknames attached to them such as Tiger's Head, Celestial Telescope (because the eyes are in this instance on the top of the head) and Toad Head,[1] be so many different species. . . . Nevertheless, here these creatures are what — to paraphrase Walter Pater — in the ways of a thousand years, men have come to desire.

Two other distinctively Chinese features of the gardens are the peony terraces and the stone mounds. To take peonies first, these will not be out for another fortnight, but the straw under which they are kept warm in the winter has long been removed, and their buds are already thick and well developed. Their coming is awaited with much eagerness, since they are the national flower of China, and more care has been lavished for centuries upon their cultivation than upon that of any other plant. No one who

[1] The Japanese call it " Dutch Lion Head ". (See Arlington and Lewisohn's *In Search of Old Peking*.)

has not seen the magnificent tree-peonies of Peking, and, next to them, of Korea, can imagine the fragrance and beauty to which they attain, as a result of this devotion, in a climate that suits them. Those in English gardens bear the same relation in beauty to the Peking peony as an ordinary pheasant bears to a golden or Amherst. Moreover, in spite of the much more considerable size of the flowers, they possess more shape, are less opaque, seem to retain the light within the dazzling clusters of their petals, the frilled outline of each of which is delicate as a Chinese drawing. These blossoms attract to themselves a crowd all through the day, and the terraces whereon they grow — and of which the cement border is claimed to be made according to a secret formula of the masons of Peking — are calculated so that connoisseurs can walk round, examining each tree as an entity and in detail, noting how each stem is disposed, how each flower opens and each petal unfolds.

The peonies, as I have said, are not yet out : but this is just the time to climb, and appreciate the purpose of, the neighbouring stone mounds : which must not be confused with the odd-shaped natural rocks we have already discussed. These are little heaps of rocks, cemented together, so as to look like a miniature mountain. In themselves, they help to diversify the aspect of a garden court, but, in addition, there is a reason for them. A wayward path ascends each one to the summit, which varies between ten and twenty feet from the ground. Here is a flat space, with a pretty, painted bench, sheltered at the back by the stone, where we can sit. For the whole of this has been planned and devised so that you can quietly and at your ease survey the top of an apple or cherry tree or a Judas-tree in blossom at your feet, or nearer, at your knees. . . . I am told that flowering fruit-trees are equally beautiful elsewhere, and certainly I have often admired them on the slopes of Etna, in Corfu and in English orchards, but I have never met with any that appeared to be as lovely as these. Never, I think, have I seen such loads of blossom, contrasting with such ancient, gnarled trunks. But it may be merely that I was thus enabled to see them from a new, insect-like level, very near, but from above.

It was easy to spend, after the manner of the Chinese themselves, a full morning watching the apple tree, to which in this case the small climb led me, revealing a hitherto unsuspected world of beauty. The whole air over it was scented and humming with thousands of fluttering wings. Even the deleterious wasp, in his uniform of a Papal Guard, seemed now to be so fully occupied as to be almost pleasant. Drones vied with workers in an appearance of industry — very irritating, no doubt, to those in the know. Butterflies (which must, too, it seemed, have been bred by Chinese amateurs), with sails painted and striped and dotted and chequered, with goggling eyes and long antennae, hovered with quick-beating wings and then alit on the gold-speckled, quivering, sun-soaked blossom, which, as one waited there, could be seen coming to life. Tight little pink buds and rosettes began to lose a little of their colour in this heat, became more luminous, turned to a more transparent gauze, then crinkled open right to their golden hearts. A subtle intoxication immediately emanated from them, and the bees, their furry bodies dusty and powdered as a miller's from their trade, turned drowsy and lingered on in the swaying cups that enclosed them, there to praise incessantly with deep drone and buzz the creator of apple-trees. . . .

Then a small bird blundered cheerfully through the curtain of petals and, his wings freckled now with gold, stayed there, tilting a branch with his weight, until it swung up and down and a petal dropped slowly, somersaulting as it turned, to the ground. . . . It was a world lovely and fresh as a poem by Herrick.

As I sat there, I tried again to compare the Chinese national sensibility with our own. It was possible, I thought, to detect the continuance of the Chinese Middle Ages in the Peking of today, and, equally, to discover the eighteenth century in the China of a thousand years ago. And many times, too, I had been reminded here, by things I saw, of the sensuous levels of Herrick's poetry ; a consciousness, I suppose, that belonged strictly to his age, though no one but he expressed that particular feeling — except occasionally Marvell — with the same perfection. Often, because of this, I had urged Chinese friends to translate Herrick's poems into Chinese, but they were always too busy with Karl Marx, Freud or Paul Valéry, to be able to bother about him. . . . Yet it could not be doubted that the Chinese would appreciate such poems as " How Lilies came White " and " The Weeping Cherry ". Equally Herrick, I was convinced, would have immediately comprehended the feelings and esthetic sensibility of the Chinese. He would have enjoyed their food and wine, and would have written a poem to the bird he would have taken out for a walk here upon every fine spring morning. And, as we know from " To Larr ", he liked the song of crickets.

> No more shall I, since I am driven hence,
> Devote to thee my graines of Frankincense :
> No more shall I from mantle-trees hang down,
> To honour thee, my little Parsley crown :

No more shall I (I fear me) to thee bring
My chives of Garlick for an offering :
No more shall I, from henceforth, heare a quire
Of merry Crickets by my Country fire :
Go where I will, thou lucky Larr stay here,
Warm by a glit'ring chimney all the year.

To the Chinese — as, indeed, to the Florentine — ear,
the music of the cricket is enchanting, and, though now
they no longer employ these little creatures, at any rate in
the north, as gladiators, they had been equally sought after
for their powers of fighting. Cricket-keeping — rather
than, as with us, wicket-keeping — had constituted the
national pastime. In former times it had been a passion.
. . . Cages for butterflies, little porcelain prisons, that, notwithstanding their delicacy, have always appeared to me
too stout a cell for such fragile captives, I had seen often
enough to know what they were — though not to this
day have I seen them in use — but, though I had met with
one or two in the antique shops of Europe, I had never
grasped the purpose, somehow or other, of a cricket-cage,
had deemed it just a box of odd shape such as the Chinese
like. Nor had I comprehended the great value that the
Mandarins had formerly placed upon them. So high were
the prices to which their own determined competition drove
them, that the nobles of Peking, " not content merely with
music, women and precious stones ",[1] ruined themselves as
eagerly and completely over the buying of these cages as
ever did the more stolid Dutch merchants in gambling for
their tulip bulbs. The largest sums of all were given for
those made by the Imperial Porcelain Factory in the reign
of the Emperor Yung Lo,[2] and next after them were esteemed

[1] See Tun Lich'en's *Annual Customs and Festivals in Peking.*
[2] A.D. 1402–1424.

the so-called " gourd vessels ", which, both in colour and shape, rather resemble an *aubergine*.

Some grigs were valued, then, only for their golden voices,[1] others for their duelling ability. Some, again — but very few — possessed both attributes to perfection. Such were those born in Hu Chia Ts'un, a village some fifteen miles from Peking; super-crickets against which no others could match their music or their strength. " Their sound is that of *shang*, and their nature is that of conquest." [2] In the course of time, the citizens of Peking learnt how artificially to rear them at home during the winter. Within a month of their ceasing to be larvae, they would sing " even more delicately than in the autumn ".[3] But at the coming of spring, they would die.

These hot-house crickets, as it were, remained very expensive : but there were many less costly breeds. From the end of May they were sold in the streets, growing cheaper as the summer deepened. Those for sale in June were bought only for their voices, the favourite kinds being called Little Golden Bells, Noisy Ones, Old Rice Mandibles, Clothes Beaters' Heads and Oily Ones.[4] Little Golden Bells were imported into Peking from a distance, and Lich'en records of them, " When one listens to them while lying in bed, their chirp is surpassingly clear, musical but not sad, as if they were born to be creatures of large rooms and lofty halls. Surely their title of Golden Bell has not been one extravagantly conferred on them." [5] On the other hand, the song of the Oily Ones was " vibrating yet pro-

---

[1] Other kinds of singing insects are also esteemed for their voices, and bring comparatively high prices.

[2] See Tun Lich'en's *Annual Customs and Festivals in Peking*. Dr. Bodde explains that *shang* is the Chinese scale of five notes.

[3] *Ibid.* pp. 81-83.      [4] *Ibid.* p. 115.      [5] *Ibid.* p. 63.

longed ", and " one may feel both joy and sadness as one listens to it on a winter night. Truly is it a sound appropriate to the man of leisure. . . ." [1] But the most costly of all were those bred alone for fighting, which made their short and seasonal appearance in mid-August. These were named Bamboo-Joint Whiskers, Crab-Shell Greens, Yellow-Mottled Heads, White-Mottled Heads, Plum-Flower Winged Ones and Guitar-Winged Ones.

Sitting there above the warm hum and throb of the apple tree, I continued to think about the grigs, and recalled a thing I had forgotten ; how bitterly disappointed a Chinese friend of mine had been in visiting England, when, on taking a ticket for a " cricket match " at the Oval, he had found so different and lengthy a combat in progress ! He had visualised it all so well, for he had asked questions beforehand ; the Oval, a green pitch, similar to their own red cloths laid down for the fight, the little " cricket pavilion " in which the insects were kept, the white-coated umpires, the boards for scoring. . . . I wondered, looking round, if any cricket combats had ever taken place within these courts.[2] Cricket-song there must have been : but, at the moment, the insect orchestra above the blossom furnished the only music. This world of painted wood and coloured tiles and flowers and green things growing seemed made, indeed, more for the use and setting of

[1] *Ibid.* p. 63.

[2] The most famous contests between crickets took place in restaurants before feasts. The insects were first weighed on very precise scales, and then placed in a pot on a red-covered table. . . . At the end of the contest the winner, uttering cries of triumph, would pursue the wretched vanquished grig round the red cloth. The loser, however, would be rapidly rescued by his trainer before he was badly injured.

The trainers were not paid outright, but took a percentage of the owners' profits. Sometimes the betting was very heavy, and men would risk their whole fortunes on one battle. (See chapter on " Various Professions " in *Sidelights on Peking Life*, by Robert W. Swallow.)

insect life than for that of human, as though some Imperial Locust or Butterfly and his suite had inhabited it. . . . And, alas, though all these things appeared to be blending together into one entity, it was the trees that would out-live the buildings. Within the space of a few years, if integration and disintegration proceeded at the same pace, there might be left here no more than a rock or two and an apple tree in bloom. (On the site of Yüan Ming Yüan, even less than that remains, though it was built of stone.) Yet never, I am sure, will the Chinese cease to produce lovely things of the same kind : there will always be dragons and pools and pavilions and flowering trees in China, for their attitude to nature arises from their very hearts and beings.

It was now close on noon, and I climbed down the steps to leave, thinking how happy the Manchu Princesses must have been, resting in the peace of these gardens during the long lacquered days of spring and summer ; a peace only disturbed by the occasional rumours of a disappearance in the Forbidden City, a death of favourite or eunuch, the news of which, though unexpected and sudden, did not take those who heard it quite so much by surprise as might have been presumed by newcomers unused to Peking palace-life. How happy, too, those calm and listless hours spent in the canopied Imperial Barge on the waters of the North Sea Lake. . . . Now, since I was due to lunch in a restaurant there, I turned my feet in that direction. And, walking by the side of this lake, so loved by two monarchs as remote from each other in time and temperament as Kubla and the Empress Dowager, I was by chance the witness of an incident typical of country and people.

A fine avenue of cedars led away from the lake at an

angle.  Something, I did not know what, drew my attention
toward them.  They were very old, and I wondered whether
any of their magnificent, rough-grained trunks could possibly have still been there in the time of the Grand Khan,
when the deer used to assemble in dappled pools in the
shade, as though in an English park.  But, all at once, a
movement — the same thing, presumably, that must in the
first place have directed my gaze toward them —, a curious
flickering in the air round one of the trees, made me concentrate upon it.  It was on fire !  And before long, fanned
by the spring breeze, flames, the pale golden flames of daylight, were licking all its limbs, flowing and twisting round
them.  I do not think I had ever seen a tree on fire before.
It was burning like a torch upswept by wind, branch after
branch, right up to its top.  A tremendous crackling and
spluttering began to sound out in the noon stillness, and
showers of golden stars exploded and fell round. . . .
Now, however, another noise asserted itself, coming ever
nearer from the distance.  It was a fire-engine ; which
dashed up, snorting in fine style.  Within a few moments,
ladders had shot up into the air from nothing, like the
mythical mango-trees of Indian conjurors, while Chinese
firemen, in the livery of their calling, and wearing the
Roman brass helmets that were formerly its pride all the
world over, had begun to swarm up them, sending great
jets and arcs of water over the tree and into its hollow trunk,
subduing the flames and getting them under control.  I
think the men themselves — it was my impression at the
time — vastly enjoyed the union of fountains with fireworks which their present task entailed.  Certainly they
showed the greatest agility and fearlessness, and before
long the charred trunk and its branches were covered with

this swarm of golden locusts. A lovely sight it was, too, this phoenix tree, its old form, still smoking, full of these gesticulating but intent beings in their incongruous attire, and one not to be encountered, I believe, elsewhere ; as unmistakably Chinese as the gardens described by Robert Fortune, as cricket-cage, ambulatory bird or the flowering cherry I had seen long ago in that garden in England. . . .

But now we must return to winter.

### CHAPTER SEVEN

## THE ANCESTRAL HALL
## OF THE
## EXALTED BRAVE AND LOYAL

Some readers of this book may wonder what has happened to the inhabitants of this wonderful series of halls, pavilions and gardens which I have attempted to describe ; they will know that the Emperor of China, Hsüan T'ung, became, first of all, Mr. Henry P'u Yi, and then Emperor of Manchukuo, the original ancestral domain of his house, but they may think of all the others, Court officials and dependents who peopled the Palace City, and for a moment speculate concerning their fate, how many of them are still alive, and what they are doing ? . . . One group of them, indeed, I encountered, surviving and still living together in a community.

The flatness of the plain which surrounds Peking is broken in a few instances by little rolling hills that, bare and brown, resemble in the winter vast tumuli, and in the narrow clefts between them are hidden many dying temples. Sometimes, when the golden dust-clouds whirl across Eastern Asia from the Gobi Desert, and an icy wind insinuates a layer of dust between the pages of every book in the house, it seems, if you go in their direction, as though these buildings must have been translated into heaven, as if the crumbling stone and brick must have ascended in the cloud of its own disintegration and there been assembled again among the blue distances and snowy peaks that are today obscured. A thick golden haze blurs the outline of roof and wall and tree until you are a few yards off them. . . . Such a day it was when, on the advice and in the company of a great friend who lives in Peking, we set off one afternoon on an expedition, the object of which, buried among these tomb-like hills and now so seldom visited, is yet quite near the city in space, though many hundreds of years, it seems, removed from it in time, and, therefore, perhaps, so difficult to find : Kang T'ieh Miao, the Temple and Refuge of the Palace Eunuchs.

No road led to it, that much we knew. So, leaving Chang's motor at the roadside (today he had not accompanied us), we started to walk over these small, dry, rounded hills in the whistling, frosty wind — or rather, winds ; for two systems of dust fought and swooped in the air, throwing into action squadron after squadron of flying particles, one the invasion launched from the Gobi Desert, the other, defensive, rising from the ground itself. Yet, through the cold, stinging bombardment of these atoms upon our faces, the sun, a golden fleece that showed but dimly, yet shone, unexpectedly, a little warm. Only in the valleys, round sheltered corners, was it possible to speak : elsewhere your breath was wrung from you, your words were snatched from your mouth in the act of talking. . . . And so, the story of Kang T'ieh, which, as we struggled along, trying to find the temple named after that

Chinese General of long ago, our friend essayed to tell us, was fragmentary, although he flung his words boldly in the teeth of the wind, and endowed them with all that feeling for *morbidezza* (by which I do *not* mean morbidity), for high lights and shadows, which a childhood spent in Italy had bestowed upon him (a feeling which gave both to his written and spoken words a special sensitiveness in their application). But I shall tell it in a short and businesslike way, although it is, indeed, an extraordinary tale, and belongs as much to the *Arabian Nights* as to history.

A little over five centuries ago, the Emperor Yung Lo decided to place Kang T'ieh, a very distinguished and reliable officer, in charge of the Forbidden City in the newly built capital of Peking, during his own absence on a hunting expedition. Pleased and proud at such a mark of the Imperial confidence, nevertheless the General was dismayed by it, being only too well versed in the plots and intrigues of palace-life in China. The probability was, so his observation and experience taught him, that, on the return of the Emperor, some powerful enemy, actuated by jealousy of so open a display of favour, would allege that the Governor of the Palace had taken advantage of his position of trust by making love to the Imperial Concubines. Since, above all other things, Kang valued the trust of the Son of Heaven and his own honour, and because he felt so certain of the course of future events, in order to anticipate them and frustrate all such machinations, he reached an unusual decision : voluntarily to castrate himself before the Emperor left, without telling him, but making sure that proof of the date upon which it took place could be produced if necessary.

Directly he returned, the Emperor, his mind inflamed by the lies of one of his ministers, sent for Kang and, as this faithful servant had expected, accused him of these misdemeanours. In reply, the General informed his master that, before the Imperial departure, he had emasculated himself, and had hidden the mutilated parts in the Emperor's saddle, so that he could prove his innocence of the charges which he had foreseen his enemies would bring against him. . . . The Emperor ordered the saddle to be produced, so that he could examine it, and there found the evidence of Kang's assertion.

Touched by such ingenious, unselfish loyalty, Yung Lo at once promoted him to the post of Chief Eunuch, and, after his death, deified him. In his memory, the Emperor had founded a temple, and had built by its side the accompanying Refuge for Distressed Eunuchs for which we were searching these hills (for, though they work the land and are, to a certain degree, a self-supporting community, it is a home and not a monastery). This charitable institution had been endowed as well by many subsequent Emperors, but, since the fall of the Imperial Family, these funds had largely vanished, and the life led by the inmates had become increasingly impoverished. . . . Indeed, they had suffered in several ways : for example, Yung Lo had also bestowed upon them in perpetuity a large piece of land about a mile and a half distant, to be used as a burial ground. In it had reposed the bones of some seventeen hundred Palace Eunuchs from the early fifteenth century down to modern times, each with a finely carved stone or marble headstone, giving particulars of name and rank, and details of the dead eunuch it commemorated. . . . But alas ! these, and the cypresses which grew among them, have been for the most part wantonly destroyed by soldiers and bandits.

The story had, perhaps, made us a little lose our bearings : but, choked and blinded, we still plunged on. . . . Surely we should be there by now ? We had left the road well over twenty-five minutes ago, and it was only a mile. . . . But now we found ourselves up against a large building in the golden haze : this must be it ! . . . At last we found a door, and outside it a rather smartly dressed young Chinese. (Indeed, he seemed to us unexpectedly young ; for all the surviving eunuchs in Kang T'ieh Miao, we had been told, were old.) In halting Chinese one of our party asked him, " Excuse me, sir, but have we the honour of finding ourselves in the Ancestral Hall of the Exalted Brave and Loyal ? " only to receive, in very good English, the startling reply, " No, gentlemen, this is Pa Pao Shan Golf Club ". . . . He did not know where the temple lay : perhaps one of the members could direct us. And so — for the temple could not be far off — entering into the sanctuary, we asked various of them, clad in the strange garb of their recreation, in baggy, thick breeches, falling below the knee, and strange coats of a chequered pattern, and sitting before small tables, to help us on our way, for indeed the temple could not be far off. Red Face and Purple Face, English and American, all sank their differences, over stymie and bogey, to turn a shade paler. Eunuchs' Temple, indeed ! Never heard of it, they were thankful to say. Shouldn't have thought a feller would want to go there, when he could spend a healthy afternoon on a golf-course instead ! As for a Eunuch General, didn't believe there was one, never heard of him ! (Certainly the description did not apply to their fellow member,

General Cruiklebury, who was universally respected. . . .
There was not one of them, they might say, who would
sit there and hear a word against him, not one. . . . Extraordinary chaps, coming here and asking us for the Eunuchs'
Temple, don't you know !) Never heard of it, they were
thankful to say ; and all the little beaded bubbles in the
glasses round which their hands were clasped seemed to
rise to the brim in thanksgiving.

Discouraged, we shambled away across endless rough
fields in the thick dust : but we had not far to go, for
almost under the shadow of that refuge for weary Europeans and Americans, we found, covering a good extent
of ground, a large group of low buildings ; looking,
indeed, lower than they really were, by reason of the cedars
and pines, and the massive, rough-hewn, yet tapering
trunks of the gingkos, that rose above them.

We turned aside into a court, and immediately, from
behind the paper windows of one of the wings on the right,
could distinguish the chinking of tea-bowls and a sound of
high-pitched gossip and chatter. Knocking at the door of
this apartment, a momentary silence ensued, and then a
hubbub of eager voices bade us enter.

When we opened the door, we found a cluster of excited, inquisitive old faces round us ; though a few figures
were still seated. Perhaps there were fifteen or sixteen of
them altogether in this long, low hall, with its dark, painted
walls. (Besides this number, we saw later two or three
working in a desultory manner in the garden, and a couple
of them in the kitchen.)

It was not, I think, a regular meal, but one of many
little snacks, " elevenses ", as it were, instituted to enliven
the tedium of these lonely and forgotten lives. . . . The

future of the eunuch is in itself a contradiction in terms, his life must always end with him. At any rate, however, in former times, a similar being who had long been on the waiting-list immediately inherited any place that fell vacant owing to death, or, more rarely, to retirement : thus every inmate knew that he would have a successor. Moreover, this meant, to the much larger community of former times, a continual influx of confreres from the Palace, liked or hated by the various individuals, but, at any rate, known to all of them, and bound to all of them by the selfsame mutilation. Each newcomer talked the identical language of the Palace, was cognisant of the names of all the streets and pavilions in it, and brought with him a fresh flow of Palace gossip, of how, in the end, it had been necessary to employ the Lesser Slicing Method in order to punish the recreant Eunuch Wang for those misdeeds and embezzlements which all his subordinates had so long suspected, of the flirtations of the newest Concubine, or of how it was said that the Emperor had again endeavoured to evade the Dowager Empress, and, as a result, now found himself locked in a room with a window which, if it were not blocked up, would look over the Lake of the Summer Palace. And, soon after his arrival, each of them, too, would deplore the deterioration, which all in turn had noticed, in the standard of the Imperial School of Deportment for Eunuchs, and of the lack of poise and respectability shown by the new recruits when compared with their elders. . . . But now there was nothing to discuss ; no Emperor, no Concubines, no Palace, no School of Deportment, no young and worthless eunuchs to criticise, no new inmates and no successors ; a world void of interest, and in which nothing worth discussing could ever happen. And without such quickenings of the spirit, without such aids to their self-esteem, the solitude, combined with hard work, of their present mode of life opposed almost too harsh a contrast to that of their former existence in the Palace ; for who knows what wealth had not passed through their hands, or into what luxurious ways of life they had not fallen in former days, when they had controlled the destinies of favourites and, even, had, some of them, by the courses they pursued or to which they advised their masters, doubtless affected the trend of Chinese history ? Even this tea — which, they told us, had been sent to them at the New Year by the famous Eunuch Yüan-Chi, still alive (though he and the evil he wrought are nearly forgotten by now) in one of the cities of Szechuan, and amply supported in his retirement by the great fortune he had amassed — even this tea, first-rate though it was, and far beyond their means, compared very poorly, if they allowed themselves to think of it, with the numerous and sumptuous meals over which they used to linger in one of the courtyards of the Summer Palace, while dwelling with gusto on some new scandal, reviewing every aspect of it, hammering away remorselessly at its every facet. . . . But gone now were the luxury, the cere-monials and the high-flown insolence of their prosperous days. They wore no splendid or impressive robes, but these dark-coloured and stained gowns. No one ever visited them, and so there was nothing about which to talk ; for, having been powerful, some of them, once, they still possessed many enemies, though no friends, from the old days, and did not dare very often to visit the city. Besides, money was scarce.

They had sat down again now, in groups, their old, yellow faces full of innumerable lines, their wisps of hair coiled at the back of their heads. At first they were silent, watching us intently, and then they began to talk together once more, wondering, I imagine, who we were and why we had come. In spite of the animated babble that arose, the hall had about it something of the air of a Women's Club or Institute, in which only constant cups of " nice hot tea " could keep up the spirits of the members. Old and alone with their strange and now expiring kind, in a decaying refuge, lost among fields uprising in a bitter wind, there was no one to protect them ; except, standing behind the chief altar of the temple, the magnificent contemporary wooden effigy of their Patron Saint, who by his example had done so much to improve their lot and to lessen the world's contempt for them. Moments they still had, such as this one, of exhilaration ; but under the surface prevailed, I believe, a distressing poverty (though, of course, it *may* have been assumed), and also, I thought, a continual sense of tedium, momentarily dissipated by tea and the timely but rare arrival of three strangers. Even now, their vivacious cackle and prattle and toothless laughter were punctuated in one direction by the low, continual groaning and muttering of two or three old creatures who sat by themselves over a brazier, staring into their little bowls of tea. They still suffered from the results of the operations undergone half a century before, but performed upon them with that appalling cruelty ordained by the unbroken Palace ritual of a thousand years. No anaesthetics were administered at the time, and after the untold barbarities to which they had submitted, the poor wretches were left to recover as best they could without medical aid. The operation had always to be performed in the same manner, and in the precincts of the Palace. The only marvel is, not that many of them were afflicted with pain for life, but that any survived, still more, recovered.[1]

My readers may well demand why any human beings should voluntarily surrender themselves to such treatment, especially when they must have known beforehand what was in store for them, and when, further, the Chinese emphasis, civil and religious, on the virtues of paternity, and belief in them, are taken into account ? . . . But the answer is a very simple one : China was a country vast and poor, and the profession of Palace Eunuch was the only certain road in it to riches for the man who was both destitute and uneducated. In order to qualify, no competitive examinations were necessary, as in almost every other walk of life. Not seldom, too, it led, through the favour of Emperor or Empress, to a great career. Moreover, the Palace Eunuch lived at the centre of things, in Peking, in the Imperial Palace. For these reasons, the appointment to such a post was eagerly sought after, and its drawbacks minimized in the popular mind. Thus, quite apart from those whose parents had chosen them, and prepared them, for the role at an early age, hoping themselves to profit by it, or whose cast of mind had, to a certain extent, fitted their characters in advance to their new situation, manifesting a cunning and love of intrigue, a feeling for dress and ceremonial, and, above all, for money, that sought its outlet in such an existence as only the Forbidden City could supply, in addition many a poor married man, with wife and children, and without any special ability for the life of an oriental palace, would have the operation performed upon him in order to obtain the chance of

[1] The reader who wishes for details can find them in *The Harem*, by N. M. Penzer (Harrap & Co., 1936), p. 324.

providing for his family after his death.

The interest, then, of the eunuch as a specimen of humanity is to be sought not only in the continued existence of so ancient an artificial sept, one originating in the remote palace-civilisations of Babylon and Assyria, and placed apart for ever from the ways of the normal man — and which, moreover, will not continue to exist beyond our own day, — but still more in the fact that a badly performed surgical operation can to such an extent modify the whole character of its subject. After this fashion can an ordinary Chinese husband, hard-working and, in his own way, conscientious, be converted into an idle, gossiping, avaricious creature, living for secrecy and intrigue. If all Chinese are inquisitive, the curiosity of the eunuch surpasses that of a whole crowd together. . . . And, indeed, the chief impressions of this unusual tea-party were of a transcendent, all-consuming curiosity, a love of machinations, all the stronger because here frustrated by circumstance, coupled with a passion for saving up and secreting money : (no doubt, in spite of the existing poverty, little hoards of copper coins were hidden away here in cell and dormitory, under floors, in chimneys and in the trunks of trees).

Many months must have elapsed, I apprehend, since anyone had been to see them, and the long winter had been full of ennui. They would have found almost any excuse, gone to any lengths of prevarication, in order to detain us, so that they could talk : though, since only one of us could speak Chinese — and he, at that time, by no means perfectly — it might be imagined that our conversation would pall. . . . But then, they could talk about us, to one another, at the same time as they could talk to

us ; and, without undue conceit, I am confident that exactly
what we did, exactly what we said, employed their sadly
unoccupied minds for many subsequent weeks. Time after
time, just as we were getting up to leave, they would prevent
us from doing so by pretending that they had omitted to
show us one of their treasures, a painting or piece of
sculpture, and then, on our return, would insist on our
having another cup of tea because we must be tired. (By
this time, even the few eunuchs who had been working in
the garden had made their way indoors, so as not to miss
the treat of visitors, of *foreigners*.) Cup followed cup, to
the accompaniment of more talk, excited squeaks and spurts
of talk. But the subjects it covered were limited ; their
interests did not range very far. The state of the world
did not affect them. They had in their own lifetime travelled
beyond its horizon, the last, lost refugees of a dead past.
. . . No, it was the small points of dress, for example, that
concerned them, the make and texture of our clothes.
(Surreptitiously, their soft, wrinkled old hands fingered
them, to gauge their quality and consequent cost.) What
price, they could not resist asking us — though, since they
had never worn such clothes, it could mean nothing to
them — had we paid for them ? When enlightened, they
babbled tremendously, and made a parade of disbelief. . . .
But above all they displayed a technical interest in how
many times a day we were obliged to shave ; a matter
which, having thrashed it out with us, they then proceeded
to discuss among themselves in corners for a full half hour,
though some of them would always continue talking to us,
so as to prevent our going away. Indeed, so electrifying
an effect did the information produce, that even one of the
poor old wrecks groaning over the brazier ceased for a

while his melancholy music, and got up, temporarily re-
vived, to take part in this pleasant *causerie*.

But we must see over the Temple again — they had
stupidly forgotten to take out two bronze vases, they remembered now, and they were sure we should admire
them. We could not leave without seeing them, one of
the chief possessions of the whole Refuge. And then, since
it was so cold crossing the court, it would be time for a
nice hot cup of tea again. . . . There was so much, they
averred, that they wanted to ask us, and, not having expected our visit, they had not been given time to think out
all their questions. . . . But, did they drink tea in England ?
And were there still eunuchs in the Palace ? No ? . . .
Everywhere it was the same ; true civilisation was dying
out. Very sad . . . but they had heard that they had
been recently abolished. Two years ago, an Englishman
had visited them and said so : but they still survived, he
had told them, in one place in London . . . in . . . a difficult word for them . . . Bloomsbury. It was, he had
said, a Refuge for Eunuchs, like their own. . . . How
they longed to visit it, and see for themselves English ways
of life.

The hall and living-room, in which we were thus liberally
provided with tea, was not of any very great beauty, though
its length, its dark walls and dark clothed figures in this
now failing light, and with the glow of the braziers, made
a most curious and effective scene, like an oriental version
of a picture by Magnasco. In the court outside, however,
under the tall trees, were several beautiful carved tablets of
stone, engraved by Emperors of the Ming Dynasty, and by
later Manchu rulers : and on the main walls of the grand,
lofty hall, facing us across it, hung two large paintings,

illustrating some of the incidents in the life of their Patron Saint, Kang T'ieh, and one or two of his victories. These are still in magnificent condition, though painted, it is said, soon after his death, and are interesting because of the very individual decorative quality they manifest, somewhat similar to that of an ancient European map, only without the naïvety. A fine painting of the General also hangs here : but, in retrospect, the whole of this cluster of buildings is dominated by the gigantic painted effigy, already mentioned, of the General, which stands behind the altar : a statue instinct with vigour, life and personality, one of the most superb pieces of sculpture of the Ming epoch. . . . Moreover, there was something not a little touching in the veneration of these poor creatures for their benefactor and hero.

After seeing the vases we made a determined effort to leave, for the winter sun was quickly sinking, a huge red lantern, toward the hills, and we ought to make our way back to the road before its light expired. In spite of the cold, the eunuchs clustered together in the doorway to see us off. The air outside was still thick with particles, but the wind had died down, though yet strong enough to make the candles flicker behind the paper windows. Though the group behind us had fallen quiet, watching our departure, we could, as we walked away, nevertheless distinguish from within the melancholy groaning of the afflicted round their brazier. . . . In the lighted kitchen two figures could be seen busily preparing supper over a stove, and the smell of garlic, supreme above all others, asserted itself, floated round the building, imparting to it a certain matter-of-fact air, a certain feeling of life. . . . And then we had passed out of the court and were in the

MING POLYCHROME WOODEN EFFIGY OF KANG T'IEH,
THE EUNUCH GENERAL, SUBSEQUENTLY DEIFIED AS
PROTECTOR AND GOD OF THE PALACE EUNUCHS. *See p.* 322

ordinary world again, among the dusty, rounded hills beneath the Golf Club.

.      .      .      .      .      .

Once more, a few weeks later, I saw some of their kind,
when a friend took me to pay my respects to the last Prince
of the Imperial House to reside in Peking.

This Manchu Prince, a cousin of the ex-Emperor, is,
though still a young man, not only a remarkable artist in
the traditional school, but — which appeals still more to
the Chinese — the greatest living exponent of calligraphy.
Indeed, his fame extends through the whole of China, and
hundreds of pounds are given for specimens of his writing.
For these reasons the people of Peking have always looked
up to him, and none of the various governments that had
at different times controlled the city had ever attempted to
eject him from his ancestral palace, though all the other
Manchu Princes had long ago been forced to leave.

The palace, built by the Emperor Ch'ien Lung, consisted of a group of tiled and painted pavilions with loggias
and marble terraces, similar to those of the Forbidden City,
placed in the middle of ancient water-gardens, now dry,
and surrounded by immense old flowering crabs, at this
moment loaded with blossom. . . . However, we had
reached it by way of a long drive, rather unusual in Peking,
and had found the gates shut. Scarcely had we knocked at
these stout wooden barriers than they were flung wide open,
and we found that a troup of twenty or so tall, middle-aged
individuals in long, vellum-coloured robes had run out of
the two small lodges, one on each side of the drive, to
welcome us.

Something in their air made me enquire who they
were. . . . In reply, I was informed that they were the

last-recruited eunuchs from the Forbidden City, younger by some fifteen or twenty years than those I had encountered at the Refuge. On learning this, I regarded them more closely, and came to the conclusion that they more nearly resembled my preconceived European idea of them, for they showed in their manner both a certain servility and smooth aplomb.

In former years they had been in the service of Hsüan T'ung, the ex-Emperor, right up to the last day he spent in the Forbidden City, in 1924. The deposed monarch had resided there for many years, in retirement, injuring no one and making no plots for the recovery of his throne. Notwithstanding, the officers of Feng Yu-hsiang, probably with that Marshal's connivance, had eventually forced an entry into the Palace, had begun to loot it, and, too, had plotted to shoot the Emperor, thus obliging him to seek sanctuary in the Japanese Legation. Realising in time what their fate would be if they were caught, these eunuchs had waited until their master had made good his escape, and had then avoided the massacre by seeking safety in the palace of his cousin. They had remained here ever since that day.

### CHAPTER EIGHT

PEKING : SERENADE AND AUBADE

W E stayed on in Peking until the beginning of the summer, when the peonies were nearly over, and had long been sheltered from the sun by mat awnings, and every day the temperature had stood at ninety in the shade.

The memories of the city that return to me chiefly, and most easily, are two.

One was of an evening just before I left. I was standing on the terrace of the Observatory, examining the bronze seventeenth-century instruments. (Unfortunately the last of those of an earlier period, which Marco Polo saw, have been removed.) Since the winter had passed, I had not been here, and, turning round, I discovered that the whole panorama of streets and temples and courts had sunk beneath the motionless green tide of leaves. Gone were the grey houses and bare twigs, and in their place stretched a still and silent forest, which, for the moment and at this extremity of the city, life seemed entirely to have deserted. Not a voice spoke.

All trees and simples, great and small,
  That balmy leaf do bear,
Than they were painted on a wall
  No more they move or stir.

.    .    .    .    .    .

My other memory, perhaps more true to the character of Peking, the Capital of the North, is of a winter's night, and its sounds ; which an accidental note or clinking together of metal or wood sometimes revives for me with the instantaneous and false lucidity of a dream. . . . No less than the day, the Peking night has its own music, in no way muted by the snow that wavers down in the glow of lanterns and braziers. Some sounds, such as the cries of the sellers of water in summer and charcoal in winter, persist, hour in and hour out, for the whole twenty-four, and form a background for the different acronychal clamour that now rises. But, for the most part, directly one system of sound is born, the other dies.

Many of those whose trade is entirely nocturnal carry lanterns and little stoves, for it is their business to supply nourishment at all hours to ricksha coolies and night workers, or they may specialise in foods suitable to the palate of the various revellers of the city, drunkards and opium-smokers ; articles specially spiced and suited to their condition. Thus you will observe Mohammedans — if you are wise enough to know them — retailing cakes fried in oil to their co-religionists. Then, again, at the time of every feast (and several fall to each lunar month) the delicacies associated with it are on sale everywhere. Thus at the New Year the dumplings mentioned more than once in these pages were in great demand, and, a fortnight later, at the time of the Lantern Festival, there were little white balls,

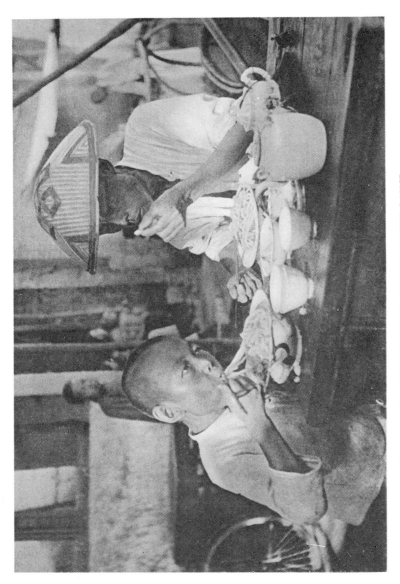

TEA AND NOODLES. PEKING STREET SCENE

made of sugar and barley-flour surrounding a kernel of walnut and red fruit jelly — but, in all truth, the foods attached to the Chinese calendar by long Peking custom are not to be numbered. (In the matter of cakes alone, there are New Year cakes, spring cakes, sun cakes, elm-seed cakes, dragon-scale cakes, cold fried pastries — to be eaten when wheat ripens — flower cakes, moon cakes — some more than a foot in diameter, and with prints of the Three-Legged Toad and the Rabbit of the Moon, creatures which inhabit that cold planet, pasted upon them — mimosa cakes, powdered with points of red sugar, rose cakes, cakes of the Five Poisonous Creatures and wistaria cakes.[1]) Thus, nearly every fortnight, there is, in addition to the ordinary articles of consumption, some special food, with its own special cry to advertise it, for the citizen to buy in the streets.

But before entering their cold darkness to consider all these things more closely, we must first take notice, if only for an instant, of the beauty and strangeness of the particular scenes which the Peking night frames. We must glance at the blind singer or flute-player, as he walks home, sounding his gong, and prodding at the ground so carefully with his long staff ; he needs no lamp, for darkness and light are the same to him, and this shows in the wary, staring blankness of his upturned mask, as he slowly rounds a corner into one of the broad, well-illuminated thorough-fares. Or let us turn to regard the seller of chestnuts, who, in a narrow lane, bends over his stove, and how its glow catches the furry edges of his cap and the upper part of his head, emphasising the gleam of his narrow, up-slanting eyes as they strain out, beyond the range of the nimbus round him, to search for possible customers in the darkness, or his

---

[1] See Tun Lich'en's *Annual Customs and Festivals in Peking.*

gesture, of putting one hand up to his ear, as he gives a
deep, hollow cry: or we can observe, in an alley, the flicker
of his lantern upon the deep golden, tarpaulin face of the
old, bearded, trudging pedlar, who has so little to offer, but
whose whole countenance is creased with thousands of dead
smiles that come to life again with each new one, as he
greets a buyer. And we must look, too, with attention at
the beauty of the lamps and lanterns themselves, and
examine the bowls and plates handled by those who deal in
cheap foods, for the ordinary coolie china of Peking is among
the most lovely articles of everyday use in the modern world:
not coarse, after the manner of peasant pottery elsewhere,
but little green celadon bowls and plates of exquisite workmanship, though without decoration, or with a fish or a
spray of flowers sketched on them with a fantastic grace.

Now, of a winter's night was the time for " hot salted
fish " — usually a euphemism for a portion of the smoked
head of a pig — " succulent beef " and " rose-flavoured
night-balls ", and their vendors were in no mood to pass
over the merits of them in silence. The country boys, too,
come into Peking at this season to sell the crab-apples [1]

---

[1] Mr. Robert W. Swallow tells us, in *Sidelights on Peking Life*, that these
" crab-apples are supposed to have medicinal properties, and in former times a
criminal, as he was going to the execution ground, would be given a string of
them to eat, so that during his last journey he might feel cheered and elevated ".
This bears a curious resemblance to the favourite description of the last meal of
the condemned man, so often reported in the press after an execution in England :
" Before walking to the scaffold, the prisoner's last request was for an apple for
his breakfast ".

Lich'en informs us, in his *Annual Customs and Festivals in Peking*, that these
crabs " are baked with sugar until sweet and stiff, and then cooled ", and en-
lightens us concerning their medicinal properties, for he adds that " when one eats
them on a winter's night, they can disperse the effect of coal and charcoal fumes " ;
in other words, of the gas from the braziers and stoves of Northern China ; very
effective contrivances for warming a house, but ones that not only often cause the
Peking sybarite a headache, but not seldom render him unconscious.

they have plucked ; little, sour, scarlet fruits, like red beads,
which, as though in reality they were such, they carry strung
in several huge necklaces round their necks, the ends hanging down on each side in front of them, as low as their
hands ; and could be heard crying, in rough, rustic accents,
" Only two strings left ! " Other hawkers were offering
with free voice " hard biscuits ", which are only sold at
night, though very popular with those gathered together
for " red and white ceremonies " (weddings and funerals),
and are the monopoly of those same men from Shantung
whom in the day-time we have heard crying " sugared horse
blossoms " : and others, again, were dispensing radishes
and water-chestnuts[1] — true men from Peking, these, with
that particular burr in their tones, as they called out, which
marks them. A few vendors were boiling eggs over a
stove, and were shouting about it, though this, you would
have thought, was a simple accomplishment, and one that
did not need the extravagant musical paeans they lavished
upon it : while, with the humility of the great, a clashing
together of brass cups — their manipulator carries them in
his right hand and, with a dexterity born of a lifetime's
practice, throws one up into the other — announced that
the chief of all street vendors was drawing near ; who, with
his free hand, was pushing along a barrow loaded with
many articles besides the one he chooses to cry : " Fruits
in Syrup ! ". (This call he changes in summer to " Sour
Prune Soup ".)[2] Others, strolling about with trays, were

[1] Water-chestnuts, a very popular Chinese *hors-d'œuvre*, consist of a kind of
root or bulb found in the mud at the bottom of certain streams. The cry is :
" Old Chicken-heads, fresh from the river ".
[2] In his *Annual Customs and Festivals in Peking*, p. 58, Tun Lich'en tells us that
" Sour Prune Soup " is made "from sour prunes boiled with sugar, to which rose
blossoms and olives are added, and is cooled with iced water until it chills the
teeth ". But this, of course, was an edition-de-luxe of the drink sold in the streets.

shouting, in preparation for the Lantern Festival, their willingness to sell paper lanterns, many of them in the shape of a fish, with green gills and red scales, and the seller of turnips was bearing along his supply in a basket (which, in a month or two, when the heat comes, he exchanges for a wooden tub of water, wherein, scraped and planed, they look as cool and frosty as winter moons), at the same time whinnying out repeatedly, " Roots that taste like pears, if bitter they may be returned ! " There were, too, more prosaic, but no less enthusiastic, proposals to furnish bowls of hot soup, of varying quality, peanuts, sweets of a hundred different kinds, dried melon and sunflower seeds, cigarettes, sarsaparilla, and regional dishes such as " fried bean curd " ; this last, consisting of squares of crushed beans fried in oil of sesame, being a favourite delicacy of the Peking night-worker. Fruit was scarce in the street at this season, both by day and night, but pears were being sold (different to any I have eaten elsewhere, being of a hard and yellow flesh, and seeming to possess a scent rather than a flavour),[1] and the vendor of persimmons, too, was doing a good trade, as he stood under a lamp and wailed out at intervals, his large round basket full of this flame-coloured autumn fruit, whose glow survives into winter to remind us of the warmth of the suns that make blossom the peony and lotus, and ripen peach and melon. . . . But these estival pleasures are as yet far ahead. Roasted chestnuts are being sold, and dumplings and hot soup against the bitter-rinded wind that sweeps round each corner, and against the snow that every now and then

---

[1] *Annual Customs and Festivals in Peking*, pp. 73-74. Lich'en mentions a kind of pear called " Duckling Yellow ", which seems to resemble this one ; it is " shaped like a quince, and like the yellow of ducklings in colour ".

flickers down to the ground, thickening the silence under
the cries and grasshopper-like clickings and clinkings.

    ·      ·      ·      ·      ·

Some Europeans and Americans may find these cryptic
and traditional sounds a source of unending irritation to
their nerves ; others may think them romantic, almost
lovely. But there is another side to it. . . . At the moment
such destitution in both buyer and seller as these so often
aptly express (for some of them seem the very voice of
poverty, screaming aloud to God above to witness their
rags, their filth, their sores and maimed or lost limbs), is
only to be found in the East, and especially in China, a land
of overflowing cities. Nowhere else in the world today
does so much ingenious and witty labour meet with so
little reward, nowhere in the most backward European
states can these crowds of blind people, beggars, cripples,
lepers and afflicted of every sort, be seen : and no amount
of accidental beauty can excuse their suffering, even though
the national temperament of the poor creatures makes them
laugh, as they do, between their bouts of professional
whining and cringing, at their own misery.

Perhaps these human beings, subjected to an existence
that is sub-human, may seem more utterly lost in the dust-
clouds of the spring, through which you can hardly distinguish their individual infirmities, or as they lie under a
piece of matting in the downpour of the summer rains ;
but it is in the winter that the terrible and aching pathos of
those who are not sunk, but who can just scrape together a
living, is best realised. Returning late, at two or three in
the morning, to house or hotel after some party at the other
end of the city, sometimes you will cross a big, well-lighted
open space, with groups of men talking cheerfully and doing

good business over stoves ; but you will also traverse endless streets and lanes, and old, deserted thoroughfares with broken walls, of which no one today can recall the purpose ; were they temples or palaces or shops ? And here, worn out by walking and by his cries, trying to shield himself from the onslaught of Siberian winds and so sitting in the shadow of a high and ancient building or by the edge of a low, squat house, with a small lantern lighting an endless expanse of snow, so tired that in spite of the iron cold he is all but asleep, the eyes shut in his yellow, emaciated face, you will find the poorer street-seller in his tatters. Sometimes he stirs to shout his wares vainly, in a voice as forlorn as the scene of which he is part, and his breath, as he gives his cry, hangs like dragon's breath on the air round him, or sometimes to stamp his feet, which seem bundles, for they are encased in torn layer after torn layer of rags. Possible buyers are scarce, and, when they come, so poor that often they just look in the basket and then turn away again ; but he must not leave his pitch or he will lose it, for others are already on the look-out to supplant him in the little custom he has, and thus habit and conscience bind him to this particular corner, and to serve the particular alleys down which he walks. . . . So he stays on, walking or sitting, all through the long night. Sometimes a ricksha man, his heart still pounding against his ribs from the run, his body still drenched with sweat, his feet already ice-cold, will stop to buy a bowl of this thin soup, reduced from pigs' bones, or a beggar, returning to his open-air hutch by the city walls, will choose a small meat-ball, made of offal, and give for it all the small cash he has been carefully collecting for twenty hours.

From every wide space and from every recess, equally,

in this great city, these innumerable cries and sounds rise up to shatter the crisp stillness of the infinite, star-spangled cold that lies here, high above men and their houses, until, at four o'clock in the morning, this symphony is crowned by a tremendous diapason : the frantic screaming of pigs whose throats are now being slit in the slaughter-house, four or five thousand of them killed and cut up every day for shops and street vendors ; the return in cruelty which men exact from the animal world for the labour it knows not.

As this haunting, trumpet-mouthed anthem of death, which continues at the same intensity for a full hour, begins to shrink in volume, the pedlars and hawkers start to pack up and go home. . . . But the day is beginning at the same time : the edge of the horizon lightens. Already the seller of almond tea [1] is going from house to house, and already the actors and female-impersonators of the Peking stage, who are his chief and most appreciative clients, are buying it, for they keep their voices in training by issuing out of the city walls just after dawn, when the air is said to be at its most beneficial, and by indulging in the most curious howls and moans (much as a prima donna might sing a scale) while facing these huge blocks of masonry. Already " fermented bean syrup " [2] is being sold in the street, from an iron pot over a stove, and the blue-covered baskets of " steamed bread " — a hot, dough-like substance that, like

[1] A drink made from ground rice and sugar with a little almond flavouring added to it. Though prepared the previous afternoon, the vendor has to boil it in the small hours, and then put it in a pot over a travelling charcoal stove, before he sets out at five in the morning on his rounds. (See *Sidelights on Peking Life*, by Robert W. Swallow.)

[2] The sale of this liquor, and so no doubt the taste for it, is confined to Peking. The beans are first ground on a stone mill by a donkey, and then the flour is boiled in water. Subsequently the liquid is strained through a rough sieve into a jar, partly buried in the ground and already containing some of the fermented liquor. *Ibid.*

" hard biscuits ", is a monopoly of men from Shantung — are soon emptied by eager buyers just off to work. For the bright winter sun has risen, melting the snow carpet that lies everywhere on the ground, on roofs and trees and the tops of walls, so that now its light can fall again upon its own stretches of orange tiles and on the glittering webs of the bare trees, from the branches and twigs of which water begins to drip, can shine on the vast old walls and towers, which the quality of its light seems to wash and renew, and, penetrating further, can model for us the distant, green contours of the Western Hills. And, with the light, the cries and sounds increase every instant in number, until soon we have again the whole, full, more prosperous day-light song of the sellers of toys and clothes and jewels, of silks and porcelains, of flowers and fruits and linen and sweets and lotus roots preserved in sugar, and hear again the flutes and gongs and drums of the fortune-tellers. . . . Only now do the magicians appear ; since what fortunes could they have told for those poor creatures starving and freezing through the night in hope of so meagre and pitiful a reward ?

# INDEX

Actors, Pekingese, 333
Acupuncture, Chinese science of, 193 n., 200
Albazin, Cossack colony, 253
Almond tea, 333
Altar of Heaven, Peking, 220, 243, 267
Angkor, 25, 32, 45, 82, 84, 86, 90, 91 ; discovery of, 86, 87, 124 ; boundary of French Indo-China moved to include, 87 ; architecture, 88, 89, 90-91, 92
Angkor Thom, 91, 112 ; date of origin, 92 ; Dr. Quaritch Wales on, 93, 94, 103, 130 ; religious system, 95 ; Royal Palace, 122-123, 125-127 ; gates of, 115, 117-118, 129, 142
Angkor Vat, 99, 100, 104-112, 121, 129, 140-141, 145, 146 ; " model " of, 70, 99 ; history of, 91-97 ; Pra Khan, 120 ; Pra Rup, 120 ; Neak Pean, 121 ; Ta Prohm, 121 ; Henri Mouhot's account of, 87, 91, 124 ; Tcheou Ta-Kouan's account of, 127-142 ; kingfishers of, 140-142 ; dancers of, 160-161
Annam, Kings of, tributary to China, 264
Annamites, their lacquered teeth, 31, 32, 48 ; as elephant keepers in Peking, 265
Antique shops, Peking, 228, 251
*Apsaras*, Angkor Vat, 98
Architecture, Chinese, 90, 281-285
Arlington, L. C., and William Lewisohn, *In Search of Old Peking*, 180, 182, 190 n., 191 n., 229 n., 265, 279 n., 292 n., 297 n., 299 n. ; on

Chinese food, 235, 240 ; on Chinese wine, 241 ; gods and goddesses, 249
Attiret, Jesuit artist, 221 n.

Ba-Khêng, Mount, 93, 120
Bandits, Chinese, 175, 215
Barbers, in Peking, 186-187
Bats, of Angkor Vat, 119 ; at Renishaw, 148
Baudesson, Captain Henry, *Indo-China and its Primitive People*, 133, 134
Bayon, the, Angkor, 92, 100, 103, 115, 116, 118-120
Bean syrup, 333
Beggars, Chinese, 173, 174, 242-243, 245-246, 331, 332
Bell Tower, Peking, 180
Betel-chewing, 31, 61
Birds, as pets, in China, 16, 288
Bird's Nest Soup, 235
Blake, William, 119
Bodde, Dr. Eric, translator of Tun Lich'en's *Annual Customs and Festivals in Peking*, 17, 167, 168 n., 262 n., 264 n., 286 n., 287 n., 295, 298 n., 304 n., 305 n., 327 n., 328 n., 330 n.
*Boddhisattvas*, Angkor Vat, 98
Bon-po Lamaism, 268 n.
Borghese, Princess Pauline, 10
Brahmanism, 95
Brahmans, 43, 130, 135 n., 136
Brass Thirsty Bird, the, Peking, 180 n.
Brighton, Royal Pavilion, 10, 156
Bruce, James, *Travels*, 35
Buddhism, 95, 247
Buddhist priests, Cambodia, 136

## THE END

Printed in Great Britain by R. & R. CLARK, LIMITED, Edinburgh.